LEVELS

of

POWER

LEVELS

of

POWER

THE FOREIGNER

MIKE GILMORE

authorHOUSE®

AuthorHouse™ LLC
1663 Liberty Drive
Bloomington, IN 47403
www.authorhouse.com
Phone: 1-800-839-8640

Published by AuthorHouse 09/30/2014

ISBN: 978-1-4969-4381-1 (sc)
ISBN: 978-1-4969-4380-4 (hc)
ISBN: 978-1-4969-4379-8 (e)

Library of Congress Control Number: 2014917487

Other Books

by

Mike Gilmore

Levels of Power:

The Senator

The Legislator

The Diplomat

The Chairman

The Toilet Salesman ... The oh so ... Necessary Guy

Acknowledgments

Many years ago, at the age of fifteen, I started my professional career. It was the summer holiday from school, and my uncle needed help at his wholesale sales company, the Home Candy Company. My uncle, Richard G. "Dick" Olinger, was the owner. He recently passed away at the age of eighty-six.

My job was far from important in the scheme of things. I unloaded and loaded trucks. I put freight away and stocked shelves. I carried orders out to customer's cars and trucks. I loved the work and the people.

It was a male-dominated business at the time. My uncle's father worked in the business, and my uncle's father-in-law, my grandfather, was the bookkeeper. He checked in the drivers and kept a record of the accounts receivables.

The other men who worked there were survivors of the Great Depression, and many had served in World War II. They understood the value of a job and steady income. Each morning they arrived and immediately started to work—no talk about last night's sports events or some crazy party they attended. They were simple men with a quiet dignity. They taught me the basic work ethics I have used throughout my career. Every one of them I remember with great fondness.

As with many characters in my novels, I have used the names of relatives, either first or last names, and sometimes both. I have used the names of high school classmates, like Brad Guilliams and Renee Stockli, and I thank them. I have also borrowed names of my fellow employees at American Standard Brands, an excellent company. I have used their names with great respect.

This book features the name of the last survivor of my old original friends at the Home Candy Company, John R. Laird. He was a sales representative and later a tavern owner. He is one of the best friends I have ever had. My wife and I always visit with him at his home in Coshocton, Ohio, on every trip back to our birthplace.

Thank you, John, for a lifetime of wonderful memories and funny stories.

Chapter 1

Washington, DC
Tuesday, November 24, 2015
7:45 a.m.

President Harold Miller was relaxing in his private office in the White House residence. The surface of the desk was invisible under the normal complement of six to eight daily newspapers from major metropolitan cities across the country that he scanned each morning. The two papers whose front page he paid the closest attention to were the *Washington Post* and *New York Times*. Both papers used large font for the headlines on the front page.

The *Post* proclaimed, **White House Corporate Tax Bill Heads to Senate.**

The *New York Times* referred to the same subject, **Senate Talks Taxes After Thanksgiving Recess.**

The sixty-five-year old president leaned back in the comfortable executive swivel chair until the chair's mechanism reached its stop. He was holding the *Times* newspaper in his right hand and ran the fingers of his left hand through his thick salt-and-pepper hair. His hair was grayer now than three years before when he took office, no doubt a side effect from the responsibilities of being president of the United States.

It was a slower than normal day in Washington. The Thanksgiving holiday approached. Congress was in recess until December 1. The White House barber was due shortly for his weekly trim. Afterward

Miller would head down to the basement gym for his daily workout, knowing it was important to maintain a healthy, trim figure for the American voters.

He continued to scan through the top story in the papers. As a native New Yorker, Harold favored the *Times*. The *Post* editorials tended to favor his rivals, but he could not ignore the paper. Its large readership carefully read the stories and followed the columnists.

If there was one topic in politics that would provoke a response in almost every American citizen, it was taxes. Increased or lowered taxes, deferred or deducted taxes, someone always felt on the short end of the stick. Taxes could make the gentlest person offer a cuss word or two.

Two months ago, the US Senate had confirmed Miller's nomination for the new chief justice of the Supreme Court. Any president would be happy when their nominee was sitting on the high court. Their legacy, shaped by the court's decisions, would be a subject for historians for many years, long after the office holder left the White House. Every court historian will review the decisions and ask if a different Supreme Court justice might have made a difference.

Miller should be riding high now that his successful nominee replaced the longest-ever sitting chief justice, Arnold Allen Lansdale. However, his first nominee, guilty of having used his position on the Federal Court of Appeals for personal gain, had marred the nomination process. The judge's inside information on court decisions had allowed his wife to make millions of dollars to fund her failing business.

To make the situation even worse, it was the Democratic senator for South Carolina, Randy Fisher, who discovered the backroom activities of Judge Wade Titus Walker. Even after the president's handpicked team had conducted their own investigation into Walker, the senator and his staff had discovered the Walkers' secrets. Walker and his wife were now starting their prison sentences, which included two counts of murder for Jennifer Walker.

To some degree, that disaster had dampened the president's victory, which was to be the springboard for his upcoming reelection campaign, starting very soon. Now he needed something else to drive his approval rating higher and bring the voters back to the Republican side of the ledger.

Before the confirmation process for his Supreme Court nominee, Miller had taken a long weekend at Camp David to plan for the upcoming election and ponder his next step. What could he do to attract the moderate conservative Republicans and moderate Democrats? He needed to move the voter's perception of his presidency more toward the middle. He had no hope of earning the very left liberal Democratic voters. His fight against the new Path to Citizenship bill, passed by Congress over his objections just before the mid-term elections, would put those voters behind his rival.

Miller threw the newspaper on the desk and laced his fingers together behind his head, remembering the long weekend with his most trusted senior staffers. To say the least, it had strained their relationships, but in the end, they came away with a plan.

Chapter 2

Camp David, MD
Sunday, June 14, 2015
1:00 p.m.

The group had been arguing since they arrived on Friday morning. The president had opened the long weekend of meetings with an unusual statement. "I want you to clearly understand this meeting. I know what the polls are saying. If we held the elections today, the Democrats would win the White House. Therefore, we are here to develop a plan to get the American public to take a new look at my presidency. I'm currently considered too far to the right and hard-headed, and we've got to develop a plan to move my image slightly to the left to attract a larger portion of the voters."

The president paused for several moments to allow his words to sink into the minds of the people at the meeting. "Everything is on the table for discussion and everybody must speak their mind. We must not withhold any idea, no matter how unusual, from consideration. If we are to figure out a way to get my approval rating out of the low forties, we need a plan. I do not want you to be afraid to speak your minds. Any questions before we start?"

The three team members gathered in the main lodge of the presidential retreat looked at each other as they settled into their chairs or on the sofa. Early Friday morning they had all arrived at the private retreat used by presidents going back to FDR's time in the White House.

The wooded hills were about sixty miles north-northeast of Washington in Catoctin Mountain Park near Thurmont, Maryland. Naval Support Facility Thurmont was the official name of the retreat, technically a military installation. The public knew it simply as Camp David.

The team was small but trusted. His chief of staff, Warren Fletcher, was both the former Republican governor of Virginia and the chairman of the National Republican Party. The president highly valued his opinion.

Allison Warden, the White House press secretary, was a slender, attractive woman in her mid-thirties with long red hair. Married and the mother of two boys, she had earned her position as a trusted staff member. Before she went to work for Harold Miller, she had a strong reputation as a crisis manager. Miller considered his presidency to be in a crisis.

Lewis Drake was Miller's campaign manager from his first run for the presidency. Together they had unseated a popular Democratic president, assisted by some questionable television ads about former president Blakely's ability to protect the country against terrorists. Shortly before Election Day in 2012, a nuclear device planted in Columbia, South Carolina, by a still-unknown terrorist had changed the election outcome. The bomb had been discovered in time to prevent a terrible accident affecting the eastern portion of the country, but Drake had immediately ordered a series of television commercials showing the old 1950s nuclear test explosions; onscreen captions asked people if they could sleep at night with Blakely as their president. The ads had worked. Miller erased a 5 percent deficient and won the election. Now Drake was here at Camp David to help plan a framework for a new strategy for the 2016 election.

The subjects discussed by the group covered the entire political spectrum. Civil liberties, welfare, education, and family values dominated the domestic agenda. Foreign relations, cuts to foreign aid to puppet governments, and aid to foreign militaries drew a lot of conversation.

Everybody had their pet issues, but nobody seemed to be able to convince the others their idea would work. For his part, the president asked a few questions, but mostly he sat in his overstuffed chair and allowed his advisors to argue among themselves. Usually the two White House insiders tag-teamed against the campaign manager, but he would stubbornly hold his position against their ideas while defending his own.

After a brief break for lunch, Alison asked if the president would excuse her so she could take a short walk around the cabins and in the woods. President Miller suggested they all might benefit from a walk in the fresh air.

Alison stood at the lunch table. "Sir, please don't take this wrong, but I need to walk alone. I think best on my feet, and I want to review an idea that is developing in my mind. I would like about thirty minutes alone, if you don't object."

The president allowed a small smile to break over his face. "Never interfere with a woman on a mission." He glanced at his wristwatch. "It's just past one o'clock. Why don't we all agree to be back here by one forty-five?"

Alison grabbed her light sweater. It was June, but Camp David was in the mountains and the temperature was a little cooler than she preferred. Leaving the men to organize their walk, she hurried from the room and headed for the outdoors.

The sun was bright, but the wind still had a chill to it. She was glad for the extra layer. She pulled the sweater around her body and flipped her thick red hair up, free of the clothing, with both hands. She decided to stay to the roads and out of the woods. With all the security provided by the United States Marines deployed for the president's protection, she would not get lost. She did not want to trip and fall while walking in the wooded area.

She simply followed the road system, which allowed her to concentrate on her idea, not any specific path within the confines of Camp David. The new idea had developed late last night as she prepared for bed. They needed something that every person would like, democrat or republican, man or woman. They also needed an idea that the president could call his own. Ever since Miller had entered the White House two and a half years ago, he had either been playing catch-up with ongoing issues or responding to the Democrats in Congress. He needed something big to bring the focus of the voters back to him rather than Congress, specifically Senator Tom Evans, who would, in all probability, be his Democratic rival next year.

Evans had already formed his presidential exploration committee and would no doubt be making his own big announcement very shortly. If Miller was to have a chance to reverse his place in the polls, he needed something before Evans started his campaign. They needed to put Tom Evans on the defensive for once until the voters went to the polls next year.

Alison walked, ignoring the beautiful surroundings. Sometimes she walked with her arms folded across her chest. When she worked the idea within her mind or envisioned making her presentation to the president and the other members of the group, her arms would swing beside her. She knew her habit of wildly swinging her arms as she talked sometimes distracted her listeners. During White House Press Room briefings, she always maintained her position at the podium and kept her hands locked on the wooden platform. As a self-taught remedy, it worked well. Only when she pointed to reporters to authorize them to ask a question would she allow her right hand to leave its fixed position.

Finally, the idea was there, nearly fully developed. She glanced at her wristwatch and saw the time was almost two. She had not realized that she had been walking so long. Alison looked around to determine her location. This was her first time at Camp David, and she did not recognize the landscape. She was on a narrow paved road within the thick pine forest. From her location, she could see none of the buildings or familiar landmarks.

Unlike some people, who seemed to have a built-in GPS system, Allison could not determine which way to go. She had decided to reverse her path back the way she had come but was concerned with how long it would take to return for her meeting with the others. She had just started to walk in the opposite direction when a golf cart came over the rise; two marines were riding in the front. They pulled up beside her. The marine riding as a passenger spoke first.

"Hello, Mrs. Warren. We thought you might need a lift back to the main cabin."

Alison's mind flooded with relief. "Yes, I certainly need a lift. I'm just glad you happen to come along. I was walking and not paying any attention to my location or the path I took to get here. Can you get me back to the president's lodge? I'm already late for the next session of the meeting."

The marines politely smiled at the striking woman. "You bet, Mrs. Warden. It will be our pleasure."

The marine who had spoken to her quickly hopped out of the passenger seat and offered a hand to Alison. She took his place in the golf cart. He quickly reseated himself on the backbench, and they were off. Neither man mentioned that the president had sent word to have someone follow his press secretary at a discreet distance in case she got lost.

Chapter 3

Camp David, MD
Sunday, June 14, 2015
2:15 p.m.

Alison burst into the cabin and hurried into the main room to rejoin the three men. The president glanced at his watch to see how tardy his press secretary was. Warren Fletcher simply wore a small smile. Lewis Drake stopped talking about his latest proposal to the president to see who was causing him to lose his train of thought.

Alison did not wait until Lewis finished his comment or allow him to pick up the thread of his conversation. "I've got it. I've got the idea that will bring the voters back to your camp, Mr. President."

She didn't even stop to remove her sweater or retake her place on the sofa that she had claimed on the Friday before. Ignoring the angry look from the campaign manager, she jumped into her idea.

"Mr. President. What is your biggest strength? What do you know about as much as any other person in government or business?"

She waited several heartbeats; she did not really want an answer. Her face glowed, her nearly full smile showing perfect white teeth. She simply said one word. "Money."

Harold Miller had spent many years on Wall Street before the political bug hit him and had accumulated hundreds of millions of dollars. Stock deals, mergers and acquisitions, and financing for business expansion all ran through his offices in New York City. By all standards,

9

he was the wealthiest person too ever occupy the Oval Office. To date, they had always tried to downplay his great wealth so as not to turn off the middle class in America. How can a wealthy president identify with middle-income voters and their struggle to pay their home mortgage and college education bills for their children? He had always followed the advice of his previous advisors—never talk about personal wealth.

Alison knew she had spoken a "dirty" word within the Miller presidency, but she plowed ahead with her idea. She asked the same question. "What is your biggest strength? Money ... and that is where you can nail the Democrats. You will use your many years of experience on Wall Street to propose a simple piece of legislation to fix one of the biggest tax problems, which upsets every middle-income person in the country."

She waited to see their reactions. Fletcher still had the smile on his face. He had hired Alison Warden to help the Miller White House out of an embarrassing situation last year when a cabinet secretary had fathered a child by a woman who was not his wife. He could tell by the gleam in her eyes that Alison had something big to spill.

Lewis Drake was still fuming about being interrupted and had not been focusing on her words.

President Miller was trying not to lose his temper at the mention of his great wealth. He hoped his press secretary was going to make some sort of sense with this wild outburst.

Alison still wore a wide smile. Some people did not realize her beautiful face fronted a brilliant mind. "Every year the press runs a number of stories about how American and foreign corporations pay no or very little income tax. Some of these companies will make hundreds of millions of dollars and not pay one red penny, while middle-income Americans pay any number of taxes. Payroll deductions for federal, state, and local income taxes. Car tag taxes, property taxes, and school taxes. The list continues, item after item. When they hear the stories about these companies that make millions and pay no taxes, they go through the roof."

Her body was quite warm from her excitement and the constant pacing in front of the three men. Alison quickly removed her sweater and tossed it on the empty seat on the couch as she continued to explain her idea. She forced herself to calm down just a little. "You will propose a new tax on the gross income of all American companies that make an income above a certain amount of money. We don't want to hurt the small self-employed people, only tax the largest corporations."

She paused for a few moments to form her next thought. "I suggest any company that has gross sales over fifty million dollars. I did a little research on the Internet last night, and I came up with almost eleven trillion dollars in US sales. If we charged a tax rate of .0025 percent, a quarter of one percent that would bring in over twenty-eight billion in new tax revenue."

She paused again in case the president, Fletcher, or Drake had any questions. They simply continued to stare at her, as if she was speaking in a foreign language. She thought that perhaps they considered her idea too ridiculous or simply unworkable.

Warren Fletcher was the first to speak. The elderly political operator moved around the room to stand next to Alison. His slender six-foot frame towered over Alison by several inches. "Yes. Middle-class Americans will love the idea. A Republican president who grew up on Wall Street finally brings the big oil companies and giant tech companies to task for all the years they have made money and not paid their fair share of taxes. Alison, I think it's a great idea."

Lewis Drake spoke up—and loudly—against the idea. "Mr. President, if you take this idea and run with it, then corporate American will take you to the woodshed. Campaign funds from some of your major donors will dry up very fast. This could be disastrous for the campaign."

Alison jumped back into the conversation to defend her idea. "Lewis, corporate America doesn't walk into the voting booth on the first Tuesday in November. Middle-class American taxpayers do, and when they do, they will have finally witnessed an American president standing up to the high and mighty and telling them their free tax ride is over."

Harold Miller had been silent during the entire discussion. As he had said earlier, he wanted his people to have a free rein over the conversation and not hold anything back from the discussion. Finally, he could not contain the question in his mind.

"Warren, how do we sell this to Congress and corporate America to try to keep them in our corner?"

Fletcher's blue eyes stared out from his heavily lined face as he looked from the president back to Alison and then over to Lewis Drake. The campaign manager still had a deep scowl on his face.

Once again, Fletcher was wearing his old hat as the former Republican Party chairman. "What does every company want from the government in control of any country where they do business?"

He was still standing next to Alison. He waited only several seconds before supplying his own answer. "Stability."

He waited for a reaction. His smile spread across his face. "Without stability they will not risk any stockholder money to build company infrastructure or other investments. They need to know up front that the local national government will not step in and privatize their assets."

They could all tell from his expression he was warming up to Alison's idea. "The United States government has provided stability for 239 years, and they've had a free ride for the entire time. If they want to see the federal government stay stable and provide a secure country for their own economic growth, they need to financially support the government with their fair share of taxes."

Alison took a step closer to Fletcher. She laid her right hand on his left shoulder to indicate another thought had entered her mind while he had been speaking. "We also mandate the new taxes be applied one hundred percent to the federal debt. Twenty-eight billion will be a drop in the bucket against the fourteen-trillion-dollar debt, but the American public will eat the idea up."

Miller looked to his campaign manager. "Lewis, are you still against the idea?"

Lewis now displayed a small grin. A heavy cigarette smoker, he coughed once into his right shirtsleeve to clear his lungs. "We can push this through the House of Representatives. It is a tax bill and must originate from the House side of Congress. We have control of the House, and we can make this happen. The fun part will be the Senate and the Democrat's very small control over the Senate Republicans. The Democrats must vote for the bill or face an angry electorate in the polls next year. Either way the vote goes, Mr. President, you win. If the bill passes, you pound your chest because your administration has made corporate American pay its fair share of taxes. If the Senate votes it down, you can pound the pulpit that the Democrats care more about corporate America than middle America. It's a campaign speech you can make every day until November 1, 2016."

Chapter 4
Washington, DC
Tuesday, November 24, 2015
8:15 a.m.

The president leaned toward his desk and roughly gathered the newspapers; he folded them together for the cleaning staff to remove. The newspapers would end up in the recycling bins in the White House basement.

The four people at Camp David had spent the balance of the weekend fine-tuning Alison's idea. They even decided to use an idea from one the president's most antagonistic foes in Congress.

South Carolina Senator Randy Fisher had arrived in Washington by way of special appointment by the governor of the state. Having saved the country from the nuclear device planted at the state fairground and survived the two gunshot wounds fired by the terrorist; he was the country's newest hero. One of the first rules he had adopted in his Senate office was the one-hundred-page limit on any new legislation. During interviews, he often stated if Congress could not write the bill in one hundred pages or less, it was probably too expensive for the country to bear.

Miller had to smile. His new Corporate America Fair Share Tax Bill had made it to the House of Representative on August 17. His team had spent weeks since the three-day weekend rewriting the bill several times to get the wording letter perfect in only ninety-seven pages. The response had been everything they had hoped. Americans across the country were immediately enthralled by the idea that finally corporate America would pay its fair share of income taxes.

E-mails, telephone calls, and letters flooded the offices of the members of the House of Representatives. Any congressman who discussed the bill at a town hall meeting and mentioned they should really take a closer look at the negative consequences of the bill were almost booed off the stage. The American public had been watching corporate America use its high-priced lawyers to avoid paying taxes for years, and now they wanted their revenge.

The House of Representatives, under the direction of Republican Speaker Larry Frye from Iowa, sent the bill to the Ways and Means Committee, and several Democrats attempted to bury the bill behind other legislation considered more important.

However, the American press knew a good story when it was right in front of them and continued to pepper the Speaker and the committee chairperson about the status of the Fair Share bill. As with many pieces of legislation, for the sake of brevity the press and politicians alike referred to the Corporate American Fair Share Tax Bill by a shorter name: the Fair Share Bill.

Never in recent years had the members of Congress felt such pressure from their constituents to pass the Fair Share Bill. Any House member who voiced disapproval about the bill found their local office the focus of irate citizens who accused the representative of protecting big business over middle-class citizens. Carefully working within the laws, citizens groups obtained permits to "walk the line" in front of the representative's office until he promised to support the president and the new piece of legislation.

The Ways and Means Committee finally voted the bill out of committee and back to the full House on November 13 with its recommendation for passage by the House. The committee vote was fourteen yeas and only three nay votes. The three negative votes were by Democrats who had an almost certain chance of reelection by their voters at home.

The full House of Representatives reluctantly took up the issue voted out of committee on Friday the 13th. Larry Frye was not a superstitious person, but he truly wished the president had left this bill on the drawing room floor. Unfortunately, that was not the case, and the full House began its deliberations.

The writing on the wall was clear for all the House representatives to see; perhaps the voting was already determined. The members knew the feelings of their constituents. On Friday, November 20, just before Congress recessed for the Thanksgiving holiday, the House of Representatives passed the measure by an overwhelming 369 to 66. Within minutes of announcing the vote results, the House recessed.

Next, the measure would move to the Senate, controlled by the Democrats. As a whole, the smaller chamber of Congress had been strangely silent about the Fair Share Bill. Perhaps they were hoping to see the House vote the bill down and save them from the same pressure faced by their brothers and sisters on the other side of the Rotunda in the Capitol.

Chapter 5

Washington, DC
Tuesday, November 24, 2015
2:15 p.m.

Capitol Hill and the congressional office buildings emptied quickly. Most members of Congress left Washington for home and their plans for the Thanksgiving holiday with their families. Many hoped to forget the last few months and the Fair Share Bill for a short time.

In the Russell Senate Office Building, the suite of offices assigned to Cameron A. Saunders, Chip to his friends, was empty except for his private office. The Republican junior senator from Virginia was sitting behind his desk talking with his two favorite Republican senators. The five-foot-ten, 145-pound senator was two weeks past his forty-second birthday. He possessed thick, dark blond hair and had a ready smile for almost any person, friend or stranger. When he was a young man still in high school, his hair was dark. After graduating from Richmond High School, he spent his summer vacation working on his uncle's tobacco farm. The summer sun bleached his hair to a light blond color. Over the years, the blond color darkened slightly but never went back to the dark brown of his youth.

The second senator was John R. Laird from Ohio. The tall, slender fifty-three-year-old senator was married with two grown children, his son now a Methodist minister and his younger daughter a schoolteacher, married to another teacher. Between his two offspring, he was a grandfather four times.

In his early thirties, Senator Laird's dark black hair he was born with slowly turned prematurely white. He had considered dyeing it back to its original tint, but his wife convinced him the new color gave him a very distinguished look, so his hair stayed natural.

Senator Laird had entered politics after making a small fortune in the wholesale beer distribution business. He had owned the franchise for a number of popular brands in his home state. Until he was in his late forties, he ran a business that required fifteen trucks to supply the taverns and restaurants within his protected market area. Only after growing tired of the business did he look to his second passion after his family: politics. He ran a clean campaign, won the primary election, and went on to unseat a Democratic senator who had run afoul of the IRS and the Senate Ethics Committee.

The third senator in the room was Roberta "Rickie" L. Hanley from Florida. The forty-six year-old single woman was not gay; she just had not yet found Mr. Right. Five-foot-two and 125 pounds, she wore her hair in a pageboy style. She still took delight in the male eyes that looked her way when she jogged through the National Mall most mornings before coming to the Senate. She was a native born Floridian and spent her entire life in the Sunshine State, and she had lots of passion for the elderly citizens retiring in her state. They were the largest segment of voters that put her into office.

The three senators had several things in common besides being members of the Republican Party. They were first-term senators, and all came to Washington in 2012 after defeating the incumbent Democrats in their homes state. More importantly, they were the biggest success stories for the Tea Party movement in the first national election for the new political party. Their movement's slogan: "No more taxes ... Not now ... Not ever!"

The three had been discussing their position on the Fair Share Bill. It was a tax increase, and they were trying to decide if they would hold to their campaign promise to vote against any new tax.

Rickie sat in a straight chair in front of Chip's desk. "This bill will pass no matter what we say or how we vote. That is a forgone conclusion. We can sit here all day and discuss what we say or do on the floor of the Senate, but we are only three votes against the rest of the Senate. The bill will pass in the Senate, the same as in the House."

John Laird sat on the sofa. He had wanted to be out of Washington and on his way back home to Ohio and his family by then, but Chip was adamant the three meet before they left Washington. "I agree with Rickie. We have no chance to sway enough senators to vote against the tax bill. It is going to pass. I wish we could stop it but I don't see any way to convince enough of the other members to see it our way."

Chip Saunders adjusted his body into a more comfortable position in his office chair. He had been listening to his friend's words carefully. They were correct. They had no chance to stop the vote for the bill.

"You are both correct in your assessment. If the bill comes to a vote it will be passed by the Senate and become law." He gave them a small smile; they could see his eyes light up. "But what if the bill never came to the floor for a vote? What if it got tied up on the Senate floor before it was assigned to the Senate Finance Committee?"

Rickie and John looked at each other and then back to their leader. Chip, willing to take risks and step into the public eye, had always been the strongest of the three. Some members of the Senate called him the show horse; others were the workhorses.

John Laird asked the question on both his and Rickie's minds. "There is only one way to stop this from going to committee. Are you talking a filibuster?"

Chip's small smile formed into a big, all-knowing grin. He nodded. "A filibuster."

Chapter 6

London
Saturday, November 28, 2015
6:00 a.m.

United States senator Randy Fisher slowly came awake in the hotel room he was sharing with his wife Annie. Their bodies were in the "spoon" position, his left arm draped over her waist and his right arm pinned under her slender neck.

The automatic mental alarm clock in his head would normally wake him within several minutes of when he wanted to rise in the morning. Today the time difference between London and Washington, DC, on their eighth day on vacation in England had set his internal clock slightly askew.

Careful not to wake Annie, he started to remove his arm from beneath her neck. He had just worked his elbow free when she gave a little sigh and asked what time it was.

"Early, babe. Go back to sleep. I'm just going for a run."

Out of bed, he walked into the bathroom and closed the door to prevent the light from shining into Annie's eyes when he flipped the switch. Randy had stayed in hundreds, perhaps thousands, of hotel rooms during his years as the sales manager for the entire southeast when he worked for Emerson Electrical Apparatus, traveling every week. The biggest difference in hotel rooms in England versus the United States was the bathrooms.

The electricity was 220 volts instead of 110 volts as in the States. Luckily, the hotels normally provided one electrical outlet that operated at the lower current in the bathroom for charging shavers and cell phones. While he was not an expert on plumbing fixtures, specifically toilets, he could tell the European fixtures operated a little differently than what he was accustomed to in the States. He was not certain how their internal hydraulics functioned, but one had to think that no matter where you were, water still flowed downhill.

He washed his face, brushed his teeth, and rinsed his mouth out with cold water. He quickly donned his heavy, warm running outfit and then laced up his running shoes. Grabbing the plastic room key-card and his BlackBerry, he quietly opened the suite's outer door and headed for the elevator.

A few minutes later, he gave the hotel door attendant a quick wave and started to go through some warm-up exercises to stretch his muscles before he began his run. He had forced himself to maintain a jogging/running routine since he had left the army nearly twenty years ago. Now, at forty-two, he was still in great shape. He kept his six-foot-tall body at 175 pounds; his muscles were still firm and lean.

He started at an easy pace but within minutes was at a full jog. He would normally run between five and eight miles, depending on his available time. Several times during the run, he would increase his speed to a flat-out run until his lungs and legs burned from the effort. His heartbeat would increase until he could feel the pulse in his temples. Today was no different. After the second maximum-speed burst, he settled back to a normal jogging rhythm.

As he reached what he estimated to be the three-and-one-half-mile mark, he started to think about the last full day of their vacation in England. Actually southern England. Annie had planned the overnight stays. Randy had focused on their daily activities.

Normally during the holiday seasons, Annie and Randy would travel from their apartment in Alexandria, Virginia, south on I-95 to Glenn Oaks near Richmond to spend about half of their holiday with Annie's parents. Then they would fly west to California and spend the balance of their time with Randy's only living relative, his aunt, Frances Ward. This year, Annie decided the whole family was going to spend the Thanksgiving vacation in an entirely different way.

She had told all of them that Randy and she were going to England for the holiday. She wanted her husband to get away from Washington, DC, and the American press coverage of his activities in the US Senate. Annie decided since she was an only child and Frances Ward had no other relatives, her parents and Frances could come with them to England.

To Randy's surprise, Frances quickly agreed to fly east to Washington. She spent a few days with them in their apartment before they joined Arthur and Millie Willis for the long overseas flight to Heathrow Airport in London.

Randy could not remember when he had had such a great time. Ever since he came into the national spotlight slightly over three years ago by stopping a terrorist from completing the setup on a nuclear device, he had been moving at a nonstop pace.

After the incident in Columbia and two months recovering from his gunshot wounds, he received an appointment to fill the vacancy in the United State Senate when his friend Robert Moore retired from the Senate with two years still remaining in his current term. A few months later, Randy met Annie Willis at the Department of Energy. Together they unwrapped a plot by the cabinet secretary to steal millions of dollars from his own department's research budget. During the process, Annie had nearly lost her own life when one of the co-conspirators attacked her.

It was an embarrassing moment for the president to have one of his political appointees caught with his hand in the proverbial cookie jar. Randy ran afoul again of the chief executive when he spearheaded two controversial pieces of legislation on immigration and border security. He thought he would have a relatively quiet time when he received an invitation to attend the ASEAN annual conference in Southeast Asia. Suddenly he found himself in the middle of a war between China and Vietnam. He and the president, whom he was growing to dislike and distrust, joined forces to keep the war from escalating outside the South China Sea.

Only a few months ago, the Senate had selected Randy as the temporary chairperson of the Senate Judiciary Committee. He led the Senate's efforts to confirm the president's nomination to fill the open chief justice position on the high court. The meeting in the White House when Randy exposed the nominee wife's corruption and murder was still making news back in Washington.

Randy crossed Trafalgar Square, approaching Nelson's Column. His hotel was located a short distance from the famous landmark in Central London. He slowed his run to a fast walk and finally down to a normal walking pace. To look back at the last three years was to acknowledge his busy schedule. The highlights of the period were his marriage to Annie and his reelection to the Senate during the last midterm elections.

He was glad for the break in his hectic life, traveling to England together with his whole family. Upon his return to Washington in a few days, his upcoming schedule appeared to be very busy. The Fair Share Tax Bill would be the first item on the Senate's agenda when it reconvened next week. There would certainly be a vocal group of senators as they tackled the bill recently passed by the House.

Randy was approaching the entrance of the Hilton-Trafalgar Hotel at 2 Spring Street. He crossed over the street that circled Trafalgar Square onto Cockspur Street and walked the short distance to the intersection of Cockspur and Spring streets. From the front entrance, the Hilton Hotel appeared triangular. The main door faced the intersection at an angle. Four stories directly above the main entrance was a large clock, showing the time at nearly eight thirty. He must have run near the limit of his normal eight-mile distance.

He wondered if the others would be up. They had arrived in London eight days ago, in the morning, after an overnight flight from Reagan National in Washington. As recommended by most travel guides, they stayed up and visited Winsor Palace and some tourist spots close to the hotel. Randy went to the British Imperial War Museum on his own. He had been a history major and wanted to see the many displays from the Second World War. He had been surprised at the number of British taking their grandchildren through the exhibits. The most popular section had been the film of the London Blitz. Many of the grandparents had been very young children during the war. They wanted their grandchildren to remember the sacrifice made by the British people almost seventy-five years before.

Chapter 7
London
Saturday, November 28, 2015
10:30 a.m.

Randy and Annie were waiting in the lobby of their hotel when Aunt Frances walked down the hallway from the elevators. She sent them a little wave of her hand and walked over to meet them.

Randy rose from the lobby table. He was drinking a cup of coffee, and Annie was working on something on her own new BlackBerry Q-10. Randy thought that Annie had selected England for their vacation to get him away from his heavy workload back in Washington, DC, but she had spent considerable time keeping up with her own projects back in the States. As the senior electrical engineer for the Global Architectural Firm, Annie was involved in overseeing a number of schools and hospitals under construction in third-world countries.

Frances went up to Randy, and he wrapped his long arms around her shoulder and accepted the light kiss on his cheek. Released from his bear hug, she leaned over to give Annie a kiss on the top of her head. Annie responded by lifting her head up and leaning forward to apply a kiss of her own on the older woman's pale cheek. The two women had grown very close over the three years they had known each other since Randy and Annie had married.

"How did you sleep last night, Frances?" she asked?

Frances settled down in the chair next to her nephew. "Wonderful. I never thought I could sleep so well away from my Pacific Ocean, but this London night air seems to do wonders for me."

She looked over toward Randy. "That doesn't mean I'm not ready to head back toward California tomorrow. I can feel the waves of the ocean pulling me home."

Randy laughed with his aunt. She lived in a small two-bedroom bungalow overlooking the Pacific Ocean in Malibu, California. When constructed back in the nineteen forties, it was an equal to the other homes nearby at the time. Today it was the smallest home in the neighborhood. The other homes from the same era were long gone, replaced with grand palatial constructions. Her little home almost seemed out of place. Randy knew Frances had turned down almost seven-figure offers from several real estate agents. He also knew she would never sell the home she had retired to after the death of his uncle.

Randy looked at his aunt. "Did the food at the Spice Market give you any problems last night?"

Randy was referring to the restaurant located five or six blocks from their hotel. The swanky W Hotel provided space for the Thai- and Asian-accented food created by superstar chef Jean-Georges Vongerichten's US-based chain.

Frances gave a little wave of her right hand to emphasize her answer. "Not a bit. I loved it. I can still eat just about anything as long as it is properly cooked. You can keep all that raw fish stuff to yourself, but other than that, I am ready for the next meal."

Randy was about to mention he was allergic to most of the raw fish dishes himself, but Arthur and Millie Willis walked up to their table.

Millie looked at her daughter, still working the BlackBerry. "Annie, put that darn thing away and greet your father. Beside, you're supposed to be on vacation." She walked up to Randy and planted a good morning kiss on his cheek in almost the same spot Frances had selected only a few minutes earlier.

Mille leaned over to kiss her daughter's cheek, continuing her light scolding. "After all, you told us Randy was the one who needed a vacation out of the country. He has spent more time not thinking about his heavy workload than you have."

Randy saw the look on his wife's face. Two years ago, he could not decide if Millicent Willis really liked him or not. Now, after three years of marriage, he noticed her siding more with him, against Annie. The last time he brought this up with Annie in the kitchen of their apartment she had smiled but stuck out her tongue at him. He had just laughed at her.

Arthur gave Randy an affectionate pat on his right shoulder. "Randy, I just want to thank you again for last night. After almost eight days away from Virginia, it was nice to have a touch of home. That was one of the best shows I've ever seen."

Everyone chimed in with words of appreciation. Knowing they might be getting a little homesick, through the Internet he had purchased five tickets for "Sinatra in London" from the apartment in Alexandria.

After the late crooner passed away, relatives had discovered nearly one hundred fifty reels of thirty-five-millimeter film taped during his television program back in 1957 and 1958. The recording technicians did not use the cheap quality film used by the television networks at the time but the best available in its day. Shot from only one camera in a fixed location, the film showed Frank Sinatra singing some of his best work, with three or four musicians providing the background music. Specialist removed the film from the family vault and restored it to almost original quality. Listening to the best music from their own time proved a wonderful experience for the older members of the group.

Frances had to speak up. "You know, I met Frank and some of the Rat Pack boys back in my old days in Hollywood, when my husband was producing movies at Warner Brothers Studios. I have never met a man more full of piss and vinegar. I loved being around him, and his talent was unbeatable, but he was a rascal."

Randy leaned over to kiss his aunt again. "Someday you need to write your memoirs about the old Hollywood. It would be a bestseller."

Frances shook her head. "Oh, no, Randy. I would not trade my days in Hollywood or with your uncle for all the gold in Fort Knox, and I would never make any money on my wonderful memories. They are just for us—when you can force me to talk about the secrets this old memory contains." She lightly tapped her temple. Randy knew she loved to tell stories about her time on the old Hollywood film studios. Maybe she was in her seventies, but her body and mind still behaved as if she were in her middle fifties.

Arthur spoke up, rubbing his stomach. "Hey, folks. Last night's wonderful dinner is long gone, and I am ready to eat. Where are we going for lunch, or brunch, or whatever you call it?"

Annie responded with a smile as she turned off her BlackBerry and stowed it away in her large shoulder bag. "That's Randy plan for today. He said we would probably want to eat something closer to home after eating British food all week."

The group turned their attention to Randy. "I thought we would eat a little American food and then do some sightseeing right around Trafalgar Square. We've got a long flight out of Heathrow early in the morning, and I didn't want us to get too tired from sightseeing today."

"Sounds like a plan," Frances said as she rose from the chair. "Lead on, Macduff. We will follow you."

The group gathered their coats and gloves, followed Randy out of the main hotel entrance, and turned left to walk along Cockspur Street. They chatted about the many historic locations they had visited during their eight days in England. The foot traffic was heavier than typical for this time of the year because the weather had been warmer than normal. However, the local weather forecast was promising a change back to normal conditions, starting with a drop in temperature, with rain moving in during the early afternoon hours. The weak sunshine seemed to indicate the forecast was accurate.

They reached the end of the block and crossed the street at the intersection. They only needed to walk a few yards before they came to a building with the Texas flag swaying in the London late morning breeze.

Randy stopped and raised his arm toward the flag. "Welcome to the Texas Embassy Cantina and some of the best Tex-Mex food you will find in London."

Chapter 8

London
Saturday, November 28, 2015
11:00 a.m.

Even in London, Randy Fisher's fame could not escape him. One of the managers of the restaurant chain was an American working in London who recognized the famous senator. He insisted on seating them at a large round table next to a window, allowing them to look out onto Pall Mall East Street, with a view of the Londoners out for their own lunchtime.

Randy's family settled into their chairs and opened the menu to browse the food selection. After eating bland English food for most of eight days, their appetites were looking forward to a taste of home.

Mille had to speak up. "Randy, this is wonderful. We've stayed at some really nice hotels on this trip, but the food is simply too bland for my taste."

Annie said, "Hey, don't forget the French restaurant in Bath where we had dinner. My waistline is still showing the huge plate of beef stew and mashed potatoes I consumed all by myself."

Mille smiled toward her daughter. "I seem to remember telling you about the three secret ingredients always used in French cooking." She was about to continue, but the other four people chimed in.

"Butter, butter, and butter."

Millie looked around the table, and they all burst out laughing.

The group placed their orders and continued to talk about the castles and palaces they had visited. One commonly unknown fact by most Americans was that castles by design were fortifications and used to protect the land. Palaces with their grand designs became the home for the royalty of England. The consensus among the group was it made no difference if the structure was castle or fort; they were physical proof of what real financial wealth was all about.

Their food arrived, and the group tore into the American-style food that reminded them of home. It might be lunch, but all of them had ordered steak and baked potatoes. Not having eaten since an early dinner last night, they were all famished.

Afterward, with the main plates cleared away, they were content to just sit and sip their coffees. It was their last day in England, and the nonstop pace was catching up with Annie's parents and Frances Ward.

Annie looked at her husband. "Randy, what are you going to do with the Fair Share Bill when we return to Washington?" Annie knew it was never too far from his mind.

"I'm not really sure. My feelings toward the president have not changed in any way. I will support Tom Evans in his run for the White House. I will make speeches and conduct fundraisers, even though I hate to ask people for money. I'm determined to see that Harold Miller only has one term in the White House."

He paused for a few moments as he gathered his thoughts. "The president's bill certainly addresses the corporate tax problems, and his drum-beaters have stirred the public to a high fever. However, all that said, I think the president has taken a Band-Aid approach to fixing a tax problem that should be resolved by fixing the basic problem. That means rewriting the corporate tax codes to close all the loopholes corporate America and the foreign companies have been exploiting for years. The new tax bill would probably be two thousand pages long."

He paused again. "All of you know how I feel about huge pieces of legislation."

Before he could continue, they all spoke together. "If it's more than one hundred pages, then we probably can't afford it."

Randy looked at the people around the table and started to laugh with them at their jab at one of his personal mantras. He reached for the cloth napkin still in his lap and wiped his mouth. During the meal, he had been facing Pall Mall East Street and occasionally watching the people walking by the restaurant. He had just laid the napkin on the table next to his water glass when his hand froze in place.

His eyes locked on a figure on the other side of the street. The younger man, dressed in a heavy black turtleneck sweater and blue jeans with black walking shoes, looked very familiar. His hair, showing beneath a wide-brim hat, was black and curly. His skin tone was dark, an uneven, thin beard pattern on his face. He was not a black man: probably European, Persian, or maybe Arab.

Randy watched the man use a cell phone to take a picture of Trafalgar Square, almost a full block away. The man dropped the hand holding the phone to his side and glanced over his right shoulder, shifting Randy's view from profile to full-face.

Even though the hat partly hid his face, Randy was certain about the man's identity. He was looking at a ghost from his recent past. Only three years earlier, the man across the street had shot Randy Fisher twice in the chest from a fifteen-foot distance.

Chapter 9

London
Saturday, November 28, 2015
12:30 p.m.

Annie was the first to see the strange look cross Randy's face. She had been waiting for him to finish his answer to her question. She looked at Randy and then quickly swiveled to look over her left shoulder at whatever had drawn his attention from the group at the table.

"What is it? What are you looking at?"

Annie turned back to Randy. The others took a quick look out the window but then turned back to Randy. From the look on his face, something was certainly upsetting him.

Randy watched the stranger across the street who had paused to take some pictures with a cell phone camera. The man adjusted a backpack slung over his right shoulder and then walked on toward Trafalgar Square.

Randy Fisher was no longer a tourist. He looked at Arthur Willis and pointed his right index finger at his father-in-law. "Arthur, pay the check and take everybody back to the hotel. Stay there. Stay together in Annie's room. I want to know where everybody is at all times."

He rose from his chair and turned toward the nearest door from the Texas Embassy Cantina that would exit onto Pall Mall East.

Annie Fisher called after her husband. "Randy, what is going on? Where are you going?"

Randy paused only long enough to turn his head and talk over his right shoulder. "Do as I say; now!"

Without another word, ignoring the stares from other restaurant patrons and his own family members, he rushed out the side door onto Pall Mall East Street. He turned right toward Trafalgar Square in the distance, looking for the man.

He could not see him. He quickly looked back the other way. Had the man turned around in the few seconds Randy had taken his eyes off the person now consuming his attention? Was he walking away from Trafalgar Square?

No. He had been taking pictures of the square from outside the restaurant. Randy started to jog toward the square. He was a long city block away, but he covered the distance in less than thirty seconds. He had to pause for heavy traffic when he came to where Pall Mall East curved south and became Trafalgar Square Road.

Over the top of the cars making the turn from the Trafalgar Square Road to Pall Mall East, he searched for the man as he waited for a break in the heavy noontime traffic. He could not see him. He had to remember the traffic pattern flowed right to left and not step into the fast-moving combinations of taxis, private automobiles, and trucks supplying goods and services to the hotels, restaurants, and shops in this busy tourist location.

Directly across the street from where he stood was the fourth plinth, located on the northwest corner of Trafalgar Square. This particular structure was different from its three counterparts, also located within the boundary of the square. The two southern plinths carry sculptures of Henry Havelock and Charles James Napier.

Major General Havelock, born April 5, 1795, died November 24, 1857, at the age of sixty-two, was a British general associated with India who had recaptured Cawnpore from the rebels during the Indian

Rebellion of 1857. During the final year of his life, Havelock commanded a division during the Anglo-Persian War. He was present at the action in Muhamra, and later his troops were engaged in the Indian Rebellion.

Throughout August of that year, Havelock and his troops pursued and destroyed all mutineers and insurgents, despite being heavily outnumbered. His years studying the theories of war and his experience in earlier campaigns by the British Army came to good use. His goal was to relieve Sir Henry Lawrence at Lucknow and Wheeler at Cawnpore.

Three times, he advanced toward Lucknow but decided to hold his position to preserve his troops, nearly wasted by disease and the hardship of battle. Finally, with the arrival of reinforcements on September 25, he was able to take the fort, only to be forced to take shelter from a second group of rebels who had arrived to retake the stronghold once again.

The attack by the rebels failed, and Havelock was again successful. But the strain of battle and fatigue had taken a terrible toll on the general. He died on November 24. He lived long enough to learn his new title of baronet, earned for his victorious march. He never knew of his promotion to major general.

Sir Charles James Napier, born August 10, 1782, died August 29, 1853 at the age of seventy-one, was another general of the British Empire under Queen Victoria. He was the commander-in-chief in India and most notable for conquering the Sindh Province in what is now Pakistan. Perhaps one of the most interesting stories about General Napier involved a Hindu priest complaining to him about the prohibition of Sati by British authorities. This was the custom of burning a widow on her husband's funeral pyre. According to his brother William Francis Patrick Napier, the general had taken very little time before delivering his response.

"Be it so. This burning of widows is your custom; prepare the funeral pile. But my nation has also a custom. When men burn women alive we

hang them, and confiscate all their property. My carpenters shall therefore erect gibbets on which to hang all concerned when the widow is consumed. Let us all act according to national customs."

The northern plinths, larger than the southern plinths, were designed to have equestrian statues, and the northeastern plinth had one of George IV. The plinth directly across the street from Randy never reached completion due to lack of funds. Today the location is special to the square and used to display a changing scene of various works from contemporary artists.

To Randy's right he could see the main attraction of Trafalgar Square, Nelson's Column. To his left was the huge National Gallery building that was to have been his recommendation for the group's last day in London. Now his focus was far from sightseeing as he tried to catch sight of his target. The traffic cleared enough for him to dash across Trafalgar Road into the square. As he walked past the fourth plinth, he approached the first of the two great fountains inside the square.

The fountains, built in the late nineteen thirties, replaced the original two structures, which failed to work properly. The water spurts from the original fountains received comparisons from local citizens to the opening of a bottle of beer. Removed by local artisans, the fountains found new homes in Ottawa, where they are still sputtering away. The newer models can shoot water as high as eighty feet on a very quiet day without a breeze. The addition of LED lights of various colors added to the attraction of the fountains.

Hundreds of tourist and local Londoners were spending their lunchtime sitting around the edge of the fountains. Randy continued to try to locate his target. He kept turning in all directions. He finally walked to the edge of the closest fountain and stepped up on top of the outer rim near the north side of the fountain that kept water from overflowing into the square. Several people nearby were giving him dirty looks and wondering what the stranger was up to.

From his slightly elevated position, Randy continued to look around. He was about to drop back down to the pavement when his target walked out from behind the second fountain in the direction of Nelson's Column. The hat was distinctive from what other people on the square were wearing. His target was still taking pictures with his cell phone.

Randy jumped off the concrete lip of the pool and ran around the northern outer perimeter of the fountain toward his quarry. He had to step around the many people between himself and the man who had shot him three years ago.

Past the fountain, he finally caught sight again of his target. Randy's position was sixty-some yards away, but he moved faster and in a straight line, fewer people now separating him from the man. He had only taken a few long strides before the man suddenly turned and saw Randy coming out of the thick group of people near the first water fountain. Even with the distance between them, Randy could see the man's facial expression change to recognition and shock.

Suddenly the hunt turned into a chase. The man turned toward the most populated spot on Trafalgar Square and broke into a run. His object was Nelson's Column and the four large bronze lions guarding the monument, surrounded by hundreds of tourist.

The man had only about twenty yards to travel to the northeast lion. Randy was more than twice that distance from the popular tourist attraction. He would never reach his target before he lost him among the spectators.

The four magnificent lions were almost 148 years old. According to legend, the lions will come to life if Big Ben chimes thirteen times. The film producers of the 1967 James Bond movie *Thunderball* ignored this myth when they used thirteen chimes of the world's most famous clock to accede to the evil Specter organization's demands for the return of two stolen twenty-megaton nuclear devices.

Randy increased his speed as he raced toward the object of his attention, now approaching the closest lion. He remembered reading that the original designs for the lions called for granite but instead were cast from bronze said to come from captured French cannons. Another tidbit of information he found amazing was that the casts were hollow. Sir Edwin Landseer designed the magnificent creatures using a cast taken from a dead lion that belonged to the King of Sardinia. When first revealed to the British public, the lions were ridiculed for their reclining posture instead of standing tall and projecting strength and dignity. Today they are one of the biggest tourist attractions in London and pay for all the attention they receive from the tourist and local visitors. Recent examinations had shown extensive damage inflicted by tourists climbing on the backs of the lions, especially at the tail sections. Some experts have warned of the possibility of the lions collapsing under the weight of their "riders". The lion considered to be in the worst condition was the northeastern lion, Randy Fisher's destination as he hurried to catch up with his target before he was lost among the tourists.

Randy covered the distance to Nelson's Column and stood between the two northern lions. All four statues, positioned in a perfect square and spaced twenty yards apart, protected the column located directly in the center of the lions.

The centerpieces of the square was the 170-foot tall column composed of Dartmoor granite and bronze, constructed between 1840 and 1843, honoring Admiral Horatio Nelson, who died at the Battle of Trafalgar in 1805. William Railton designed the column, and the Craigleith sandstone statue of Nelson is by E. H. Baily. The eighteen-square foot-bronze panels were cast from other captured French cannons.

The original cost for the monument in 1843 was £47,000, but the statue received an overhaul in 2006 at a current-day cost of £420,000. At that time, the workers discovered the statue to be fourteen feet, six inches shorter than previously thought.

Randy decided to move east around the northeastern corner of the monument and dodged between the sightseers. He made the turn at the corner and walked quickly along the outer edge toward the southeast lion. His quarry was no longer visible.

He had almost reached the lion on the southeastern spot of Nelson's Column when he caught sight again of his quarry. The man had already crossed the street beyond the monument and was now running past the statue to King Charles, still maintaining a fifty-yard advantage on Randy.

Randy knew he needed to increase his speed if he wanted to catch up with his target. He broke into a fast run toward the street. The traffic at the intersection of Cockspur and Strand Street was just a heavy as when he had tried to cross from Pall Mall East into Trafalgar Square—perhaps heavier because cars and trucks from Northumberland Avenue also entered the traffic pattern around the Charles statue.

Randy saw a slight break in the traffic flow when two cars suddenly tried to occupy the same spot. Amid the honking car horns, screeching tires, and angry drivers, he made a dash across the busy street into the center island occupied by King Charles sitting astride his horse on a granite pedestal.

Randy had learned a little-known fact. The specific location of the statue was also the exact spot that all road distances to London are measured from within the country. All information about the distance to London on any signpost throughout the country was determined from that central point.

Randy continued his mad dash over the traffic island and crossed through the heavy traffic again onto the eastern sidewalk of

Northumberland Avenue. While dodging the heavy traffic moving in the seemingly wrong direction, he had lost sight of his objective. He tried to reacquire his target, but the man was nowhere in sight. He had lost him.

Chapter 10

London
Saturday, November 28, 2015
12:50 p.m.

Randy stood still among the Londoners walking past him as he searched for the man. That was the only way he could think of him. He had no name or nationality with which to identify his target. Only the fact that someone possessed the mirror image of the man who shot him three years ago and tried to set off a nuclear device in his home city in South Carolina made him continue in his search. There was no doubt the man he was chasing was not the terrorist from three years ago. Randy had absolute proof the terrorist was dead. However, the fact they looked exactly alike meant he needed to catch the man and determine his identity.

The wind was starting to pick up; dark clouds were moving in overhead to block the sunshine. It appeared the warm, moderate weather London was enjoying was about to end. Randy had left his overcoat at the Texas Embassy Cantina and was wearing a long-sleeve white cotton shirt over dark brown slacks. His sports jacket started to flap in the strengthening wind.

He stood at the intersection on Northumberland Avenue and The Strand. The entrance to the Charing Cross Subway Station was only a few feet away. If the man had entered the subway system with other pedestrians as Randy crossed the heavily congested streets, then he probably had lost him.

Randy looked south down the length of Northumberland Avenue, but there was no sign of his target. He looked east up The Strand. The busy city street, congested with traffic, sidewalks filled with noontime pedestrians, offered a wealth of sights and sounds, adding to potential hiding places. Huge buildings and many doorways offering dozens of spots for his adversary to hide filled both sides of The Strand.

Randy was about to look back down Northumberland when he noticed a body leaning out from the doorway entrance to the Waterstones store, located in a huge building nearly seven stories tall, with over sixty yards of frontage along The Strand. Was that his man?

The answer came almost immediately. When his target noticed Randy looking back, he stepped backward, out of Randy's view. A few seconds later Randy saw the man break from the bookstore entrance and dash east toward the train terminal. Randy broke into a full run. Now it was a race between one man and another.

The area was one of the busiest in all of London, among the most heavily populated area in the City of Westminster. Hotels like the Corinthia, the Royal Horseguards, and the Guoman were all within a few minutes' walking distance. Dozens of restaurants were located there, offering almost any style of ethnic food to satisfy any person's taste buds. Centers for higher education, like the King's College Medical School and Courtauld Institute of Art, were within the confines of the area. Tourists could find many spots of interest, like the Cenotaph, which became the center focus of the British population every year on the Sunday closest to November 11 as they paid homage to the victims of two world wars. No serious student of architecture would want to miss visiting the historic St. Martin-in-the-Field Church designed by Scottish architects James Gibbs.

Randy moved as quickly as possible as noon lunch ended, dodging pedestrians on the street and people leaving the restaurants and shops.

He could see the railway station and ran for the entrance. His target had already entered the hotel directly connected to the huge transportation hub complex.

London was one of the most densely populated cities in the world. During the Cold War of the nineteen fifties and sixties, thousands of Europeans escaped from their countries, fearing the domination of the Soviet Union during that time. Travel to the United States was difficult and the shorter distance to the United Kingdom was more attractive. Over time, the population of London changed with the addition of different ethnicities. London was a magnet, and more people moved there to live with family members. Of the city's thirty-two boroughs, thirteen were in Inner London and nineteen in Outer London.

To facilitate inner-city travel by hundreds of thousands of people every day, London offered one of the world's most extensive railway and underground systems. Charing Cross Railway Station was located in the center of the magnificent city and was the hub of the transportation system. People could enter or leave the station using the two London Underground tunnel stations located at each end of the huge building housing six sets of railway tracks. Charing Cross and the Embankment Tunnel systems conveyed thousands of people every hour.

Randy finally reached the entrance to Charing Cross Station. From the sidewalk, he rushed through an opening in a brick-and-wrought-iron fence that separated the street from a driveway access that allowed motorists to pull out of traffic to drop off passengers for the station or the hotel in front of the station.

He ran into the Guoman Hotel foyer. He had to assume the man would pass through the hotel into the train station to access the extensive transportation system and elude capture. His hard-soled shoes clacked loudly on the marble floor. The interior foyer was round and filled with dozens of men and women. Randy had to stop to get his bearings.

He finally located a sign with an accompanying arrow indicating the direction to the railway terminal. He followed the sign down a hallway, past several meeting rooms and public restrooms. He went through several turns and finally came to the large glass doors leading into Charing Cross Station.

Randy emerged into the huge interior lobby of the train station. Hundreds of people were checking train schedules, purchasing items from the dozens of shops, or having a cup of tea or a bite of food in the restaurants. Natural light flooded through the clear roofing system, creating a blend of light and partial shadows across the lobby floor. The ceiling, forty or fifty feet above his head, was supported by rows of steel I-beams. The top flange of each beam lay against the roof with about a three-foot space between the lower flange, connected by a series of internal webs of V-shaped steel support structures.

Randy had entered the north end of the rectangular structure; the long axis ran north to south directly ahead of where he stood. The building was longer than an American football field.

He quickly pivoted in several directions, trying to locate the man. A long row of ticket stations filled most of the outer western wall. A queue of people were working their way through a network of blue polyester tapes stretched between steel poles to keep customers in some sort of organized line.

Magazine shops, small restaurants, and coffee and teashops advertised their products with bright neon lights, including stores selling cell phones and accessories among other retail outlets. Pedestrians were entering or leaving, mixing with the general traffic inside. Many looked above their heads toward the master clock to compare the time with wristwatches or cell phones. Other people stood near the ticket counters, looking at the electrical boards showing the schedules of the trains leaving or arriving at the station. Nobody was yelling, but the natural noise level inside the station was loud and added to the confusion.

Randy felt his heart beating in his chest. He was in good physical shape; the chase from the restaurant, across Trafalgar Square, and into the train station had not worn him out. But he was extremely apprehensive. He had lost his man, perhaps hiding in one of the dozens of shops, the many exits back to the streets, or the escalators with large illuminated numbers helping travelers locate their correct train one floor down to the tracks below. There were too many ways and places for a man to hide and escape discovery.

Chapter 11

London
Saturday, November 28, 2015
1:15 p.m.

مادر مقدس محمد (ص)

Holy mother of Muhammad. Shir Mohammad Moez Ardalan silently muttered a curse as he considered his escape options from the man who had been chasing him. If he could kill him, then the problem would be resolved. He felt no hesitation about killing the United States senator. In fact, he had dreamed of the day when he would slice the man's throat and watch the life bleed from his enemy's body—the man who was responsible for killing his twin brother.

Shir was thirty-five years old, a few minutes younger than Ali Nik Moez Ardalan, who had nearly accomplished the ultimate goal: smuggling a nuclear device into the United States and delivering a crippling blow to the one country that continued to exploit all of the Muslim countries in the Middle East. The United States would use whatever excuse was necessary to continue the flow of oil to their country while denying the Muslim countries the right to take their own place as the rightful leader.

Shir Mohammad Moez Ardalan and his brother had been born in Yazd, Iran, to a family that could trace their linage back to when Marco Polo visited the city during the thirteenth century. Yazd, the capital city of the Yazd Province in Iran, was 306 miles southeast of Tehran, home to almost 450,000 people and known for its unique architecture, sweet shops, and high-quality handicrafts, like silk weavings. In his diary, the famous Italian explorer wrote about the Iranian city located almost in the center of Iran.

Yasdi also is properly in Persia; it is a good and noble city, and has a great amount of trade. They weave there quantities of a certain silk tissue known as Yasdi, which merchants carry into many quarters to dispose of. The people are worshipers of Mohammad the holy prophet of Islam.

When you leave this city to travel further, you ride for seven days over great plains, finding harbor to receive you at three places only. There are many fine woods [producing dates] upon the way, such as one can easily ride through; and in them there is great sport to be had in hunting and hawking, there being partridges and quails and abundance of other game, so that the merchants who pass that way have plenty of diversion. There are also wild asses, handsome creatures. At the end of those seven marches over the plain you come to a fine kingdom which is called Kerman (*The Travels of Marco Polo*, translated by Henry Yule).

Their father was a medical doctor and very respected within the city. Many times when they were young boys, he would take Shir and Ali to the famous Marco Polo Restaurant in the city. They would laugh and enjoy themselves as their father told made-up stories about the explorer. Life had been very good for Shir and his brother until their father's death while he was in America.

When the brothers were still in their early teens, their father had obtained a hard-to-get visa to travel to the United States to attend

47

several medical conferences in New York City and to visit the Medical University of South Carolina (MUSC), a teaching hospital in Charleston, South Carolina. He was to be away from his family for almost a month. He promised to write letters to his sons to reduce their loneliness during his extended absence. The first letter took almost three weeks to arrive from the United States. He faithfully mailed additional letters almost every other day. They were still receiving letters for over a week after the local government officials had called upon their mother. With her two sons, she had learned the news about their father's murder in his hotel room in Charleston during a robbery. It seemed bad news could travel faster than the letters filled with love and humor. Each one received after the news of his death would end with the number of days before he would return to his loving family. The postmark on the last letter they received from their father was on the same day he had died.

Local village elders took over their education. One man in particular would visit each day with the brothers. He talked how great a doctor their father had been and the terrible loss to their family and the community. He would tell stories about living in the United States and how the Americans there used others to their own advantage. It was not hard for Shir and Ali to learn to hate America and the decadent people who lived far away, to understand that they would enter another country and force their own type of government and beliefs on people who really meant nothing to America.

As the brothers grew into young men, the Elder continued to talk about how America would keep expanding its influence. It seemed there was no country or army strong enough to defeat them. He told them the only way to stop the Americans was to take the war to their own shores and to the homelands of their friends.

When they reached their early twenties, they lived in camps with other young men from different countries and learned how to handle small arms and automatic weapons. They learned about assembling bombs and developing complex detonators that would explode long after they were gone and safe from the enemy. When not in training classes they attended lectures given by other men who lived far away from Iran and learn how the Americans, the English, and the French were trying to take the riches from beneath their land. Shir and Ali learned they were not alone in their hatred for the Americans.

As their training continued, it became clear that Ali was the more aggressive. He seemed to be able to handle the weapons better. He had a natural ability to understand the construction of bombs and the wiring required to make them explode at different times. He developed his own unique method to wire the devices, leaving bobby traps in case someone came upon one of his presents and tried to deactivate it. He would call them little presents and laugh because he would kill many Americans.

One day the Elder introduced Ali to a new stranger. Ali was delighted. He left the camp with the stranger for a special assignment, a mission of great importance requiring special training that would force him to spend many months or even a year away from his family. The last time they were together, Ali whispered to his brother that the success of his mission would avenge their father's death.

The two brothers were sad to go separate ways, but the Elder promised one day they would meet again. As they stood outside the tent they shared with four other young men, they hugged each other and promised to somehow stay in contact. Ali had left with the stranger, and Shir had never seen him again. No word of the work he was doing or the mission he had been assigned ever came back to Shir. No contact of any kind.

Almost two years had passed since their last morning together when word came of an incident in America. Newspapers headlines and broadcast news outlets proclaimed a terrible weapon was uncovered in a southern city. The American authorities claimed a terrorist, identity yet unknown, had tried to set off a nuclear device. Only the heroic efforts of one man had prevented the terrorist attack from succeeding.

Shir had listened to the news over the camp radio as he prepared for his own mission to send arms and small bombs into the insurgents' camps in Iraq, hoping to kill more Americans. He was ready to leave for his own mission when the commander of the local group called him back and told him he would not be on the mission. Instead, he would travel back to his village for further instructions. He arrived home to spend several days with his mother and finally received word to meet with the Elder. The old and wise man told him it was no longer safe for him to leave the country. The Americans knew his face.

Shir could not understand the reasoning behind the new order. Why were they forcing him to stay behind while others continue with the fight? What had he done wrong to deserve this punishment? For the first time since they met many years ago, he argued with the Elder. He demanded an answer. The Elder sat quietly without speaking a word. He would normally never accept this type of disrespect from a soldier under his command. He looked into the face of the younger man and saw the same look in his eyes as in the man who had been his best friend … the young man's father, now dead for many years.

He patiently indicated for others in the room to leave them alone. The room emptied of all others except the Elder and Shir. Patting the carpet next to him, he spoke to the younger man. "Please sit down beside me, Shir. I will show you something that you will never share with another person." Instead, the younger man took a seat on a rug near the center of the room so they could face each other. The room was bare of all things consider a luxury. There was a single rug in the center, soft and warm; a simple cot for the Elder to sleep on was set up in the corner.

When Shir settled before the Elder, the old man looked directly in his eyes. "Again I tell you, you must never speak of this to any person. Not even to me. Are you perfectly clear on this?"

Shir understood the seriousness of the Elder's words and simply indicated his understanding. "I am perfectly clear. Never will I repeat your words."

The old man nodded and reached for a backpack on the floor. He unbuckled the straps that held the cover flap sealed and removed a wallet-size photograph. He looked another time into Shir's eyes before making the final decision to show the photograph to the young man. He simply said, "Ask no questions about where this came from", and then handed the photograph to Shir.

Shir might have been looking into a mirror. The only light in the room came from one small light bulb. He could not make out the few facial details in the picture that showed the difference between him and Ali. As he focused on the picture, he could tell it was a full frontal photograph of his brother from the waist up. The *Y*-shaped surgical incision and the closed eyes were enough to tell him his brother was dead.

His hands begun to tremble and tears formed in his eyes, but he kept silent, despite the words he wanted to scream. The old man leaned forward and laid his right hand on Shir's shoulder. "Ali died trying to destroy America. He was only a few hours away from succeeding. Some day we will complete the mission, but you must never be seen by them. The American intelligence organizations know his face, and now yours. They are unaware of his identity, and we must keep it that way."

Shir did not say another word but rose from the floor and put the photo in his pocket. The Elder had not wanted him to take it, but he decided to keep his thoughts to himself.

Two and one-half years went by. Shir Mohammad Moez Ardalan continued to help the cause by returning to the training camp and working with others preparing for their missions. He asked to revenge his brother and strike a blow against the Americans. Each time, his request received the same response: not this mission.

He taught tactics and logistics to new recruits. Better-skilled men taught weapons training, but he kept up with his own training with the many different types of handguns and the knife. All the while, he heard about the successful missions and the failures. He continued to ask to become part of a mission, but still the answer was no. When he became aware of a new mission that would strike at the heart of England, he walked into the office of the camp leader and demanded that he be part of the mission. The leader listened to his arguments and promised to take the idea up with the people planning the mission. To his surprise, several days later he received a summons to the camp leader's tent and was told to prepare to leave camp within twenty-four hours. He would be part of the mission to hurt the enemy in London.

A quiet cough behind Shir broke his reminiscence about Ali's death and brought him back to the present. The store clerk stood next to him. "Can I help you, sir, with a selection?"

Shir felt sweat rolling down the center of his back. There were beads of sweat at his temples and mixed within his thin mustache. He shook his head no. "I'm just waiting for a friend."

There was hardly any accent in his words; his English was nearly perfect. The clerk simply nodded and turned away to return to the sales counter, where he kept an eye on the stranger.

Shir had ducked into the clothing shop to avoid the searching eyes of the US senator. Now he visualized his appearance. The Tie Rack store's product offerings prevented him from blending properly with the few other people in the shop. With his current clothing, picking a tie would not look quite correct. He would have to move soon or the clerk would become more suspicious.

At the corner of the store's front window, he leaned forward slightly to check if the American was still in view. His hat brim tapped the glass surface. He pulled back and removed it. He had earlier tried to hide among the hundreds of people in the train station, and now he had to locate one man among the same number of people milling in the station lobby. He could not afford to be captured by the single man who might be able to warn the English authorities that a terrorist plot was developing in their country. He could not see the American, nor could he see to the end of the long station lobby.

There was no doubting Shir's conviction. If the American came too close, he would have to kill him.

Chapter 12

London
Saturday, November 28, 2015
1:30 p.m.

Randy Fisher was pissed at himself. He had lost the man. Now he would have to contact the authorities without proof that there might be a terrorist threat developing in London. He walked around the train station for a few minutes, looking in all directions in hope of locating his adversary. He was reaching for his cell phone, not quite knowing whom he was going to call, when a man in a dark outfit emerged from the Tie Rack store.

He had noticed the store during his earlier scout of the retail shops. The company's logo featured a picture of a tie instead of the letter *T*; the logo had stuck in his mind. The man looked familiar. Randy quickly walked about fifteen yards to stand in front of the store, continuing to watch the stranger heading for the south lobby exit. He took a few seconds to look through the front shop window inside the clothing store and noticed a collection of men's black leather jackets along the left wall of the shop. A mannequin in the storefront displayed the same type of jacket.

Randy looked sharply again at the stranger. Except for the leather jacket and the missing wide-brim hat, the rest of the clothes he wore were the same as the man he had been following. The backpack slung over his right shoulder was the giveaway. Apparently the man had purchased a jacket to wear over his heavy sweater.

The chase was on again!

Randy put on a burst of speed and raced to close the distance; it seemed they were always forty or fifty yards apart. His quest was moving at a walk, and Randy quickly shortened the distance between them.

Shir Mohammad could almost feel the eyes of the senator boring into his back, and he threw a look over his left shoulder. He should have avoided the impulse to check on the senator, but he could not force himself to keep looking ahead. The decision was the correct one. The senator had discovered him, even with the jacket as a disguise, and was now running to catch him.

Randy saw the man hurriedly glance over his shoulder, jam the hat he had held against his chest firmly back onto his head, and suddenly break out into a full run, heading toward the escalator down to the train tracks running under the main floor of the station.

Randy ran at full speed, closing the distance between them. He was only about twenty yards behind the man when a young boy ran out of a magazine store and collided with him. The boy, about five or six years old and only forty pounds or so, bounced off Randy's left thigh and crashed to the floor. His mother, a few steps behind her son, quickly scooped her son up, offering her apologies to the stranger. She alternated between apologizing to Randy and scolding her son for running out of the store.

Randy was forced to stop for precious seconds and ensure the boy was unhurt, but quickly he left the pair staring at his back as he resumed the chase.

His target was no longer heading toward the escalators to the train tracks but had diverted to the exit doors on the south end of the lobby that opened outside the terminal building.

The gap had increased while the English boy and his mother held up Randy's pursuit. When he burst through the terminal exit, the man was running south on Craven Street in the general direction of the River Thames.

Craven Street was slightly narrower than The Strand, with less pedestrian traffic. Randy increased his speed and slowly decreased the separation between pursued and pursuer. The street ran along the terminal, and then turned south to follow a long, gentle curve, finally connecting with Northumberland Avenue. The tall buildings took on unusual shapes to match the street configurations. They had wide foundations on the northern ends that narrowed down to much smaller footprints as the various streets came together at sharp angles.

Randy reached the intersection of Craven Street and Northumberland Avenue. There was no doubt in his mind that he would soon catch up with his quarry. Why the man had not taken one of the dozens of trains from the terminal or gone down into the underground tubes was a mystery. The decision was the one piece of luck that allowed Randy to stay in pursuit of his target.

Some of the pedestrians the two men ran by were stopping to watch the unusual event happen around them. Among the pedestrians and inside the terminal the two men had recently left were the normal force of English bobbies. Several officers had notified their dispatchers that something might be developing; two men were apparently in some sort of dispute, and one was chasing the other. Although most bobbies still did not carry firearms, their utility belts held the typical equipment one would expect to see on a law enforcement officer. Moreover, they had radios to keep in contact with their regional headquarters.

Northumberland Avenue ended as it neared the Victoria Embankment and the River Thames. Randy watched the man jump off the curb to cross Northumberland Avenue. He headed toward the multi-tiered steps leading up to the Golden Jubilee Bridges that ran parallel with the Hungerford Bridge, which handled the trains in and out of Charing Cross Terminal.

The steel truss railway bridge had a confusing past, little known outside of London. Originally constructed in 1864, it spanned the River Thames for almost three hundred and fifty yards. The first Hungerford Bridge was a suspension footbridge built in 1845. It received its name after the Hungerford Market because it connected the south bank to Hungerford Market on the north side of the Thames. In 1859, the railway company that was extending the Southeastern Railway into the newly opened Charing Cross Station purchased the bridge. Under the direction of Sir John Hawkshaw, the old footbridge was replaced in 1864 with a larger construction of nine spans of wrought-iron lattice girders. Later, several more additions increased the capacity of the walkway, but over time, further expansion of the rail system required the elimination of one walkway.

Other footbridges accommodated the growing traffic for the Festival of Britain in 1951. However, the footbridges earned a questionable reputation for being narrow and dangerous, and their physical condition deteriorated. In the mid–nineteen nineties, the decision to replace the old footbridges with new structures running on both sides of the Hungerford Railway Bridge seemed imperative. The construction was difficult. The old footbridges needed to be removed and the new replacements constructed while keeping the railway bridge open to train traffic. Other complications included the Bakerloo Tunnel line, which ran only a few feet under the riverbed, and the possible danger of unexploded World War II bombs buried in the Thames mud.

Inclined outward-leaning pylons support the decks of the completed bridges with fans of slender steel rods called deckstays. There are 180 of these painted white rods on each bridge. The deck stays receive additional support and are held in position by other rods called backstays. The deck is held in position by steel collars fitted around the pillars of the railway bridge attached to the pillars by tie-down rods. The entire structure remains in place through exploiting the tensions between the pylons and the various stay rods and struts.

The two new footbridges, completed in 2002, were named the Golden Jubilee Bridges in honor of the fiftieth anniversary of Queen Elizabeth II's accession. However, the public continued to refer to the three bridges at the Hungerford Bridge.

Randy was getting closer. When he reached the first set of concrete and steel steps leading to the footbridge, he temporary lost sight of his quarry. As he reached the bridge walkway, he again saw the running man. Now it was a race to catch the man before he crossed the River Thames and escaped in the crowd of tourists on the other side. Randy ran as fast as his legs would carry him, dodging among the pedestrians making their own way across the footbridge. Randy guessed his quarry was seven or eight years younger than he was. His physical fitness routine was now paying off. He was faster, with better wind management.

Quickly he was closing the gap. He was within twelve or fifteen feet, and they were only about three-quarters of the distance across the bridge. He noticed the man slowing; he seemed to be favoring his left leg. Had the man pulled a muscle or tendon, forced to give up?

Randy never broke stride as he quickly approached his adversary. He was not going to try to tackle the man but planned to just grab him and try to restrain him against the side railing of the footbridge. With only a few feet now separating them, Randy started to slow down. He was reaching out with his right hand to grab the back of the man's leather jacket when suddenly his quarry turned and pivoted on his left foot. Using his momentum, the man lifted the backpack from his right shoulder and with all of his strength slammed it against the side of Randy's head.

Awkwardly positioned with his right arm outstretched and his left foot far ahead of his right, Randy lost his balance with the impact of the backpack. His forward momentum carried him several more steps before he tripped over his own feet and slammed into the steel tubular guardrail at the same time as he glanced off the body of his adversary. His legs went out from under his body and his right temple struck the railing.

A dazzling array of small white stars filled his vision as he fell to the concrete deck of the footbridge. He threw out his right hand to help break his fall, but his momentum rolled him over, leaving him with his left shoulder against the railing looking back toward the train terminal.

Shir Mohammad was on one knee near the east side of the walkway. He had lost his balance after the backpack impacted with the senator's body. The force had knocked him to the opposite side of the bridge, where he tripped over his tangled feet. His lungs were burning from the fast run, and his legs felt like rubber. He held the backpack in his left hand. Still breathing heavily, he reached inside the main compartment for the Browning Titanium Gray Red Acid Quick Open knife. He needed to kill the American while the senator was dazed from his fall.

In his haste to grab the knife, it slipped from his hand. He rummaged among the other items in the bottom of the bag. Once he had the knife free, he tossed the backpack off to the side. The deadly knife blade was folded within the red handle. He moved his forefinger to the indentation just in front of the handle and depressed the release mechanism by feel alone. The twelve-centimeter titanium blade snapped open and locked into position.

Shir had never felt such hatred before. His father had died at the hands of some unknown person in America during a senseless robbery. His brother had died at the hands of the very American in front of him right now. At this moment, the purpose of his mission to London was far from his thoughts. He only had one desire: to kill the American.

He could tell the senator was coming back to his senses. The glazed look in his eyes was gone as he struggled to get back on his feet. Blood was running down the side of his face from a cut above his right eye. Shir needed to make his kill move with the knife now.

Randy Fisher saw the man rising from his kneeling position with the knife in his right hand. From a position of confidence a few moments ago, he realized he was now in serious trouble. The two men locked their eyes on each other. Randy observed the hatred in the other man's eyes and the determination to finish him off in his expression. He forced himself to his feet and regained his balance. The perfect mirror image of the man who shot him twice three years ago moved across the bridge, the knife held low by his right hip.

Other pedestrians suddenly realized some sort of dangerous confrontation was taking place nearby. Everybody scrambled to get away from the two antagonists.

Randy felt his foe would bring the knife up and around, intending a strike to his lower abdomen. The four-inch blade was long enough to deliver a killing blow. He would bleed to death within minutes. Randy watched his foe take two steps forward until he only needed one more step to launch his attack. Randy needed some way to throw his adversary off balance. "Your brother tried to kill me with a knife three years ago after he shot me twice with his gun. He received very poor training by his handlers. You're no better."

Shir Mohammad Moez Ardalan felt the blood pounding in his brain as the man before him spit out words of insult against his brother. He paused his attack. "You know nothing about my brother, but know this, American. I will be the one to avenge his death. You will die here on this bridge."

Randy paid little attention to the words of hate spoken by the twin brother. Instead, he watched the body language of the man intent on killing him. The space between their bodies changed with each man's attempt to find a better position for attack or defense. Shir continued to scream words at Randy, spittle flying from his open mouth. Inhaling oxygen deep into his lungs, Shir screamed out a loud final cry of pent-up anger and hate. With only a split second of hesitation, he committed the next step and launched his attack.

Twenty years had gone by since Randy Fisher left the United States Army as a private and an experienced military policeman. As an auxiliary deputy sheriff on the Richland County Sheriff's Department, only a few times had he participated in additional training programs; none of them dealt with hand-to-hand combat. But training stays with an ex-soldier. An old memory flashed through his mind. He remembered his hand-to-hand combat drill instructor screaming in his face to move faster. The DI was so close to him that day he could still remember the smell of the instructor's breath from his morning coffee. Randy's body suddenly reacted to the killing move from the terrorist out of long-past training and self-preservation.

He saw the killer make the first move with his right foot and the forward movement of his right shoulder. The knife was still clasped in his right hand, the knuckles white and bloodless from the tight grip. The killer's left hand and arm started to pull back as he twisted his body to force every ounce of strength he possessed into the knife thrust meant for Randy Fisher.

Randy moved without forethought. He quickly shifted his body to the right, a subtle leaning motion, without moving his feet. It was enough so the killer changed his body motion to adjust to the moving target. As the right hand of the terrorist came around, Randy could see his adversary's body move slightly to correct for his feint, moving the terrorist's body into a slightly off-balanced position. At the same time, Randy suddenly moved quickly to the left and a half-step back. The right arm holding the knife sliced through the air between their bodies, missing Randy's abdomen by less than an inch.

Shir could not believe he had missed from so short a distance. He could feel the flap of the American's sport coat graze the back of his right hand when his momentum carried his body farther around.

Randy stepped back toward the Iranian. He shoved the terrorist's right hand farther away from his body using the side of his right hand. He grabbed the sleeve of the leather jacket to help maintain control of the arm with the knife. With his left hand closed into a hard fist, he delivered a powerful blow to the right side of the terrorist's temple, just below the hat. He felt the shock from his fist colliding into the man's skull all the way to his shoulder. For a few seconds, he saw the man's eye roll, his focus lost, after the impact from his fist.

Stunned, the terrorist tried to pull his arm free. He dropped the knife and went down on one knee. Randy was moving in for another strike when a person plowed into his back. Randy lost his grip on his attacker's leather jacket. The fast-moving assailant approached from his blind side, and Randy found himself thrown hard against the side railing for a second time. He felt pain in his left shoulder from the blow to his back and a stinging feeling in his right wrist. He slowly started to rise to his feet a second time.

Another man, five or six feet away from Randy, was assisting the Iranian up and yelling at his partner in a foreign language. They took six or seven steps before the first terrorist seemed to recover enough to move under his own strength. He began to head back toward Randy, but the second man grabbed him by the left sleeve of the leather jacket and roughly pulled him toward the end of the bridge and the stairs leading down to the embankment. They were yelling at each other before the first man seemed to realize they needed to escape. The terrorist turned away from Randy along with his partner. Both men started to bolt as fast as they could run.

Randy Fisher was back on his feet and slowly recovering. His left shoulder hurt, and blood was running into his eye from the cut on his right temple. There were a number of abrasions on the heel of his right hand. He quickly accessed his wounds. They were not life-threatening, but he would require medical attention. He looked around and noticed the heavy knife on the east side of the walkway. The terrorist's backpack was several feet away. He walked over and stood next to them so they would not be disturbed and any evidence damaged.

Off in the distance he could hear whistles blowing, but his primary focus was still on watching the two men. They reached the set of stairs on the south end of the bridge that led down to a tree-lined pathway along the River Thames. At full speed, they leaped the final two steps of the concrete stairway and ran toward the London Eye off in the distance. For a few seconds he could follow their progress by the bobbing hats they both wore. Finally, he lost sight of them when they moved among the thick trees and the hundreds of tourists walking alongside the river, popping open their umbrellas against the growing strength of the rain.

Chapter 13

London
Saturday, November 28, 2015
2:30 p.m.

Randy Fisher, cold and wet, sat in one of the interrogation rooms in the Metropolitan Police Station on Agar Street east of Trafalgar Square. An unarmed bobby stood quietly against the wall next to the only exit from the room.

The rain had started to fall almost as soon as he got back to his feet, at first only a few heavy drops against his face. As he lost sight of the two men mixing with the tourists, he saw the wall of rain moving from the west toward the Golden Jubilee Bridges. The chase was over. He had lost his adversary.

Westminster Bridge was over six hundred yards west. In a few seconds of the heavy rain, it was almost invisible. As the bridge disappeared, the weather front moved closer. The London Eye became hard to discern, and then the hard rain was upon him, moving east.

People quickly whipped out their umbrellas, or brollies. He had learned the newer modern accepted term was tote. But Randy was without any protection from the cold rain. His sport coat became heavy as the material absorbed the rain. He lifted the collar against his neck, but the rain was simply too heavy. He could feel the water running down his back; he used his hand to clear his eyes. Each time, his right hand came away showing watery blood from the cut above his brow.

He reached for the cotton handkerchief in his back pocket to cover the cut on his right temple.

Several British bobbies arrived on bicycles and quickly took a firm hold of his arms. He needed to clear up their concerns and explain why the chase after the other man had ended in a skirmish. They were trying to talk above the noise of the rainfall, but they simply gave up when a motorized police cart with a hard-shell top arrived. They indicated for Randy to take a seat next to the driver. Another bobby climbed onto the back bench to watch him. The driver made a U-turn on the footbridge and headed back toward the Charing Cross Station side of the River Thames. They did not try to ask him any questions as they hurried back across the bridge.

At least he was out of the direct rain, but the brisk wind still blew the rain on him, and his wet, cold clothing was sticking to his skin. It all added to his sense of failure.

At the other end of the Jubilee Bridges, the driver steered the cart down a wide ramp to access the walkway below. A police car with a flashing rotating blue light was waiting for them. Randy received instructions to transfer to the car with three other officers. They motioned for him to enter the back seat. He was surprised they did not restrain him with handcuffs as probably would have been done in the States. At least he was out of the blowing cold wind and rain and inside a heated cruiser.

The drive was short: north on Northumberland Avenue to The Strand and a right turn. They only drove a few blocks before the police cruiser turned left onto an authorized-only access to Agar Street and the modern police building located at the next intersection.

Once through the entrance lobby, they escorted him to a chest-high counter where he received instructions to empty his pockets. After the officer at the counter logged his possessions, they walked

Randy deeper into the building and placed him inside an interrogation room. Typical of police interrogation rooms around the world, the solid walls contained only a basic heavy wooden table and four chairs. They motioned for him to take a seat. A male officer, left in the room, stood near the door, his hands clasped in front of him, to watch Randy. A few minutes later, a female police officer entered the room with a black bag like those carried by doctors in old movies. She requested permission to examine his wounds. She gently probed his head wound and examined the abrasions on his right hand and wrist.

She was probably twenty-eight or thirty years old and about five feet four inches tall. Her face, framed by curly dark hair, was pretty, with soft-looking skin that required little makeup. She reminded Randy of his wife. She looked into his face and offered a small smile. She seemed to decide he was no threat and sat down in the chair next to him. She peered at the wound over his right eye as she opened her medical kit.

"The cut on your forehead looks worse than it really is. I do not think you will need any stitches. Maybe just a couple of butterfly plasters." She gave him another smile. "Sorry ... you Americans call them a Band-Aids, right?"

Randy smiled back. She had a nice accent. Then he remembered he was the foreigner in the room. "Yes. How do you know I'm an American?"

She gave him a bigger smile and then laughed, showing straight white teeth. "Your clothes and shoes are all made in the United States. You are also wearing a Timex wristwatch, so I made a guess based on my observations. How did I do?"

Randy laughed. "Your observations were spot on."

"Good. Let me get you fixed up, and I'll see about a towel and a hot cup of coffee or tea."

Randy nodded his head. "Thanks … a large hot cup of coffee would be great. Do you suppose I could speak with whoever is in charge of this station? I really need to call some people."

She offered a small smile as she removed a Band-Aid from the sterile wrapper. "I'm sure someone will be here shortly."

A few minutes later, she finished her work and closed the medical kit. "That will hold you for a little while. I'll be back in a few minutes with your coffee and something to help you dry off."

Randy examined the dressing she had placed around his right wrist. "Thank you again."

As she opened the door, she nearly bumped into the first of two men trying to enter the room. The plainclothes man stepped back to allow her to leave the room and then walked in, followed by an older man in uniform.

They nodded to the uniformed officer in the room, who closed the door after they entered and resumed his position off to the side of the table. They took the two chairs across from Randy and laid Randy's passport and driver's license plus a file folder on the table. Randy could not see what the folder contained.

The younger unshaved man was about Randy's six-foot height but heavier by maybe twenty-five pounds. His dark hair was cut so short Randy could not determine the color. Every dip and curve of his skull was visible, giving him an ugly look. His suit coat showed many wrinkles, and his shoes needed a coat of polish. There was no wedding band on his left hand so Randy guessed he was single. With his sloppy dress and poor personal grooming, Randy did not foresee a wedding any time in the near future for the man. He could understand Annie's comments about men who thought the unshaved look adopted by television and movie stars was stylish. It only made them look like bums.

The uniformed officer appeared to be around fifty-five years old; his uniform was properly pressed and looked custom made. His black hair was thin, his scalp showing through in several places. His shoulder epaulet was black with what looked like a wreath of leaves arranged in a circle not quite closed at the top. Within the wreath were two round red-tipped poles. To Randy, the poles resembled two cigarettes with one of the ends lit. This man appeared to be the senior officer; his overall appearance was more in keeping with his rank.

The younger man spoke first. "I'm Inspector Lonny Watkins, and this is Commander Corley. He is in charge of the center part of London and most of the area where you were seen chasing a man, ending up in a scuffle." He flipped open the folder, pulled out a half-dozen photos, and laid them across the table for Randy to see. Randy recognized the various locations in the photographs. Apparently, traffic and security cameras had recorded his bizarre chase through Central London.

Watkins picked up Randy's passport and looked again at the name. "Now, Mr. Fisher. You haven't broken any laws except perhaps disorderly conduct, but we are very interested in why you were chasing that man and why he tried to kill you."

Randy had been sitting in the hard wooden chair at an angle that helped the medical officer examine his wounds. Now he turned to sit squarely on the chair and face the two officers. "Do you have the knife he used to attack me? His fingerprints might be on the blade. What else was in the backpack?"

Watkins shook his head. "I'm afraid we will be asking the questions first, sir. Why were you chasing that man?"

Randy knew he needed to end any confusion. "My name is Randy Fisher, and I'm a United States senator. The man I was chasing is an exact look-a-like of the man who shot me three years ago after trying to set off a nuclear device in Columbia, South Carolina."

Their facial expressions froze. Randy allowed them to recover. "I noticed the resemblance and decided I needed to catch him and discover his identity." Randy proceeded to tell them about his chase from the restaurant to the south end of the Jubilee Bridges. As he reached the part of his story that aligned with a photo, he touched the photo and sometimes changed its position on the table to match the timeline of the chase.

The commander listened to Randy's detailed description of the chase before finally breaking his silence. "First, Senator Fisher, let me apologize for the way we treated you. We had no idea who you were."

Randy was about to reply, but the door opened again. The medical officer entered, holding a tray with a small coffee pot, a china cup with the Metropolitan Police logo, and several small plastic cups holding packets of sugar and powdered creamer. She set the tray on the table in front of Randy and then removed the heavy cotton towel draped over her left shoulder. She wrapped it around his shoulders. Randy thought her kindness was touching; it contrasted with Inspector Watkins's impatient look at the interruption.

Randy quickly poured a cup of coffee and took a careful sip to test the temperature. It was perfect. He took a deep drink from the cup. He gave the medical officer an appreciative smile. "Thanks. This really hits the spot."

"You're welcome, sir."

Watkins watched the interchange between the officer and the witness. His fingers tightened along the edge of the papers in his hands as his frustration grew. "Perhaps we can continue now."

The woman's eyes snapped toward the plainclothes officer. "A few moments of civility never hurts, Inspector Watkins."

Her snub toward Watkins was noticeable to all. The uniformed officer still guarding the door coughed to cover his small chuckle.

Commander Corley decided to make the introduction. "Officer Davis, this is United States Senator Fisher. Senator, this is Anne Davis … a very capable officer."

Randy smiled to Officer Davis. "We've met, just not formally. Thank you again, Officer Davis."

She stepped back from the table. "My pleasure, Senator." As she turned, she nodded toward Commander Corley and left the room.

Randy took another sip of the hot brew and then set the cup back on the table. He used the warm towel to rub his hair and face. Most of his hair had already dried, but it felt good to move the cotton fabric across his face and around the back of his neck.

Corley turned toward the officer still standing against the wall. "See if you can find the senator some dry clothes until we can get this mess sorted out and him back to his hotel."

Randy suddenly sat back in his chair. "I need my cell phone. I left all my relatives in the restaurant. They have no idea what is going on."

Corley looked again at the officer, who was moving toward the door. "Bring his belongings first and then try to get some other clothes."

When the officer left the room, Randy picked up the photographs on the table. He flipped through them, looking for the face of the man he had chased. It was not evident in the photos.

"How is it you caught my face in all the photos but not the man I was chasing?" Randy quickly decided he had been rash. He had been hatless, while the few times he had seen his adversary, the wide-brim hat hid the man's face. Avoiding the cameras was probably the reason why both men were wearing the fedoras in the first place.

Their faces started to color from embarrassment, but further discussion of the subject seemed redundant after the uniformed officer reentered the room with Randy's cell phone. Randy accepted the device and looked at them again. "Do you think I can have a little privacy to talk to my wife? I don't know about an English wife, but mine will be asking a lot of question that I'm not prepared yet to answer."

Corley answered, "Of course, Senator. Just step out of the office when you're ready to resume our talk."

He began to follow Watkins out of the room but turned back. Randy was accessing the contacts in his smart phone. "What hotel are you staying at, Senator?"

"The Hilton next to Trafalgar Square."

"Good. The hotel is only a few blocks away from the station. Please tell your wife that one of my officers will be over there shortly to pick up a set of dry clothes for you."

Randy hit the speed dial for Annie's cell phone. He was not sure what he would tell her.

Chapter 14

London
Saturday, November 28, 2015
3:15 p.m.

Randy Fisher ended his telephone conversation with Annie. She had immediately launched into a series of nonstop questions, but he had finally calmed her down enough to let him answer a few of them. When he mentioned that someone from the police department would be there shortly to get a fresh set of clothes for him, the questions started again.

Finally, she seemed satisfied with his answers; other questions could wait until he got back to the hotel. He laid the phone on the table next to the photos Corley and Watkins had left on the tabletop. He gathered the photos up and flipped them on their sides before slapping them against the tabletop to align them. Afterward he again flipped through them, looking for a picture of the man he had chased.

He suddenly slapped his right hand against his head. The contact caused both his head and wrist to hurt. "You deserved that, you fool," he said aloud to the empty room.

He finished the second cup of coffee and as he rose from the chair and headed toward the door, he grabbed the folder cover. On the other side of the door, he saw a number of officers gathered in several small groups. Their discussion faded quickly as they looked at him in the open doorway.

"Where's Commander Corley?" Randy asked.

The officer who had brought Randy his cell phone stepped forward. "Please walk with me, Senator Fisher. I'll take you to the commander's office."

Randy followed the officer deeper into the building; they came to a bank of elevators. One of the doors was just opening as they approached so they did not need to slow their pace. The officer pushed the button for the top floor and the door closed.

Several floors higher, they stepped off the elevator and walked straight down a hallway to a set of double glass doors. Corley was sitting behind his office desk, talking on the telephone. He had seen Randy exit the elevator and watched his approach.

Corley quickly finished his telephone call as Randy walked into his office without waiting for permission. Randy had his cell phone in his right hand.

"I've got a photo of the man I was chasing on my cell phone."

Corley looked back at his guest. "I didn't think you had time to snap a picture of him."

Randy's lips pulled to the side as he tried to determine how to explain his next statement to the commander.

"Commander, have you ever been shot?"

Corley was slow to answer. He readjusted his body in the office chair. "No. I have been very lucky in my years of service. I have never been required to fire a weapon in the line of duty or been faced with someone who was trying to kill me. I am, of course, somewhat aware of your personal history, Senator."

Randy nodded. "Then you know my government never identified the man. Nothing ... no name or nationality. No clue who he was or who supported him in his efforts to obtain the weapon and bring it into my country." Randy paused to plan his next words. "I hope you don't think what I'm about to tell you is strange. Someone tried to kill me, and I think it would be natural for everyone to realize I would want to know everything there is to learn about my assailant." He looked from Corley back to the uniformed officer still in the room.

Corley simply nodded at the American. "Yes. Quite correct."

Randy nodded in return and plunged ahead with his explanation. He lifted his smart phone to indicate it. "I used my position on the US Senate Committee on Intelligence to obtain the complete file on the man who shot me. I have all the information stored on my phone right here. It is stored behind several layers of encryption, but it will have all of that information, plus a photograph of the man I chased. Remember, he acknowledged the man who shot me was his brother. You have to believe me when I tell you they were identical twins."

Randy opened a file on the smart phone and entered a password. The file opened, but the letters were a scrambled mess of unintelligible words. He entered a different password, and slowly the scrambled letters took shape; readable words appeared.

He moved around the room and laid the phone on the commander's desk. The other officer did not ask Corley for permission before he moved around to the other side of the desk to look at the phone.

Randy slowly scrolled down the file. Finally they came to the photograph of the terrorist. He had not looked at the file for the almost two years since he had originally loaded the information on the phone. He had not told anyone he had copied the information, which probably was in violation of several security articles of the United States government. Regardless, he had wanted the information, and now he could put it to good use.

Corley sat back in his chair. "We need you to send us this file, Senator. With this information together with the contents of the backpack, we might be able to identify your man and perhaps learn what he's up to here in London."

Randy agreed. He picked up the phone from the commander's desk, about to ask him for an e-mail address, when the face of his phone changed to show an incoming call. The number ID indicated the call was from one of Randy's best friends.

"Please excuse me while I take this call, Commander."

Randy pressed the accept button on the phone and raised it to his right ear with his bandaged hand. The different time zones between England and the United States made the time in Washington about nine fifteen in the morning.

"Good morning, Marion. How are you this fine day?"

Randy heard the voice of his best friend, Marion Bellwood. The voice of the deputy director of operations for the Central Intelligence Agency came in very clear from across the Atlantic Ocean.

"I'm fine. Thanks for asking, MP. I understand you've been playing some sort of English variation on hide and seek and have gotten yourself hurt."

Randy chuckled to himself at Marion's use of his "MP" nickname. They had both served in Europe back in the nineteen nineties. Randy had been a member of the army's military police, and Marion had been a CIA case officer. They had spent many evenings in one of the bars near the army base at Mannheim, Germany. Marion had tagged Randy with the nickname, and he would use it whenever he thought the younger man was getting himself into some sort of trouble.

"Well, you know, Marion, it wouldn't be any fun if I didn't see a terrorist every time I came to London."

Marion's voice took on a serious tone. "Annie called Marci and told her you've been hurt and need help. I got the call coming out of a meeting with the national security advisor. What is going on over there?"

Randy spent thirty seconds bringing his friend up to date on his morning's activities. There was silence for several moments after he had filled in the details.

Marion came back with a question. "Where are you now?"

"I'm at the Agar Station of the Metropolitan Police. It's close to Trafalgar Square."

"I know where it's at," Marion said. "I'll make a few calls while I'm on my way to the airport. I will see you in six or seven hours. Try to avoid any more trouble until I get there."

The phone ended with a loud click in Randy's ear.

Randy was about to explain to Commander Corley who the caller was when he saw the elevator door in the hallway open. Annie Fisher walked off the lift next to the medical officer who had treated his wounds. Annie carried a small suitcase in her hand, a very determined look on her face.

She saw Randy through the glass doors of the commander's office and made a beeline toward him. The sight of his bandages quickly changed the hard look on her face into concern, and she simply asked a short question. "Oh, Randy. What have you gotten into now?"

Chapter 15

London
Sunday, November 29, 2015
9:45 a.m.

The location for the next meeting moved from the Agar Metropolitan Police station to the main headquarters building for New Scotland Yard. Many people thought the police department was a separate entity from the famous Scotland Yard, but in fact, they were the same organization. New Scotland Yard was simply the name of the building for the senior-level officers of the Met, as the locals called it. More than 49,000 full-time employees made up the department; nearly 38,000 were uniformed police officers under the direction of Commissioner Sir Alistair Stanley-Moore.

Stanley-Moore had held his current position for almost three years after approval by a committee comprised of the home secretary, the mayor of London, and the chairperson of the London Police Authority. Once past the committee, he received a formal appointment by the queen. He was one of the leading experts in criminology in the British Isles.

Randy Fisher stood next to Marion Bellwood, recently arrived from the States. They shared a small space at the window on the top floor of the large steel-and-glass-façade building. Randy looked down at the top of the famous revolving triangular New Scotland Yard sign, recognized around the world.

He had arrived back at his hotel with Annie yesterday afternoon to face the concerns of his aunt and in-laws. They had nearly as many questions as Annie. After promising to answer every question to the best of his ability, he put them off until he took a shower and changed into the same clothes Annie had brought with her. Commander Corley had taken the information from Randy's smart phone and contacted his superiors for further instructions and consultation. He promised to contact Randy later with any new developments and bring him back to the station the next day for a meeting to update the senator. He offered to have Officer Anne Davis take a department car and transport Randy and Annie back to their hotel.

Once out of the warm shower and back into dry clothing, Randy gratefully accepted a thick ham and Swiss cheese sandwich and another cup of coffee ordered from room service and settled down in their hotel room. Surrounded by his loved ones, he told them the entire story of his adventure since he had left them with their mouths open at the Texas Embassy Cantina earlier in the day.

Millie asked the questions on everyone's mind. "You think there will be some sort of terrorist attack here in London by this man and his associates?"

Randy tossed the cloth napkin that came with his lunch back on the serving plate. "There's no telling for certain just yet, but it is a possibility. Now that the man has been seen, the group might call off their plans or at least delay them."

Frances spoke next. "You said group, but you only know about two men, the one you were chasing, and the other one who hit you from behind."

Randy set his empty coffee cup back on the tray. "Yes. I only know of the two, but these terrorists usually work in a group of four or more, depending on the size of their operation."

Millie laid her hand on her husband's arm. "Well, I'm glad we will be leaving for home early tomorrow morning. I want to be out of London in case there is a problem. I hope the authorities can catch these men. I am very glad you were not seriously hurt, Randy. You need to stop taking these risks."

Annie looked at her husband's face as she spoke to the group. "I hate to break your bubble about this, Mother, but I'm willing to bet a very large amount that my dear husband will not be on the plane tomorrow. Not unless the police can perform a small miracle today and capture these men quickly."

All the adults looked at Randy and waited for his comment. His face took on a determined expression. "I can't leave until this had been resolved. The man's brother shot me twice and killed David Bechtol at the fairgrounds in Columbia. It is almost a forgone conclusion he knows who was behind the attempt to place a nuclear device within our country. This is the first solid lead we've had in three years, and I'm not about to give up the chase."

He stopped to allow them to understand the reasoning for his decision and then continued. "That being said, I want all of you on the flight out of here tomorrow. I will not be able to focus on my work here knowing that you might be in danger."

Annie moved to sit on the edge of the sofa she was sharing with Randy. "Now wait just a moment, buster. I am not leaving you here by yourself to deal with these damned terrorists. If you stay, I'm staying right here with you."

Randy turned toward his wife. He kept his tone calm, but there was firmness in his words. "Yes, you are going. Your parents and my aunt have had enough vacation excitement to last them for a while. I want them on their way home, and you're the only one who can get them safely home and keep me from worrying about them."

Annie had seen the look of determination on Randy's face several times in the past. She knew it was no use to argue further. She decided to change the subject and maybe get him on the plane with the rest of the group. "What about your work in the Senate? The Fair Share Bill is to be taken up on Monday when the Senate goes back into session."

Randy rose from the sofa and walked past his aunt on one of the straight upholstered chairs in the large sitting room. He walked to the window of their sixth-floor room to look out at the traffic below. After a moment he turned back to face the others. "The bill will be introduced into the Senate on Monday and then assigned to the finance committee. I'm not on the committee. This mess in London should all be over with before the bill comes back to the full Senate."

Annie was not quite ready to give up. "And if this thing over here is still unresolved after a week or two? How long will you stay?"

Randy remained quiet for almost half a minute before he answered Annie's question. "Whatever these people are planning could be a dress rehearsal for another attack in the States. I will stay here until they are captured or killed."

Randy looked away from the view through the Scotland Yard window toward Marion Bellwood. His friend had arranged a Metro Police escort to the airport that morning. Randy rode with his family to Heathrow. At the curbside for US Airway's overseas check-in, he had helped his in-laws and Aunt Frances with their luggage and then spent several minutes giving hugs and kisses. Aunt France placed both hands on the sides of his face and pulled his head down to whisper her final words into his ear. "You get these bastards and come home safely."

Annie had tried to show a brave face, but a few tears escaped and ran down her cheeks. She gave him a firm kiss on his lips. "You and I are still planning on a family together, and I need you to keep up your side of the deal. You clear on that, mister?"

Randy kissed his wife again and looked down into her eyes. "Never out of my mind."

He now looked at his wristwatch and back at Marion Bellwood. "They should be in the air by now."

Marion reached out and gave Randy a light slap on the shoulder with his right hand. "Don't worry. They are in the air, and Marci will meet them when they arrive at Reagan National. In addition, I have arranged for a couple of my people from the Protective Division to be at the airport with Marci. Frances will love the special treatment."

Randy gave his friend a grateful smile and turned to look at the group of high-ranking London law enforcement people and several representatives from Her Majesty's government. They were waiting for the representative from 10 Downing Street, the prime minister's office.

The room was large and rectangular. The heavy wood conference table could hold at least sixteen people. Tubular steel chairs with cloth-padded seats waited along the outer wall of the room for fifteen or more attendees. The number of people talking quietly in the room would fill most of the chairs.

Marion Bellwood looked over toward a new person who had entered the room. He gave Randy a little head nod toward the new arrival. The man was in his middle sixties and tall, well over six foot two. Marion noted that his once-slender body had grown heavier, but his movements were smooth and fluid. He caught sight of Marion and changed direction to come over to them by the window. As he drew near, Randy could see the small broken capillaries in his large Roman nose. His eyes were bright and crinkled at the edges as he offered a smile and his hand to Marion.

"Ah, Marion, you old rascal. How nice to see you again."

Marion took the offered hand and affectionately patted the shoulder of the older man with his left hand. "I'll answer to 'rascal,' but I think

81

you've got at least ten years on me. If anybody in this room is an old rascal, your name would be the first on the list."

He made a slight head movement to indicate Randy. "Sir Huddleston, let me introduce to you United States Senator Randy Fisher; the reason we are all together today. Randy, this is Sir Lawrence Huddleston of MI6. Behind his back, they call him 'the Chief'."

It was Randy's turn to offer his hand to England's top spymaster. Many Americans failed to understand the difference between Britain's MI5 and MI6. The American Federal Bureau of Investigation was the equivalent of MI5. They were responsible for protecting the UK at home and overseas against threats to national security. The more secret MI6 was the equivalent of the Central Intelligence Agency. Its mission was to gather intelligence outside the UK in support of the government's security, defense, and foreign and economic policies.

The two men shook hands as they sized each other up. Marion decided to make sure his English cousin was aware of Randy's background. "Sir Lawrence, I'm sure you are aware of Randy's efforts to capture the two North Koreans in California several months ago."

Huddleston was still holding onto Randy's hand. "I'm quite aware of this man's record. Well done, Senator. We had been searching for those two *gentlemen* for some time. They were two very dangerous men who needed removed from circulation. When your government is finished with them, we have a court of law that will add to their prison sentence. Yes, well done indeed."

He looked Randy directly in the eyes. His demeanor no longer showed any humor. "Now it appears your own history had decided to pay you a visit. Of course, I read the reports of your activities yesterday. For a politician, you handled yourself very well when you went up against a trained terrorist with a knife." A small smile broke out on his face. "Of course, you've had some experience with that sort of thing before, if I remember my reading from several years ago."

Randy was about to answer when someone rapped their knuckles on the tabletop. The three men quickly turned to the front of the room. Sir Alistair Stanley-Moore cleared his throat. "Ladies and gentlemen, let's all take our seats so we can begin."

Randy and Marion moved to take the two chairs assigned to them according to the double-sided place cards with their names. Randy could identify others in the room from their nameplates but not their positions or responsibilities. He moved the nameplate farther back from the table's edge to make room for the booklet waiting at his place. He was a little surprised at how quickly such placeholders could magically appear on short notice before such meetings.

In front of each person at the table was a folder with the Scotland Yard emblem embossed on the cover. Randy opened the folder and examined the information inside. Some of it he quickly recognized as information he had provided to Commander Corley from his smart phone.

Marion leaned toward Randy and whispered close to his ear. Randy could hear a touch of whimsy in his tone. "Some people might think you're a bit of a ghoul carrying photographs of a dead man in your smart phone. Most of us have family photos."

Randy leaned toward Marion as the CIA operative pulled away. "It's not something I want the voters of South Carolina to know about, though hopefully they would understand."

Sir Lawrence Huddleston walked past Randy and Marion, giving them both a light squeeze on their shoulders, and moved to his place at the table. He was on the other side from the Americans and closer to the front of the room. He stopped several times to shake the hands of other people in the room and offered a quick smile and a few words.

There were about thirty people at the table or in the chairs against the outer walls, a four-to-one ratio of men to women; the number of those dressed in civilian clothes versus either military or police uniforms was about equal. Randy was not very familiar with the various uniforms, but he guessed there were only one or two from the military.

He recognized Commander Corley from yesterday, seated to Randy's right on the other side of Marion. They had already spoken briefly when Randy arrived earlier.

Commissioner Stanley-Moore was in his midfifties with graying hair, wearing a long-sleeve white shirt with shoulder epaulettes and a black tie. He stood at the head of the table after the others had taken their seats. His epaulettes were about the same size as those worn by Commander Corley. One of the insignias was similar—the circle with the two burning cigarettes. An additional diamond and crown made his uniform appear a little more elegant. He looked up from papers on the table in front of him. "Good morning. I know that most of you are acquainted, but we have several guests here today. I will begin with their introductions and move around the table and then the room for their benefit."

He held a pen in his left hand and used it as a pointer. "At the end of the table are our two American friends. The man farthest away is United State Senator Randy Fisher, responsible for our gathering here today. It appears he has stumbled onto a possible terrorist plot. Next to him is the deputy director of operations for the Central Intelligence Agency, Marion Bellwood. I'm sure all of you will want to meet these men before you leave here today, but please wait until after the meeting."

He turned to the man sitting to his left. "This is Deputy Commissioner Jonathon Shepard, who will be in direct charge of this investigation until it is brought to a successful conclusion. He will be taking over this meeting as soon as all the introductions are completed."

Stanley-Moore then quickly went about the table. To his right was the minister of defense, Gordon Naismith. Gloria Merd was a cabinet minister without portfolio assigned by the British prime minister to any special but limited engagements. She sat next to Minister Naismith. Next to her was Paul Andres, the director general of the security service who headed MI5.

Stanley-Moore continued around the room, introducing additional members of his staff. Some would be in charge of the physical search for the men wanted for questioning; others were part of the Met's Intelligence Division. When he finished with the introductions, he turned to his deputy. "All yours, DC."

Randy had paid close attention during the introductions. Certainly, the British authorities were taking this possible terrorist attack very seriously. Representatives from the highest levels of the British government and law enforcement agencies occupied chairs in the room. He would compare this to a meeting of the president's National Security Council back in the States.

Deputy Commissioner Jonathon Shepard was a few years older than Stanley-Moore. A daily regimen of exercises and jogging coupled with a rigid diet kept his body lean and in great shape. His haircut was longer than younger officers, who favored the more modern buzz cut worn by Inspector Watkins. A wavy curl gave Shepard's hair body. He rose from his chair to make his presentation. He pointed to a young female officer sitting at a desk in the back corner, away from the room's entrance. Most people in the room had not noticed her.

She activated some switches, and a screen slowly unrolled from the ceiling in the front of the room, behind where Stanley-Moore had stood. The room's interior lights darkened, and a projector mounted to the ceiling flashed a faint picture against the screen. The projector's bulb took a full minute to reach maximum brilliance, and Stanley-Moore used the time to move out of the blinding light shining slightly over his head.

Shepard moved from the side of the table to stand in an angled position so he could see the screen and easily swivel to look back at the assembled group of people. He was holding a sheaf of papers as he addressed the group for the first time.

"Well, now. I am going to take you through the events of yesterday with Senator Fisher. If you have any questions, speak up."

The presentation started with the photographs and video clips taken by the CCTV cameras located in Trafalgar Square, Charing Cross Station, and from the south end of the train station down the length of the Jubilee Bridges. Between the pictures, a rudimentary map of the square and surrounding areas showed Randy's locations during his chase. In the bottom, right-hand corner of each picture and duplicated on the map was a time stamp.

There were sixteen or eighteen slides in the first part of the presentation. Randy was as interested as everyone else in the room. He was hoping to see someone who might be the second suspect. Finally, the part came when the camera caught the fight near the end of the bridge. There were several murmurs or gasps as Randy dodged the knife thrust and then delivered the blow to the terrorist. Someone in the back of the room muttered, "Good show there."

Finally, the camera captured the second man hitting Randy from behind. During the few seconds the new arrival was within the field of view of the camera, his hat blocked any view of his face. The group watched the silent digital replay as Randy wiped away the blood flowing from the wound to his eyebrow. The look of dejection on Randy's face was the last picture captured by the camera.

Marion Bellwood leaned toward Randy. "Your luck held again, MP. You must be like a cat with nine lives."

Randy simply nodded and moved to whisper back to Marion. "Yeah, and I'm using them up too fast." He shook his head. "If only I could have captured him."

Deputy Commissioner Shepard addressed the group. "Does anybody have any questions for Senator Fisher?"

The defense minister spoke first. "Did you have any idea there was a second man before he struck you from behind on the bridge?"

Randy shook his head. "No. He was a complete surprise. I am afraid I lost sight of my target many times during the chase. It is entirely possible they met briefly or communicated by cell phone and planned the attack. My instinct tells me he might have been somewhere close by and acted on his own. Maybe they were going to rendezvous and I caused them to rethink their plan."

Gloria Merd spoke for the first time. "You're quite certain about the words the first man spoke to you? His words about his brother were clearly understandable?"

Randy never hesitated. "Absolutely. He had very little accent. He told me he wanted to avenge his brother's death by me three years ago. There is no doubt in my mind he is the brother of the man who tried to set off the nuclear device in my country three years ago."

Chapter 16

London
Sunday, November 29, 2015
10:35 a.m.

Randy Fisher's words about a nuclear devise caused small pockets of conversation to break out in the room. The big elephant in the room had suddenly made itself visible. Was London about to face a similar threat from a terrorist group?

Only one known terrorist had been behind the American incident, and he was dead. Here in London, at least two men were involved in a possible terrorist plot, and the threat of a nuclear incident brought terrible images to the people assembled in the conference room. The Central London population exceeded eight million residents, and thousands of tourists were always within the city at any given time. In comparison, Randy's entire home state of South Carolina had a population just under five million people.

Paul Andres, head of MI5, rapped his knuckles on the table. He gave Shepard a look that hastened the DC of the London Metropolitan Police department to use his own knuckles to get the meeting back under control.

"All right, all right. Let's settle down. Director General, do you have questions?"

Paul Andres was a large man. At six-foot-four, he was the tallest person in the room. His large girth nearly overfilled the chair he was currently commanding. "What have we learned about the two men, other than what the senator and our friend from the American Central Intelligence Agency have provided?"

Shepard looked back toward the projectionist at the small desk in the back of the room. "Officer Langhorne? Would you bring up what we have developed so far on the two suspects?"

Several slides quickly flashed across the projector screen before Officer Langhorne finally settled on one from the digitalized information Randy had provided Commander Corley yesterday at his office on Agar Street. The people in the room quieted down as they focused on the new slide.

It was clear to all in the room that the photograph before them was of a dead man lying on a laboratory table. The closed eyes and Y-shaped incision from the autopsy were visible. On the side of the abdomen was the narrow wound from a knife blade that was the cause of death. Shepard resumed his briefing. "This is the snap of the man killed three years ago in America. The Yanks have provided all the information they have on their suspect, and we added that to the portfolio provided to everyone here. Next slide, please, Officer."

Randy looked at the picture blown up on the large screen. Before today, it had been a small photograph from the original file when viewed on the smaller screen on his computer or cell phone. His memory of the fateful day quickly filled his thoughts.

Randy's mind cleared itself of the past as the screen filled with a new slide. The previous slide had showed a nearly naked body lying on an autopsy table, devoid of color. This photograph contained vivid colors and details. Four people were in a clothing shop; a red arrow superimposed onto the photograph signaled out one man in particular at some distance from the camera's location. As Randy and Marion focused their eyes more closely on the photograph, they could tell it was a men's clothing and accessory store.

Randy suddenly recognized the location. It had taken a little longer than might have been normal because the picture was from the back of the store facing the lobby of the train station. The tie shop.

Shepard continued. "We were not able to locate the suspect in any of the snaps taken by our security cameras as we did the senator. However, our investigators had a bit of luck. The officers retraced the entire route of the chase and asked every street vender and storeowner if they remembered seeing the man in the autopsy photograph. We got this picture off the security camera at the haberdashery shop inside Charing Cross Station. It seems our suspect stepped inside to hide from the senator, and over time, the store manager became suspicious. He approached the man several times to ask if he needed any assistance. The first time the man simply told him he was waiting for a friend, and that might be the truth, as the second suspect showed up soon afterward on the bridge. When the manager approached him again, the suspect decided to purchase a leather jacket. The manager claimed it was the quickest sale he had ever made."

There was light laughter around the room.

Someone from the back of the room called out a question. "How did the suspect pay for the jacket?"

Shepard's eyebrows popped up slightly. "Well, now. I am afraid our luck did not extend far enough. He paid with cash."

Shepard looked over at Randy in the reduced light in the room. "Senator Fisher, can you confirm the man in the picture is the same man you chased yesterday through the train station and later confronted on the Jubilee Bridge?"

"Yes. In the picture, he is wearing a heavy wool sweater, and he is holding his hat in his left hand. He put the coat over his sweater to try to disguise himself. You can also see the backpack he was carrying. It is still over his right shoulder. The backpack is what I noticed as he was walking away from me. When he realized I had recognized him, he jammed the hat back on his head, I assume to prevent any camera from capturing a good photograph of his face, especially the elevated cameras."

Someone in a chair along the wall spoke up. "Good show, sir, not to lose your focus on the suspect."

Shepard nodded again toward the projectionist. "Next slide, please."

The next slide showed a close-up photograph of the backpack and all the contents found inside arranged on a white surface. Slowly the projectionist flipped through several more slides that showed a close-up of every item. In addition to the backpack were the knife, a cell phone, a spiral notebook bound along the side, a cotton handkerchief, a bottle of water, a folded map of London, and several English currency bills of various denominations.

The police lab technicians had displayed the notebook from the backpack by itself for the next slide. A small plastic ruler lying next to the notebook provided a two-dimensional reference. The notebook was five-by-eight inches.

Shepard continued. "From the knife, cell phone, and bottle of water, we were able to lift several good sets of fingerprints. No positive returns so far within our own database, but we are still awaiting the response from Interpol and from our American friends, thanks to Mr. Bellwood. We are hopeful in this respect."

The next slide was the cell phone. "Our suspect was taking snaps with the camera in his cell phone. We have almost 150 snaps of high-traffic tourist spots: Nelson's Column, the National Portrait Gallery, the London Eye, Westminster Abbey, and the House of Parliament. At any time during the day there can be upward of several thousand people at each location."

He turned from the screen to look at the people in the room. "That's not all. The notebook also contained a short list of some of the same locations. Our translators worked out the conversion."

The screen flipped to a page showing handwritten Persian words next to the English translations. The room was silent as each person read the list of some of the most popular tourist locations within London. Even Paul Andres was quiet as he worked the security problems through his mind.

خانه مجلس	**House of Parliament**
چشم لندن	**London Eye**
کاخ باکینگهام	**Buckingham Palace**
وستمینستر کلیسای	**Westminster Abbey**
ستون	**Nelson's Column**
گالری ملی پرتره	**National Portrait Gallery**

Randy and Marion looked at each other. They were quietly thankful the page in the captured notebook did not contain a list of high-traffic tourist locations in Washington, DC. The realization of a possible terrorist attack in Central London quickly sobered their thoughts.

A person could have heard a pin drop on the hardwood floor before Deputy Commissioner Shepard broke the silence. "All right. Let us review our security procedures and every department's responsibility in the investigation and search for our suspects. Please turn to page fifteen of your booklets."

Chapter 17

London
Sunday, November 29, 2015
2:30 p.m.

Due east of London, as the River Thames flowed generally east, was the historic dock area. For hundreds of years, London's supply of food, spices, and many other goods entered England by boat to be sold at the markets.

As the River Thames cut through the land, it made a huge southern bend shaped like a horseshoe with the open end on the north side called the Isle of Dogs. On the open area close to the river, it was natural over time to construct docks and warehouses within the horseshoe-shaped land. One development included the markets to sell the imported goods and food products. One of the oldest markets was located at Billingsgate. Several large facilities to handle trade included the two West India Docks buildings, the South Dock, and the Millwall Docks. They closed in 1980, and the business owners built the Canary Wharf Development on the site.

Established by special charter in 1327 by Edward III, Market rights prohibited rival markets within 6.6 miles of the city, determined by the distance a person could walk to market, sell his produce, and return in the same day. Through the years, other laws granted by charter allowed the population to collect tolls and customs at Billingsgate and other locales like Cheap and Smithfield. Since then the Billingsgate Market

Acts of 1846 and 1871, followed by the City of London Acts of 1973, 1979, 1987, and 1990, have confirmed the city's role as the Market authority.

The name Billingsgate evolved from predecessors like Blynesgate and Byllynsgate, used by the locals until they finally adopted the present form. The origin of the name, still unclear, could refer to the water gate at the south side of the city. It was originally a market for corn, coal, iron, wine, salt, pottery, fish, and many other miscellaneous goods. It seemed to become an exclusive market for fish around the start of the sixteenth century.

In 1699, an act of parliament declared Billingsgate a "free and open market for all sorts of fish" except eels. Eel sales were restricted to the Dutch fishermen who helped to feed the British people in London during the Great Fire.

Until the mid-nineteenth century, merchants sold fish and other seafood products from stalls and sheds. As the population grew and the demand for fish increased, it was decided to build a market designed to handle the fishing trade sales. In 1850, the first Billingsgate Market building was constructed, but it proved to be inadequate and later demolished in 1873 to make way for the current building. Designed by city architect Sir Horace Jones, today most of the Market is located in a more upscale neighborhood called Docklands.

Both police and fire services for Billingsgate fall under the protection of the City of London. As one of London's twenty-five wards, Billingsgate elects an alderman to the Court of Aldermen and commoners to the Court of Common Council of the City of London Corporation.

North of Billingsgate is the community known as Poplar. It is a quiet, mostly residential area of East London, about 5.5 miles east of Charing Cross. The district center is Chrisp Street Market. Notable public housing includes the Lansbury Estate and Balfron Tower.

Named after George Lansbury, a Labour Party MP, the development started in 1949 after the war to rebuild an area heavily damaged by German bombing. The developers used the design philosophy that new development should comprise neighborhoods and the neighborhoods should have all that a community required, including flats, homes, churches, schools, a retirement home for the elderly, and a shopping area with pub.

The Greater London Council selected a building site on the Brownfield Estate for Balfron Tower, and the construction crews completed the project in 1967. The 27-story, 276-foot-tall building holds 146 homes. A separate attached structure enclosed the lifts, or elevators, and accessed the main building with walkways located at every third floor. Should a person live on the eleventh or thirteenth floor, they would take the lift to the twelfth floor and then the stairway up or down one floor.

Other areas of interest include the Poplar Recreation Grounds, Robin Hood Gardens, and the Follett Street Seaman's Mission built in 1898. The Poplar Hospital for Accidents opened in 1855 on the north side of East India Dock Road with the main intention of treating injured dockworkers. Notable people born in Poplar include Angela Lansbury and Jennifer Worth, author of *Call the Midwife*, which was adapted for television.

All Saints Church lies in the southern half of Poplar and is the Church of England parish church. The church laid the first foundation in 1396. The foundation stone of the current structure followed in 1821. During the Blitz of the Second World War, the building received extensive damage from a V-2 rocket, and postwar reconstruction begins in the nineteen fifties. Today the church's main body is two stories tall; a steeple located on the west end added another fifty or sixty feet to the structure's height. The church sits on a large lot, taking up an entire city block. The long axis runs north and south, with Bazely Street to the rear and Newby Place along the front. The north and south streets bordering the church are East India Dock Road and Mountague Street.

Directly across Newby Street from All saints Church resides a large, square, brown brick home. The two and one-half story structure was originally a retirement home for the elderly. The building fell on hard times after the war. The owner, killed during one of the German Luftwaffe attacks, left the building in disrepair, and the surviving relatives had no funds for improvements. In the midfifties, the city was close to ordering the structure removed, but an Arab family owning a rug-importing company purchased the home from the owner's estate for a value well below its previous worth. They poured thousands of British pounds into the renovation and saved the structure. They used the downstairs for a retail sales showroom and offices; the family members lived on the second floor and in the attic.

Their business did well over the years. In the late 1980s, the father passed his company to his eldest son and his family. Some of the daughters continued to work in the business until they were married off.

In 1979, one son decided he needed to take a different path in life from his father and older brother. He returned to Iran shortly after the fall of Mohammad Reza Pahlavi, better known as the Shah of Iran. He quickly inserted himself into the new Islamic Republic led by Ayatollah Khomeini. He rose rapidly within the ruling religious order and was soon leading the Revolutionary Guards insurgency efforts against other countries. He name was Seyyed Reza Nikkhad. Over many years, he went by many names for security purposes, but eventually he became known as the Elder.

In the early part of 2008, he learned of his older brother's fate. The rug business was failing; the crippling world economy affected nearly every business, including the sale of Persian rugs. His brother was looking for a way out of the business and enough money to move to a more modern location in the northern part of England.

The Elder convinced his superiors to purchase the property under the cover of a false business incorporated in France. They planned to use the property as a base of operation and a safe house for future missions against the United Kingdom.

His older brother never knew Seyyed was behind the sudden offer from the French company. They had not seen or spoken to each other since Seyyed had left England in 1979. The financial arrangement was more than he had hoped for from the sale. The sale included a generous amount to cover the purchase of his business name, the buildings, current inventory, and the two old panel trucks he used to deliver what few rugs the company sold.

Using false French identity papers, several Iranian men moved into the house and operated the rug business under the same name. The new owners had purchased the company's name under the lie they wanted to keep the name due to the reputation developed by the original owners. Today it was the base of operation for the Elder's plan against England—more specifically Central London.

Shir Mohammad Moez Ardalan was in a second-floor room of the house. From the front corner window, he could see the trees lining the yard that ran parallel with Newby Street, as well as the highest portion of the church steeple beyond the trees. The rusted wrought-iron fence surrounding the large lot encompassing the rug building was invisible from his position, but it would keep anybody from entering the property. Two walk-in gates, always chained and locked, prevented anyone from walking in off the sidewalks. The only access for potential customers was by the driveway. There was a small public parking lot near the front entrance to the retail shop. The shop window displayed rugs for sale, but they were of obvious low quality with extremely high prices. They were open for business but did everything possible to discourage customers. The same driveway provided access to the back of the old retirement home, where a storage shed built several years ago was located. They could enter or leave the rear of the building and storage shed unseen through the thick woods surrounding the three sides of the property. Their business cover and the secluded location were perfect for their purpose.

Shir turned from the window and walked to the small mirror hanging on the wall near the doorway that led to the main upstairs hallway. He was holding an ice pack against his right temple to help reduce the swelling from the hard blow delivered by the senator from the United States. When he removed the ice pack, the mirror showed the dark, angry bruise on his face. The swelling was very noticeable. He touched the bruised area with his right hand. The skin was still very sensitive. Despite the swelling, he felt a depression below the skin. He was certain the senator had broken the bone beneath his right eye. He had tried to cover up the spot by wearing sunglasses, but the bruised area was too large.

Shir had been in England for almost a month, helping to prepare for the operation. He was one of five men who would be involved in the attack to destroy vital infrastructure within London and, with much planning, kill thousands of British people. With any luck, they would kill hundreds more staying at the hotels within the city. Their ultimate plan was to cripple the city by destroying one of its most precious lifelines. Before Shir could continue, he would have to endure another temper tantrum from the group's leader.

He left his bedroom, entered the hallway, and walked to the staircase leading to the first floor. The house was very large, with six rooms on the first floor. Two rooms were set aside for the showroom rugs that nobody would visit. The only room visible from the showroom was the office.

The rug company had not seen a customer for months. The telephone on the line assigned to the rug company had rung only twice since Shir had arrived. One call was an incorrect number, and the other had been someone trying to sell them a new credit card system. However, from a local citizen's viewpoint, the rug business was thriving. The two panel trucks leaving the property and returning several times each day indicated lots of business activity. With the church across the street only occupied several times each week, the few people living in the neighborhood accepted the comings and goings as normal business.

Shir reached the bottom of the stairway and turned toward the back of the house. He could hear music coming from the front showroom. Iraj Malek-Mohammadi would be in the office, watching the showroom for any intrusive customers. He reached the kitchen area and walked to the back door. He could see the storage building through the glass windows. Hossein, Ali, and Gholam would be working in the building, expecting him to help prepare for the attack.

Leaving the house, he crossed the fifteen feet separating the two structures and entered the side door, passing into the corrugated steel storage structure. The building had no windows, and the two overhead doors on the north end of the building stayed closed unless the trucks were leaving or entering the building. All the lighting inside was provided by fluorescent overhead fixtures.

The two old white panel trucks were parked in their normal spots inside the building, awaiting their lethal loads. The sides of the truck still displayed the fading lettering and logo of the rug company. Both trucks showed scratches and small dents along the sides and on the bumpers. One truck had a long crack in the front windshield that started down near the dash in front of the passenger's seat and continued across the windshield. The crack rose up toward the middle of the window near the halfway mark but dropped back to the lower edge before it reached the driver's side. The tires on both trucks were old and worn and would normally need to be replaced soon.

Three sets of eyes turned toward the sound as Shir opened and closed the side entrance door to the storage building. The sounds within the building vibrated off the bare steel walls. Normally a paper-lined blanket of fiberglass, installed between the joists of the walls, would act as a sound-deadening and insulation layer, but only bare steel separated them from the outside. They took no risk of discovery and always spoke in low voices. Shir hoped the risk of excessive noise would keep Hossein from berating him for having to come to his rescue from an older man on the Jubilee Bridges.

He walked past stacks of rolled carpets, most about five or six feet wide. They lay inside the same wooden bins used to ship the rugs from France. Each wooden crate, encased with a fine steel-wire mesh to hold the wood together, supported the weight of the rugs within.

For months, their dummy company had been receiving crates of rugs. Each rug was rolled and tightly wrapped with a thin plastic ribbon that required a sharp knife to cut. The rolled rugs were laid on their sides inside the wooden bins and neatly stacked. Each layer consisted of eight rolled carpets about twelve inches in diameter; each bin had four layers, making up thirty-two rugs per bin.

Shir had not bothered to count the number of wooden bins stacked inside the thirty-two-by-forty-eight-foot building that was twelve feet high. He would guess the number was well over one hundred and fifty shipping crates. The top layer of rolled carpets was completely normal. Should anyone bother to check the rugs during the transits from France, the rugs would agree with the shipping manifest. All the paperwork was perfect, and there was nothing detectable by security equipment or specially trained dogs within the rugs.

Nevertheless, the other three layers of carpets concealed long flexible plastic tubes of material. Each tube was four feet long and only about two inches thick. The tubes were heat sealed on each end; a knife was required to slit open the plastic lining. Inside the tubes was a fine white powder they would carefully transfer to large yellow fifty-five gallon plastic drums sitting on heavy wooden pallets. Once the powder filled the drums, they would be loaded into one of the panel trucks with the old forklift sitting behind the trucks.

Chapter 18

London
Sunday, November 29, 2015
3:15 p.m.

Hossein Rahim Bonab stopped his work on the plastic sleeve of fine powder. He had been carefully slitting open the tubes with his Browning Titanium Gray Red Acid Quick Open knife and slowly pouring the powder into the large plastic barrel next to his workbench. He kept his dust mask and plastic latex gloves in place; the fine powder lingered in the air, and he did not want to breathe any of the powder into his lungs.

In another part of the building, Mohammad Javen Nik Khah and Gholam Reza Rasoulian were slowly and carefully unrolling the carpets from the last three crates and removing the plastic tubes. They carried them over to Hossein's workbench and laid them carefully on the tabletop. The plastic was eight millimeters thick, much heavier than a normal trash bag. Nobody wanted to break the plastic, have the contents spill out, and get on their skin or into their lungs. While the contents would not burn or immediately kill them, they knew they could become very sick without proper medical treatment.

Hossein watched Shir put on his latex gloves and dust mask. This was not the proper time to scold the man again; they needed to get their work done and then plan the actual attack. Because of Shir's near capture and doubtless being recognized by the American, they needed to complete their preparations and reschedule the operation.

The planned attack was to begin this coming weekend, starting on Friday night. They would have had the entire weekend to contaminate the London water system with the powder. Now they would have only one night to complete their work.

The fine white powder was odorless and looked like baking flour. To help with the deception, the yellow heavy-duty plastic barrels they were using carried labels with the name of a well-known commercial brand of baking flour.

The others could not see the smile on his face as his thought about the contents of the powder. A scientist in his beloved Iran had developed the powder from the dried dropping of animals infested with cryptosporidium. The droppings had been specially treated to remove odor and color, leaving behind the protozoa that caused gastrointestinal illness.

Each bowel movement of an infected animal could contain millions of crypto parasites. The human host would begin to feel the effects of the organism very soon after consuming infected food or water. The symptoms could last for weeks and had proven fatal in the young and elderly or people with compromised immune systems, such as AIDS patients. That alone would be enough reason for Hossein and his men to wear the masks and gloves. However, the scientists had improved the concentration levels of the cryptosporidium and predicted a much higher fatality rate. They claimed any person with a common cold would become very sick and, if not treated quickly, die from the illness.

A number of cryptosporidium species infect mammals. In humans, the main causes of disease were *C. parvum* and *C. hominis*. Environmentally hardy cysts, or oocysts, transmitted the parasites. Once ingested, they harbored in the small intestine and infected the intestinal epithelial tissue. The cryptosporidium oocysts could survive for lengthy periods outside the host and resisted many common disinfectants, notably chlorine-based disinfectants. Cryptosporidiosis was typically an acute, short-term infection, but it could become severe, chronic, or deadly. In humans, it might remain for up to five weeks in the lower intestines.

Most modern water-treatment plants took their raw public drinking water from rivers, lakes, and reservoirs. They used conventional filtration technology to safeguard the public. Direct filtration, slow sand filters, diatomaceous earth filters, and membranes removed 99 percent of cryptosporidium. One of the largest challenges in identifying outbreaks was verifying the results in a laboratory. The oocytes might appear under microscopic examination of a stool sample, but they could be confused with other similar organisms. If drinking water were potentially contaminated by cryptosporidium, the safest option was to boil all drinking water.

Hossein had consulted with the scientist on the best method to contaminate the water system in London for the longest possible time. The goal was to infect as many people in London as possible with the concentrated levels of cryptosporidium. Many, if not all, Londoners would get sick, and many would die. The secret was to infect the water and keep the authorities from finding out and broadcasting the alarm.

Their original plan had called for them to strike this coming Thursday afternoon and early Friday morning. They would create several diversions with small explosive devises planted at popular tourist attractions. The threat of further terrorist attacks would pull security personnel into the city, away from the outer areas where the water-treatment plants were located. Shortly thereafter, during the confusion from the attacks, they would enter several water-treatment plants that supplied water to Central London. They would kill all the plant personnel and dump their fine white powder into the water.

Now their original plan had been jeopardized by Shir's recklessness. Shir was to have photographed the tourist spots so they could decide the best locations to place explosion devices. Hossein was to have picked Shir up in one of the panel trucks when he left Trafalgar Square. He had arrived in time to see him running from the square with the stranger in pursuit.

Finding a parking spot close to the pedestrian bridges had been pure luck. Hossein had arrived in time to knock the man down and pull Shir out of the area. Later he had gone back to get the van, and they had returned to the house on Newby Place.

Later today, he would devise a new plan. It was certain they needed to move the date of the attack up.

Chapter 19

Washington, DC
Monday, November 30, 2015
10:00 a.m.

The clock mounted above the rostrum in the United State Senate showed it was a few minutes before ten. Senate Majority Leader Tom Evans was reviewing the schedule for the day's session in preparation for leading the members into the day's main event.

The Senate had been in recess for the extended Thanksgiving holiday, and many members had used their time at home to meet with politicians, business leaders, and voters to gauge their reactions to the upcoming debate on the president's Fair Share Bill.

Tom Evans wanted to get through the day and back onto the campaign trail. He had declared his candidacy for the presidency just thirty days before. His campaign manager, Cheryl Williams, had suggested he make his campaign announcement on the steps of the Capitol. The setting would provide a dignified backdrop for the kickoff speech for his run for the White House. Tom and his wife Betty had overruled Williams and selected a different venue for his first speech as a Democratic candidate for president.

The Pico-Union section in Central Los Angles, considered by many to be the poorest neighborhood in the city, offered a diverse population. Almost 85 percent Latino, mostly immigrants, and the fourth most-crowded neighborhood in the City of Angles was home to more than

42,000 residences in the 1.67-square-mile area. Tom and Betty chose one of the daycare centers for children of working parents for the kickoff speech. Tom wanted to show that his presidency would be about the people in America. He wanted to show that the government needed to focus on basic building blocks, to improve society with better schools and educational programs.

He had stressed in his speech that America's educational system was falling behind other countries. Without the best possible schools for its children's future, the United States could slip back into a country dependent on engineers, architects, and highly skilled workers from other countries. He wanted to use the renewal programs in Pico-Union as an example to the country. It would show how the same spirit duplicated throughout American would rebuild other inner cities and keep America the greatest country on Earth.

The huge crowd of supporters cheered their candidate, and the press reported the campaign was off to a powerful start. Tom had hit the campaign trail every day, crisscrossing the country, but now felt he needed to be back in Washington for the introduction of the president's Corporate American Fair Share Tax Bill.

Tom glanced at his wristwatch and up at the clock above the rostrum. They were within a minute of each other. He looked around the Senate Chamber. His bench was near the front of the chamber one level up from the main floor of the multi-tiered semicircular platform.

The carpet throughout the eighty-by-one hundred-thirteen-foot area of the chamber floor was a royal blue with a pale gray fleur-de-lis imprint woven into the polyester wool. The three-sided marble rostrum, large enough for four people to work at the built-in desktops, was in the front of the chamber. The president of the Senate had a large desk on an elevated platform behind the rostrum.

Surrounding the second level of the Senate Chamber was the gallery for visitors and guests of Senate members. The portion behind and above the rostrum was reserved for members of the press, American and foreign; Tom noticed the area was already filled. The Senate would receive full coverage today as they begin to wrestle with the Fair Share Bill.

Avery Doaks, the Republican minority leader from Virginia, approached Tom and gave him a friendly light slap on the shoulder. The sixty-two-year-old senator had been a member of the Senate for eleven years and was up for reelection in 2016. "You're pulling a lot of people to your campaign rallies, Tom. I not sure about the president, but I would think your other Democratic rivals for the nomination would be ready to concede."

Tom smiled back at his Senate rival. Avery's comment was true. The number of people attending his campaign events had been large, and he drew energy from the crowd's enthusiasm. A slight decrease in the size of the crowds since the president's Fair Share Bill had passed the House was also true.

"I've been very encouraged by the initial turnouts, Avery, but there're still almost eleven months until the election. Many things can happen between now and then. How is your campaign coming?"

Avery smiled back. "I wouldn't want to raise your hopes for a change of colors on the political layout for the Senate in 2017. I'm fairly certain my Senate bench will still be listed on the red side of the map."

Tom slowly shook his head as he returned his old friend's smile. "Well, I'm certain you're correct, Avery, but the Virginia state representative from Roanoke seems to be drawing a lot of interest from the voters. You had better watch out for her. I hear she is a real up and comer in your state. Plus you have a Republican governor who will be out of a job when his term expires next year. I hear he might want your seat."

Tom was referring to Governor Tom Postman, who would be concluding his second and last term at the end of 2016.

Avery's smile faded slightly. "Postman has had his eight years in the spotlight. Taking on a fellow Republican will put a bad taste in the party's mouth. I don't think he is as smart as others give him credit for."

Tom nodded in understanding before offering a last warning. "He's good-looking and makes a good impression on camera. You had better watch your back, Avery. He could sneak up on you before you're aware of it."

Tom decided to change the subject. It was near time to call this session of the Senate to order, and he had enough work ahead of him without giving election advice to a political rival. Secretly he hoped the young Democratic Virginia representative would pull off an upset and improve the Democratic numbers in the 2017 Senate. "Are you going to introduce the Fair Share Bill for the president?"

Avery shook his head. "I'm letting Candy have the honors on that one." Candy DuPont was the Republican senator and the minority whip from North Dakota, up for reelection next year. The forty-seven year-old married mother of two girls possessed a strong work ethic, likeable personality, and high level of respect in the Senate and thought to have an easy path to reelection from the voters in her home state.

Avery Doaks noticed Vice President Jimmy Diamond enter the Senate Chamber from the set of wooden double doors to the right of the rostrum. He was about to walk back to his own bench. "I see the vice president has decided to make an appearance. Probably the president wants to make sure we do a good job of introducing his bill into the record today."

Tom could not stop from needling his opposite number. "Perhaps he's worried his own party members in the Senate might not want to support this questionable piece of legislation."

Avery laid his right hand on Tom's shoulder, the smile remaining on his face. "Come on, Tom. The country expects you to play nice with everybody, and that includes the president. Besides, you've already told the press you would not stop the bill from going to the finance committee."

Tom smiled back at Doaks. "I'm a man of my word. Fair Share will go to committee. I will only voice my disapproval of the bill when and if it comes back to the Senate floor for a vote. I will not use any influence to bury the bill in committee."

Avery nodded and moved away toward his bench seat as Jimmy Diamond brought the gavel down hard on its wooden base to bring the chamber to order. The vice president of the United States held the position of president of the Senate, a largely ceremonial position granted under the Constitution. He only had voting privileges if the Senate's vote on any legislation ended in a tie.

Jimmy Diamond was a former governor of Florida and had been the vice president for less than one year. The president had selected him after the former vice president resigned over disagreements with Miller.

For the next fifteen minutes, the Senate went through the daily opening procedures for each session. Under the rules, several discussions about old business rose to the floor, but the assembly discussed nothing major that consumed much time.

The only new piece of legislation scheduled for today's session was the president's Fair Share Bill. The schedule for introduction was at or about eleven thirty. The bill would receive an abbreviated first reading by Senator Candy DuPont. Once receiving the required seconding, the chamber would vote to assign the bill to the finance committee. Afterward, the Senate would recess for lunch. At the expected time, Candy DuPont rose from her bench seat and requested the floor from Vice President Diamond.

Diamond stood behind the raised desk and pointed the gavel toward the woman from North Dakota. "Senator DuPont has the floor."

The members of the press were scribbling the details leading up the introduction of the bill in their notebooks. Would the president's legislation hit a roadblock from the Democratic-controlled United States Senate?

Candy DuPont waited for two heartbeats and began her prepared remarks. "Ladies and gentlemen of the Senate, it is with great pleasure that I introduce into this chamber a new piece of legislation that finally corrects a terrible injustice to all tax-paying middle-class Americans. Each year these millions of Americans dig deep into their financial pockets to pay their fair share of taxes that fund the operation of our government, military, Social Security, and Medicare and provide for the continued security and stability of the American way of life.

"For years, many American and foreign companies have failed to pay their fair share of the taxes used to provide them a stable government and risk-free environment in our country for their businesses to grow and thrive. All any person has to do is look back into history and see how many other companies have lost ownership and control of their investments to friendly governments that suddenly changed to a dictatorship.

"This bill addresses the loopholes in our current tax system by requiring any company, American or foreign, operating in the United States with retail sales in excess of fifty million dollars, to pay a quarter of one percent in a new federal income tax. It is fair and a responsible move by our government to ask these companies that makes hundreds of millions of dollars from the sales of their products to American citizens to pay their fair share.

"In addition, the new revenue received from the Corporate America Fair Share Tax Bill will be directed exclusively toward the reduction of our federal deficit, further ensuring our government remains financially stable and provides a prosperous future for our citizens and future generations of Americans."

Candy DuPont stood tall at her desk, her feet planted firmly to support her slender five-foot-two frame. She held the papers containing her speech in both hands and used her left hand to push her glasses up farther on the bridge of her nose. She paused in her delivery to allow her fellow senators to hear her closing remarks with perfect clarity.

"This bill is asking for only a quarter of one percent—*a quarter of one percent!* Our average middle-income taxpayers hand over between twenty-seven and thirty-five percent of their annual household income. Most of it comes right out of their paychecks before they even see it. Now we want businesses to pay their *Fair Share.* Thank you, senators, for your time and consideration of this important piece of legislation."

Candy sat down. The bill was out on the floor, and she was waiting for Avery Doaks to offer a second to her bill. After a quick vote by the membership, the legislation would be on its way to the Senate Finance Committee.

Vice President Jimmy Diamond shifted his eyes from the far side of the chamber where Candy DuPont was sitting toward the center of the room and Avery Doaks. The minority leader, still seated, was preparing to rise from his bench seat. He would simply say, "I second the measure, Mr. President."

As Jimmy moved his eyes toward Doaks, a hand rose from the Republican side of the Senate from the back of the room. "Mr. President, may I have the floor?" The other Republican senator from Virginia, Cameron Saunders, stood at his desk, asking to be recognized.

Jimmy hesitated for several seconds. When any new piece of legislation first reached the Senate or the House of Representatives for the initial reading, it normally proceeded under a very controlled process, all the details worked out far in advance. For a young senator to ask for the floor during this crucial time was slightly unusual.

Diamond looked at the freshman senator and assumed he wanted to get his name into the official Senate records for supporting the legislation. Seeing no harm, he looked over to Doaks and then back to Senator Saunders. "The chair recognizes the junior senator from Virginia."

Avery Doaks settled back on his bench seat and turned his head slightly to more easily hear the new senator state his seconding of the bill.

Chip Saunders felt a nervous tremor run across his shoulder blades. He stole a quick look at Senators John Laird and Roberta Hanley, both seated to his left and right. Part of their coalition had been born from their close seating proximity in the Senate Chamber.

"Mr. President, I rise today to voice my protest against this piece of legislation that proposes to apply a new tax against American business—a tax that is unfair and unjust. I was voted into this respected chamber by an over whelming number of citizens in my state that have adopted a policy—no new taxes. No way. No how. For me to allow this piece of legislation to be further introduced into the Senate, where it is expected to be quickly passed by the membership and allowed to become the law of the land would be a violation of the pledge I swore to adopt and support. I'm afraid this process can't be allowed to be continue."

All heads in the Senate suddenly shifted to look at the forty-two-year old senator from Virginia. Saunders was dressed in an expensive dark blue suit, white shirt, and red striped tie. His face, topped by perfectly combed dark blond hair, projected a look of sincerity and confidence.

He waited until the noise in the Senate Chamber quieted down enough to allow him to proceed. "I am, at this time, prepared to stop the Senate from proceeding any further with discussion of this bill."

Avery Doaks was out of his chair immediately. "Will the senator yield the floor to at least allow the bill to be seconded?"

The other senators held their breath to hear the response from Saunders.

Chip Saunders knew this was when the proverbial crap was going to hit the fan. "No, Senator, I will not yield the floor to allow the bill to be seconded and proceed to committee. This bill stays right here. It should never had been introduced in the first place."

Chapter 20
Washington, DC
Monday, November 30, 2015
4:00 p.m.

Filibuster! The word alone sent reporters scrambling from the Senate Chamber to their camera operators and whipping out their cell phones to blast out the news. Only in the United States Senate can a minority of senators prevent the advancement of legislation they feel is wrong for the country.

A filibuster could go on forever under the current Senate rules, until it received a successful vote of cloture. The procedure required a favorable vote from a three-fifths majority, or sixty senators, to stop a filibuster. Prior to the 112th Congress, the filibuster and cloture process was used an extreme number of times when Republicans and Democrats failed repeatedly to agree on issues before the Senate.

At the end of the 111th congressional term in 2012, Leonard Graham, the Republican Speaker of the House from Pennsylvania, retired. He had lost his second bid for the Republican presidential nomination to Harold Miller. In 2013, the newly elected Speaker, Lawrence Frye, spoke passionately of how the House of Representatives would enter a new era of bipartisanship between Republicans and Democrats and with the Senate.

After the near-disaster of the nuclear event in South Carolina was narrowly avoided and Randy Fisher's appointment to replace retiring

Senator Robert Moore of the same state, a new desire to work together came to the Senate. Some members gave credit to Fisher and others to the national security event in the Palmetto State, but a majority of senators and members of the press credited the combination of both events. It had been some time since the Senate had faced a new filibuster.

For four hours, Senator Saunders listed the reasons for his stubborn refusal to release the Senate floor to any other person. When he completed the list, he simply started over at the beginning and repeated the same list of reasons again.

Senator Roberta L. Hanley rose from her bench seat and asked if Senator Saunders would yield the floor. This was the eighth or ninth attempt by other senators to wrestle the Senate floor away from Saunders, and the members were surprised by Saunders's response.

"I yield the floor to Senator Hanley from the great state of Florida."

The ambient noise level in the Senate increased as members turned in their chair to look at Hanley or closed a newspaper or magazine they were reading. How had the forty-six-year-old woman convinced her friend to yield the floor?

Handley picked up her notepad. "Thank you, Senator Saunders. Like you, I too signed a pledge to never vote to raise taxes. In support of the pledge, I offer you my support to refuse to allow the Fair Share Bill to proceed to committee."

The audible groan throughout the Senate Chamber almost overshadowed the voice of Roberta Hanley as she began with the same list of reasons to stop any further progress of the bill to further tax retail sales of corporations conducting business in the United States.

With Hanley now holding the Senate, Chip Saunders walked off the floor to use the men's facilities. Proper decorum allowed him to take about one step outside the restroom before Avery Doaks was standing in front of the younger senator.

"What the hell do you think you're doing?" Doaks demanded of his Republican brother.

Chip Saunders quickly stepped around the older senator and took a bottle of water from one of his staffers, who had been waiting for his exit from the restroom. Saunders calmly ignored the hard look from the Senate minority leader, twisted off the plastic cap, and took a small sip of water. His throat was dry, and the cold water provided quick relief. He wanted to remain properly hydrated but not consume too much water; that would create a problem for him during his next shift on the Senate floor.

Doaks was fuming. "Son, I asked you a question, and I expect an answer right now."

Saunders twisted the cap back onto the water bottle. "I will be happy to provide your answer as soon as I have refreshed my throat." He spoke without any disrespect in his tone of voice. He did not want to cause further hard feelings than he had already.

Doaks looked at the other people in the hallway outside the men's restroom. He looked at his own staffer, Harry Donaldson. "Harry, clear out the nearest room so Senator Saunders and I can have a private word together."

Two minutes later Doaks and Saunders were alone in a small conference room off the Senate Chamber. Doaks was about to repeat his question when the door burst open and Candy DuPont blew into the room. Her face was red with anger, her shoulder-length hair slightly mussed.

"I can't believe you would stab me in the back with this ... this filibuster. Do you have any idea how hard we have worked over the last few years to avoid this kind of crap? Any idea how this looks to the American people and the press?"

Avery Doaks never allowed Saunders to speak. "If you had a problem with the bill that you felt so strongly about that you needed to resort to this type of tactic, why didn't you come forward and say something before we were on the Senate floor?"

Saunders used the time before he answered their questions to take two steps toward the heavy wood conference table and rest one hip on the shiny surface. He looked to Avery and back to Candy, trying to decide which question to respond to first. "If I had voiced my concerns and told you I would not allow this bill to proceed, you would have both used your Senate authority to keep me from speaking on the floor. I am sorry about ambushing you like this, but I know how things can work around here, and this was the only way. This bill went through the House like an out-of-control freight train not because a majority of representatives truly favored the bill but because they were afraid to vote against it. Either the president would have done everything in his powers to hurt them in the press or he would have gone on national TV and told the people of their districts they were siding with big business. They were afraid and simply caved in to the pressure from the White House."

Avery Doaks stepped away from Saunders to circle the conference room until he was back in the nearly same position. During the time required to do so, he realized Saunders was not using the filibuster to fuel some ego trip. The thought allowed him to cool down, but the look on DuPont's face showed she was far from satisfied by Saunders response.

Doaks took a position next to the minority whip and placed a hand on her shoulder to calm her down. Looking toward Saunders, he asked his next question. "How long do you and Senator Hanley think you can hold the floor?"

Saunders could not keep a small smile from his face. Still keeping any tone of disrespect out of his voice, he gave them a simple answer. "What makes you think Rickie and I are the only senators who have joined this filibuster?"

Chapter 21

Washington, DC
Monday, November 30, 2015
4:30 p.m.

President of the United States Harold Miller pressed the "off" button on the television remote; the face of CNN senior news anchor Barry Cooper faded from the screen. He had just watched the news network's coverage of the events in the United States Senate. The highly rated news program had allocated a full thirty minutes to coverage of the filibuster, with reports from Karen Phillips, senior congressional reporter, and David Hope, senior White House reporter.

The president looked at the people in the room. Vice President Jimmy Diamond was back from the Senate, allowing the president pro tem to take over the chamber in his absent. He was sitting in a straight leather club chair in front of the president's Resolute desk.

Next to him, in an exact copy of his chair, sat Alison Warden, starting to feel the anger from her boss. Behind the president, Warren Fletcher stood with his arms folded, looking at the pair in the chairs.

The president looked at his vice president. "How did this happen? How did we not know that bastard from Virginia was going to block our own bill?"

Diamond never waived. Unlike the others in the room, he had no fear of the president or his temper. He was not up for reelection next year like Miller. As part of his deal to come on board as the new vice president, the seventy-two-year-old former governor told the president in their first meeting that he would only accept the position for the two years left in Miller's first term of office. At his age, he did not want the stress of the job to kill him off sooner than necessary and the mild diabetes he controlled with oral medication must not get worse. The president and Jimmy agreed that the former governor would provide the president with a candidate the Senate would confirm, allowing Miller two years to find a new person to run as his VP candidate for his second term.

Keeping his tone of voice calm and respectful, Diamond answered the president's question. "Sir, I'm of course sorry for the problem. Had I known in advance the senator from Virginia was going to pull this stunt, I would not have recognized him. I really didn't think it was going to be a problem."

Miller was still fuming. "Why didn't you go back to Doaks for the second? It was what we planned for in the first place."

Jimmy looked the president directly in his eyes. "I thought it would look better if we had someone besides Doaks offer to second the bill. In addition, Saunders was on the list of senators in favor of passage. This list was prepared by our own legislative affairs people, so I thought there was no risk of a problem."

Miller leaned back in his chair and ran the fingers of his right hand through his hair. He swiveled his chair around to look up at Warren Fletcher. "Warren, what do you think? Can we get the sixty votes to end this and then get the votes to send the bill to committee?"

Fletcher was about to speak when the door to the Oval Office opened; a secretary brought in a pink message slip and handed it to Fletcher. She turned immediately and left the room, closing the door behind her.

Fletcher read the note and then handed it to the president. He looked at Jimmy and Alison. "That message is from Avery Doaks. He says it is apparent there is at least one other senator prepared to help Saunders and Hanley with the filibuster. He acknowledges that with three Republican senators working together, he doubts if he can get a cloture invoked under Senate Rule XXII any time soon."

Miller rose from his chair and moved over to the windows overlooking the Rose Garden. Warren stepped around from the back of the president's desk to give the chief executive more room. The president folded his arms across his chest. This bill had been working as he had intended. The voters were in favor of the bill, and the polls were showing his improved ratings. All their hard work had been paying off—until this moment. Now they had a mutiny from within his own party.

He turned back to his senior staffers and the vice president. "Okay. What do you recommend we do to stop the filibuster?"

Fletcher knew it was his job to speak for the others. "With a Democratic-controlled Senate and Tom Evans likely to be their contender for your office next year, we can't count on them for help to end the filibuster. We need to bring pressure on the ones causing this problem. We use the office of the president and the American voters to pressure Saunders, Hanley, and whoever else they have lined up for support to give up the Senate floor."

Alison spoke in support of the chief of staff. "I agree. With two or more senators tag-teaming, they can hold the floor indefinitely, until enough other senators get tired of the whole mess. They might secretly hate the bill, but we can make the Senate look very foolish the longer the filibuster lasts. Eventually they will get enough votes to bring it to an end."

Jimmy Diamond voiced his thoughts. "I also agree, Mr. President. Alison can talk about the disruption from the Press Room, and you can make several speeches to condemn the senators' actions. In the meantime, Warren and I can work behind the scenes with our legislative aides to persuade other senators to join together to vote to take control of the floor away from Saunders and company."

Miller looked down at the two people sitting in front of his desk and then toward Fletcher. His chief of staff gave him a silent nod to confirm his agreement with the plan as laid out by the vice president. He made his decision. "Okay, that's the plan." He looked directly at Alison. "I want you to hit them hard from the Press Room. Do not talk about them being renegade members of the Republican Party but about how they are stopping a bill highly favored by the American people. We need the voters to overload them with e-mails and letters condemning their actions so big business will pay their fair share."

The president watched his vice president, chief of staff, and press secretary exit the Oval Office, leaving him alone. He resumed his seat, leaned back in his chair, and began to form his plan of revenge against the cabal of renegades. Two or more made no difference to him. Once the bill was passed by the Senate and on his desk for his signature, he would make them pay for their treason.

Chapter 22

Washington, DC
Monday, November 30, 2015
5:00 p.m.

Even when he was on an extended leave, the work in Randy Fisher's office, located in the Russell Senate Office Building, continued. Sally LaSalle replaced the telephone handset on the cradle disconnecting the call from another senator. Why was Senator Fisher not in the Senate today? When would he be back?

All good questions Sally thought and no answer from the senator still in London. The South Carolina senator's chief of staff in the Washington office was also chief over his four state offices. She was at a loss for why Randy was extending his stay in London. It could not be an extended vacation as had been listed on his office's website for the last seven days. She knew Annie Fisher and her parents, as well as Randy's aunt, had arrived back in the country early yesterday afternoon.

Yesterday morning Sally had gone on the senator's computer using the password he had provided when she took the position in his office several months before. Checking on his return status, she had looked to see if he and his party had checked into the airport for their return flight. She had found confirmation for Annie Fisher and the others, but the airline website still listed the senator's personal flight status as unconfirmed.

Early that morning she had received a call on her cell phone at six forty-five while driving to work; it must have been early afternoon in London.

"Good morning, Sally. How was your weekend?"

Sally had smiled. She had previously worked in the same position for retired Senator Moore but had left when she became pregnant with her one and only child. At the time, she had been forty-one, and her obstetrician had urged her to reduce her workload and stress. Now she was back in her former position, working for one of the most respected men on Capitol Hill.

"I'm fine, Senator. Are you ready to get back to work? The Senate has a very busy schedule until the end-of-year recess." She did not ask why he had not yet confirmed his return flight. Maybe he had taken a different plane back to the States and she was not aware of the change.

"Sorry, but I'm going to have to play hooky today, and maybe a few days more. You'll have to handle things until I can leave here."

Sally was slowing driving in from Rockville, Maryland. The traffic was already at its normal frustratingly congested level. Slowly hundreds of cars tried to occupy the same narrow two lanes for miles behind her. She had finally made it to Whitehurst Freeway and the light at Twenty-Ninth Street NW.

The senator never missed work. Never once since she had been working in his office or since the South Carolina governor had made his appointment. She was at a loss for words. A horn blast from the car behind brought her back from her thoughts. The light had change to green, and Washington drivers were impatient to move farther down the street to the next red light. She hit the gas and moved the car through the intersection and another fifteen or twenty feet until traffic forced her to stop again.

"Are you still there, Sally?"

"Sorry, Senator. It's the normal morning rush hour here. When will you be back?"

The voice from 3,700 miles away came back clear over her cell phone. "I'm not sure yet. Something has come up over here, and I've got to stay until the picture clears up."

Sally was an experienced Washington, DC, political operative. She knew double talk when she heard it. She hoped the senator's picture would clear up soon, because her picture was suddenly dark as mud.

Fisher had told her he would update her if his status changed and to call him if any serious problem arose in his absence.

Her thoughts were interrupted when June Little walked into her office. The holder of the dual roles of secretary and receptionist stood a full six feet tall; the staff believed she tipped the scale at 250 pounds. No one in the office would dare to ask her to confirm the estimate.

"The senator's website still has him on vacation. We are getting calls from some members of the press, wanting to know where he is and why we haven't updated the schedule." June stood in front of Sally's desk. She did not have to ask the obvious question.

Sally made her decision. "Put on the schedule that the senator is taking some personal time off. If anybody asks what he's doing, just tell them ..."

June completed the statement. "It's personal and none of your damn business."

Sally laughed. "That's as good a response as any other, but I suppose we need to be a touch more diplomatic."

June laughed back. "I know. It's personal, and when the senator is back we will update the schedule again."

June was back at her desk in the front lobby of Randy's office when Sally's intercom buzzed. June informed her Senator Tom Evans was on hold for either Randy or her.

Sally hesitated for a few moments to prepare what she was going to say to the majority leader. She grabbed the handset once again and spoke into the mouthpiece. "Sally LaSalle."

The rich voice of the man she believed would be the next president of the United States came over the phone. "Where is your boss, Sally?"

Sally knew she could not double talk Tom Evans. "He is still in London, Senator. I talked with him early this morning on my way into work. He's not sure when he'll be back in Washington." She remembered a wise piece of advice from her former boss Robert Moore. "The truth can never get you into too much trouble, if you haven't caused the trouble in the first place."

The senator came back with more questions. "Is he sick over there? Are Annie and all the relatives with him?

More truth time. "I believe he's fine, Senator. Annie and her parents and Randy's aunt all came back yesterday as scheduled. Senator Fisher stayed longer than planned."

She could almost hear other unasked questions, but Evans simply offered two statements. "Keep him informed on what is happening in the Senate. Also inform me if Randy's in trouble and needs help."

Chapter 23

London, England
Tuesday, December 1, 2015
7:30 a.m.

Randy Fisher stepped out of the shower and grabbed a thick towel to dry his body. He could hear the television from the bathroom, and he walked out into the bedroom naked to stand in front of the set. Two news anchors from CNN International sat side by side, rehashing the same information he had listened to earlier.

He had risen at the normal time to take a run before he showered and then had some breakfast. A quick look at his BlackBerry before he dressed for the outdoor weather showed a number of e-mails.

The first one he read was from Annie, letting him know they had gotten home safely and all were fine. She mentioned that his aunt Frances and her mother had both enjoyed the VIP treatment offered by Marion's men from the CIA's Protection Division. She closed the e-mail by telling him how much she loved him and said she wanted him to come home very soon.

The next message was from Sally LaSalle. Her e-mail was very much unlike his wife's. Instead of being filled with endearing sentiment, it was very cryptic. "Senate in uproar over Fair Share. Check out CNN."

As he dressed for the run, he watched the news reports about the filibuster started by Senators Saunders and Hanley. At eight in the evening EST in Washington, the American public was surprised again when Senator John Laird from Ohio rose from his desk and asked Senator Hanley if she would yield the floor.

To the disappointment of the Republican leadership in the Senate, the filibuster continued, with Senator Laird repeating the six reasons why he and his partners could not allow the Senate to vote the Fair Share Bill into committee.

Other reports were broadcast by Washington-based CNN reporters, who interviewed senators about the filibuster and members of the House of Representatives who had supported the bill and voted for its passage. Interviewed in his office in the south end of the Capitol building, Speaker Larry Frye spoke about the bill and the senators. "We're disappointed with our Republicans brethren. This bill is favored by a very high percentage of Americans and should be assigned to the Finance Committee in the Senate."

Karen Phillips of CNN caught Tom Evans as he left his office in the north end of the same building. "The filibuster has been used for many years by senators in a minority position to stop legislation that would have sailed smoothly through the chamber. The Senate has had many discussions about changing the Senate rules of procedures to eliminate the filibuster option. However, no senator wants to eliminate the rule and prevent themselves from the same ability later."

The dainty reporter had to stretch out her arm holding the microphone to reach high enough for the very tall senator not to have to bow down to reach it. "Senator, have you met with any of the three members who are part of the filibuster?"

"Not yet. They have the floor. Until enough senators are willing to organize sufficient votes to invoke cloture, the filibuster will continue."

Phillips came back with another question. "Senator, you are running for your party's nomination for president. If you receive enough ballots during the primary campaign to win the nomination at the Democratic convention, you will be trying to dislodge a sitting president. It appears the longer the filibuster continues, the more harm is done to the president and his reelection to office. Are you using your position as the Senate majority leader to stop others senators from talking to the three freshman senators and convincing them to release their hold of the Senate floor?"

Tom Evans's face took on a very serious look. "Let's be clear on this, Karen. It is no secret that I am opposed to the president's bill. I think it is the wrong way to force corporations to pay more federal income taxes. Yes, I am the Senate majority leader, and I could attempt to apply pressure on the three senators to stop the campaign. I could have also made it more difficult for the legislation to even be introduced on the floor in the first place." Evans stopped to look at the camera. "But I discussed this with Speaker Frye of the House of Representatives and told him I would keep presidential politics out of this legislation process. It is important the election next November is not be used to decide what is happening now in the Senate."

Randy left the TV running when he left his room a few minutes after six to head to the elevator and down to the lobby. Washington, DC, was five hours behind him, and he had plenty of time to consider what he might do about the filibuster and the Fair Share Bill. When he walked into the lobby, two tall and muscular men were sitting near the front entrance door. They were dressed in heavy sweat suits with hooded sweaters pulled over the tops of the exercise outfits. Expensive running shoes enclosed their feet. They rose to greet him as he approached.

The older of the two by several years offered the first words. "Good morning, Senator. My name is Agent Phillip Booker, and this is Agent Charlie Reader. You can remember our names by just thinking of BookReader." He smiled and continued. "The weather outside is very cold. Are you sure you want to run this morning?"

Randy looked at the two men. There was no doubt that Marion Bellwood had ordered the two operatives to provide protection for Randy. Booker looked to be in his midthirties, his hair trimmed short and his blue eyes sparkling with amusement. Reader was several years younger than Booker and three inches taller than Randy. His black skin was very dark. He looked like he should have been playing basketball instead of working for the CIA. "I suppose there is no choice in whether the two of you come along for the run?"

The younger man spoke first. "The DDO told us with or without your consent. Your consent would make the time more enjoyable."

Randy gave a little laugh. "All right. Try to keep up. I like to maintain a certain speed."

To his surprise, the run was enjoyable. The two men responded to his questions and remained silent when his thoughts turned inward. He took the same route as he had the day he spotted the terrorist through the Texas Embassy Cantina window. When they were almost back to the hotel, Randy was slightly amused to see both younger men breathing heavily. Their breaths left their mouths in heavy white streams in the below-freezing air.

They crossed Trafalgar Square for the second time, only minutes away from the hotel, when Randy slowed to a walk before stopping completely. The two CIA operatives came to a halt and took positions on both sides of the senator. Their eyes moved continually, scanning for any possible danger. They would have preferred that their protectee kept moving back to the hotel.

Randy looked around the square and finally rested his eyes on Nelson's Column. "If you guys were going to set off a bomb or bombs in London, would you select Trafalgar Square?"

Both men shifted part of their thinking process from pure protection to analysis. Booker spoke first. "The square would be an easy target.

They could walk in and drop off the bomb in some sort of backpack and be a safe distance away within thirty or forty-five seconds."

Agent Reader shook his head. "The kill ratio would be lousy this time of the year."

Randy looked directly at Reader. "What do you mean by 'kill ratio'? I've never heard that expression before."

Reader pointed to the open area within the square. "In the early morning hours the square is almost devoid of tourist. The only people here right now are on their way to work. They are crossing through the square to save time rather than following the meandering streets. As the day goes on, the number of people will increase slightly, but the weather this time of the year in London will reduce the possible target number considerably. If this were summertime or the weather better than normal, a terrorist with a bomb would have a higher kill number. It makes no difference to the bomb material if the weather is cold or hot. However, the number of targets in the wintertime is a lot fewer. Your kill ratio is much lower in the wintertime."

Randy felt a shudder run up his back. In the Senate later today they would be trying to break a filibuster over taxes. These men were talking about kill ratios and how the body count would be better in the summer than winter.

Randy rubbed a gloved hand over his face. "Okay. Let's get inside the hotel. I am meeting Marion for breakfast. Are you guys going to join us?"

Chapter 24
London, England
Tuesday, December 1, 2015
8:15 a.m.

Randy was at the table in the hotel restaurant, where breakfast was being served. BookReader sat across from each other at another table, keeping an eye on all the people moving in the restaurant. Marion Bellwood chose that moment to come in and took the chair across from Randy. He gave his two men a little head nod to acknowledge their presence. He placed his hand carefully against the side of the coffee pitcher in the center of the table. Satisfied with the results of his test, he flipped the coffee cup at his place upright and poured a full cup. After adding two packets of sweetener, he used his spoon in a slow swirling motion to blend the powdered crystals into the brew.

Randy watched the entire process without a word. Some people needed their first sip of morning coffee without any conversation.

Marion took his first sip and apparently was happy with the results. He took another drink and then traded the cup for the menu lying on the table. "What do you recommend here?" This must be your third or fourth morning at this hotel."

Randy had already finished his breakfast. "Eggs and tomatoes. The British are great gardeners, and their vegetables are wonderful. I'm not sure about you, but I've found eggs to be the same in every country I've visited."

Marion face changed a little to show he appreciated Randy's comment and suggestion. When the waiter came to their table a few minutes later, Marion ordered scrambles eggs and sliced tomatoes. He requested a side of wheat toast with light butter.

When they were alone with the exception of BookReader, he brought up the subject of the Senate. "Do you need to fly back to Washington and help with breaking this filibuster?"

Randy was quiet as he formulated his response. "No. Not yet at least." He waited a few moments. "I'm fully against the bill. The filibuster gives me time to see how this event in London will play out. Besides, even if the Senate insisted I return, a bill on taxes just does not rank up there with the brother of the man who tried to kill me three times. Two bullets and a knife." Randy sipped his coffee. "No. Right now I'm more interested in how we're going to catch these guys and stop whatever they have planned before it's too late."

Bellwood set his empty coffee cup down. He picked up the pitcher and poured a refill. "What's this 'we' stuff? You're no field agent, and I'm not letting you get hurt playing some sort of Rambo."

Randy looked at his best friend. "What makes you think I'm willing to sit on the sidelines and just let something happen?"

Marion pointed his right index finger at Randy. He kept his voice low, but there was no mistaking the intensity. "Listen, MP. We are not playing games over here. The British are the best at covert affairs, and their anti-terrorist training is the best in the world. You were in the meeting on Sunday and heard DC Shepard lay out their program to catch these people. We've got to rely on their procedures and wait for them to sniff these guys out."

Randy laughed quietly, pointing his right forefinger at the two security men at the next table. "You're willing to quietly sit by and wait until the British authorities find these guys?" He did not wait for Marion's answer. Instead, he came back with another question.

"Tell me, old friend. How many men did you bring with you from Washington or pull in from other stations once you knew who we were chasing?"

Bellwood stirred sweetener into his second cup of coffee. He kept his voice low. "Let's just say the American Embassy here in London has about fifteen more cultural attachés than their normal complement."

Marion's breakfast arrived, and he dug into the food. Randy let his friend eat in silence; Marion finished his food in less than ten minutes. "You're right. The tomatoes have real flavor to them. I spent most of my foreign service time in Germany first and later the Middle East. Most of my travel in this part of the world was simply catching connecting flights at Heathrow."

He decided on one more cup of coffee. "All right. You do not want to sit on the sidelines. I can understand that. What do you suggest? You are the anti-terrorist expert at this table."

Randy drained his coffee cup and used his napkin one last time before laying it on the table. He picked up the check, glanced at the amount, and removed his credit card from his wallet.

"I'm not going to tell you what to do with BookReader over there or their brothers, but I'm going back to Scotland Yard and go over all the evidence they collected from the back pack again."

Marion looked at his two men. He thought about asking for some clarification of the names Randy was calling them but decided it was not worth the time. "What do you think you can find that Scotland Yard's experts might have missed?"

Randy shook his head. "I don't know, but it beats sitting around here with my two bodyguards, waiting for something to happen. I'd rather be proactive."

Chapter 25

London, England
Tuesday, December 1, 2015
9:45 a.m.

Hossein Rahim Bonab was in the room on the second floor he used for planning their operation looking at a large paper map of London. Shir Mohammad's near-miss capture by the American was forcing Hossein to change their timetable for the attack.

Originally, they had planned to start their attack on the London water supply system this Friday. The plan had called for them to have the entire weekend to complete their work. They would have introduced the fine white powder infested with the cryptosporidium oocysts into the water system after the drinkable water had passed through the treatment facility. The number of water-treatment technicians they would have to dispense with would be at the lowest levels from late evening on Friday until the first shift arrived on Monday morning. By that time, his team would have mixed all the powder into the water, with enough time for the poison to move through the entire water supply system. Now he had to devise a new plan. They could not take the risk of waiting any longer and the British authorities finding them.

The street map was open on top of a four-by-eight sheet of plywood supported by the wooden crates used to ship rugs. In addition to the city streets and the larger thoroughfares accommodating cars and trucks, he had marked the location of the pipeline for the Thames Water Ring Main.

London's water supply infrastructure had developed over hundreds of years. For much of London's history, private companies provided water taken from the River Thames and the River Lea without regulations with regard to purity. A crisis occurred in the middle of the nineteenth century, with outbreaks of cholera from the polluted Tideway. Over many years, nearly a dozen private water companies were organized; some merged with others or went out of business.

Enacted in 1852, the Metropolis Water Act made provisions for securing the supply of pure and wholesome water to the metropolis. It became compulsory for all water companies to filter their product for purity. In addition, the authorities created the Metropolitan Commission of Sewers and organized a new program to properly handle wastewater and prevent it from contaminating the source of the drinking water used throughout the great city.

At the beginning of the twentieth century, the private water companies were nationalized by the government under a new program. The Metropolis Water Act of 1902 created the Metropolitan Water Board. The sixty-seven-member board voted to acquire nine different companies supplying water to London at the time. The board added new water-treatment facilities to increase the supply to meet the growing demand by the population. The Metropolitan Water Board, with several other local water boards, created the Thames Water Authority. Currently water was supply by four companies. Thames Water provided 76 percent of all demand. Affinity Water, Essex and Suffolk Water, and Sutton and East Surrey Water supplied the final 24 percent.

The single largest infrastructure project in recent years was the creation of the Thames Water Ring Main, the backbone of London's water supply. Eight kilometers of mostly concrete pipe with a diameter of one hundred inches transferred potable water from water-treatment plants in the Thames and River Lee catchments for distribution within London.

Thames Water Authority constructed the initial ring between 1988 and 1993. Soon after, two other extensions were completed, with additional plans for further extensions through 2025. The average daily flow was approximately 0.3 gigalitres (0.3 x 109 liters), which represented about 7 percent of the daily demand for London.

From the southwest end of the system, the northern portion of the pipeline connected water-treatment facilities at Kempton, Mogden, Kew, Barnes, Holland Park, and Barrow Hill. The Southern line ran east through Walton, Hampton, Surbiton, Hogsmill, Raynes Park, Merton, Streatham, Brixton, and Battersea, connecting with the northern line at Barrow Hill. The two extensions connected the huge water reservoir at Honor Oak to the Water Ring Main at Brixton, and the Stoke Newington facility connected at New River Head and tied into the Main Ring at Barrow Hill. The Water Ring Main ran between 33 and 213 feet below ground level and 33 feet to 98 feet below sea level.

Hossein traced the Thames Water Ring Main along its path on the map with his index finger. Somewhere at one of the storage or pumping stations was where they needed to dispatch the powder. The insertion location had to be after the treatment phase of the system. There were a number of treatment locations, and the water needed to remain in the main only long enough to get into the local city water lines without passing through another treatment facility. While the enhanced concentration of the cryptosporidium oocysts possessed thick protective walls and could live a long time outside of the host, passing through a water-treatment facility would degrade the pathogens or kill them off completely.

The water-treatment plants processed water through several stages before moving into the local water lines servicing the consumers. The water arrived from underground wells, rivers, or lakes into a storage tank. The next stage was a series of filters to remove contaminants. Water from rivers and lakes might contain any number of contaminates, including the remains of dead animals, animal excrement, leaves, and sediments. The water passed first through a set of filters designed to remove large objects from the water. Subsequent filters continue to remove smaller and smaller items.

The next set of filters normally included a sand filter, a duplication of nature's own method for purifying water. As surface water soaks down deep into the ground, passing through layers of sand, it becomes clean once again. The sand filters acted in the same manner.

Diatomaceous earth filters used at the next stage were similar to swimming pools filters. The final particle removal procedure was achieved through reverse osmosis water filters, where the water passed through a series of membranes.

The final water purification stage was the chemical treatment process. A specific mixture of chlorine and fluoride provided final purification of all possible living organisms, like cryptosporidium oocysts and other pathogens, which might have somehow survived the numerous earlier stages of filtration.

Hossein grew frustrated in his efforts to find a new plan that would work within their reduced allowed time. "Damn," he muttered. Had he the time, he would have killed Shir Mohammad and found a replacement, but he was short on time and needed the damn fool's help.

He needed identify a location on the Thames Water Ring Main close to where they now were. They could not spend too much time in traffic with their cargo. He looked at the closest location to the pipeline. Battersea or Brixton were the closest, but they were pumping stations; the water would be under terrific pressure and more difficult to access.

He moved his finger to the western stations but then stopped and pulled it back to Honor Oak. He remembered there was something special about that location. He reached to the far corner of the plywood table and picked up the three-ring binder where he stored all the collected information about the London water infrastructure. The binder was almost three inches thick, filled with the results of his research. He quickly opened the cover and flipped through the pages and brochures. He located the section on the city of Honor Oak and the information on the underground storage reservoir.

The small community covered two boroughs: London Borough of Lewisham and London Borough of Southwark. The distance from their Newby location was almost five miles in a straight line but probably closer to seven or eight once they crossed the River Thames and followed the city streets.

He wanted to learn all about Honor Oak and the underground water reservoir. The city had originated hundreds of years before. On May 1, 1602, Elizabeth I had picnicked with Sir Richard Bulkeley of Beaumaris by an oak tree at the summit of a hill in the Lewisham area.

Shortly thereafter, the local citizens referred to the famous tree as the Oak of Honor, and the city name grew from there.

In 1935, King George commemorated his Silver Jubilee at the summit, and later it was used by Queen Elizabeth II for her Silver and Golden Jubilees. During World War I, a gun emplacement was erected on the hill to protect the residence from zeppelin raids, added more history to the site.

Hossein felt his heartbeat quicken slightly as he came to the part that had stuck in his memory. In 1896, the open space within the community was due to become part of a golf course, but the local people forced the cancellation of the idea. The Metropolitan Borough of Camberwell purchased the land, and the open space became a public area in 1905. The authorities built a nine-hole golf course on top of the Honor Oak Reservoir between 1901 and 1909 and called it the Aquarias Golf Club. At the time it was completed, the reservoir was the largest brick underground reservoir in the world and remains one of the largest in Europe even today. The reservoir forms part of the southern extension of the Thames Water Ring Main.

Hossein flipped back to the information on the Thames Water Ring Main. He found the sheets devoted exclusively to the cavernous water reservoir. Now more than one hundred years old, the facility had recently undergone an upgrade. Another tidbit of information informed him that the water main lining was constructed with over nineteen million bricks. The storage capacity was equivalent to the daily supply for 800,000 people.

Hossein sat back on the three-legged wooden stood and thought about the information. That location could poison over three-quarters of a million people. The nuclear bombs dropped by the United States on Japan during the final days of World War II killed between 150,000 and 246,000 people. His project could effectively poison nearly four times that many; a great many would subsequently die from the effects of the cryptosporidium.

He walked over to the laptop computer on the old wooden desk and entered "Honor Oak Reservoir" into the search engine. There were several different articles about the historic site, but the picture of the main building was what drew his attention. It was located in the middle of several golf course fairways. The building, constructed of red brick, was a basic rectangle. On the long sides of the building, a rounded bump out broke the smooth lines of the structure. A marble pilaster at every corner of the building provided a structural accent. The roof was slate shingles, finished with a cupola at the top.

The amazing part was the location. The field the building lay in was completely open on all sides for many yards. Golfers would play past the building. He noticed small square concrete boxes at various locations on the grounds. They all ran in straight lines from the building on all four sides and were spaced twenty to forty yards apart. The open field was nearly three hundred yards long by about one hundred seventy-five yards wide.

He looked at the outer perimeter of the property. It was completely open and accessible by a number of city streets. There would be no security guards to deal with. If they arrived after sunset, they would be able to break into the building and have the entire night to access the underground storage reservoir and dump their complete supply of powder into the vital water supply.

If they all worked together, including Shir Mohammad, they could finish their preparations and have the trucks loaded and ready to go tomorrow night. They could take advantage of the short daylight period and be on their way by five in the afternoon.

Chapter 26
Washington, DC
Tuesday, December 1, 2015
9:00 a.m.

Alison Warden stood in front of the White House Press Room on the raised dais, confronting the members of the press corp. The forty or fifty reporters would listen to no other news stories but the filibuster still going on in the Senate. She was ready to blast the three senators and had decided to start with her own prepared remarks before taking questions. She wanted to bring up different points from those that President Miller would be making during his own speech later that day in Memphis, Tennessee.

She faced the reporters hungry for her comments. All were ready with notepads and digital recorders to capture every word. "The Congress of the United States has for the past three years experienced an improved public rating and has been able to complete a larger volume of important work than the previous assemblies due to the cooperation between the Miller White House and the congressional leadership. Today we are seeing a return to the old, unproductive ways that had led to the lowest approval ratings in congressional history.

"The American public has provided all the reasons for this filibuster to come to an end. They favor the Corporate America Fair Share Bill by a wide majority. They are flooding their respective senators with e-mails and letters telling them to force a vote of cloture and allow the Senate to assign the bill to the Finance Committee.

"The president has put together a fair and equitable program that would require large corporations to pay their fair share of taxes to support the country they live and work in. They demand protection from our police departments. They demand a fast response from our fire departments. They demand security from foreign terrorist who would destroy their way of life and the millions of dollars of profits they earn each year.

"Fair Share is right for the country, and three senators are abusing their Senate privileges to hold up important legislation. The filibuster needs to be stopped and the bill moved into committee."

She then pointed to a raised hand near the front of the room. She had seen David Hope of CNN News sitting in a chair near the outer edge of the room with his hand outstretched. The news network tried to offer an unbiased program, but over the last few years, they had been the first network to break several stories that put a bad light on the Miller Administration. She could not totally ignore him, but he would not be the first to get her attention.

Michael Rennie of the *New York Times* stood to ask the first question. "Alison, the filibuster has been going on for nearly twenty-one hours. What has the White House done to placate the three senators into giving up their hold on the floor?"

Alison liked the question. She wore a firm but friendly look on her face. "We have requested an audience with any one of the three senators, but to date they have refused to meet with a member of the White House. The president has refused to cave into their demands. He is fully committed to the American people to ensure hundreds of large corporations producing fifty million dollars of retail income pay their fair share."

She looked to Patty Neal of the United Press International. The tall, slender reporter stood her full height, only two inches short of six feet. She was as tall as or taller than most men in the room were. "Alison, the three senators, Saunders, Hanley, and Laird, are members of the Republican Party. It would be no surprise to anyone if the Democrats, who hold power in the Senate, had voted to refrain from sending the Fair Share Bill to committee. To have members of the president's own party block the bill is quite unusual. Has the president lost touch with his own party?"

Alison responded in a firm tone. "Absolutely not. The House of Representatives passed the bill in near-record time while the Senate was dealing with other issues. As you know, all legislation concerning taxes must originate within the House of Representatives. The overall response from both Democrat and Republican voters has been overwhelmingly in support of the bill."

The questions and answers continued for another twenty minutes. Finally, Alison recognized David Hope from CNN. Hope was in his middle forties and retained his good looks and thick crop of black hair. Standing in front of his chair, Hope seemed not to notice he was probably the last reporter called at the end of the press conference. "Alison, do you think the American voters will start to pay more attention to the three Davids in the Senate as they wage their battle against the White House Goliath the longer the filibuster continues? Will the other senators begin to feel that maybe this bill is wrong?"

Alison secretly groaned. She knew almost every reporter in the room would reuse Hope's reference to the three Republican senators. Perhaps it would be worse if the same name were used again by one of the reporters traveling with the president at his speech in Memphis. "I'll leave the Bible out of this question and simply say the American people have clearly let their feelings be known about the Fair Share Bill. They want the federal government to bring justice to the payment of taxes in this country. The three senators knew who and what they were taking on before they walked onto the floor of the Senate."

She gave a little hand wave to indicate the press briefing was closed. "That's all until our 1:00 p.m. briefing."

Some reporters were shouting questions as she left by the side door leading back to her office in the West Wing. She heard several calls with questions referring to the three Davids.

She passed other people working in the executive mansion and made a beeline for her office. Once in the privacy of her own little kingdom within the White House, she picked up the receiver of her desk phone and placed a call to Warren Fletcher.

Chapter 27

Memphis, TN
Tuesday, December 1, 2015
9:30 a.m. CST

Warren Fletcher was riding in the president's limousine, facing the chief executive as the car raced through the city of Memphis, Tennessee. The governor of Tennessee, Lance Wooten, sat beside Harold Miller, urging him to reconsider the Fair Share Bill. The car was in the middle of a caravan of Secret Service vehicles and vans carrying support personnel. The members of the press were in a bus they were to reimburse the White House for providing.

The president's people had recommended Memphis as his first stop of the day. He was scheduled to fly west to Denver, Colorado, later and then northeast to Chicago for an early evening speech before returning to Washington. The president had ordered his staff to select locations in the middle of the country for the Fair Share speech. Memphis was located on the Mississippi River at the junction of two major interstate highways.

Interstate 40 began near Wilmington, North Carolina, and stretched 2,552 miles west to Barstow, California. Interstate 55 ran from Chicago, south through Memphis, and continued to La Place, Louisiana, providing interstate transportation to more than twenty thousand trucks every day.

The city of Memphis was the birthplace or home of many famous Americans. Perhaps the most famous was the late Elvis Presley, as well as Johnny Cash, B. B. King, Isaac Hayes, Al Green, and Justin Timberlake.

The population demographics for the nearly 670,000 Memphis residents were 62.6 percent black Americans, 29.6 percent white, and 5 percent Hispanic, leaving the last 2.9 percent to other ethnic races.

The combination of interstate traffic and the Mississippi River helped to fuel the economy. The city was home to the corporate offices of Federal Express. Any person traveling to or from the Memphis International Airport could not help but notice more FedEx jet aircraft than all the other commercial airlines combined.

Fletcher received the telephone call from Alison Warden as Air Force One was nearing Memphis International Airport. He was in the president's office space on the plane reviewing with him the possible questions he might be asked.

"Watch for the reporters to refer to the three senators as 'the Davids' in a battle of willpower with the White House Goliath. They will want to try to get a reaction from you; we don't want to elevate them to any sort of celebrity status."

Miller nodded in agreement. "The only status they will get from me will be at the bottom of the ladder when they need my help on some pet bill of their own after this is all over."

Once on the ground with the 747 parked at a remote location, Miller walked down the stairway and met Tennessee governor Wooten waiting with a big smile for his favorite Republican, the press cameras catching the president's arrival in Memphis. The two friends shook hands and then walked to the waiting limousine. Once the Secret Service was ready, the line of cars, vans, and one large bus headed for the airport exit.

The presidential motorcade passed hundreds of people along the travel route from the airport who wanted to see a glimpse of the president or who could not obtain tickets to the president's speech. The motorcade travel I-240 north to Popular Avenue, turned right onto Central Avenue, and approached the Holiday Inn Hotel and Conference Center across from the University of Memphis campus. The president was to give his speech in the hotel's grand ballroom.

On the drive from the airport, Governor Wooten warned his friend about the mixed crowd awaiting him. Most would be in support of the Fair Share Bill, but the president needed to expect some negative reactions mixed in with the cheers.

"This is home to Federal Express, Harold. You have to expect some of the people in the crowd to be supporting the company's position. The company thinks they are already paying their fair share, and your new tax will just take more profits from their pockets. I looked at the figures for their 2013 taxes. They paid almost nine hundred million dollars in various taxes to Memphis, the state of Tennessee, and the federal government."

Miller looked out the window as his motorcade sped past men and women waving their hands, some carrying miniature American flags. He used his left hand to indicate the people lined along the street. "Do you want to tell them they need to pay more instead of these billion-dollar corporations?"

Wooten simply shrugged. "I'm just giving you some advance warning. The corporations are not happy with you. We should have taken a new look at the corporate tax rates and some of the crazy deductions Congress has passed over the years."

The president sat in silence for the balance of the trip. Shortly his motorcade reached their destination.

The three-story Holiday Inn Hotel and Conference Center, constructed in early 1995 of modern brick and glass, had a huge portico entrance in the middle of an all-glass front wall. A large parking lot on the east side would accommodate most of the guests and their transportation, but the Secret Service deemed the front entrance too exposed for the president's safety.

The motorcade pulled into the main entrance by the portico as directed by uniformed Memphis police and supported by Secret Service agents. The president's limousine turned left onto Deloach Street and traveled a short distance to the rear of the hotel. Assured that all pathways were clear and under constant supervision, the senior agent of his security detail opened the door for the president to exit the vehicle.

Harold Miller entered a hotel back door and passed through a short entrance hallway that came to a tee. His lead agents turned left, followed the hallway another twenty-five feet, and entered the kitchen area. Extra agents, assigned to other doorway exits along the hallway, would remain there until the president left the hotel.

The hotel kitchen staff, forced to stop their cleanup work from the morning breakfast, watched their president and governor, along with members of their staffs, quickly move through their work area. The president waved, smiled, and even stopped to shake a few hands with the closest staff. Wooten joined in on the festive mood to spend a few moments with some of his supporters.

The hotel manager waited inside the kitchen next to the large set of double doors that opened into the grand ballroom. Miller stopped to shake hands with the fifteen-year hotel veteran as Wooten continued on to make the introduction for the chief executive.

The sound of the crowd through the doors made conversation inside the kitchen area difficult. As the governor reached the end of his short introduction speech, Miller grew quiet as he mentally prepared for his speech. All the people around him stopped talking so as not to break his concentration.

On stage in the grand ballroom, Governor Wooten looked out over the assembly. The packed room of nearly fifteen hundred people must have reached the maximum limit allowed by the local fire marshal. He had them pumped up and full of excitement. He finished his opening remarks with a fanfare of words.

"This is a great day for Memphis and Tennessee. We have our country's leader waiting to speak with you, so let us not delay any longer. Ladies and gentlemen … the president of the United States."

Two Secret Service agents stood inside the ballroom doors from the kitchen. Their protectee waited for them to open them. They heard their supervisor authorize them to open the doors when ready before they made a final sweep of the room through their dark sunglasses. They each had a hand on to the edge of the doors and quickly opened them to allow the president to enter the grand ballroom. The Munford High School band, winners of the latest Bandmasters Championship under the direction of Robert Preston, had been playing before the governor came onto the stage. They now struck up "Hail to the Chief", and the president walked out of the kitchen area at a brisk pace and took the four steps up to the stage area two at a time.

Governor Wooten was waiting for him. The two men shook hands and exchanged big smiles for the cameras. Wooten then stepped back to take a seat with the other dignitaries behind Miller at the podium. The president's speech was already showing on the monitor, ready for him to refer to as needed.

Miller waved to the cheering crowd with outstretched arms and looked around the huge ballroom. Three seventy-two-inch LCD monitors, mounted at strategic locations, would allow people farther back from the stage to see the president. Miller let the cheering continue. He wanted the television crews to capture the audience's high spirit and enthusiasm. After several minutes he started to speak.

"Thank you. Thank you. It's wonderful to be here in the great state of Tennessee, home to the best country western music in the world."

The fifteen hundred people cheered again in support of his statement. Miller continued to smile, feeling the emotion coming off the people. He raised his hands once again to bring the audience noise level down and slowly they retook their chairs.

"Thank you again. I want to acknowledge some people here who helped to make this event a success. Thank you, Lance Wooten ... a great governor for Tennessee."

Again, the crowd rose from their seats to show their approval.

Maintaining his smile, Miller again waved them back down. He then mentioned the members of the local Republican Party and their position in the Memphis or Tennessee community positioned around the raised platform at various locations. It appeared he was just selecting their names at random from memory. In reality, the names appeared in his speech and displayed on the teleprompter. After naming eight or nine people, he came to the last person on his list.

"I wanted to thank Dr. Amy Carnes for being here today. Dr. Carnes is the chairperson of the Robert Wang Center for International Business Education and Research here at the University of Tennessee. The center, designated since 1989 by the US Department of Education, is a place where students, business executives, and academic professionals can join to become culturally conscious and globally competent in our diverse global society. This school is helping to develop business leaders not only for companies doing business in the United States but anywhere in the world. Dr. Carnes, please stand up."

Dr. Carnes, fifty-two years of age, had long, thick curly red hair. She held a doctorate in international economics. Seated next to Governor Wooten, she stood by her chair to the cheering of the audience. The president turned from the podium to locate her and acknowledge her smile to him.

When the crowd had quieted down President Miller resumed his speech. "Economics, business, taxes. Those subjects are the reason we are here today. American and foreign corporations are selling their products in the United States, which you are purchasing. Maybe you even work for them. They are earning millions and in some cases billions of dollars in profit each year and not paying any income taxes. Is that fair? Do you think that is fair?"

The crowd was on their feet yelling, "Not fair. *Not fair. Not fair.*"

President Miller, a small polite smile on his face, let the chanting continue for almost half a minute. He finally raised his arms to urge the crowd to retake their seats. Before resuming his speech, he raised his hands a short distance off the podium. "Why are federal income taxes necessary? Nobody likes to pay taxes. I came from Wall Street, and I certainly did not want to pay income taxes any more than you do. However, just like you, I did not have a choice.

"Federal and state governments must collect taxes to pay for the services provided to every citizen. States provide schools for your children. Cities provide for your police and fire departments. They do this to provide for a stable community for you to raise your families."

He paused for several seconds. "The federal government needs the tax dollars to pay for the men and women in our armed forces. We have federal construction projects like roads and bridges. We have federal agencies, like the Department of Agriculture, to ensure the food you purchase is safe to eat. Most importantly, your tax dollars allow the United States government to provide a safe and stable form of government for companies to develop, manufacture, and sell their products. Without that ... without government stability, their investor's money and the money you invest in your 401-Ks would be at risk."

The president paused to look over the crowd. They were listening closely to his words. Other than an occasional cough or the sound of cameras snapping digital photos, the room was quiet.

The president had an open business portfolio on the podium that contained his speech, though he felt more comfortable using the teleprompter. He reached to the back of the portfolio, pulled out several stapled sheets of papers, and held them up for the crowd to see. "This is a portion of the 2014 tax forms of a publically held US company. They are required to release an annual income statement to their stockholders. Many of you probably have stock in this company. In 2014, they made over forty billion dollars from their worldwide operations. Their tax obligations amounted to just below two percent."

The crowd remained quiet as he continued. "Two percent. That is around eight hundred million in taxes. The average American is paying thirty percent or more of their total income toward their tax obligation."

He paused as he waved the tax forms above his head. "Two percent." He dropped the papers onto the podium and pointed toward the middle of the fifteen hundred people sitting quietly in the room. "Thirty percent.

"Two percent by a big company making billions. Do you think that's a fair share?"

The crowd was instantly on its feet. Some were yelling, "No!" but others were chanting, "Fair share!" Slowly voices all switched to the "Fair share" chant.

The president allowed them to continue for almost a full minute before he gestured with his arms to bring them back to their seats. "A fair share. That is what I am fighting for in Washington. The House of Representatives passed the Corporate America Fair Share Bill in a very short time under the leadership of Speaker Larry Frye. It looked like we were going to get reasonable action in the Senate, even with a Democratic majority. Even a Democrat who announced his candidacy for the presidency said he would let the American people decide the issue has remained silent."

Harold Miller paused to make sure the crowd was paying close attention. "Yet here we are, waiting for the members of the Senate to stop the three inexperienced United States senators fighting to keep the bill from going to the Senate Finance Committee. There the bill can be debated and brought back to the full Senate for a vote. All the while, these rich companies continue to use tax loopholes to avoid paying their fair share."

He again pointed his finger toward the center of the audience. "Remember this. The federal debt will be the recipient of all the income from my Fair Share bill. We are using this money to continue to ensure the stability of our government and country."

The fifteen hundred people reacted to the president's last statement, rising to their feet with applause and loud cheering. Many tried to restart the "Fair Share" chant.

Harold once again waved them back to their seats as he prepared to deliver his final words. "I need your help. I need you to tell your senators to stop this filibuster. Stop abusing the powers of the Senate and let this bill proceed. These representatives were not sent to Washington to be obstructionist but to work for the good of the country."

He pointed toward the right side of the ballroom this time. His voice increased in volume. "Call your senators. Tell them to make it stop." He pointed to the center of the room. "E-mail your senators. Tell them to make it stop." He pointed to the left side of the room next. "Text your senators. Tell them to make it stop."

The crowd yelled and clapped their hands.

He used both hands to point over the crowd, his energy building to a climax. "It's time for everyone to pay a fair share!"

Chapter 28

Washington, DC
Tuesday, December 1, 2015
12:00 p.m. EST

Karen Phillips took the empty seat beside Tina Lewis in the Senate Press Gallery. The two CNN congressional reporters had been alternating to cover the Senate filibuster. Normally Tina would cover the House side of Congress, but with the Senate in session around the clock and activity in the House now on the back burner, CNN Washington Chief Bud Wilson had asked her to help with the network's coverage of the US Senate.

Karen, thirty-two years old, was well under five feet tall; she had long, thick black hair. Her dark eyes, offset by the red lip-gloss she wore, sparkled when she was on camera. She was dressed in a dark blue business suite and matching shoes. She was still looking for a husband outside the news industry who would put up with her busy schedule.

Tina was two inches taller and two years younger, with short brown hair with natural curl. She was the mother of two boys; her husband worked at the Capitol Power Plant on SE East Street as a third-shift supervisor.

Karen leaned in so she and Tina could talk quietly. "I listened to your coverage on my way in this morning. Anything happening that you couldn't put on the air?"

Tina shook her head. She had been following the activity in the Senate for the last eight hours. "Nothing. They have been repeating the same drivel since this thing started. You would have thought they could be a bit more creative."

She opened her six-by-nine top-bound spiral notebook to consult her records. "If they keep to the established schedule, Saunders should be here anytime to replace Senator Laird. They've been keeping to a four-hours-on, eight-hours-off schedule." Tina closed the notebook and slipped it into her shoulder bag. "Well, I'm off. Don Bailey should be coming on as the camera operator if you need him, but so far this thing has been boring as all get-out."

She grabbed her coat from the empty seat next to her and got up to leave the gallery. She turned back to Karen when one new thought came to mind. "There *is* one thing, but it doesn't have anything to do with the filibuster. Your special senator Fisher has not been seen since the filibuster started. I only know this because I heard Senator Shelba Mace asking Tom Evans where Fisher was. With the senators rotating in and out, it is hard to keep track of who is on the floor. It seems he never returned from the Thanksgiving break."

Karen gave her colleague a smile and playful slap on her left buttock. It went unnoticed by the few members of the press remaining in the gallery. Most of the reporters were bored with the speech down on the floor of the Senate Chamber and were probably in the Senate dining room for lunch. "He is not my special senator. I've just been lucky to score more interviews with him than any other reporter."

Tina whispered a little laugh and called out, "Have fun" before she started to walk up the stairway toward the nearest gallery exit.

Karen Phillips had been covering Congress for almost five years since promoted from a special-features reporter. One of her biggest news stories had been the scandal at the Department of Energy uncovered by Senator Randy Fisher and his wife, then Annie Willis. She had been in the middle of her broadcast from the sidewalk in front of the Forrestal Building, home to the DOE, when Energy Secretary Raymond Cleveland had shot himself in his office inside the building.

She had made it a point going forward to monitor the South Carolina senator's activities. He had been the center of several other major news stories during the past few years. Her balanced reporting of the stories had earned her several exclusive interviews with him.

She looked over the railing above the chamber floor toward Randy Fisher's Senate bench seat. It was empty and looked abandoned. Old newspapers covered the tops of desks in other senators' benches. Some desks held open Senate rulebooks; a few of the Republican senators were trying to find a way to break the filibuster.

She looked toward Senator Laird. The tall, slender, fifty-three year with a head full of thick snow-white hair, stood out among his fellow senators on the chamber floor. He was still repeating the same six reasons for why the Fair Share Tax Bill must not go to the committee. Karen reached inside her shoulder bag, which matched her outfit, for her smart phone. In all the initial excitement over the filibuster, she had failed to notice if Senator Fisher was in the chamber earlier. Currently, the minimum number of members required by the Senate Rules Committee to maintain a quorum occupied the floor. The senators had been rotating in and out of the Senate Chamber.

Karen had the Senate's membership websites programmed into her smart phone. She was in the process of bringing up Senator Fisher's to check his office calendar when she heard some commotion on the floor of the Senate below her. Leaning forward, she looked over the railing.

Senator Saunders was walking in to take his seat. He stopped briefly at Senator Laird's bench as a sign of support and then stepped over to the bench seat beside his friend. He quickly arranged a few papers he had taken from his desk and then rose from his seat. "Will Senator Laird yield the floor to me?"

John Laird tuned to the right and nodded. "I yield to the senator from Virginia."

Laird sat in his chair. Their plan was to change their current talking points to examples of companies that were already paying their fair share of income taxes. The new plan would show the Senate members and the American public the number of companies who did not take advantage of every loophole their accountants or CPA could find. He opened a short note from Chip Saunders, slipped to him during their handshake, describing the president's speech delivered several hours before in Memphis. He wanted to wait a few minutes to see what Chip would say in his opening remarks.

Chip Saunders looked refreshed and rested after his eight hours off the Senate floor. He took a few moments to organize his thoughts and then looked around the chamber. He thought about requesting another call for quorum but decided the act would antagonize his fellow Senate members.

"Members of the Senate. I watched the news coverage of President Miller's speech from Memphis, Tennessee. He used some harsh words to play on the feelings of his audience and gain their sympathy for his Fair Share Bill. As he requested of his audience, my office has been receiving a large number of e-mails and other forms of communication to attempt to stop these proceedings. I am impressed with the quick reaction in such a short time. I have to wonder about the work behind this effort from President Miller and his organization. It does make me ponder if my fellow senators and I are making a mistake and should release our hold on the Senate. The filibuster rule is controversial, and the Senate has considered abolishing it a number of times. Wisely, this chamber has refused to discard the rule, which simply allows the minority side of any issue to ensure their voice is heard above the volume of the majority."

He paused for a moment to look at the other senators in the chamber. There were fifty-two members in the chamber, counting John Laird who was still sitting at his desk. "It also allows time for the minority who are abusing the patience of their fellow senators to reaffirm their own convictions about their cause. During the same time that I was receiving the e-mails and texts and telephone calls from American citizens telling me to stop my efforts here on the Senate Chamber, I also received a large number of e-mails and other communications asking me to continue to stop the Fair Share Bill from progressing further in the Senate. That fact that the majority of the various forms of communications were from my own state of Virginia, where I was elected under the pledge not to vote for any new increased taxes, was no surprise but very welcome.

"I was surprised by the number of American citizens from other states also offering their support. My office is keeping a running tally. At this moment, we estimate nearly twenty percent of the messages were from outside of Virginia. It renews my faith in the path my colleagues and I have taken. We realize the American public was heavily in favor of this bill when it was first introduced by the president, but we think it is wrong and hope with time and persistence our message will get across to other members of the Senate."

He stopped to pick up a few sheaves of papers stapled together at one corner. "On this list are hundreds of American corporations that do pay their fair share. I intend to share with you their names."

He looked at the top of the list on the first page and starting to call out the names of American companies. The typed, single-spaced pages were full. It would take several hours to go through the entire listing before he would need to repeat the list from the beginning.

Some of the senators, forced by the rules of quorum to be present, groaned over this new boredom. Several moved to interrupt Senator Laird as he walked to the nearest chamber exit to use the next eight hours to rest before he would again take the floor.

Avery Doaks and Candy DuPont were at the door as Laird approached. Doaks held up his hand like a traffic cop. "Let's have a little word, Senator Laird. We've got a cloakroom set aside so we're not disturbed."

John Laird stood before them. "All right. Let's talk."

The three senators left the chamber and walked a short way down the hallway. A staff member for the Republican minority leader stood guarding the door to keep the room free of any other persons. They would remain outside the door to ensure privacy for the meeting.

Once inside, John Laird took a chair at the small conference table inside the windowless room. They could not force him to remain standing on his tired legs. Doaks sat across the table from Laird. DuPont stood to the side of Laird looking down. DuPont's face was red with anger. "All right. This has gone on long enough. You three have made your point. It is time to allow the Senate to finish its business and let the bill go to committee." She was only inches from Laird's face. "If the bill is voted out of committee and back to the floor and you still feel the same way, you can still offer to speak against it. Maybe you will have enough votes to stop the bill."

Laird looked from Doaks to DuPont. He was a little uncomfortable with her proximity. He rose from his chair, walked to the far corner of the room, and turned to face the Republican leaders. "If we let this go to the Finance Committee and come back out—and right now you have enough committee votes to ensure it will come back—neither I nor my colleagues will ever get a chance to speak on the floor about the bill. You will team up with the vice president to make sure we are not recognized so this bill is run through the Senate so fast it will make our heads spin."

Doaks knew DuPont's approach would never work. "Then what do you want? We can try to negotiate something. Not on this bill, because if we change it in any way it will have to go back to the House for another vote. But we can offer you or the others something on another issue."

John Laird straightened his tired back. "No. The only thing you can do is to vote to stop this bill here and now. Anything less and we will continue with the filibuster. We have enough people to keep this up indefinitely. Now if you will excuse me, I need to use the restroom and then check in with my staff."

Chapter 29

Washington, DC
Tuesday, December 1, 2015
12:45 p.m.

Karen Phillips stood outside the cloakroom, waiting for the three senators to exit. Avery Doak's staff member had been keeping her at a respectful distance, so she had not been able to hear any conversation from the other side of the closed door.

She had seen Senator Laird stopped at the exit door of the Senate Chamber by his party's Senate leadership. She had hurried from the galley and down the stairs to the main floor. When she reached the same floor as the doorway to the Senate chambers, none of the three senators was in sight. Looking around the wide hallway, she recognized the staff member from Avery Doak's office. Seeing the look on the staffer's face, she decided to wait from a distance, among the many other people moving within the wide hallway.

Only a few minutes went by before John Laird came out of the room and turned away from Karen to make for the nearest men's restroom. She was debating if she should wait outside the restroom. She had done it before to get a comment from a senator and would not hesitate to do so again.

The cloakroom door opened again, and Avery Doaks and Candy DuPont walked out. Their expressions told her the discussion in the room had not gone their way. She had no time to contact Don Bailey, her camera operator, set up near the Rotunda. Armed only with her digital recorder, she quickly approached the two Republican senators.

"Senators Doaks and DuPont. Could you comment on your attempt with Senator Laird to stop the filibuster?" She had guessed about the reason for the closed-door meeting, but it was logical and correct based on their expressions.

Doaks quickly looked around for a camera operator from the news network and saw none; he was glad no one had captured the look of surprise on his face. He hated ambush tactics by any member of the press.

Quickly putting on a smile, he spoke toward to the outstretched hand holding the digital recorder. "Good afternoon, Karen. We did have a few minutes with Senator Laird and asked if we could get him to allow the bill to go to committee where it would receive a full review. Witnesses could have testified about whether the Finance Committee should vote to recommend its passage by the full Senate. We feel it is important to stop the filibuster and allow the Senate to continue with its normal work. As you are aware, we have other pieces of legislation that we want to work on before we recess for the year. The filibuster is stopping other important work besides just the Fair Share Bill."

Karen turned her mic toward Senator DuPont. She was much shorter than the female senator was and needed to reach up. "Senator DuPont. Were you able to convince Senator Laird to release his hold of the Senate floor along with Senators Hanley and Saunders?"

DuPont looked at the group of people forming around them. Reporters from other news outlets were already holding their microphones out to capture her words.

"We did discuss possible options with Senator Laird. He gave us a few thoughts that we can share with our colleagues, but this is very sensitive, as you can imagine, and we need to meet with other members of the Senate to discuss it with them."

Karen jumped in with her next question before another reporter could try to edge her aside. "Are you saying that Senator Laird offered to stop the filibuster if you agreed to meet the demands of the three Davids?"

DuPont kept her expression calm. The new name the press had adopted was rapidly spreading around Capitol Hill. "This is not an event that the press can apply some catchy label to, trying to hype their ratings. We have an important piece of legislation on the floor of the United States Senate that will address tax loopholes used unfairly by many corporations to avoid paying their fair share of income taxes while millions of middle-class Americans supports the government with their tax payments."

She stopped to allow her emotions to calm down. "We did not offer anything new on the Fair Share Bill to any of the senators involved in the filibuster. We simply appealed to their common sense about allowing the bill to move forward, as the majority of the country wants."

Karen was happy with her recording of the two Republican Senate leaders. She wished her camera operator had been there to record DuPont's slightly flustered facial expression. She would simply have to describe the emotions displayed by the senators during her next on-camera report. She gave them a polite smile. "Thank you, Senators Doaks and DuPont for taking the time to talk with me."

She stepped away. Other reporters moved in, trying to get more information from the senators. She called Don Bailey on his cell phone to alert him she had an update on the Senate's efforts to break the filibuster and then made a second call to Bud Wilson at the CNN Washington building with the same news.

As she made her way to the Rotunda where Bailey's camera equipment was, she used her smart phone to bring up Senator Fisher's website and his calendar. His schedule noted he was taking personal time off. That was strange. She had a good memory but wanted to check whether Randy Fisher had ever missed a Senate session since he came to office. She did not think so.

She flipped the calendar back to November to check his whereabouts during the Thanksgiving break. The last days of November, when the Senate had been in recess, began his personal time off.

Karen Phillips did not keep as close a watch on Randy Fisher as her colleagues kidded her. He was happily married to a very nice woman, and she currently had a new man of her own. Her brother, employed by a large investment company on Wall Street, had recently introduced her to the manager of a hedge fund. They had already gone on three dates, which was almost a record for Karen. So far, so good in the love life department.

As she approached an open area in the Capitol Rotunda, she saw Don Bailey. Unlike the on-air reporters who must maintain a perfect professional image, the thirty-five-year-old camera operator was dressed in blue jeans and a heavy open-collar cotton plaid shirt under an open zippered jacket. The shoulder-held camera was set up on a tripod, the legs extended, ready for her broadcast to the studio. After she had completed her broadcast, she would determine if the network could discover where Senator Fisher was located and why he was not attending to business.

Chapter 30
Washington, DC
Tuesday, December 1, 2015
3:15 p.m.

Sally LaSalle replaced the phone hand set in the telephone base and sat back in her office chair. She had the television in her office muted as Senator Cameron Saunders was broadcast over C-SPAN. He was continuing with his new pattern, reading the list of American companies who were paying federal taxes. If they held to their established schedule, Senator Roberta Hanley would be taking the floor in about forty-five minutes.

She was worried. Her boss was AWOL, absence without leave, and refused to offer any reasons for not returning from London. She had asked if there was anything she or the staff could do to resolve whatever was holding him in London. The answer on the line was more double talk.

She had just closed her eyes. A knock on her door opened them again, and she leaned forward to bring her swivel chair back to its upright position. Brad Guilliams and Renee Stockli were standing in the threshold to her office. The two legislative aides to the senator had recently announced their engagement and were planning on a spring wedding. Brad was slender, six feet tall, with close-cropped brown hair. His politics leaned toward the right, making him the office conservative. Renee was about five foot-two, solid but slender, with finely textured blond hair. Her sparkling eyes always reflected her perky personality through the wire-rimmed glasses perched on her small Roman nose. She leaned toward the liberal side of the spectrum. Three years ago, the two aides would argue like a cat and dog over most of the political issues in then-Senator Robert Moore's office. Brad had been looking to make a change when Randy Fisher took office. The new senator decided to use their differences to work out issues in any newly proposed piece of legislation and come up with solutions he could use with the other senators. To everyone's surprise, the two young staffers had discovered they had more in common than they realized. After three years of working together almost every day, they were going to be married in the spring.

Brad stood behind Renee. "Any word when the boss will return? We've got a pile of work building up that needs his attention."

Renee piped up. "Yes. We are fairly sure where he stands on this Fair Share bill, but we need his guidance on other legislation very soon."

Sally motioned for the two to take the empty chairs in front of her desk. "I have no answers for you. I just hung up from talking with him. He is still in London, and his return to Washington is still open. I've asked him if there is something we can do to help with whatever is keeping him in London, but he says he's got all the help he needs except insight."

Brad's face screwed up with confusion. "Insight! What the heck does that mean?"

Renee leaned over toward him and grasped his hand. "It means the senator has a problem and needs help. This man never misses a day of work in Washington. The senator logs as many hours as most other elected politicians in Washington does, perhaps more than most. Something happened in London while he was over there, and he needs time to figure out a solution to his problem."

Brad laced fingers with his bride-to-be. "Surly it's not a problem with his wife. I can't believe there would be a problem between the senator and Annie."

Renee's little laugh came out more like a snort. "Fat chance of that. That marriage is a solid as a rock. If there were a problem with their marriage, the senator would not be in London. He would be right back here in DC, fighting to save his marriage." She shook her head. "No. Something else is going on that we are being kept in the dark about."

Sally rested her elbows on her desktop. "I've only been here a few months. If Tim Smith were here, he would probably call Annie Fisher and just ask her what was going on. I've only met her once, so I'm not sure how she would respond."

Tim Smith had been Randy's former chief of staff prior to Sally LaSalle. The black American had left to run for the House of Representative in his home district in Ohio. Randy Fisher was planning to campaign for his friend when the election really got into swing next year.

Sally saw Renee's expression change. "What?

Renee took her hand from Brad's grasp and used it and her other hand to help formulate her thoughts. "On the day before they were all scheduled to return to Washington, I sent a text message to Annie asking if they needed someone to pick them up at the airport. She replied that Marion Bellwood would have several of his men at the airport to meet them. I didn't think anything about it at the time, but why would operatives working for the CIA deputy director of operations send men to meet them at the airport?"

Sally LaSalle was back in her element and made a quick decision. She flipped her computer to the contacts section and located Annie Fisher's cell phone number. With no hesitation, she picked up the telephone and dialed the number.

After two rings, Annie Fisher answered.

"Mrs. Fisher, this is Sally LaSalle from the office. I sorry to bother you, but we are worried about the senator still being in London. Is there anything we can do on our end?" Sally listened for almost a full minute without interrupting. Brad and Renee could only sit and wonder what Annie was telling their supervisor.

Sally finally responded to the senator's wife. "All right, Annie. If you need anything or hear from the senator about anything that we can do to help, please let us know. Yes. That is all right. Thank you."

Brad and Renee both spoke together. "What?"

Sally leaned back in her chair again and raised both hands. "Something happened over there all right, and I think it's got to do with national security. She told me Randy had to stay to take care of some old business but not to worry because Marion Bellwood was there with him."

Renee asked the question on her mind. "So what do we do now?"

Sally's left wrist rested on the edge of the desk. She pointed her index finger toward the two and moved it back and forth. "For now ... nothing. If this involves national security, the last thing we want to do is stick our noses where they do not belong. Senator Fisher will contact us if there is something we can do for him."

She was about to issue new instructions to the legislative aides when her office intercom buzzed. June Little was calling.

"Sally, Karen Phillips from CNN is on hold. She's asking when the senator will be returning to Washington."

"Thanks, June. I'll take the call."

She looked at Brad and Renee. "Stay quiet but listen in."

Sally hit the illuminated button on her desk phone and then activated the phone's built-in speaker.

"Good afternoon, Karen. How are you?"

Karen Phillips's voice came clearly over the speaker. "I'm fine, Sally, but we are wondering why Senator Fisher is missing all the fun with this Senate filibuster. It seems the other members could use a dose of his well-known common sense. Can you tell me where Randy Fisher is right now?"

Sally replied quickly so as not to show any hesitation. "He's still taking some personal time off, Karen. To protect his privacy, I can't tell you where."

"Come on, Sally. What is going on? Senator Fisher never misses work. Do not tell me he is in some sort of rehab or some other dip-shit excuse. For him to not be in the Senate right now means something more important is going on."

"I'm sorry, Karen, but there is nothing sinister happening with the senator. I am sure he will be back to work in a few days. Is there anything else I can help you with?"

Sally heard a slight laugh from the speaker. "There is, but I'm just going to get the same BS answer."

Sally looked at her office companions and shrugged her shoulders. "Well ... call back if there is anything else we can do to help."

Karen Phillips heard the telephone on the other end disconnect. She dropped the handset back into its cradle and looked across her desk to Bud Wilson. Her boss was sitting in the only chair in her cubbyhole of an office in the CNN Washington Bureau near the Capitol.

"Well ... what do you think?"

Bud Wilson was sixty years old and had headed the Washington Bureau for almost fifteen years. The overhead fluorescent lights made his baldhead shine. He had a slight grin on his face. "You're right. Something is going on with the famous Senator Fisher." He sat back in the chair and looked out the small office window behind his congressional reporter. "Where was he during the Thanksgiving recess?"

Karen unconsciously used her right hand to flip her long black hair behind her ear. "I think I heard someone over on the hill talking about Fisher taking his wife and some other family members to England."

Wilson rubbed his eyes using the back of his hands. "I wonder how we could find him if he's still over there? If we had an idea, we could ask our London people to look into him."

Karen Phillips had a growing smile on her face. "I've been covering Randy Fisher since the terrorist incident down in Columbia, South Carolina. He has a few habits that we might be able to use to find him if he's still in London." Karen looked at the small clock built into the decorative inkstand on her desk, a birthday gift from her parents. "It's 3:30 here in Washington. What time is it in London?"

Bud took a few moments to work out the time difference out in his head. "Eight thirty in the evening. Put the phone on speaker and call over there. Ask for Janice Curtain. She should still be in the office."

Karen took about thirty seconds to look up the international phone exchange and the local telephone number for their CNN London office. The phone rang twice before a woman's voice answered. Karen quickly asked for Janice Curtain. After a short time on hold, a rough, raspy voice came on the line. Karen could visualize someone sitting on the edge of a newsroom desk smoking a cigarette. The person on the other end of the line did not waste any time.

"Curtain here. Who's speaking?"

"Janice, this is Karen Phillips calling from Washington. I have Bud Wilson in my office with me. How are you today?"

There was a slight pause on the other end. Karen and Bud Wilson could hear muffled sounds but could not make out the words coming through the speaker. The raspy voice came back over the speaker.

"Listen, love, we got a bit of a flap going on over here, and I don't have time for chit chat. Now, what do you want?"

Bud Wilson leaned closer to Karen's telephone. "Janice, this is Bud Wilson. Have you married that old goat you've been shacking up with for the last ten years?"

They could hear the woman laughing and coughing at the same time. "Bud Wilson, as I live and breathe. Have you starting growing any hair yet? You've been bald since you were in nappies."

Bud laughed back but then got serious. "Janice, what's going on over there? You said something about a flap?"

The laughter on the London end of the phone stopped. "Something is happening here in London. Scotland Yard pulled in a bunch of extra bobbies from the outer boroughs, and our spotters have reported a heavier than normal police presence around the tourist hotspots. They are mostly dressed in plain clothes to keep a low profile, but it looks like some sort of security flap. So far the Yard's director of public affairs has been completely mum on the subject."

Bud asked, "How long has this been going on?"

There was a slight hesitation in her response. "It seemed to start Sunday morning. First it was around Trafalgar Square and Charing Cross Station, but now the extra presence seems to also be around Buckingham Palace and most of Central London, out as far as Windsor Castle." There was dead air for about ten seconds.

"Tell me something, Bud. You got a handle on any of this?"

Bud answered quickly. "It's the first we've heard of it, but maybe we've got something to help you find your answers. We've got a missing United States senator who was last known to be in London over the Thanksgiving holidays."

"Who is it?"

"Senator Randy Fisher."

"*The* Randy Fisher? The one who stopped the bomb a few years ago and the war in Southeast Asia earlier this year?"

"The one and only," Bud answered back.

They heard Curtain take a deep breath; a short coughing fit followed. "Blimey. That would get the Yard Birds' knickers in a twist. What else can you tell me?"

Karen spoke up. "The senator has some habits from his younger days. He usually stays at the Hilton hotels. You might check to see if he was registered with any of them."

Curtain replied, "Well, that shouldn't take too long. There are only two Hilton hotels in London. The best is across the street from Trafalgar Square, right where this current mess might have started. Might be a coincidence, might not. I think I'll put a few people onto this and see where it leads us."

Chapter 31

London
Tuesday, December 1, 2015
8:30 p.m.

Randy Fisher was tired. Probably not as tired as the members of the Metropolitan Police department involved in the search for the terrorist but still tired after a full day at Scotland Yard.

After breakfast, Marion Bellwood and BookReader drove Randy in their rental car to the New Scotland Yard building on Broadway in Westminster. They showed their identifications to the security guards at the rear entrance gate and parked in a VIP spot at the rear of the building. Inside the lobby, they showed their IDs once again and requested that the security clerk telephone DC Shepard's office and obtain his permission to enter the building.

Four minutes later, they exited the elevator on the eighteenth floor and met a uniformed employee of the Met. The same woman who had operated the projector at their Sunday meeting was their new guide. She gave them a cheery smile supported by very white teeth. "Good morning, gentlemen. I am Constance Langhorne. DC Shepard is waiting for you in the command center. He asked if I would escort you to the room."

They followed the woman out of the lobby area down a long hallway. They would have guessed her age somewhere in the early thirties, but her long, light brown hair was twisted into a tight bun at the back of her head, and that always shaved years off a woman's appearance.

At the end of the hallway, they came to a pair of double glass doors. The frosted glass panels prevented them from seeing through to the other side. Constance Langhorne approached a stainless steel box mounted next to the left door. It had a number keypad to punch in a combination. She kept her body close to the entry system to prevent them from seeing the combination of numbers she used to unlock the door.

"We all have our own unique set of numbers, so there is a record of who is in the War Room at all times. Please follow me, gentlemen." She opened the door to allow them to enter the room. Agent Reader hurried to grab the door from Langhorne and gave her a big smile. She smiled back. "Thank you, Mr. ..."

"Thomas. Thomas Reader. It's very nice to meet you."

Randy and Marion were first to follow Constance into the room. Marion gave his younger agent a stern look. Phillip Booker grinned a little at Thomas Reader and shook his head. As he walked past his partner, he dug his left elbow in his midriff and quietly mumbled a warning. "Let's stay focused, shall we, Tommy."

Inside the room, eighteen or twenty people were working to monitor the Met's operation to find the two terrorists. The room must have been fifty feet square, with a ceiling at least twenty-five feet above the floor. The glass wall to the left was the same opaque glass of the entrance doors, allowing a limited amount of natural light into the room. A number of glass-enclosed offices lined the right wall. However, the first thing to draw every one's attention when they entered the room was the front wall of flat-screen monitors. A series of seventy-two inch high-definition plasma screens in a large block, six screens wide and six screens high, displayed a number of complicated maps of Central London and the surrounding area.

Randy and his fellow Americans stared for several minutes at the screens, trying to make sense of the massive amount of information in front of their eyes.

Constance Langhorne offered an explanation. "We can put up almost any image we want from the Earth satellites. It quite similar to Google Earth that you look at on your computers screens, but now we have it focused on Central London. The center screens show a compilation of different pictures to make up one large picture. The outer row of screens on both the left and right side and along the top row show individual locations that we can monitor. If needed, we can bring any one of them into the large center screen and enlarge the image. We can redirect the satellites images to any part of London, or England for that matter."

She gave them another minute to watch the screens. "Let's move a little closer, and I will give you a more detailed explanation of what you're seeing."

The center of the room was an open area of about ten square feet. A single row of desks placed in a large L-shape lay along the back wall and ran against the outer opaque glass wall. A man or woman occupied each of the desks, each with their own twenty-seven-inch monitor, keyboard, and telephone. As new information from the security teams in the field arrived at their desks, they would update the screens with the new information.

In the open space, the group took a closer look at the screens. Constance pointed with her left index finger to what she was describing. "As I said, the main group of screens in the center shows most of Central London and the immediate surrounding area. You can see we go west to Warwick Road, west of Kensington Palace. The northern boundary is the A-40 Highway, Westway Road, which becomes Marylebone Road and then continues east to become City Road. We go farther east to Shoreditch High Street where it meets with Commercial Street and the intersection where the A-11 and A-13 come together. The east screens show White Chapel and the Tower of London, crossing the

River Thames on Tower Bridge. We show Druid Street and most of Southwark down to the intersection of New Kent and Old Kent Roads. We go west to the intersection of Battersea and Latchmere Road and then back north to Kensington Gardens."

She pointed to the sides of the large screen array. "Some of the other individual screens show locations far away from Central London that we want to monitor but will not fit on the larger center screen. As I said, we can bring any of the images into the center screen if we need to enlarge a particular image."

She allowed them to process that information and then continued with her explanation. "We are watching this from the Earth satellites, but we can change the image to any of the hundreds of CCTVs. Traffic cameras or security cameras are inside buildings like Charing Cross Station or any of the underground tube lines. It's all very sophisticated."

Marion pointed to the screen. "What do the orange circles and blue and white dots indicate?"

"Oh yes. The orange circles are the locations indicated in the notebook recovered from the suspect who got away from the senator. Those areas are high-priority locations. The blue dot represents a uniformed bobby, and the white dots are plainclothes officers. We can track them by the GPS chip in their radios."

She moved to one of the desks where a young man dressed in a long-sleeve white shirt, blue striped tie, and dark pants was sitting. His fingers were moving across the keyboard at his desk but stopped when Constance approached. "Erik monitors all the security personnel at every location so we know what assets we have available to respond to any situation."

She pointed to Trafalgar Square on the center group of screens. "Eric, who do we have at Trafalgar?"

Eric entered a few keystrokes on the keyboard, and one of the side screens changed to show Trafalgar Square. The background image of the square was lightly shaded, but the blue and white dots glowed more brilliantly. A list of names for the supervisors of the security people assigned to the square appeared off to the right side of the monitor.

From the smile on Constance's face, it was obvious how proud she was of the amount of information at their fingertips. "Now ... you can see we have four officers on the immediate square. Three are plain clothed. The other one is a uniformed bobby. You can also see we have a few more around the surrounding streets, close enough to respond to any situation within the square itself."

Randy pointed to the screens. "What if you need more support than these dots represent?"

Constance's smile grew a little bigger. "That's a good question, Senator Fisher. Eric, change the screen to show the armed forces we have ready to deploy."

Eric quickly tapped the new set of instructions into his keyboard. The entire center screen changed to show a dim background of Central London with a series of green dots. Again, off to the side were the military unit numbers and the type of personnel available. "This doesn't give us individual names, but we know what unit is there and the type of equipment they have."

She stepped a little closer to the screens and moved her hand to indicate several of the units. "We keep them out of sight from the public. Some are located at the Agar Street Police Station or inside one of the bays of a fire station or a public garage— any place that is close to where we want them to be but out of sight of our terrorist."

Deputy Commissioner Shepard came out of the corner office. He caught sight of Randy and Marion and the two CIA operatives and diverted his path. After a round of handshakes and introductions to BookReader, he looked at the screens.

"I see Constance has given you a tour of our War Room. It is quite similar to what Churchill had during the Second World War with maps of Europe and Africa, but with all the electronic tools at our disposal today, we have real-time imaging. Its real name is the Command Room, but people working here simply call it the War Room when we are facing a possible terrorist plot."

He continued to look at the screen for several more seconds before turning back to the Americans. "Well now. Why don't you come with me, and I'll give you an update on the current situation".

They followed him back to the largest of the three offices. It was nearly ten feet in depth and fifteen feet along the outer wall. There was a basic government-issued steel desk and swivel chair, along with two steel-framed straight chairs in front of the desk. In the corner to their right as they entered was a smaller round table for four people. Two chairs were at the table. Another two were stacked in the corner.

Shepard indicated that Marion and Randy take the chairs near his desk. BookReader settled in the two chairs at the table. Shepard walked around the desk, dropped into the padded swivel chair, and released a little sigh between pressed lips. He dropped some papers and used his feet to pull the chair closer to the desk. "Well now. Let's see what's happened since last evening."

He picked up a spiral-bound notebook with letter-size sheets of paper and flipped a few pages back and forth. Randy noticed it was of better quality than a typical office supply brand, where the side of a notebook had the normal wire curved into a spiral and woven through the miniature holes along the edge of each sheet of paper. When the writer removed a sheet from the notebook, the holes in the paper were torn and small bits of paper remained inside the coil of stiff wire. Sometimes the ribbon of paper was almost the length of the sheet of paper. Other times, many little paper remnants fell out of the notebook onto the desk surface or floor.

In Shepard's notebook, the coil of wire wove through the network of holes, but each sheet also had a small perforation about one-half inch from the edge of the paper sheet parallel to the line of holes. A person could hold a finger down on the edge of the perforation and carefully tear the sheet out of the notebook without creating a mess with little bits of paper. From Randy's seat, he could not see any paper remnants, so he assumed Shepard would use the line of perforations to remove sheets of paper.

Shepard finally located where he wanted to start his briefing. He unconsciously started his sentence with the same two words. "Well now. We have had no increase in signal intelligence before your incident with the man on the footbridge or afterward. History shows an increase in e-mails or cellular phone traffic from suspected sites before an operation commences and then a drop-off and finally complete silence just before they start the campaign. Everything so far is quite their normal routine."

Randy spoke up quickly. "Are you assuming this might be a false alarm? Are you downgrading your efforts to locate the men?"

Shepard looked at Randy for a few seconds longer than comfortable. "No, Senator. Not at all. Her Majesty's government still considers this operation a high priority. We have sufficient information to continue on for another day or two."

He went back to his notebook and ran his right index finger down the page. "Well now ... Where was I? Oh, yes ... Nothing from signal intelligence. Well now, we have been watching the airports, bus stations, and the underground very closely for any persons fitting the description. Of course with this being London, we have many assets down by the docks and at every major place along the Thames. If your men, Senator Fisher, are still in London, they are keeping their heads down until they are ready to make their move."

Marion shifted in the chair as he spoke up. "This is your city, Deputy Commissioner. When would be the best time to strike to get the most out of their efforts this time of the year?"

In the outer War Room, all the windows were frosted. The window in DC Shepard's office was clear. Perhaps it was a sign of his rank. He rotated his chair and looked out the window at the December weather. The sky overhead was heavy and dark for the time of the day. There would be no sunshine coming through the heavy cloud cover; it appeared the rain could fall again at any minute. Randy remembered from the morning report on the hotel television that the local weatherman predicted the temperature was to drop throughout the day and bring in rain mixed with ice, possibly heavy at times.

Shepard turned back to face his guests. "Well now. The weather is in our favor for keeping the tourist numbers down. I would think we are rather safe until this weather front blows through and the temperature and sunshine return to more favorable conditions to bring out the numbers. I say we need to watch this thing at least through the weekend. Then we will probably reassess the latest information and issue new instructions."

Marion looked at the deputy commissioner but kept his thoughts to himself. He glanced at his wristwatch. "I appreciate your taking the time, Deputy Commissioner, to bring us up to speed. I've got an appointment with some people over at MI6, so I need to leave."

He rose from his chair and offered his hand to the deputy commissioner. He turned to Randy, who was just getting out of his chair. "Randy, are you staying here or coming with me?"

Randy looked at the Englishman across the desk and then at his friend. "If DC Shepard doesn't mind, I would like to stick around here for the time being. I would like to look through the information we have on the personal effects found in the suspect's backpack."

Shepard gave a little shrug. "You're quite welcome to stay here in the War Room or down in the evidence room. Wherever you feel comfortable, Senator."

Randy made a quick decision. "I think the evidence room would be best. I do not want to be in the way here. This must be the busiest room in the building."

Shepard wanted the Americans out of his way but remembered his manners. "No problem at all. Perhaps the evidence room would be best. I'll have one of the lads escort you down."

Randy turned in time to see the sorrowful look on Agent Reader's face. The beautiful Constance Langhorne would not be walking with them.

Outside his office, Shepard got the attention of another young man and ordered him to take Randy down to the fourth floor to the evidence room next to the CSI laboratory for their unit. He wished them a pleasant day, shook hands all around, and returned to his office.

Once outside the War Room, Randy asked their escort to stop before they reached the elevator. He pulled Marion and BookReader off to the side. The two agents stayed a few feet away and kept a watch on the traffic in the hallway so their boss and the senator were not disturbed.

Randy looked in his friend's face. "Do you agree with Shepard's opinion about the risk of an attack being low until the weather clears up and more people are outside?"

Marion looked around to ensure no other person was within hearing. "No. If I were a terrorist, I would use the lousy weather to cover my activities. Maybe the kill ratio would be lower, but the chance of a successful mission would be higher. I would strike now."

Randy was in full agreement. "All right. You head over to MI6 and put your head together with their analysts. I will stay here. I still want to look over the physical evidence. Something is bothering me about it, but I can't put my finger on it just yet." He looked at BookReader. "Why don't you take BookReader with you? They would probably be of more help to you than me."

Marion shook his head. "Sorry, Randy. You've had your lot of excitement on this trip." He looked at the two men and then back to his best friend. His expression changed to a look of slight confusion. "BookReader? Whatever you call them, they stay with you until you step on a jet back to Washington."

Chapter 32

London
Tuesday, December 1, 2015
9:30 p.m.

Randy stepped out of the shower and used the thick towel to dry his hair and body. He had turned on the exhaust fan to keep the mirror from fogging over so he could see his reflection. The scar from the bullet wound inflicted by the terrorist in Columbia was still visible through the thick mat of layered chest hair. The red around the wound was long gone, and he thought the rough scar tissue was a little smoother than before.

The scar was an everyday reminder of how close he came to death slightly over three years ago. He rubbed his left shoulder to ease the slight pain that developed on cold and rainy days. The local weatherman had nailed it. Just after the lunch hour, the rain and temperature began to fall. When it got into the low thirties, small pellets of hail mixed with the steady rainfall. It was nasty weather for the balance of the day.

He stepped closer to the mirror and ran his right hand over his cheeks. He decided to wait until morning to shave again. He had a thick beard pattern and many days he would shave twice. His eyes went from the whisker stubbles to the two butterfly bandages above his right eye. They needed changing, and he opened his toiletries bag and rummaged inside for two fresh bandages.

He carefully removed the old ones so not to pull off the scabs that kept the wound from reopening. The deep cut was healing. Maybe after another day or two he could go without the small bandages. Finished with the wound, he checked out the deep abrasion on his right wrist just behind the outer pad of his palm. The large gauze pad needed changing as well, and he once again dipped into the small bag that contained his electric shaver and other toiletries. The new gauze pad was the last one provided by Officer Davis at the Agar station. He would need to find a drug store tomorrow and purchase some new medical supplies.

Finished in the bathroom, he walked into the living room of his suite and put on a clean set of undershorts and a pair of cotton jersey pants he normally wore in their apartment in Alexandria, along with a T-shirt. He went to the mini refrigerator and removed a bottle of London Pride beer. He twisted off the cap and tossed it into the nearby trashcan. He took a sip from the bottle and walked over to look out the window. His top-floor suite gave him a good view of the next buildings. Off to his right the lights of Trafalgar Square allowed him a view of most of the square. The hotel building prevented him from seeing Nelson's Column.

As he looked out the window, he decided the day had not been a complete waste of his time. From the War Room, their escort took them to the evidence room on the fourth floor of the twenty-story building. He discovered he could only look at photographs of the evidence. The actual items were tagged and bagged and could not be touched by anyone except the CSI personnel and case investigators. Otherwise, Randy might contaminate the evidence and make it unusable for criminal prosecution if they captured the men and brought them to trial.

Looking at photographs all day was brutal. He took pity on BookReader and told them they could move about the building. He promised the two security agents he would not leave the small unused office off the evidence room provided to him for anything except to use the restroom down the hallway. Booker told him they would compromise; only one agent would stay with the senator. They would switch off every hour to stay vigilant and fresh.

Randy took the file folder of pictures and arranged them on the desk in two rows. The top row was the items he had seen handled by the suspect. The second row included photographs of the other items discovered inside the backpack. The top row documented the backpack, knife, and cell phone, along with copies of all the pictures taken with the cell phone. The bottom row photos showed each page inside the notebook, the handkerchief, the map of London, British paper money in various denominations, and a single bottle of water.

He started with the items he had seen handled by the terrorist and carefully looked at the photos. He forced himself to look at each part of each item. The backpack photo had two long rulers on two dimensions to provide the size. It was fifteen inches tall and ten inches across. The depth probably averaged seven or eight inches. The color was basic black, and the manufacture's logo was located on the top right side. It appeared to be a lightning bolt. No name was visible. Two shoulder straps, slightly wider at the top, attached at a horizontal seam and continued down the back of the bag. The straps were sewn to the top of the backpack about three inches apart but turned outward at the bottom, where a cross strap was attached to keep the two larger straps from flopping around too much. Once placed over the shoulder, snap clips attached the cross strap to the larger shoulder straps.

Another photo showed the backside where the top flap came over, sealed shut by a plastic snap clip. The bag's interior padding prevented any sharp objects from sticking into the back or sides of the wearer. Randy spent nearly twenty minutes looking at the two photos of the backpack before he set them back down in their top row position.

The next item was the knife. As knives go, it was not as nasty looking as those used by members of the Armed Forces. As an MP in the army, Randy had carried a knife as part of his standard equipment package. He had now faced the wrong end of a knife twice in his life and would be happy never to repeat the incidents.

The experts described it as a Browning Titanium Gray Red Acid Quick Open knife. The wooden handle was red oak with a downward tip at the end to ensure it would not slip through the closed fingers of the user. The front part of the handle had an indentation where the spring release mechanism was located. After depressing the metal release, the knife would spring open and lock into position. The user would have to press the spring release a second time to release the locking mechanism and fold the blade back into the closed position. The maker manufactured the blade from titanium for its ability to hold hardness and to retain a sharp edge. The blade ended with a very sharp point. The Browning logo and name were etched into the hardened metal. There was no doubt in Randy's mind the knife was of quality material and construction. Again, he spent almost twenty-five minutes looking at the photo, but he discovered nothing to ease the nagging suspicion still bothering him. There was something that he was seeing but not recognizing. What was it?

The next picture from the top row showed the cell phone. It was the latest model from the largest manufacturer in Europe, made in China. Randy had seen many of the exact same type: a black plastic body with a black glass front. It contained a high-quality phone and camera for taking several types of photos or even a video clip. Randy clearly remembered seeing the twin of his attacker from three years ago taking pictures outside the Texas Embassy Cantina restaurant. The photo in his hand contained two images, front and back views. He could learn little from just the pictures. The camera itself contained dozens of photos stored on its memory chip. The CSI lab had printed the images; each sheet of photographic paper displayed four photos from the camera. One by one, he carefully reviewed each set of photos.

Each sheet contained four photos of London's popular tourist spots, many from different angles. The pages were marked to indicate the order in which the locations were photographed. Many of the locations were the same Randy and his family had visited on their vacation: Buckingham Palace, the Queen's Gallery, the Duke of York Column, and then on to the National Portrait Gallery, Trafalgar Square, and Nelson's Column. There were four photos of Charing Cross Station from various angles and then across the walking bridge to the London Eye. Looking at the photo of the famous tourist attraction, Randy remembered his own trip on their first full day in London. They had been lucky to book their tickets in advance. The crowds were heavy as the weather was nice.

The Eye stood 443 feet tall, contained thirty-two sealed, air-conditioned or heated capsules designed to hold up to twenty-five riders. The entire rotation traveled at ten inches per second; it took a full thirty minutes to make one complete circuit. The view was breathtaking. Randy hoped the financial difficulties surrounding operational cost were resolved. It would be a shame if the London Eye was shut down and removed.

After the London Eye, the photographs indicated his suspect next moved to Hyde Park and Kensington Gardens and the magnificent palace located on the western edge of the huge garden area. Randy could remember seeing the Palace on the large screens in the War Room.

The other dozens sheets of four photos seemed to confirm the suspect had made an extensive trip around London to determine possible targets. With so many places to cover, enhanced security would place a strain on the Metropolitan Police Department and their resources.

He returned the thick batch of photos back to its place on the table.

He had spent two-thirds of an hour on the photos of the backpack and knife and another ninety minutes on the cell phone and all the photos it contained, but he had nothing to show for his time. *Time,* he thought. *Yes, it was time for a cup of coffee to refresh his mind and eyes.*

Randy stepped out of the small office. Agent Reader was leaning against the wall. He looked at Randy and pointed down the hallway. "The men's room is down the hallway and toward your left. There is a small coffee and snack shop on the next floor down."

Randy nodded. "Pit stop first and then coffee."

Reader stood outside the men's room and fell into step beside Randy when the senator emerged. They located the elevator and took a short one-story ride to the next floor below. The coffee shop was located directly off the elevator lobby area. Randy saw a queue of six or eight people. As he and Reader entered the shop, he felt his cell phone vibrating in his right pants pocket. He stepped off to the side where several tall pedestal tables and stools were set. One table was empty, and he took a stool to read the e-mail coming in on his BlackBerry.

Needing to focus on the phone, he reached inside his left pants pocket and removed the money clip with his British money. He pulled out a twenty-pound note and handed it to Reader. "If you get me a black coffee and a muffin, I'll happily pay for whatever you would like."

The agent nodded, took the money, and stepped into the line. Every thirty seconds he turned and glanced over his shoulder to check on his protectee. Finally, he reached the counter and took a minute to order their coffee and then make a final review of the muffins, cakes, and cookies. Satisfied with his selection, he gave the server a final nod and moved to wait in line at the cashier to pay. He watched their order being prepared and placed on a small plastic tray resting on a stainless steel platform and slid down toward the cashier. Theoretically, the plastic tray and the customer would arrive together at the cashier.

This time the system worked. Reader handed over the senator's money and received his change, which he laid on the tray as he picked up their order. He walked around the final post that channeled customers in an orderly queue and turned toward the table and Senator Fisher.

Reader noticed an immediate problem. Randy Fisher was not where he had been sitting thirty seconds ago. Two women sat at the table, smiling and chatting happily with each other.

Chapter 33

London
Tuesday, December 1, 2015
11:30 a.m.

Reader hesitated only long enough to collect the plastic tray with their order as he hurried from the coffee shop back to the elevator. As he approached the lobby area, he saw the elevator doors closing. Several uniformed officers were talking to each other a few steps from the doors.

Charlie reached the elevator doors and pressed the up button. He turned to the men who were quietly talking a few steps away. "Excuse me, gentlemen, but did you see another man get on the elevator from this floor? He was in his early forties, about six feet tall with average-length brown hair?"

Both men stopped talking and stared at him for a few seconds. One finally looked down at the tray with two cups of coffee and the two muffins. He looked back to Reader's face. "Yes. I believe the man you are looking for stepped onto the lift just after we stepped off. Is there a problem?"

Reader just shook his head. "No problem. Just someone who doesn't understand security procedures."

There were six elevators in the lobby. The floor light suddenly popped on to indicate a car had arrived. Reader made sure it was going up and sent a little head bob toward the two men. "Thanks for your help", he said quickly and stepped onto the lift. He used his free hand to press for the next floor.

Ten seconds later the door opened on the fourth floor. Reader hurried out of the lift, trying not to spill the hot coffee. When he rounded the corner, Booker was standing outside the office doorway in the same spot Reader had been several minutes ago. The senior agent was giving him a hard look.

Reader gave his partner a look and then stepped past him to glance inside the office. He looked back to the senior agent. "Where the hell have you been?" Booker asked. "You know what DDO Bellwood would do to both of us if something happened to that guy? We'd probably be guarding some damn politician's mutt, or worse."

Reader shook his head. "I'm telling you. I took my eye off of him for thirty seconds, and when I turned around he was gone."

Booker just shook his head. No excuse would be good enough. He glanced down at the plastic tray in Reader's right hand and reached up to take it away from him. He took a sniff of the hot coffee. A small smile appeared on his rough face. "All right, you're excused this time."

He turned and stepped into the office. "We have your coffee and muffin here, Senator Fisher."

Randy Fisher looked up and turned his body slightly as the two men approached the table. He reached for the coffee and took a sip. "Thanks. I have a question for both of you. The evidence man who gave me these photos told us the photos were printed from the cell phone in the order they were taken by our suspect." He pointed toward the first photo of four pictures. Each had a small day and time stamp in the lower left corner.

Agent Booker claimed the second cup of coffee meant for his partner and took a quick sip before he set the plastic tray on the far edge of the table. He heard a slight growl escape from Reader's throat. He could not keep a little smile off his face as he stepped closer to the table and looked past the senator's shoulders at the array of photos again spread out on the table.

"That's right, Senator. There were almost one hundred and fifty pictures in the phone. Each had a time stamp to indicate when it was taken by the suspect."

"Right," Randy said. He pointed to the first set of photos and then pointed at each page. "Here are the photos of Trafalgar Square. They are located in the middle of the group of photos. All the following ones were taken by the suspect after he took the photos in Trafalgar Square."

Reader had stepped to the other side of Randy and was looking at the photo. "I don't understand, sir. I see when the photos were taken, but what is significant about the order of the photographs? How does that help us determine where they might attack?"

Randy shook his head. "It doesn't narrow down the possible targets, but something is definitely wrong. I was having lunch around noon when I saw the suspect standing outside the Texan Embassy Cantina. He was taking a picture from Pall Mall East Street down toward Trafalgar Square. First, there is no picture of the square from that angle in this lot. Second, I started chasing him within a few minutes of when he took the picture that is not in this batch. We played the cat-and-mouse game for more than two hours, and then he lost the backpack on the foot bridge."

Randy stepped away from the table and walked past Booker around to the other side of the small room. He turned to the two agents. They could see a sparkle in his eyes. "The photos are out of sequence, and the photo he took when I saw him is missing."

Reader called out first. "There are two phones!"

"Yes," Randy said. "That's what's been bothering me. I did not see him when I first ran out of the restaurant. I guessed he was walking toward Trafalgar Square, and I headed in that direction from the restaurant. I did not see him again until I stood up on top of the edge of the fountain. Then I saw him walking out from behind the second fountain."

Randy stopped, thinking back to the memories of that moment. He could see the terrorist, the backpack slung over his shoulder. Then it came to him. He remembered seeing the cell phone in his right hand, down along his right thigh.

"When I caught sign of him again he still had the phone in his right hand. He was not taking any pictures but just holding the phone. Within seconds, we were into the chase. There was hardly any time from that moment until he lost the backpack to remove the backpack, open the pocket cover, and place the phone inside the backpack."

He looked at the two agents. "All right, guys. If you were either me or the suspect and involved in a cat-and-mouse chase, would you take time to put the cell phone inside the backpack?" Randy answered his own question. "No. You would slip it in your pants pockets to make sure you didn't lose it."

Booker nodded in agreement. "Or if you're concerned about being caught or tracked by the GPS signal inside the phone, you would ditch it. There would be many opportunities—in any trash receptacle or entrance to a drainpipe. Even better, when your man was running over the bridge he could just drop it into the river. We would have a hard time finding something that small in the River Thames."

Reader had to point out the one flaw in their theory. "You said he ran into the Tie Rack shop and purchased a leather jacket. He could have put the phone inside the backpack at that time. We know for certain he took the backpack off to put on the jacket."

Randy smiled at the younger man. "You're correct. He might have put the phone in the backpack when he was in the tie shop, but that doesn't explain the missing photo from outside the restaurant and that the others photos are not in the proper sequence."

He reached down to pick up the single sheet with the front and back photos of the cell phone. "There was a second phone. Maybe this one was left along with the backpack to throw us off their real target."

All three men were silent as they contemplated the ramifications of Randy's last statement.

Booker was moving his right index finger over the many photos of the London tourist spots. "If we're correct, then London might have thirty thousand members of their police department looking in the wrong place."

Chapter 34
London
Wednesday, December 2, 2015
12:15 a.m.

In the bathroom of his hotel suite, Randy Fisher plugged his BlackBerry into the charger. He had been using it a lot lately and the battery was low.

He had made a call to Annie. His Aunt Frances was still staying at their apartment in Alexandria. She was not returning to California until Randy was back in the United States. Her decision had been firm. Frances was not going back home to worry alone about her only living relative while he was in another country chasing some damn terrorist.

Randy had to smile as Annie explained all that. He envisioned his aunt standing in their living room and talking to Annie. She had put the phone into Frances's hand and let her talk with Randy to make sure she knew he was safe and under the protection of Marion Bellwood's men. Randy had assured Frances that BookReader was watching him closely. Once satisfied with his safety, Frances had returned the phone to Annie and left the room to allow the two to speak privately.

Randy again explained the security procedures Marion had put in place around him. The two agents were in the same hotel, across the hallway in another suite. Marion was staying only several doors down the hallway. Randy's protection was solid.

Annie seemed to be satisfied with the precautions but warned her husband to leave any new chases to the professionals. She wanted him back in their apartment safe and in one piece.

They talked about her work. The time allowed Randy to forget about why he was still in London and not home with the woman he loved. He had just disconnected the call when the BlackBerry showed another incoming call; the screen displayed the caller's information. Tom Evans was calling.

Randy had been ignoring all calls from other members of the Senate or their staffers, but he knew he could not hit the ignore button on this one. Instead, he pressed the answer button.

"Hi, Tom. How are things in the Senate today?"

Randy could hear the chuckle in Tom's voice. "You are missing one hell of a show over here. Three Republicans senators are holding up a Republican president's bill. If it were not so serious, we Democrats would be laughing our asses off. In fact, I'm sure a few chuckles are taking place in the privacy of some people's offices or homes."

After a silence, Tom's voice came back on the phone. "You want to tell me about the security threat going on in London right now? I got a briefing on it right after the White House received theirs."

Twenty minutes later Randy had the Democratic candidate for president up to date to the point when he had discovered evidence there was a second cell phone. "I had another meeting with the deputy commissioner of Scotland Yard, who was forced to agree with me. That led to another smaller meeting among the heads of Scotland Yard, MI5, and MI6. The same two cabinet ministers also attended, and they were all forced to conclude the coverage watch area needed to be enlarged."

Tom replied, "It sounds to me like they need to include almost all of London, or even England itself. The photos might have been taken to pull security forces away from the coastline and other outer areas and into London itself."

Randy agreed. "Yes. That was the two-ton elephant in the room. Every procedure set up to find these people might have all be for naught. We've back to square one in our search."

There was almost thirty seconds of silence on the line between the two friends. Tom finally broke the quiet. "If you're at a dead end, then why don't you come back to Washington? We could use a little of your famous common sense over here to kill this bill and end the filibuster. All three of these senators came into the Senate when you were reelected. You have common ground with them. Especially Senator Laird. You two sit across the aisle from each other where the Democrats and Republicans physically separate on the Senate floor."

Randy did not answer. Tom took the lack of a response as a sign to continue. "I also know your office is having a problem explaining why you are not on the floor of the Senate or at least in Washington. I spoke to Mrs. LaSalle. CNN and some of the other news networks are starting to ask about your absence. The longer you're not here, the more likely they will come up with wild speculations to explain your absence."

Randy still remained silent.

Tom decided to prod his friend a little more. "Randy … I understand you want to catch this twin or look-a-like. I would feel the same if I were in your place, but maybe it's time to leave it to the professionals and come back to DC where you can do some real good. We need to end this in the Senate, and you've got a relationship with the three Davids."

Randy stood at the window looking out over portions of London. He shook his head. "The professionals had the photos, but none of them realized they were not in the proper sequence. If I hadn't noticed, then all the security would still be focused on Central London." He paused for a few moments and then continued. "I know these people are the professionals, but something is telling me to stay. I still have a nagging suspicion something was overlooked in the evidence. I can't leave until I figure it out."

Tom answered quickly. His voice was soft, but doubt was starting to creep into his words. "Randy … you just spent a full day stuck in a small office staring at the physical evidence. How much more do you think you can get from looking at the photographs?"

Randy felt some irritation building inside his chest but kept his voice calm. Tom Evans was a good friend and he respected him. "I don't know, Tom, but until I know for sure these guys are out of the area and we haven't any reasonable chance to catch them, I'm going to stay. This is the first time in three years I've had a chance to get some answers about what happened at the fairgrounds in Columbia. I'm not going to stop until I get those answers to my questions."

Chapter 35

London
Wednesday, December 2, 2015
12:45 p.m.

Hossein Rahim Bonab walked into the spare room on the second floor of the safe house on Newby Place Street. The room was almost bare. No bed or dresser. No chair to sit in. Only a threadbare carpet to cover the hardwood floors. Lying on the carpet were Hossein's items of interest.

Five sets of clothes and equipment. First were the uniforms: gray cotton coveralls for each. They were identical to those worn by field employees of Thames Water Utilities Ltd. in every detail. The front right breast had the name of the employee above the pocket. On the left breast was the logo of Thames Water Utilities, a blue circle open at the top with what appeared to be water waves on the bottom. The words embroidered inside the larger blue ring were THAMES WATER.

No uniform was complete without a cap. The baseball-style hat was gray to match the coveralls and included the logo on the front above the visor. To complete the physical disguise was an identification badge. A plastic envelope attached to the chest pocket flap of their coveralls would include their photograph, false nametag, and position.

To any common person or even a local police officer, they would be just as they appeared: field technicians for Thames Water. No one would question them about being out on an emergency repair. Of all the water utilities firms servicing greater London, Thames Water was the largest. It also had the highest record of water leaks within the supply system. It would be normal to see a Thames Water technician out on a service call at any time of the day or night.

On the wall were several large photographs taken of Thames Water employees working on hydrants or other equipment. Their white vans were included in several of the photos.

Hossein was kneeling on the floor holding one of the uniforms when Mohammad Javan walked in. Hossein dropped the coveralls and looked at his most trusted man. "How are things proceeding in the garage?"

Mohammad was the largest and perhaps the most intelligent of the five men. Finding a set of coveralls large enough to fit his huge frame had been an impossible challenge. It was not the height but the girth that had been a problem. Mohammad was an inch or two below six feet tall but tipped the scales at nearly 275 pounds.

"We will be ready by tomorrow afternoon. Rest assured, my brother, I will have the vans ready. The cold weather is giving us problems with the paint drying, but Gholam brought in some electric heaters and we are keeping the building warm enough. We will be prepared."

They both looked at the clothing. In addition to the uniforms, each man had a pair of black work shoes, all with a decent shine—not too bright, but good enough to maintain the impression of a good Thames Water employee.

Winter coats with the company's logo were folded and lying beside the other clothes, along with a pair of heavy cotton work gloves. Here they had not needed to worry about a company-approved look. From the photographs of the work crew, each member wore whatever glove style suited his or her purpose.

Each man would have a heavy-duty gray canvas tool bag with a zippered closure along the top that would allow easy access to the bag's interior. The bag was sixty-one centimeters, or about twenty-four inches long. Two heavy straps, sown completely around the bag to provide support to the bottom and looped above the bag, provided a handle grip. Lying next to each tool bag were the individual equipment and supplies each man would need to perform their job during the attack. The most common item for each man was his weapons. The bag was the perfect size to hide a Micro-Uzi machine pistol.

Major Uziel Gal developed the Uzi in the late 1940s. The prototype was finished in 1950. The Israeli Defense Force started to see the Uzi first in 1954, and it became a general issue weapon two years later. The weapon had become very popular with many official armed forces and terrorist groups. The Uzi came in four different versions, and sales exceeded ten million pieces. The original, the submachine gun, fired six hundred rounds per minute of 9 mm Parabellum or a slightly slower rate of five hundred rounds per minute with an effective range of two hundred meters with the .45 ACP.

The Mini Uzi, introduced in 1980, was a smaller version of the regular Uzi. It had a faster recycling time and an effective range of only one hundred meters. The Micro-Uzi, introduced in 1986, was an even smaller version, quite suitable for Hossein and his men. The weapon was 486 mm long (19.13 inches) fully extended but reduced to only 282 mm with the stock folded. Its muzzle velocity was 350 meters per second, and its cyclic rate of fire was twelve hundred rounds per minute.

Beside each weapon were six magazines: one to be loaded into the weapon before they left the property and five for back up. The magazines held twenty rounds of the 9 mm ammunition, but the six magazines would provide 120 rounds of ammunition.

Next to the Micro-Uzi was a Korth 9 mm semi-auto pistol manufactured in 2006. Few Americans were familiar with one of the highest quality German manufactures of handguns, located on a small island in the Schaale River in northern Germany. Ratzeburg, Germany, was located in the northern part of the country, home to the Korth Firearm Company. Willi Korth was forty-one when he founded his company in 1954. His first models were basic revolvers manufactured from high quality steel obtained from MG-34 machine guns scrapped after World War II. The steel used had a 1,700-psi tensile strength; heat-treated to Rockwell 58C.

The current 9 mm model, released in 2001 as a single action, worked with a trigger pull release of 2.4 to 2.6 pounds, with only a .06-inch trigger travel. To manufacture these high-end custom European guns involved as much as 70 percent hand labor and hand fitting in each pistol. The magazine for the Korth held ten 9 mm rounds. Each man would have one clip in the weapon and two spares clips.

Their main weapon was laid out off to the side and against the room's outer walls. Beneath the hidden firearms, each tool bag would contain a four-pound block of C-4 explosive and blasting caps. The blasting caps were currently safely stored in another room away from the C-4.

C-4, or Composition C-4, is a common variety of plastic explosive. C-4 is composed of explosives, plastic binder, plasticizer, and usually a marker or odorizing chemical to identify its source. The explosive RDX, cyclonite, or cyclotrimethylene trinitramine, was 91 percent of C-4 by mass. The plasticizer diethylhexyl, or dioctyl sebacate, made up 5.3 percent. Other ingredients to complete the chemical make-up include polyisobutylene as the binder at 2.1 percent and a SAE 10 non-detergent motor oil at 1.6 percent. Normally 1.25 pounds of C-4 can destroy a pickup truck. An eight-inch steel beam would require eight to ten pounds of the stable but dangerous explosive.

In their group, Iraj Malek-Mohammadi was the explosive expert. He had taken the cakes of off-white explosive and blended within the putty-like substance hundreds of metal BBs that would be propelled at a high rate of speed, wounding or killing almost anyone within close range of the tool bags when they exploded. However, the killing of bystanders was a secondary target for the C-4. Each bag's configuration of C-4, carefully designed, was meant for a unique target. Hossein had selected specific targets to draw the authorities away from their main objective: the Honor Oak Water Reservoir, the new prime target.

He and Shir Mohammad would take the powder laced with enhanced cryptosporidium to the huge water reservoir. They had to assume security cameras around Trafalgar Square or Charing Cross Station had captured Shir Mohammad's face. Even under the wide-brim hat, Hossein also concluded his face was now in some British government databank from his rescue of Shir Mohammad, so all public locations were off limits to both of them. Not that Hossein cared. He wanted to be the one to pour the powder into the reservoir and kill anyone who drank the poisoned water. If they did not have enough time to pour the powder into the reservoir, they would use the two bags of explosives to destroy the huge water supply. Maybe they would not kill as many people in London, but they would cause a huge disruption in the clean drinking water supply.

Target Two was intended to be a diversion from their main target. Hossein had selected Trafalgar Square, specifically Nelson's Column. To cripple the national monument, a symbol of Britain's history of world domination, and perhaps damage it to the point where the massive column might collapse would be a very symbolic blow. Since it was a popular tourist location, they could also hope to kill or maim many dozens of people. For this target, Iraj had shaped a four-pound block of C-4 to fit against the base of the column. The shaped explosive charge would cause tremendous damage. Iraj Malek-Mohammadi, their bomb expert, would be the one to deliver this blow to the British.

Target Three was another diversion that could impose a deadly impact on the British. Charing Cross Station. The largest passenger station in Central London would be very crowded at the time of the attack, allowing them another opportunity to divert attention from their primary goal and to kill many British citizens. Gholam Reza Rasoulian would be the person to deliver that deadly blow.

The confusion from the explosions would draw hundreds of British security personnel into the very heart of Central London, away from Hossein and Shir as they approached the reservoir at Honor Oak.

Mohammad Javan Nik Khah would be the driver for the second van. His huge girth made him too noticeable and he moved too slowly for other assignments. His huge size would not hinder his ability to handle the van. He would drop Iraj off near Trafalgar Square and then deliver Gholam in front of Charing Cross Station at the main entrance on The Strand. Afterward he would travel northeast up The Strand to Lancaster Place and turn right to cross the River Thames over the Waterloo Bridge. Once on the other side, he would park near the London IMAX Theater and wait for Iraj and Gholam to rejoin him. They would have three possible avenues of escape: continuing on Waterloo Road or east on Stamford Street or west on York Road. If all went as planned, they would drive south to Honor Oak and help finish dumping the powder into the reservoir and provide additional security.

Hossein and Mohammad moved toward the doorway and turned to look over their equipment one last time. Clothes, weapons, and explosives. The only things not into the room were the blasting caps. Iraj had insisted on keeping them in his own bedroom. He would insert the electric detonators into each individual block of C-4 just before they left the building tomorrow.

Chapter 36
Washington DC
Wednesday, December 2, 2015
9:30 p.m.

Harold Miller, president of the United States, pressed the off button on the television remote in his private study on the second floor of the White House.

He was happy but slightly concerned. The good news was from his legislative affairs staff members. They were telling him the three Davids were in a precarious position. The campaign by his media staffers was continuing the pressure for the three senators to give up their fight to hold the floor. They were also keeping the pressure on the other senators to force a vote to invoke cloture; once the three senators lost control of the Senate, they would have enough votes in their back pocket to force the bill into committee.

The thing bothering Harold Miller was the letters and e-mails they were receiving at the White House. The percentage for passage of the Fair Share Bill was ever so slightly decreasing.

Why? Were the three senators being that effective in their broadcasts from the floor of the Senate? Would his lead still hold and persuade voters to perceive that Harold Miller was moving his political thinking more toward the center, away from an extreme conservative position?

Two other things were bothering him. Tom Evans, who was almost certain to win the Democratic nomination and run again him in the

2016 election, was remaining silent. True, the Democratic candidate had promised on several national news networks that he would remain quiet on the subject of Fair Share. He simply stated he felt the bill was wrong and would enter his negative vote on the floor of the Senate. He would not use the bill as a campaign tool against the president. So far, Evans had kept his promise, but it would not take much to find a reason to come out and blast the bill and add his weight to the filibuster.

The second concern was the silence from his other archenemy. Senator Randy Fisher had not spoken out on the bill.

Harold Miller sat back in his swivel chair and ran his right fingers through his thick hair. How he hated Randy Fisher. His hatred grew every time the senator appeared on a news program or his name mentioned in a conversation. He simply could not stand to read another story about the famous senator from South Carolina.

Miller knew his polling figures better than anyone did. In 2012, he had been five points behind incumbent president Johnathon Blakely. Blakely was almost assured a reelection for four more years; Harold would be the "almost candidate", a one-line footnote in American history.

However, luck had changed for Blakely. An almost successful terrorist attack was Harold's path to the White House. If the nuclear device had detonated in Columbia, then Miller and Blakely would probably have died, along with thousands of other Americans. The country would have faced the worst calamity since its birth almost 236 years before.

If he had died in the explosion, then the election would not have mattered to Harold Miller. However, a young, unknown man had walked into the dock at the grandstand on the state fairgrounds and stopped the terrorist from completing his mission.

Harold Miller's political action committee had almost immediately seized the opportunity to tell the American voters they were not safe under another four years of the Blakely administration. With only three weeks until Election Day in November, to the surprise of the Democrats they had turned the polls around. Harold Miller won the election.

It was a wonderful day for Harold Miller and his family, but the one nagging irritation in the back of his mind was the unknown young man who saved the country that day in October. Randy Fisher was the unknown man. His actions prevented the nuclear blast from affecting the entire Mid-Atlantic and Northeastern portions of the country. That one man had helped Harold Miller turn the polls in Miller's favor and put him in the White House.

Now the same man was in the United States Senate, already considered one of the brightest and most popular people in Washington. As the Democratic senator from South Carolina, Fisher had proposed several pieces of legislation against Harold Miller and forced them through Congress with enough votes to override a Miller veto. The man whose actions had put Harold Miller into the White House was usually against every issue that Harold proposed before the country.

Just thinking about Randy Fisher made beads of sweat pop out on Harold's forehead and upper lip. He reached into a side drawer of the desk and pulled a facial tissue from the cardboard box. He wiped the moisture from his face.

He had been wondering why Fisher had not been heard from on the Senate floor, perhaps even joining the three renegade senators to add his voice to the growing discord with the Fair Share Bill. He had been almost afraid to ask any of his legislative affairs staffers about Fisher.

Finally, during a meeting early that morning, he received an update about a possible terrorist attack developing in London from his director of national intelligence and national security advisor. During the meeting, he learned the deputy director of operations for the Central Intelligence Agency was in London representing the American interest. There was proof that one of the terrorist suspects had a possible relationship to the man who brought the nuclear device into the United States three years before.

When he asked about the reliability of the information, he then learned Randy Fisher was not in the United States but in London. The senator had been the one to sound the alarm.

Miller shook his head. Fisher was again at the center of attention. The only good thing about the whole event was that the immediate terrorist threat was in London instead of Washington, and Fisher was not in the Capitol, where he would be working against the Fair Share Bill.

A soft knock on the study door interrupted Miller's thoughts. A Secret Service agent opened the door, and Alison Warden walked into the study.

"Good evening, Mr. President. I've got the latest poll numbers and the last-minute changes to tomorrow's bus schedule for your approval."

The tall redhead walked up to the small desk and handed the sheets of papers to Harold Miller. On the two top pages were the reports from the polling organizations. He quickly scanned the numbers.

"We're still leading by fifteen points, sir. The numbers are down slightly from earlier in the week, but they do not reflect your speech in Memphis. With the bus event tomorrow, we will reverse the numbers, and the Senate will be forced to do something to take the floor away from the three senators."

She pointed to the figures on the second page. "These figures indicate the American public is getting tired of the three senators and their hold on the Senate floor. It shows the country wants the Congress to get on with its work and not have three members of the Senate stopping all other pieces of legislation from being heard."

She waited until the president looked up toward her. "You need to hit them hard tomorrow during your three speeches. Hit them with how they are disrespecting the Senate and that they need to listen to the growing number of voters who want them to end the filibuster."

Miller's schedule called for him to leave the White House by Marine One and travel to Andrews Air Force Base. There he would board a large tour bus with members of the press. The idea was to show how close to the American people he was while delivering his message about the Fair Share Bill. They would travel to Alexandria, Richmond, and Chesapeake in Virginia, where he would talk about the bill and how American and foreign corporations needed to pay their fair share.

"What size crowds are we expecting tomorrow, Alison?"

"Very good, sir. The advanced team has distributed well over one thousand tickets for each location, and members of the press have taken every available bus seat. We are going to pull the attention away from the Senate floor and back to you and your Fair Share bill. It should be a great day."

Miller looked over the schedule. At first, it was to be a series of short flights using Marine One, the president's personal helicopter. Miller felt he needed to get closer to the people and had ordered the trip changed from the helicopter to the bus. It would also provide a lot of face time with the members of the press who were riding on the bus and hammer home his ideas about the Fair Share bill and the effects of the three senators holding the floor of the Senate Chamber.

Chapter 37
Washington DC
Wednesday, December 2, 2015
10:30 a.m.

Ohio Senator John Laird was standing his fifth turn on the floor of the Senate since he and his two friends had taken control of the Senate Chamber. As planned, they had stopped reciting the reasons against the Fair Share bill and the number of American companies that were already paying their fair share of corporate income taxes. It was useful in the beginning, but the constant repetition of the same information was even wearing on the three senators.

The new plan was to for each senator to do something completely outside politics. At midnight, Senator Saunders had brought in several children's book that he used to read at bedtime to his own two sons years ago. He started with Dr. Seuss's *The Cat in the Hat*. He was almost through with *Green Eggs and Ham* for the fourth time when his period on the floor was over. The children's books had made a very favorable impression on the members of the press, and they had broadcast the information to the American voters. The immediate response had softened their image with the voters, making them look more human: senators who cared about children.

At 4:00 a.m., Roberta Henley took over from Chip Saunders. She brought with her a book describing all the national and state parks in her home state of Florida. She jumped around within the book, starting with the parks located along the northern part of the eastern seaboard and traveling south until she hit Miami and then on down into the Florida Keys.

Fort Clinch State Park was first, followed by Amelia Island State Park. She moved south of Jacksonville to the Guana State Park and its 60,000 acres. She reported information in the book about how in 1957 the water flowing in the Guana River was intentionally blocked in an effort to flood the upstream marshes to enhance wintering waterfowl habitats. The result was the creation of present-day Guana Lake. The lake water was brackish in the southern portion near the dam but gradually became fresh water as it traveled away from the dam. Today both saltwater and freshwater fish species existed in the same body of water.

When John came in to relieve her at 8:00 a.m., Rickie had just virtually left the Florida Keys and was moving to the Florida Everglades. She would continue with her list of parks when she came back at 4:00 p.m.

John's background before entering politics had been the beer distribution business. He decided the subject would not help their image with the American citizens. He decided to try sports, in particular professional baseball. Everyone likes America's favorite pastime, right?

Since Ohio has two professional major league teams, he would start with the Cleveland Indians and move on to the Cincinnati Reds. He started at the beginning with the team along the lake. The team became a major league franchise in 1901 and were called the Lake Shores and later the Bluebirds, the Broncos, and, from 1903 to 1914, the Naps. It was after the 1914 season that the club owners requested a new name more like the Boston Braves, now the Atlanta Braves. The media chose the Cleveland Indians. Over the years, the team along the lake picked up two nicknames: "The Tribe" and "The Wahoos" because their logo was Chief Wahoo.

He put special emphasis on the Curse of Rocky Colavito. Just before opening day in 1960, Frank Lane, then the general manager, traded Colavito to the Detroit Tigers for Harvey Kuenn. Colavito was an Indian fan favorite and the 1959 American League home run co-champion. Krenn was the American League batting champion.

After the trade, Colavito hit thirty home runs four times and made three All-Star teams for Detroit and Kansas City before returning to Cleveland in 1965. Kuenn, on the other hand, would only play one season for the Indians before leaving for San Francisco. John went on to explain how *Akron Beacon Journal* columnist Terry Pluto documented the decades of woe that followed the trade in his book *The Curse of Rocky Colavito*. Colavito claimed to have never placed a curse on the Indians; he simply requested the trade over a salary dispute with Frank Lane.

John was prepared to discuss a number of topics he had listed on a series of three-by-five index cards as he held the floor of the Senate. He did not need detailed notes as he was speaking mostly from memory. He continued with the history lesson, but in the back of his mind were concerns about the filibuster and its ramifications within the Senate and Washington.

It was an understatement to say the pressure from their own party leadership in the Senate, along with legislative aides from the White House, to end the filibuster was weighing heavily on all three senators. Each of the three Davids would describe to their partners the requests to step inside the same cloakroom before and after each shift on the Senate floor and explain where they intended this filibuster to go. Unless they could get the help of the Democrats and go against what seemed to be the majority of the American voters, there seem to be no way to settle their disagreement and end the filibuster.

The White House press secretary was slamming them at every opportunity from her podium in the Press Room. The president was getting ready to hit the road again tomorrow to tell the public they were protecting big business from not paying their Fair Share.

The three continued to support each other the best they could. When one would relieve the other on the floor of the Senate, they would give each other a pat on the shoulder or back and a big warm smile. Sometimes the senator being relieved would stay longer at the desk and continue to show support by not taking the full eight hours of downtime to rest or hurry off to take a shower and change clothes or grab something to eat.

Working four hours on and eight hours off the Senate floor was having a negative effect on each. John knew they could not hold out for more than another day or two and hoped other senators would pick up the baton and help carry the load.

He was starting to talk about the great Satchel Paige. In 1948, the black American became the oldest rookie in the major leagues at the age of forty-two and the first black pitcher. Page ended the season with a six-and-one record and a 2.48 ERA, forty-five strikeouts, and two shutouts.

As he looked around the Senate Chamber, Laird's eyes once again fell on the empty bench seat across the aisle from his own. Randy Fisher had been absent from the Senate floor since Monday morning. If John could have wagered on any Democrat to help the three Republicans, it would have been his friend from South Carolina.

Chapter 38

London
Thursday, December 3, 2015
10:30 a.m.

Randy Fisher was back at Scotland Yard in his little cubbyhole of an office. He had worn out BookReader's patience with his insistence that there was more to be learned from the physical evidence. One man still stood guard outside the office, and they relieved each other every hour, but they refused to enter the room and spend any more time looking at photos.

Randy had arranged the whole batch of photographs in the same order as the day before. It made sense to continue with his examination of the evidence. He had completed the top row of pictures, but his discovery about the cell phone and the meetings afterward had interrupted his examination of the second row.

He focused now on the map of London, the man's handkerchief, the bottle of water, the money, and the notebook.

The technicians in the crime lab had thoroughly examined the map of London for marks, pinholes, or circled locations that could indicate where the attack might take place. It was the very same map of London Randy had purchased through a local bookstore in Alexandria to help plan their time in London. He had spent hours in their apartment determining how to best use their time and visit as many historic locations as possible. The planning for their trip was now helpful for a different purpose; he could visualize in his mind the physical layout of Central London. He knew which way was north versus south and east versus west. He knew most of the distances between one landmark to another and whether it made sense to take the tube versus a London bus or one of the black taxis that ferried tourists around the city.

After thirty minutes, he went on to the man's handkerchief. The technicians had thoroughly examined it for any type of trace evidence. No DNA or chemicals were identified except for a common local brand of laundry detergent and a faint wisp of chlorine from the London water. Nothing to lead to the identification of their suspect. Randy set the photograph aside and went on to the British currency.

Four photos displayed the bills, both front and back. He counted fourteen British pound sterling bills. Four £50 notes, five £20 notes, and five £5 pound notes totaling £325, or a little over $500 in American money. He was not an expert on the physical characteristics of the British pound and whether these bills were counterfeit; it would be up to someone else to make that determination. After fifteen minutes, deciding there was no reason to "follow the money", Randy set the photos aside.

The next-to-last piece of evidence was the bottle of water. A handwritten note on the photograph indicated the water bottle had been unopened when discovered. A chemical analysis of the water inside indicated nothing more in the bottle than the advertising claimed on the label: water.

The brand name was Kingshill Forest Glade; the water originated in Scotland. The photo showed the back of the bottle and the label advertising that Kingshill Forest Glade Natural Mineral Water was bottled directly from a source in the heather and forest-clad hills of Central Scotland.

Looking at the photo, Randy decided he was thirsty and needed some water to replace what his body had sweated out during his run early that morning with his two shadows, BookReader.

He glanced at his watch. It was eleven fifteen. He would review the photos of the notebook and then break for lunch around noon. If he had not finished with the pages from the book, he would start again after a break.

The notebook was shown closed in the first photos, again with a small ruler to indicate a size of three and a half inches wide and five and a half inches in height. The front cover was a plaid blend of pale blue and green squares. The logo on the bottom right appeared to Randy to be an upside down *V* with a profile of an Egyptian maiden and the full moon showing behind her. Clairfountaine was the brand name of the notebook.

The back cover was the same color theme as the front but gave more information about the notebook. There were originally 180 pages on ninety sheets of ruled paper. They advertised the paper was a blend of acid-free paper stock with an extra smooth satin finish. Another handwritten note from the CSI technicians informed Randy that of the original ninety sheets, only forty-two were still in the notebook. From the distressed cover, the notebook had changed hands many times.

He set the photos of the cover aside and concentrated on the photos of the individual pages. The first page was the one shown in their first briefing on Sunday. This showed the list of high-profile British historic sites and famous landmarks written in Arabic. Without the translation, Randy would have no idea of their meaning. Each page, previously displayed on the large screen in the briefing room, showed Randy no new information.

As the lunch hour approached, he heard a soft knock on the door, and Agent Booker stuck his head in. "How about some lunch, Senator? You have been in this office all morning. I'd be going stark raving mad by now."

Randy shoved his straight chair back from the table. "I think you've got a wonderful idea, Agent Booker." He collected all the photographs, turned them on their side to slap then against the tabletop, and arranged them into a neat stack. The top photo was the cover shot of the notebook. Randy was standing up from the chair when it dawned on him that the notebook was the same brand used by Deputy Commissioner Shepard. Obviously, the Clairfountaine brand was popular in London.

Outside the office, BookReader waited. Randy gave them quick look. "Okay, guys. Which cafeteria in the building do you want to eat at today?"

Reader spoke first. "We've been thinking, Senator Fisher. This place has lost all of its culinary attraction for us. I heard about a sandwich shop about a block over that is supposed to be great. How about we stretch our legs and give it a try?"

"Is it raining?"

Reader was quick. "Not yet. They say the rain will move back in this afternoon, so if we hurry a little we can grab some lunch and be back inside before it starts."

Randy laughed. "You've got everything checked out, Agent Reader. I would hate to disappoint you and force us to eat once again in good old Scotland Yard."

They were walking down the hallway toward the elevator lobby when Randy spotted Constance Langhorne standing next to the elevator. He leaned slightly closer to Reader as they neared the lobby. "I don't suppose Ms. Langhorne was the person who provided you the information about this wonderful restaurant?"

A slight smile formed on Reader thick lips. Under his dark black skin, Randy could not tell if he was blushing, but his smile grew larger as they reached the elevator.

Randy did not wait for an answer. He came to a stop before the young and beautiful female Scotland Yard officer. Her face broke into a smile, and her eyes dashed from Randy's face to Reader's and then back to the senator.

"Ms. Langhorne, would you like to join us for lunch? We've been given solid information that there is a great sandwich shop about a block over from your building." Randy heard Booker let out a muffled laugh but decided to ignore him. He kept his eyes on the young woman.

She sent an even bigger smile back to Randy. "Senator, I think that would be lovely. I was going that way myself, and I would be glad to join your merry little group."

"Excellent," Randy said.

He turned to Reader. "Charlie, be a gentlemen. Help the young lady on with her coat."

From the front of the building, they worked their way across Victoria Street to Abby Orchard Street. The buildings were modern for this part of London. That indicated their construction had repaired damage from the bombing during the Second World War.

They walked down Abby Orchard Street and came to the Luke House. The eight-story concrete and steel building contained apartments on the five upper floors and a combination of offices and retail shops on the three lower floors. Their lunch destination, Beverly's, a sandwich shop, was on the street level.

The restaurant's interior reminded Randy of an old diner he might see in a movie from the 1930s or 40s. Wood tables covered with red-and-white checkered tablecloths and leather padded wood chairs were set at an angle to the front window. The place seemed to be busy with the noon lunch traffic, but surprisingly there was one available table near the back. As they approached the table, a woman in her early fifties came from behind the counter. She had been watching their approach since the foursome had entered the restaurant.

She breezed over to Constance and gave her a big hug. "Honey girl. It's so lovely to see you. Your father's been wondering when you would stop in again."

Constance Langhorne was blushing. Randy was certain from her red-faced expression the chance meeting in the elevator lobby had been arranged so Constance could show off the Americans from the United States.

Constance took a deep breath and turned to Randy, who had a slight grin on his face. "Senator Fisher, this is my mum, and this restaurant belongs to my family. I am sorry, but I let it slip that you were in Scotland Yard on a visit to London. She asked if I could bring you around."

Randy stepped up to the mother of his escort. Her hair, a mixture of brown and gray strands, was tied back into a ponytail with a red scarf. It was easy to see the family resemblance to Constance. The facial features were the same, but Mrs. Langhorne had a heavier body than her daughter.

"Mrs. Langhorne. It is a real pleasure to meet you. The boys here have been telling me about the great food you serve to your customers. I've been waiting all day to give it a try."

Beverly Langhorne beamed toward her guests with pleasure and quickly got them seated at the table she had been holding in reserve. It took only a few moments for Mrs. Langhorne to place menus in their hands and offer suggestions from the lunch specials. Randy changed to hot chocolate, and the others stuck with a variety of hot teas. Edward Langhorne, Constance's father, stopped by their table after delivering a lunch order to the next table. He was a few years older than his wife, slender, with a gray handlebar mustache reminiscent of an English shopkeeper from the 1930s.

Randy decided to try the cold lamb sandwich with a little mustard for a real change of pace. To his delight, he found it was quite good, accompanied by excellent conversation during lunch. Constance was relieved that Randy had not taken offense over her little trick to have him meet her parents. She beamed her bright smile at him as she watched how well he got along with her parents. Only Agent Reader received more smiles from Constance than Randy did.

Her mother made numerous trips to the table to ensure the food met their expectations and to keep their drink cups full. Constance kept a close watch on the time and mentioned she needed to get back to Scotland Yard when 1:30 p.m. approached. Randy thanked the parents, who insisted the lunch was on the house. BookReader also offered their sincere thanks for the great lunch.

The foursome had just stepped out onto Abby Orchard Street when two women popped out of a small car illegally parked along the street curb and quickly rushed to them.

"Senator Fisher … Senator Fisher, may we have a moment of your time?"

Agents Booker and Reader quickly put their bodies in front of Randy and held up their hands to indicate the women should stop and keep their distance.

One woman was about five foot eight inches tall, maybe thirty-five years old, with long brown hair tied into a ponytail. She held a digital camera and brought it up to take Randy's picture. The other woman was in her early thirties, with short curly hair. Her head came to the top of the other woman's shoulders. "Senator Fisher. We are from CNN here in London. Our office in Washington told us you were missing and thought you might be in London."

Randy recovered quickly. "Well, you can see I'm not missing. I'm just here on some business."

The woman wrote in her notebook and came back with another question. "Senator, what do you know about the increased level of security we are experiencing in Central London? We watched you leave your hotel this morning and enter Scotland Yard, where you were all morning until you came out for a lunch break."

Randy looked both ways down the sidewalk. Londoners out for their own lunches were walking past them, some having to step out into the street to get past the small group. This was no place to discuss national security.

"Ladies, I am afraid I cannot talk about something I know very little about. I am not in any way a security expert. I suggest you contact the public information department within Scotland Yard."

The younger woman would not yield in her quest for information. "Senator, only a fool would be taken in by that statement. You have a bandage over your right eye and another one wrapped around your right wrist. Somehow, I think you know a lot more than you are willing to tell us. Do we report that you are holding back information about a security situation that has Scotland Yard all in an uproar?"

Randy's expression turned hard. "I think you'd better make sure of your facts before you upset a lot of the people in London by talking about things you have little information about. Now if you will excuse us, we have work to do." He started to move toward Victoria Street.

The young reporter called his name once more. "Senator Fisher, please speak with us."

Randy stopped and turned back to the CNN reporters. The woman flipped to a new sheet of paper in her spiral notebook and wrote down some information.

"Senator, I've given out all of my business cards. Here is my name and telephone number. If there is any information you can discuss, please contact me. Please call. Day or night."

She carefully tore the page from the notebook using the perforation along the edge next to the wire core. Randy noticed her handing the sheet to him, but his eyes remained glued to the page under the sheet where she had written her contact information.

"May I see your notebook?" he asked. He stretched his hand toward the reporter.

She hesitated for a moment, but he had asked his request so very softly. She felt compelled to hand the notebook over.

Randy carefully took the notebook in his left hand. He opened it to the page after the sheet she had just torn from the notebook. He could read the information she had written on the page torn from her book. The indentation from her ballpoint pen was clearly impressed into the paper and easy to read.

Placing his right index finger inside the notebook so he could find the page again, he flipped the notebook closed to look at the cover. The Clairfountaine logo was in the lower right corner, exactly like the notebook in the evidence room taken from the backpack.

Randy swallowed and handled the notebook back to the reporter. He looked at the sheet of paper she had handed to him. Her name was Jasmine Ainsworth.

"Thank you, Jasmine. If I can, I will contact you before I leave London. Now you must excuse us. Something important has just come to light."

Chapter 39

London
Thursday, December 3, 2015
1:30 p.m.

Randy, BookReader, and Constance Langhorne hurried off the elevator into the fourth floor lobby and continued to the evidence room at the end of the hallway. Constance used her four-digit security code to open the door.

Randy's companions were following him with blind faith. He had only told them during their fast walk from the restaurant that he needed to see the actual notebook from the backpack.

They entered a good-size room filled with rows of shelving. The actual part they could access was very small and separated from the rest of the room by a heavy wire-mesh screen and a steel counter. A small opening in the center of the counter allowed small parcels to pass through to the evidence clerk. At the evidence counter, Randy told the clerk he needed to see the notebook. The clerk shook his head and informed the American senator that only CSI technicians or case investigators could see and handle the evidence.

Randy tried to keep his cool. He had spent two days poring over the photographs. He was the person to discover the second cell phone was not the one used by their suspect and was perhaps a plant to divert the authorities from finding the real target. He was rapidly losing patience with the clerk.

He leaned close to the heavy wire mesh installed over the Formica countertop. "I want the head of your CSI division here right now!"

The man stepped back. "We call it Forensic Science over here, Senator Fisher." He seemed to get a little pleasure from correcting Randy.

Randy stepped back. He wanted to grab the mesh screen and rip it from its mounting. Instead, he looked at Constance. "Please call Deputy Commissioner Shepard and have him come down here right this very moment."

Constance Langhorne stepped up to the counter and pointed to the telephone on the counter next to the clerk. The clerk's nametag read REGINALD CLOVES. "Reggie, hand me the telephone immediately."

Grabbing the phone, Reggie set it inside the open hole at the bottom of the screen and pushed it through to the other side of the counter. "No need to be snippy, Senator. You know very well, Ms. Langhorne, I don't like to be called Reggie."

Constance pulled the telephone set closer. She hesitated for a few seconds to pull the number she needed from her memory and pressed a line button on the phone to dial an inside number.

The clerk took a step back from the counter. He curled his hands into small fists and placed them against his waist at the beltline. "You can call DC Shepard, but I'm just going by the department rules."

Constance heard the phone on the other end of her call ring twice and then a deep voice answered. She recognized the voice. "Dr. Kiley. This is Constance Langhorne."

She hesitated a few seconds as the man spoke back to her. "Yes ... it's a pleasure to talk with you as well. Sir, something has come up here in the evidence room. We need someone from your department to come here immediately to bring a piece of evidence out of storage. This is regarding the possible terrorist plot."

Silence.

"Yes. It is very important. Thank you, sir."

She hung up and pushed the set back through the screened opening. She gave Reggie a firm look. "Dr. Kiley will be here in a few minutes. I would strongly urge you to have the evidence box ready and waiting for him."

Reggie looked as if he was going to remind her once again about his proper name but changed his mind. He turned without another word to walk down one of the aisles created by rows of metal shelving that held hundreds of cardboard boxes of evidence from cases under investigation by Scotland Yard.

He arrived back at the counter less than a minute before another man walked into the evidence room. The new arrival, in his late fifties, had only a thin halo of mixed brown and gray hair. He sported a thick mustache; his sideburns were longer than the current style. He was dressed in a long-sleeve white shirt, tie, and black wool pants. He wore a cardigan sweater instead of a suit coat.

Constance quickly made the introductions and then told the chief of Forensic Science for Scotland Yard they needed to look at one of the pieces of evidence inside the box on the counter.

"Which piece?"

Randy answered; he was the only one who knew what he needed to see. "The notebook, please."

Kiley nodded and looked at the clerk. "Reginald, open the door and bring the box out here."

The clerk did not hesitate this time. He pulled a set of keys from his pocket, selected one from the batch, and stepped toward the heavy wire-mesh door. Inserting the key into the lock, he opened the door next to the counter and brought the box through the doorway; he placed it on a small table next to the main door into the evidence room.

Kiley removed the cardboard cover and lifted the plastic evidence bag containing the notebook. He looked at the evidence tag taped to the plastic cover to check the identity of the last person who had handled the plastic bag. He looked back to Randy. "I can't let you touch the notebook, Senator, so you will have to tell me what you are looking for."

He was reaching into his front pants pocket for a pair of thin latex gloves as Randy explained what he needed to see. "From the photographs, I can tell each page in the notebook has a series of small perforations in a line directly next to the holes for the wire coil. In addition, I noticed there were several pages torn from the book after the last page they used to record notes. The narrow strip of paper for those sheets was still in the notebook. I want to look at the first blank pages in the notebook. There might be impressions from what was written on the last page torn out of the notebook."

Kiley gave his mustache a little side-to-side twitch and put the gloves on. He carefully opened the seal on the bag and removed the notebook. He set the bag aside and carefully laid the notebook on the tabletop. Still using great care, he opened the notebook one page at a time.

Randy could appreciate the thoroughness the laboratory chief was using, but the slowness was maddening. Finally, Kiley reached the last sheet with writing still in the coiled-wire notebook, pages the notebook owner had not removed. He turned the sheet over to the next blank page. In between the final page with writing and the first blank page, several narrow borders remained from pages torn out of the notebook. Kiley left the notebook lying on the table and took a half step back to look at the first blank sheet, allowing the overhead florescent lighting to shine on the page from different angles.

Charlie Reader stepped in closer and reached inside his winter jacket for a flashlight inside a leather holster attached to his belt. "Here, Doctor. Try the light from my torch."

Randy and Agent Booker looked at Charlie. They each shook their heads slightly because he had used the English term for a flashlight. He noticed their looks and gave a little sheepish grin in return.

Taking the offered torch, Dr. Kiley bent at the waist and turned the beam on. He moved it around the page, letting the light beam strike from different angles. He carefully lifted the page to shine the light beam through the underside of the sheet. The lengthy process wore heavily on the patience of Randy and his cohorts. Finally, the scientist straightened his back.

He turned back to the clerk. "Reggie, I'm taking the notebook back to the lab. You can put all the other items back into storage." Reggie kept his mouth shut about the shortened name and produced a clipboard with a form attached. He noted the evidence number on the outside of the plastic bag that had contained the notebook and offered it to Dr. Kiley for his signature. Kiley was taking responsibility for the piece of important evidence.

Kiley handed the clipboard back to the Reggie. He picked up the notebook and put it back inside the evidence bag. "All right, why don't we all go back to my laboratory? We can take a closer look at that page."

The group of five left the evidence room. They followed Dr. Kiley down the hallway past the elevators and turned right at the first intersection. They came to a pair of white steel doors. One door was solid; the other had a small rectangular double-pane window, a sheet of wire reinforcement between the two panes of glass. Kiley stopped long enough to enter his own four-digit number into the wall-mounted locking mechanism and pushed the door open when he heard the buzz as the solenoid released the lock.

The group walked into the heart of Scotland Yard's Forensic Science Division. The room must have been nearly sixty feet square with several glass-enclosed offices or smaller laboratories off to one side. Kiley did not take time to explain what any of the other people in the room were working on but walked about halfway down the right side of the room until he came to a wall-mounted light box used to read X-rays.

Randy first thought it was similar to the light box his own doctor had used when he went in for check-ups for his wound from the terrorist three years earlier; however, this light box was a little different. His doctor used a rocker switch to turn the power on and off to the light panel. The light box in front of the group had a dial knob to allow adjusting the light to different levels.

Dr. Kiley took the notebook out of the plastic evidence bag and laid it down on a table under the light box. Very carefully, he removed the blank page from the notebook, using the line of perforations to separate the sheet and leaving only the narrow paper stub.

Still wearing latex gloves, he carefully secured the top edge of the sheet of paper under a metal clip along the top of the light box to hold the paper in place. He turned the small black plastic knob on the light panel to the right one click, and the light behind the glass front panel came to life.

The light was too dim. He turned the knob two more clicks and the light increased. When he had the light intensity at the mid-level position, they could see indentations appearing on the sheet. He took a few more moments to adjust the lighting up and down until the writing on the paper was readable.

The words appeared to be another Arabic list. The group as a whole tried to step in closer to the sheet of paper, but Dr. Kiley blocked them with his raised right hand.

"Hold on. Let me take a picture of this."

He reached for a special digital camera next to the light box attached to the wall by a pair of long, heavy-duty stainless steel hinges that allowed the operator to place the camera in front of the light box. The equipment moved smoothly on the hinges. Kiley aligned the camera in front of the sheet of paper and pressed the power button. The viewing screen built into the camera came to life; the sheet of paper was visible through the camera's lens.

He adjusted the camera lens to enhance the image on the sheet of paper and then pressed a button on the side of the camera. A few seconds later, a high quality digital printer a few feet away started making some clicking noises, and they could hear the rollers in the paper storage bin grab a sheet of paper and start the printing process.

Slowly the sheet of paper rolled out of the printer and slid to a stop in the plastic paper tray. Kiley picked up the paper and gave it a quick look. Shaking his head at the Arabic writing, he handed it to Randy Fisher.

Constance moved next to Randy while BookReader moved to look around his shoulders at the list. None of the four could make out the words.

"Where is your translator, Constance?" Randy asked.

"That would be the language expert in our Middle East section. That department is on the ninth floor. We share intelligence with both MI5 and MI6."

The original four hurried out of the room and back to the bank of elevators. Several minutes later, they were on the ninth floor, passing through another secure locking device at the Middle East department.

Constance led the way into the secure intelligence section of the Yard. Large three-sided cubicles divided the main room from private offices off to each side. Gray cloth-covered partition walls five feet high enclosed each cubicle. Six desks made up a mini section, three to a side. With swivel chairs, the desk occupants could work at their stations or turn to face each other. A narrow table used for group meetings divided the cubicle. Members of the unit currently occupied four of the desks.

Constance led her group into the nearest cubicle, stopped at one of the empty chairs, and looked over the cubicle wall and around the room for its occupant. The person assigned to the workstation kept the desktop very orderly. A computer monitor and keyboard rested on top of a full-size desk calendar pad showing the month of December. All the usual supplies—pens, pencils, notepads, and stapler—were neatly stored out of sight. Only the computer monitor showed any activity; the Scotland Yard logo slowly moved to different positions on the screen. Not seeing the person she was looking for, Constance finally spoke to an elderly woman at one of the desks inside the cubicle.

"Where is Mr. Sloane?"

The woman looked at the empty desk next to her own; she seemed to realize the man in question was not there. She rolled her swivel chair over to the desk and looked at his desktop calendar. "Ah yes. Extended lunch. He has an appointment with his dentist. I am not sure if he will be back today. Depends on how the procedure goes, you know."

Constance slapped her right hand against her thigh through her wool skirt. Frustration showing on her face, she turned to look at Randy Fisher. "Blimey," she muttered quietly through clenched white teeth.

Randy held the paper from the printer. He suddenly reached into his pocket for his own smart phone. He scrolled through his contacts and found Marion Bellwood's cell number. In a minute, he had his friend on the phone.

"Marion, I'm about to e-mail you a photo from my cell phone. I need the language translated immediately. It might be nothing, but it might be very important." Randy listened for a few moments. "Right. It will be there as soon as I can work the camera in my phone."

He disconnected the call and pressed the camera button on the side of the BlackBerry. Constance held the paper, and Randy leveled the camera in front of the page. He took the picture, pressed several more buttons on the keypad, and e-mailed the photo to Marion's cell phone.

Randy let out a sigh and looked at the other members of their little group. "Marion will send the photo to someone in his own Middle East department. Now we wait."

Chapter 40

London
Thursday, December 3, 2015
3:30 p.m.

They were ready. Each man was now wearing the uniform of the water company supplying the largest percentage of water to Central London. Mohammand Javan was unable to close the front zipper on his coveralls due to his massive waistline, but he would be inside the truck during the distraction phase of the operation at Trafalgar Square.

The truck exteriors were now converted. No longer were the name and logo of the rug company displayed. Instead, each truck was showing the Thames Water Utilities name and logo along with the FIELD SERVICE DIVISION lettering on each side and across the two rear doors.

Mohammad Javan Nik Khah, Iraj Malek-Mohammadi, and Gholam Reza Rasoulian would drive the first truck to Trafalgar Square. They would travel in from the east on The Strand and take Ducannon Street until it came to a dead end at Trafalgar Square. Iraj Malek-Mohammadi would exit the truck at the intersection and make his way from the northeast corner toward his target. Mohammad Javan would then drive to the second target and drop off Gholam. He would turn the van left onto The Strand, drive to the pickup location, and wait for his friends.

Hossein Rahim Bonab looked at the panel trucks. They were older than the trucks currently in service with the Thames Water Utilities but he doubted anyone would notice with the time of the attack coordinated with the setting sun and the darkening skies from the approaching storm.

The other panel truck was loaded with the twelve barrels of poisoned powder laced with the enhanced cryptosporidium. Loaded with the forklift, they rested on three heavy wood platforms. Plastic strapping material enclosed the barrels to prevent them from sliding off the skids during transit to the water reservoir. Hossein and Shir Mohammad Moez Ardalan would handle the real attack while the others created havoc exactly where the British authorities would be watching and had concentrated their forces.

Hossein looked at each man; the members stood in a straight line for inspection, almost like soldiers before a battle. Indeed, they were soldiers, carrying the battle to their enemy. Their enemy outnumbered them, but surprise and diversion would be on their side.

He stopped in front of Mohammad Javan. He was several inches taller than the massive giant was and could not wrap his arms completely around the man's wide shoulders. Nevertheless, he gave his friend a hard slap to the right shoulder and then grabbed his shoulders with both hands. They embraced.

Mohammad Javan's long curly black hair stuck out several inches along the sides and back of the billed cap. Hossein smiled at his friend and reached up to remove the hat. He placed it in Mohammand Javan's right hand. "Don't forget to shove your hair up inside the hat. We must not have you looking like a slob. You have to look like every one of the British bastards."

Next in line was little Iraj Malek-Mohammadi, the bomb maker. Taller by at least three inches, Hossein towered over the youngest member. Iraj always seemed to have a small smile on his face. He was only in his late teens, and his beard pattern was not fully developed. Unlike Mohammad Javan's hair, Iraj's hair was styled in a close-cut butch. His outer jacket was slightly long in the sleeves. Hossein reached down and rolled each sleeve up one turn. "We don't need you getting tangled up when you're working with the detonators and arming the bombs."

Iraj's smile turned to a full grin. His teeth, heavily stained from his smoking habit, were a dingy yellow color. He lightly punched his leader in the chest with a pointed index finger. "You remember what I taught you about how to insert the blasting caps into the block of explosive. Don't let Shir Mohammad do it or you will both see Allah before your time."

Gholam Reza Rasoulian was next to be inspected by the leader. He was equal in size and shape to both Hossein and Shir. He was the quietest, but Hossein knew it was not due to nervousness or fear. In fact, it was quite the opposite. Gholam was the most deadly of the group with both the handgun and the Mini Uzi.

Hossein gave him a simple nod and moved on to Shir Mohammad Moez Ardalan. Shir gave him both a smile and nod. "I am ready. I will not disappoint you tonight."

Hossein simply gave him a return nod but did not reveal his thoughts. *You will not disappoint me tonight because I will kill you myself after we have accomplished our mission.*

He took two steps back from his men. "We are ready. Allah will be with us."

Two minutes later the vans pulled out of the steel building, leaving the dark interior filled with packing crates and hundreds of Persian rugs. The promised rain was starting to come down, softly at first, but within a few minutes, as the vans neared the end of Newby Street, it was falling hard and the wind was picking up.

Hossein let Shir Mohammad drive their van. "This rain will help to cover our work tonight. The British authorities will be keeping their heads down and drinking their tea in some warm and dry place. They will not see us coming."

Chapter 41

Richmond, VA
Thursday, December 3, 2015
10:30 a.m.

The Virginia Center Commons was a large shopping mall located off exit forty-three of the I-295 outer belt in Richmond, Virginia. The shopping mall, built in a bent dogleg design, consisted of a longer leg slightly more than 1,300 feet in length and a shorter leg nearing 661 feet. As with all shopping malls, they needed large retail establishments, or anchors, to bring in the shoppers. In the case of VCC, they were fortunate to have four major outlets. JC Penny, Sears and the Sears Auto Center, Burlington Coat Factory, and Macy's were big attractions for shoppers. Together with these well-known retail outlets, the shopping mall contained nearly seventy-five smaller retail shops. Open seven days a week, the mall provided most shoppers with whatever he or she required.

One end of the long leg of the mall was vacant. It was large enough to attract a fifth anchor store, but the last tenant had moved out at the end of their lease. The leasing corporation for the mall ownership was in negotiations with another retail outlet. The talks, stalled over the cost per square foot of rental fees, were keeping a large section of the mall empty during the holiday shopping season. When the local general manager for the mall received a telephone call from a White House aide asking if they could rent the 89,000 square feet for a few days to set up before a speech by the president, the general manager had jumped at the opportunity.

As with most previous renters, the recent tenants had left the space in need a lot of cleaning to prepare for a public event. The manager quickly computed the expected cost to make the space usable and then tripled the amount. To that figure, he added the actual cost for a one-day event plus the time before the event for setup and the time after the event for teardown. When he completed all the mental mathematical calculations and added his profit, the figure came to nearly four months' worth of the normal rent he would get for the space. To his surprise, the offer was quickly accepted; the office facsimile machine returned a signed contract from the White House within a few hours.

The bus caravan conveying Harold Miller and his entourage arrived from Alexandria exactly on schedule. Along with the bus carrying the president, his traveling staffers, and members of the media, the Secret Service had a convoy of four black sports utility vehicles loaded with heavily armed agents clad in black SWAT uniforms. Four Virginia State Patrol cars spearheaded the convoy in front of the bus, and another three cruisers followed behind, effectively filling the lanes of I-95 south from Alexandria. Security personnel blocked off every intersection from Alexandria to Richmond for fifteen minutes prior to the motorcade's arrival and another ten minutes after it passed.

The bus pulled into the parking area near the rear loading docks, and the advance team of Secret Service agents took immediate control of conveying the president and his closest staffers into the building through a walk-in door and then into an office normally used by the shipping clerk. The members of the press were escorted into the building through another entrance into the open area normally filled with displays stocked with a variety of goods for sale.

The general manager for the building complex might not have recognized his own facility due to the miraculous transformation conducted by the president's advance team. One thousand metal folding chairs, divided into five large V-shaped sections filled the huge open area left vacant by the previous renter. The aisles between each section started at the large entrance from the shopping mall's common area and led up to the front of the room, where a raised platform had been constructed and covered with royal blue carpeting. The raised sides of the platform now displayed patriotic red, white, and blue plastic material. Banners hanging from the ceiling or attached to the walls displayed a variety of short slogans. SUPPORT THE FAIR SHARE BILL and CALL YOUR SENATOR TODAY emphasized the message the president would soon deliver. The American and presidential flags stood proudly on the stage.

An expensive portable sound system, rented by the White House, guaranteed that the huge crowd and, more importantly, the members of the media could hear and record the president's speech. Members of the advance team had worked right up to just a few minutes before the president's motorcade arrived to ensure every decoration provided the perfect image for the event.

Alison Warden was the senior White House Staffer in charge of the event. She made a last-minute inspection from the top of the stage as she looked out into the portable spotlights set up to illuminate the stage when the president made his entrance. Off to the right, a local high school band was playing popular selections from Broadway musicals to keep the waiting crowd entertained until Harold Miller took the stage.

The one thousand chairs were almost full. All the people attending had entered from the mall's common area and passed through metal detectors under the watchful eyes of dozens of Secret Service agents. To say the senior agent in charge had been a royal pain about this hastily scheduled public event to promote the president's Fair Share Bill was quite an understatement. To do three events in one day with less than seventy-two hours to prepare had taxed the Secret Service and Alison's own team.

So far, the day had gone smoothly. The bus ride from Andrews Air Force Base on I-395 to I-95 and to Alexandria had been uneventful. The reporters were delighted to get such close access to the president; he had spent nearly the entire thirty-minute ride of the first leg walking the center aisle of the bus, laughing and joking with member of the press. They might not be quite so happy after they learned the president would be flying back to Washington after the last event aboard Marine One from the Norfolk Naval Shipyard directly back to the White House.

From Alexandria to Richmond was about ninety minutes. Miller had used the time to answer the reporters' questions.

From the *Washington Post*: "Mr. President. The polls are showing the public is starting to listen to the three senators holding the floor of the Senate, and support for your Fair Share Bill is weakening. Will the three stops today bring the support back?"

Miller kept a full smile on his face. "We think the support has always been with us, but Americans need to take care of their everyday needs. They have jobs to go to and children to raise. If the three senators would take time to look around themselves they would find they are very alone."

From the *Richmond Times Dispatch*: "Mr. President. Why did you select Virginia for today's three stops? Are you singling out Senator Saunders? He seems to be the leader of the three senators."

Miller decided honesty was the best answer to the question. With a large grin across his face, he answered the question in a loud voice. *"Yes!"* He got the expected laughter from the reporters. "Senator Saunders informed the members of the Senate that his supporters have voted him into office after his no-tax pledge. If we are to convince the good senator to drop his stranglehold on the Senate, then we need to convince the people of Virginia and have them tell Senator Saunders to sit down."

Again, the president received a mixture of laughs from the hardened reporters.

From the *Miami Herald*: "Sir. Can we assume your trip tomorrow to Florida will be aimed at Senator Hanley?"

Miller retained his smile. He was warming up to the exchange with the reporters. "Either one of the three senators can stop the filibuster. I think what they are doing is wrong and disrespectful to the Senate as a whole and to the American people. I spent many years in the Senate, and never once did I have to resort to a filibuster. Today in Virginia, we will take our message directly to the American citizens who voted to put Senator Saunders into office. Tomorrow we will go to Florida. If the filibuster is still going on, we will travel to Senator Laird's home state. I will not give up my effort to make large American and foreign corporations pay their fair share."

The governor of Virginia stood off to the side with the mayor of Richmond. The mayor would shortly introduce the governor, who was ready to make his own opening remarks and then introduce the president. The governor had been traveling with them on the bus from Andrews Air Force Base and would use the same speech he had delivered in Alexandria. Alison Warden gave both of them a smile and thanked them for all their work to help bring the event off smoothly. When the final musical number was almost finished, she left the stage area and walked back to the room where the president was mentally preparing to deliver his speech. He looked up from wherever his mind had taken him as she entered the room between the squad of agents surrounding the president.

"We're all ready to go whenever you want to start, sir. Mayor Collins of Richmond and the governor are on stage getting them warmed up for you."

Miller nodded. "Good. Let's get this started and then move on to Chesapeake."

Chapter 42
London
Thursday, December 3, 2015
4:45 p.m.

Any driver can attest that rain will affect traffic patterns and movement in any large city. London was no exception. The harder the rain, the more congested the traffic flow.

With temperatures in the low forties, London drivers became more cautious of surfaces on the many bridges leading out of Central London. The surface area of any bridge can freeze quicker than typical road surfaces. The heat in the ground and below the surface will keep roads from freezing. Bridges, lacking heat from the ground, froze quicker than the roads.

Mohammad Javan was fuming at the congested traffic and the delay in reaching Trafalgar Square. Their plan called for Iraj to detonate his bomb at the base on Nelson's Column just before 5:00 p.m. Gholam would have entered Charing Cross Station just minutes before the first planned explosion and placed his bomb near or beneath the electric signs showing the trains' arrivals and departures at the station.

The bomb at the square would detonate and cause widespread panic within the entire area. Many would rush to the train station in hope of seeking shelter and escape on the trains or the underground tube station. Once in the station, the British would assume they were safe. Then the terrorists' second deadly explosion would detonate, leaving many dead. The diversion would be complete.

The dual explosions, along with the false information left inside the backpack and camera by Hossein and Shir Mohammad would reinforce the security services' belief that Central London was the main target. They would have no choice but to bring additional security resources into Central London, away from the outer boroughs, granting Hossein and Shir Mohammad unfettered access to the Honor Oak underground storage facility and plenty of time to pour the cryptosporidium powder into the huge tank.

Driving northwest on The Strand, they were finally approaching their first turn. At Southampton Avenue, Mohammad Javan turned right, drove two blocks to Henrietta Street, and made a left turn. The traffic congestion was less. Many of the streets in the area were one-way and shorter.

Henrietta Street came to a dead end at Bedford Street. He turned right, drove one block to King Street, and turned left onto New Road. After two long blocks, the street came to a dead end. He waited for the light to make the left turn onto St. Martin's Lane. He had three long blocks to drive before they finally made it to Williams IV Street, then a left turn and a short distance to Charing Cross Road and the A-400. From there the distance to the northeast back corner of Trafalgar Square was less than three hundred and fifty feet. To their right was the National Portrait Gallery; the Church of St. Martin's in the Fields stood on their left.

Iraj and Gholam had kept silent throughout most of the drive from Newby Street. Occasionally one would comment on the rain when it came down harder. Both were ready to sacrifice their lives to accomplish their mission. As they slowly inched their way toward the square and the location chosen for Iraj's drop-off point, they felt the wind picking up strength, whipping around the corners of the van. Off in the distance they could make out the lights of Trafalgar Square and see the people who were taking short cuts through the center of the square to shorten the distance they needed to walk to their homes or the underground tube station at the southeast corner.

The tension inside the van increased as distance to the target decreased. Mohammad Javan looked at the traffic and his wristwatch. He finally broke the silence inside the van. "Iraj, you will have to delay the detonation longer until we get closer to the train station. If you blow the bomb too soon, we will miss out on killing many of the British when they gather inside the station for protection."

Iraj remained silent. Mohammad Javan glanced into the rearview mirror to look at Iraj over his own massive left shoulder. He was about to repeat his instructions when Iraj simply said, "Yes."

Finally, the traffic moved, and they made half of the remaining distance to the square before the traffic stopped again. Mohammad Javan consulted his watch. They were running at least thirty minutes late. Hossein would have assumed the first bomb would have gone off by now. Perhaps the traffic and rain had also affected Hossein and Shir's timetable for their part of the mission.

They were now within one hundred feet of the planned drop-off at the northeast corner to the square. The huge National Gallery building loomed outside the window on Mohammad Javan's right side.

He looked around for security guards of any type but saw nothing to cause any alarm. "Iraj, arm your bomb and prepare to exit the van when we stop the next time. Try to find someplace to remain out of sight until well after we make the turn onto Duncannon Street."

Once they made the left turn onto the short one-way street and back to The Strand, they would move with the flow of the traffic and shortly arrive in front of the main entrance to Charing Cross Station. Gholam would be only minutes away from the lobby area of the station. He would have to find a place to hide the bomb, perhaps inside one of the retail shops. Once he heard the first explosion from the square, he would activate a ten-minute timer designed by Iraj to detonate when the British flooded the station seeking shelter from the danger on the square. If discovered early, they could detonate the bomb immediately. Iraj had a trigger device wired to all the explosives that would send an electrical charge from the batteries to the blasting caps; the bombs would explode.

Traffic moved again, and Mohammad Javan fed gas to the engine. The van moved another sixty feet. When the brakes brought the van to a stop, he simply said, "Go."

Iraj Malek-Mohammadi had already slid across the back seat. He opened the passenger door behind Gholam nearest the sidewalk and stepped out of the van. The rain had largely abated.

He walked behind the van and crossed the street. He stole a quick glance at the driver's rearview mirror and saw Mohammad Javan's eyes in the reflection. He reached the wide walkway separating the National Gallery and Trafalgar Square. Once it had been a through street connecting Pall Mall East to Charing Cross Road. The last renovation to the square had closed the street to vehicular traffic. He could have moved due south to a line of trees along the east side of the square just a few feet from the van to remain out of sight and give Mohammad Javan and Gholam time to make the turn onto Ducannon Street. Instead, he started walking in a straight line, two hundred and fifty feet toward the open space at the back of Trafalgar Square and then between the two plinths.

Iraj had trained a long time to reach this part of their plan. He saw the massive column in front of him rising majestically into the stormy night sky. He gripped the two canvas handles on the tool bag tightly. The tool bag weight a lot. He had almost eight pounds of C-4 instead of the four pounds originally called for in their plan. The tool bags he had prepared and given to Hossein and Shir Mohammad contained only two pounds of the high explosive. He had felt it was right to reduce their allotment. The plan was to pour the poisoned powder into the drinking water for Central London. His plan was to destroy the column ... the centerpiece of Trafalgar Square.

Chapter 43

London
Thursday, December 3, 2015
4:57 p.m.

Alfred Duncan had been an English bobby for almost forty years. He had been born in Stockwell, a district in inner South West London about two and one-half miles south-southwest of Charing Cross Station. He had attended the St. Stephen's Church of England Primary School and continued on to the Stockwell Park School. Upon graduation, he had enlisted in the British Army. Four years later, he left the army as a lance corporal and used the recommendations from his sergeant and platoon lieutenant to apply to the Metropolitan police force.

He'd settled in his hometown and used the money he had saved from his army pay to put a down payment on a little cottage near the primary school of his youth. During secondary school, he had dated Charlene Quince on a regular basis, and they had continued to write to each other when he was away in service and were always together whenever he could get approved time away from his army posting. Early in their relationship, Charlene stopped calling Alfred by his formal name and just used Alfie.

They dated only a short time once he return to Stockwell and were married in the St. Stephen's Church less than three months after he left the army. They spent their seven-day honeymoon on the Isle of Jersey.

When they returned to their home, Alfie found a letter from the Resources Directorate within the Metropolitan Police Department informing Alfred his application was accepted and he was to report for a physical examination, further testing, and interviews. Six weeks later Alfie entered the new recruit training program at the Scottish Police College in Tulliallan in Perthshire, Scotland. The academy was located in the Tulliallan Castle, built between 1812 and 1820, now turned over to the academy for their use.

The course consisted of classroom training on law, legal procedures, and physical fitness. Alfie found the workouts in the gym and the outdoor events easy compared to the training he had received in the British Army. The classroom training was interesting enough to keep his mind occupied, and he graduated in the top 10 percent of his class.

Upon graduation, he became a police constable assigned to Central London on a two-year probationary period where he would work and continue with additional training. In reality, over the years the training never stopped, and Alfie enjoyed most aspects of the work.

After the probationary period, he tried to get a transfer to the Stockwell Police Station but there were no openings, so he continued to work within the Central London division. As part of his continuing training program during the next five years, other transfers came to Alfie, and he moved about Central London. His reputation as being dependable in tough situations and knowledgeable in all police procedures grew over the years. Alfie Duncan was a good police officer.

The years passed by. Alfie and Charlene became parents of a girl first and a son two years later. They continued to live in their original home in Stockwell and raised their family. Life was good for Alfred, both at home and work. Eventually he stopped applying for a transfer to Stockwell and continued to work in Central London.

About fifteen years earlier, he had transferred to the Agar police station and received a new assignment to Trafalgar Square. He walked his outside beat around the square and the National Gallery up to Charing Cross Station. Other officers were assigned to the station interior and the underground tube system. After two years, Alfie received a chance to transfer to the armed service division within Scotland Yard. With the increase in terrorist threats within London, the Yard decided to create a new division of uniformed and armed police. With his military background, the department supervising officers heavily pursued Alfie.

He took several weeks to discuss the transfer with Charlene. It would mean an increase in pay, and he would not be walking the Trafalgar Square beat in the rain and cold of the London winters. They were sitting outside on their back porch swing on a warm spring evening when he decided he wanted to accept the pay increase. He went through a list of reasons to convince his wife that his decision was the right one.

Charlene put her right foot down on the porch floor to stop the back and forth motion of the swing. "Alfie, love. What do you like best about your job today?"

Alfie did not have an immediate answer but finally replied, "Just being a police officer."

Charlene shook her head. "Not good enough, Alfie. I will ask you once again. Why do you arrive thirty minutes early for your shift at the station every day? Why do you always work late when they ask you to stay over?"

Alfie forced the swing back into motion and used both hands to rub the crown of his head, his thumbs moving just above his ears. He could feel the hair in the middle was thinner than along the sides. He was developing the same bald pattern as his father and grandfather. He gave a little laugh as the truth flooded his mind. "I love the people. Especially the tourists from all over the world. As soon as they get out of the airports, they want to come to my Trafalgar Square. They want to climb the lions. I have to shoo them off. They want to wade in the fountains, and I have to blow my whistle at them to chase them out, even on hot summer days."

Charlene leaned over to give her husband a little kiss on the side of his face. "Alfie, do you know you've been calling Trafalgar Square your square for the last ten years, maybe even a bit longer? If you left Trafalgar Square, you would regret it within just a few weeks. We do not need the extra money. I am making enough working as the assistant clerk at the Comfort Inn at Vauxhall. Stay where you're happy."

Alfie had notified the officer who had been trying to recruit him into the new division that he was happy where he was and continued working the beat at Trafalgar Square. It turned out the decision had been the right one. Less than six months later, he received a promotion to sergeant. Charlene had cried the day he donned his new jacket with the three chevrons above his division call sign and shoulder number.

Alfie Duncan took his new position to heart. He made it his mission to learn everything about Trafalgar Square and the buildings surrounding the famous landmark. He spent time learning the names of many of the local workers as they traveled to and from their places of business. He had decided to make Trafalgar Square his place, and no one would hurt Alfie's home—not in Stockwell or in Trafalgar Square.

Chapter 44

London
Thursday, December 3, 2015
4:59 p.m.

Metropolitan Police Sergeant Alfred Duncan was trying to stay warm and dry. He stood under a protrusion in front of the windows of the Hilton Hotel off the southwest corner of Trafalgar Square. The rain had started about an hour ago, and he was close to the hotel at the time. He knew the door attendants, the desk clerks, the maintenance engineers, and the assistant managers and general manager. They all liked having Alfie around. His presence gave their guests a safe feeling, and he was always happy to provide directions. Tourists loved to talk with the famous London bobbies. They were almost a tourist attraction themselves.

Since the division commander informed the officers about the terrorist threat several days earlier during the division's morning roll call, Alfie had been working overtime. The extra pay would be nice for the coming Christmas holiday, but in truth he would have worked without overtime.

He was almost sixty-two years old and twenty pounds heavier than when he started on the force many years ago. Charlene had been retired now for two years and kept some mild pressure on him to turn in his papers and take his pension. The arthritic pain in his back and right shoulder would probably force the decision soon.

He pulled the collar up on his winter jacket and worked the scarf up a little higher on his neck against the bottom of his ears. He was careful not to dislodge the earpiece from his radio set. Alfie had never regretted his decision to stay in the unarmed division, but he was very glad to accept all the new gadgets the service provided to their officers in the field. With his radio, he could communicate with the officers under his command and with the officer assigned in the War Room to monitor the big screens showing Trafalgar Square and the surrounding area. He knew one of the white dots on the screen represented his presence near the square. He was dressed in his black uniform and heavy coat, his rainproof cover over his cloth helmet. He was also equipped with an Airwave personal radio; the signal from one of the implanted chips would show white on the monitors. White was for an unarmed bobby.

Having no pistol did not mean Alfie was unarmed. He carried an extendable baton that he was very proficient with, CS/PAVA incapacitating spray, a set of arm restraints, and now an X-26 Taser. Unarmed, but still a formidable police officer.

Alfie had been watching the traffic slowly moving past the hotel and around the square. It was about as bad as it could get, and it would probably be at least another two hours before traffic would start to thin out. The wind had suddenly lessened and the rainfall was not as hard. His field of vision was improving as he looked out toward Nelson's Column. The ground-mounted spotlights never failed to make the majestic monument shine, even in a heavy rain.

He noticed the man approaching the north entrance to the square at almost the same time as his earpiece made a mild scratchy noise and a voice popped into his ear.

"Stranger entering the square carrying some sort of tool bag."

Alfie left the hotel entrance area in the diminishing rain. He crossed the street, working his way through the stopped cars. The traffic jam was a blessing for him at this minute. He entered the southeast corner of Trafalgar Square and quickly walked toward the center of the square as the man was about to enter the middle section of Trafalgar Square in between the two fountains.

Alfie's ear mike crackled again. "Subject might be heading to the fountain. He is wearing a uniform. We think it might be a maintenance man from the Thames Water Utility. Maybe he's there to work on the fountains."

Alfie was wondering who in the hell was on the other end of the ear mike. He hit the button that activated the miniature speaker attached to the collar of his jacket. "There would be no service personnel from Thames Water here at night. Moreover, they would not be making any repairs to the fountains. That would happen under the Greater London Authority control. The pumps and controls for the fountains are located under Charing Cross Station."

He flipped the radio to a frequency that allowed all the men in the sector to hear his instructions along with the idiot back at the War Room.

"Be alert, gentlemen. We might have something going on here. Units Two and Four, move in to inspect the man with the tool bag."

In the War Room conversation dropped as everyone became aware of a possible situation developing toward the middle of Trafalgar Square. Overhead speakers broadcast the radio conversation between the officer monitoring the screen and communications with the officers on the ground at Trafalgar Square.

Randy Fisher had been waiting in the War Room for the language experts back in Langley to provide the interpretation of the unidentified Persian words found on the blank sheet of paper. BookReader sat on straight-back chairs in the rear of the room drinking coffee and following the new developments on the front-wall screens.

For Fisher, the waiting game was becoming tiresome. He could understand why some ranking military officers would rather be in the field with their men. Waiting back at headquarters until the military mission began could strain any person's nerves. With nothing else to do, it only seemed natural to wait in the War Room, where he would hear if anything was happening. It seemed his decision was correct. Something might be developing right that minute.

Iraj Malek-Mohammadi walked at a steady pace toward Nelson's Column, unaware he had already attracted the attention of six members of Alfie Duncan's security squad and the people in the War Room. His eyes were fixated on his target. Iraj was near the center spot between the two water fountains, fifty or sixty feet from the base of the historic column, when he became aware of several men in uniform approaching from both the east and west corners of Trafalgar Square. He stopped his forward movement and slowly turned his head left and right, looking at them and deciding if he could proceed. Were they a threat?

In the van, Gholam was the first to notice that Iraj had not taken shelter to wait until they were closer to Charing Cross Station. Mohammad Javan, behind the driver's wheel, had only been able to move the van a few yards in the congested traffic since Iraj had left the van. Gholam reached over with his right hand and tapped Mohammad on the shoulder. The heavyset man quickly glanced left at his partner. Gholam was leaning forward and pointing out the window to Mohammad's right. The big man twisted in his seat and looked at the object of Gholam's concern.

Mohammad swore under his breath. Iraj was not waiting near the trees as instructed but standing near the center of the square. The bomb-maker was going to ruin their timetable for the attack. Mohammad needed to make a quick decision; should Gholam leave the safety of the van and try to walk the two blocks to Charing Cross Station?

Over the radio network, officers were reporting in their assessments of the suspect. He had placed the tool bag under his left armpit, allowing his right hand to rest on the top of the bag near the zipper. One of the ground officers asked over the microphone if the higher elevation CCTVs could determine if the zipper appeared opened or closed.

In the War Room, one of the technicians changed the magnification of the CCTV camera on the suspect to center the picture on the tool bag. The image was very clear through the high-quality camera lenses. "The zipper on the tool bag is opened. The suspect seems to be moving his hand closer to the open top."

DC Shepard had been standing near the center of the room. He moved quickly past Randy Fisher to the monitoring station near Constance Langhorne and picked up a desk-mounted microphone. "This is Shepard. Do you have a clean shot at the suspect?"

Two snipers on top of the highest buildings around the square answered back within seconds. Sniper 1, positioned on top of the National Gallery, was near the front of his building overlooking the square. He had the ability to sweep the entire square with the exception of any person on the far side of the column.

Sniper 2, positioned on the South African High Commission office across Charing Cross Road, centered the crosshairs of his scope on the target. Unknown to him, the van carrying Mohammad Javan and Gholam Reza was almost directly below his position.

"S-1. I have a clear shot. Awaiting a green light."

"S-2. I have a good visual, but the water shooting up from the fountain might deflect my shot. Awaiting a green light."

Alfie Duncan was now the closest man to the suspect at less than fifty feet. He stopped moving when he heard the reports from the snipers. He was unarmed, and the only protection he could take was behind the bronze lion on the northwest corner of Nelson's Column.

He looked around at the number of other people in the square. Many were simply passing through Trafalgar Square as a shortcut to their destination and had stopped in their track. Others were already hurrying to a place of safety. Those coming from the tube stations were moving to take shelter on the south side of Nelson's Column, putting the tall obelisk between them and the man standing in the center of the square. Alfie was motioning for other people to move back and away from the suspect.

Iraj assessed his position, turning slightly to look at Alfie Duncan and the two other officers who were now in front of him. They were not blocking the path to his target but he knew they were there to stop him.

Dozens of eyes were watching the scene: close up, like Alfie Duncan and his men; the snipers through the high-powered eyepieces of their Accuracy International L115A3 sniper rifles; at a distance over the monitors in the War Room. Many of them saw the smile forming on the suspect's face.

Randy Fisher sensed movement next to him and stole a quick look to his right; he discovered Marion Bellwood standing beside him. Bellwood motioned to the big center screen filled with the scene from Trafalgar Square. "Is that either of the two men from the bridge?"

Randy was about to answer when they all saw the suspect's face almost light up with a larger smile, and then he quickly slipped his right hand inside his tool bag.

DC Shepard was preparing to yell into the microphone and give the release to the snipers when the male suspect pulled the Micro-Uzi from his backpack.

Many things happened in just a few seconds. Alfie Duncan yelled for his men to take cover. Shepard yelled into the microphone for the snipers to shoot the suspect. Exposed bystanders saw the gun appear and started to make a run for the nearest shelters.

Both British snipers made their kill decision at almost the same split second before they heard DC Shepard give them the command. Their AI L115A3.388 sniper rifles were bored to fire an 8.59 mm bullet with a muzzle velocity of 936 meters per second at an effective range of fourteen hundred meters.

The two specially trained riflemen aimed for a head shot that would cut through the medulla oblongata within the brain and destroy the eleventh cranial nerve, also called the accessory nerve—more of a motor nerve rather than a sensory nerve. The high-powered bullets would destroy the nerve and freeze the subject's motor capabilities to the head, neck, and lower muscles. A successful shot would stop all muscles from moving and prevent the terrorist from being able to activate any device inside the tool bag.

Both heavy rounds from the rifles hit Iraj within a period too quick to determine which bullet struck first. His right arm, holding the Micro-Uzi, was already out and moving toward Alfie Duncan when the weapons discharged all twenty rounds in the clips. Iraj was falling toward the paving stones of the square. He was dead when his body flopped to the surface of Trafalgar Square. He did not need to be concerned with detonating the bomb. His backup plan automatically went into a very short countdown.

The rounds from the Micro-Uzi all hit hard surfaces and ricocheted off the paving stones up into the nighttime sky. Every person in the immediate area around Trafalgar Square hit the ground. Their bodies were as low as possible when the eight pounds of C-4 exploded inside the canvas tool bag.

Chapter 45

London
Thursday, December 3, 2015
5:15 p.m.

Iraj Malek-Mohammadi had not touched the trigger mechanism inside the bag. Even if he had, the separation of his cranial nerves by the two 8.59 mm bullets would have made it impossible for him to move his hand or fingers to activate the bomb. In fact, Iraj was dead before his body hit the ground.

However, the level-sensing back-up firing mechanism he had wired into the bomb and armed just before he left the van had worked perfectly. Iraj had kept the tool bag perfectly level even when he transferred the bag from the handgrip to holding it under his left arm. Once he starting to collapse after the lethal headshots, the mercury-filled leveling mechanism inside the bag went into effect. The level in the tube went off balance and rolled the liquid to the end of the short tube, touching two bare wires and completing an electrical circuit. An energy charge left the battery and traveled at the speed of light to the electric-type fuse head blasting cap. The fuse wires delivered the electrical charge to the electric match inside the blasting cap and ignited the pyrotechnic ignition mixture that provided the explosive charge to set off the eight pounds of high-explosive C-4.

Explosive materials receive a classification based on the speed at which they expand when detonated. Materials that detonate or explode faster than the speed of sound receive a "High Explosives" classification. C-4 certainly fell into that category.

The eight-pound block of explosives detonated just as Iraj's body hit the surface of Trafalgar Square. The blast sent out a shock wave of light, sound, heat, and pressure. The shaped charge inside the bag was designed to fit against the curvature of the column and direct the destructive blast into the column, bringing the obelisk down.

Instead, the blast exploded 360 degrees. Iraj's body completely vaporized from the force. The energy waves traveled away from the epicenter at the speed of sound. Car and building windows were shattered. The waterspouts in both fountains were blown toward the rear of the square. Because Iraj had pulled out the Uzi and fired the weapon, witnesses close enough to be seriously hurt by the blast were lying flat on the pavement or behind a structure for protection.

Alfie Duncan and nearly everyone huddled near Nelson's Column suffered ruptured eardrums. Although people lay close to the ground, normally harmless debris suddenly moved at tremendous speeds, slicing through their clothing. Those lucky enough to be wearing eyeglasses avoided some damage to sensitive eye tissue.

Because Iraj was in the open space of the square, most of the energy from the bomb blast simply expanded out into the air. The light energy was blinding and the noise defeating, but the explosion lost most of it strength before it caused major damage beside ruptured eardrums and hundreds of shattered glass windows.

In the War Room, the blast was captured on the many CCTV cameras recording as the event unfolded. While the people in the room were some distance from Trafalgar Square, they could not stop from leaning away from the screens and shielding their eyes from the intense light.

However, it took a full minute for the lenses inside most of the CCTV cameras to reset after the bright flash of the blast. The cameras closest to the blast site received a direct hit and sustained damaged by the explosion. Many failed to reactivate; others provided an out-of-focus picture too fuzzy to provide any information. Operators inside the War Room quickly tried to switch the monitors to other cameras, and the big screens slowly came back to life.

Disaster training kicked in for the people inside the War Room, and they placed calls for emergency responders. Ambulances dispatched. Medical personnel were notified; fire and rescue equipment rolled out of bays. Others were trying to contact the local police officers at the scene to get updated information.

Randy Fisher felt helpless as he watched the trained professionals try to maintain their composure and go about their duties. Marion Bellwood was on his cell phone calling in a situation report back to Langley, knowing the information would soon reach the White House Situation Room. Phillip Booker and Charlie Reader stood by their chairs. Their coffee was going cold.

DC Shepard moved quickly to each station to ensure staff members were all right and able to focus on their work.

Constance Langhorne was doing the same when she heard one of the technicians over by the frosted glass wall call her name. She hurried over to the station and saw the woman staring hard at her monitor.

As Constance reached the younger woman's desk, Emily Shoreham was pointing at her twenty-seven-inch monitor. "Constance, I'm playing back the digital recording, trying to find where the bomber came from. Look here at the back corner of the square. It looks like he came from behind that Thames Water motor van. I don't see him any other place until he emerges from behind the van."

Constance watched another replay on the screen. She agreed completely with Emily's assessment. "Transfer your video to one of the larger front monitors." She turned back to the large wall screen as the image from Emily's monitor suddenly filled one of the left side screens. It took only a moment to locate where the van had been before the explosion.

Constance shifted her eyes to the main screen, filled with the disaster on the square. All around the perimeter were stalled cars, vans, and a few larger trucks. Many were sitting at unusual angles. Because of the damaged CCTV cameras, it was difficult to distinguish whether some vehicles were cars or small vans.

She went to one of the other stations and directed the man to change his camera angle to show all of Charing Cross Road. It took several seconds for the camera to move and the technician to bring the picture into focus. The area was darker than before; many streetlights were out. The technician adjusted his equipment to compensate for the low light level.

Finally, they could at least distinguish the cars from the trucks. She looked carefully and noticed the van on Charing Cross Road, almost at the Ducannon Street intersection. A car from the inner lane had tried to move away from the blast area became stalled itself and blocked the van. Some drivers were outside their cars, unable to see through their damaged windshields. From their distant expressions and unsteady motions, many were simply in shock. Nobody was visible inside the van. "Switch your screen to the main center screen."

As the man complied, Constance moved back to the center of the room next to DC Shepard. She grabbed his left arm to get his attention. She pointed to the main screen, now showing the white Thames Water van in the center of the picture.

"We think that Thames Water van was used to bring the bomber to the square. It's still stuck in the traffic."

Shepard took only a moment to bring up the portable hand radio he had switched to since the explosion. He quickly issued new orders for onsite security forces to move in on the van and take anybody inside into custody.

Sniper 1 on the roof of the National Gallery changed his position to focus his weapon and high-powered scope on the van, but he found only the solid sidewall and the small window next to the driver's door.

Sniper 2 was almost straight above the van. He leaned over to sight the van through his rifle scope. At the short distance, he hardly needed the extra magnification, but the angle of his vision was off. He could not see inside the van.

Less than a minute after DC Shepard issued his new orders, four heavily armed members of the Armed Service Department of the Metropolitan Police moved in from two different directions. The rain had almost stopped. The wind was less fierce. Lighting was bad from the loss of the streetlights, but that might help the officers remain undetected as they moved closer to the van.

The lead officer finally worked his way closer to the van using stalled cars for protection. He thought there were two people inside the van. He quietly warned anyone nearby to walk away from the area.

"This is leader A. I see two possible suspects inside the van. We are moving in. Everyone has a green light if they have a clear shot."

Chapter 46

London
Thursday, December 3, 2015
5:37 p.m.

Mohammad Javan and Gholam Reza were slowly recovering from the effects of the explosion. The safety glass in the driver's door next to Mohammad and the front windshield were gone, blown away by the force of the explosion. Light rain and wind blew into the van and on their faces. The combined effects of rain, wind, and the drop in temperature helped to restore their senses. The small pellets of broken glass had pockmarked their faces, and each had small cuts that slowly oozed blood.

They had watched as the British shot down Iraj, his body falling to the ground. The explosion from the bomb took them by surprise as much as the other people in the area. Only a short time passed before Mohammad had recovered enough to think about moving the van and escaping from the area. It was no hope; other cars boxed the van. He used the sleeve of his right hand to wipe blood from his face. He could feel tiny pieces of glass pellets imbedded in his skin. As Gholam was coming back to his senses, Mohammad looked out the open spaces of the front and side windows, trying to decide their next move.

The car next to the driver's side rested against the van and prevented Mohammed from opening his door. "My door is blocked. We need to leave through your door or the back of the van." The giant made a quick decision. "Get your bag. We will walk to the train station. We will set our explosives inside and leave any way we can, train or the underground."

Both men reached down to the floor between the front seats and picked up their tool bags. They quickly checked for their weapons; both removed the Korth handguns. There was no need to keep the weapons hidden. They would take too long to remove from the bags if they needed them.

Gholam started to open his door when he saw movement ahead about twenty-five feet. The shape was human, and he could just make out the silhouette of a rifle or some sort of weapon. Mohammad looked to where Gholam was staring and saw the same shape. He spun in his seat to look off to his right; he saw another armed officer moving in toward the van. He pointed to the slow-moving target. "It seems our fate will end right here." He reached back into the bag for the Uzi and the spare clips. "I don't want to die like Iraj, with a bomb blast. I want my death to be more personal."

He quickly fed a round into the chamber and slipped the safety off. In the darkened interior of the van he could hear Gholam readying his own machine gun.

They looked at each other, and each gave a smile and a head nod. Looking back toward the moving targets approaching them and the people still milling around the cars stalled beside the van, they stuck their weapons out the space where the front and side windows used to be and pulled the triggers.

Chapter 47

London
Thursday, December 3, 2015
5:50 p.m.

The gunfight lasted for only a short period, but the number of dead and wounded was much higher than from the bomb blast. Bullets from the Uzis cut down the two closest police officers with lethal head and neck wounds above where their bulletproof vest could protect them.

Immediately afterward, the two terrorists changed their direction of fire and took out numerous bystanders still recovering from the effects of the blast. Those people had no chance.

Both terrorists used the brief opportunity in the confusion to change the magazines in their Uzis, inserting fresh clips with another twenty rounds each. They were ready to fire their weapons again when bullets started to enter the van's sidewall behind Mohammad.

Sniper 1, on the roof of the National Galley, could not see the terrorists. He was a perfect witness to the death coming from inside the van. Still having no clear target but using logic as to their location, he opened fire on the van from his elevated position behind them. The first round missed Mohammad Javan Nik Khah, but the next three entered his back and throat. Blood spurted from his mouth and neck, and his body fell forward against the steering wheel.

Gholam saw his friend slump forward. The huge body compressed against the steering wheel, and the horn started to blare. He knew he

265

needed to try to leave the van. Safety in mobility was one of the ideas they taught at the camps. He opened his door, firing his Uzi to create whatever distraction possible. He had only taken one step from the van when Sniper 2 fired an 8.62 mm-round directly into the top of his head from the rooftop above. He died as he fell to the asphalt.

Chapter 48

London
Thursday, December 3, 2015
6:00 p.m.

The uniformed officers and civilian employees inside the War Room in the Scotland Yard building were in shock. For many, this was their first involvement in an actual terrorist situation. No amount of classroom training in the coordination of monitors and the flow of information in and out of the facility could prepare them for the scene on Charing Cross Road. Even the former military officers experienced and hardened from overseas duty in Afghanistan or Iraq were deeply affected by what they had just witnessed.

Marion Bellwood and his two security agents had seen almost every conceivable type of horror in their time working for the CIA, but they were just as speechless. Randy Fisher felt sick to his stomach.

There had not been enough time to assess the death and destruction from the bomb blast before the people inside the War Room stood by helplessly as the second attack occurred before their eyes.

They watched Londoners getting out of their damaged and stalled cars on Charing Cross Road, trying to understand what had just occurred on their beloved Trafalgar Square. Many of the drivers from the cars were just realizing they had survived a terrorist attack. Some were turning to help the wounded, only to become the targets of another attack, gunned down without mercy.

The workers inside the War Room would never forget the images on the huge center screen as the bodies reacted to the deadly hail of gunfire from almost point-blank range.

Randy Fisher felt his own helplessness and wanted to rush to the scene to provide what little comfort might be possible. He felt worthless in his safe position inside the War Room. He looked around at the others in the room. Constance Langhorne stood quietly off to the side of the open center section, her face a mask of confusion and shock. He took a few steps to reach her side. Softly he placed his hand on her shoulder.

"Constance, are you all right?"

She looked up into his face. There were tears at the corners of her eyes, and she took the handkerchief Randy offered to dry the moisture.

She nodded and used the cloth to dry her nose. She offered the cloth back to Randy, but he gave a little wave of his hand, indicating she keep it.

"Constance, I need your help. I need to get a photograph of the two terrorists from the van. We have to know if they were the two I fought with on the bridge or if those two men are still out there." He looked into her eyes. He could see her mind start to focus on his words. "Constance, if those men in the van are not the two we've been looking for, this whole mess might not be over with. These three dead terrorist might be just a diversion from their main target. We've got to see their faces, and we must hurry."

Constance nodded in understanding. "Of course, Senator. You are perfectly correct. Let me see if I can contact someone at the scene to snap their pictures and e-mail them to us here in the War Room."

Randy watched her walked to where one of her people was still working the communications system. He walked over to Marion. The CIA DDO was just ending a call to Langley.

"The president is on a bus to Chesapeake, Virginia, to give another speech against the filibuster. The Secret Service is considering cancelling the event and taking the president off the bus and back to Washington or some other place. They haven't decided."

Randy asked the first question that entered his mind. "Do they think this event is part of something larger?"

Marion shook his head. "We don't know at this time, but we've issued a higher-level warning. The network news agencies back home have already shifted their attention from the president and his fight with those three senators to this event."

Marion pointed to the center screen, still showing the devastation on Trafalgar Square. Already ambulances with flashing lights were on scene, as well as emergency workers and many more uniformed and armed members of the Metropolitan Police department. Portable lights and generators brought to the scene mixed their brilliant lights with the revolving lights from the emergency vehicles. All were contributing to the surreal image showing on the center screen.

DC Shepard walked toward them. As he got closer, Randy could see the pain in his eyes. When the deputy commander of Scotland Yard paused next to them, Randy spoke softly to the older man. "Please accept our condolences for your loss, DC Shepard. Any word on the number of people killed or wounded?"

Shepard had the requested information on a small slip of paper in his front shirt pocket. He did not need to reach for the answer to Randy's question. It would always be in his memory.

"Twelve dead ... eighteen wounded. Three of my officers are among the dead. Four were wounded in the explosion as they tried to approach the bomber." He started to move off but stopped. "Thank you for your help, Senator Fisher. If you had not provided an early warning, this would have been much worse. Now if you will excuse me, I'm on my way to the square."

He walked away before Randy could mention that maybe this mess was not over.

Chapter 49

London
Thursday, December 3, 2015
6:15 p.m.

Hossein fumed with anger. Shir Mohammad was driving the second van loaded with the cryptosporidium powder inside the twelve fifty-five-gallon yellow plastic barrels.

They had left the rug business buildings directly after Mohammad Javan and the others. At the intersection of Aspen Way they had watched the first van turn right toward Central London and their mission. Shir turned left, drove a short way to Preston Road, and followed it into the old Graving Dock area, strangely enough by way of a street named Trafalgar Way. When they reached the old Canary Wharf, he turned right and drove over the little-used road system through the old docks, too small for the huge tankers and container vessels bringing imported goods into England from China and Europe.

Once through the docks and old wharfs, they crossed the River Thames into the outer boroughs of southern London. There, the traffic had become jammed due to the weather and time of day. Hundreds of thousands of Londoners were trying to get home before the weather turned worse.

As the crow flies, the distance to the Honor Oak Reservoir was only about three and one-half miles. Hossein had allocated only twenty minutes to drive from the rug company building on Newby Street to their target. However, by six fifteen they were not yet at the small village. He had no one to blame for this but himself and thousands of cars and small trucks.

By seven, they finally arrived at Hichisson Road, which allowed them to drive into the Aquarias Golf Club. The sky was fully dark, as was natural for that time of year. The rain had stopped during their drive southwest from their starting point, but raindrops were again falling. With the overcast blocking out any moonlight, the area around the clubhouse was completely dark except for a few security lamps in the parking lot.

Shir brought the van slowly to a halt on the white pea gravel parking lot; they both rolled down the side windows to listen to the night noises. Only the splattering of the heavy raindrops on the roof of the van broke the silence.

Hossein pulled from an inside pocket the local paper map he had used to plan the mission. He opened it in his lap, with Shir holding the edge. He used a small flashlight to look at the details of the golf course and located the reservoir building that would grant them access to the pipeline system.

The Aquarias Golf Course roughly formed a large rectangle. The clubhouse and maintenance buildings were on the north end of the course. Residential homes lined the east and west sides of the fairways. Due to the water reservoir, the course was not laid out with trees and ponds mixed among the normal sand traps found on all golf courses. The fairway grounds were completely bare of trees to avoid their root systems from growing into the water reservoir or the pumping equipment.

Hossein found the club house building on the map and then the reservoir building. After turning the map to align it with their location, he pointed to a cluster of buildings and a dirt road. "Those must be the maintenance sheds for their lawn equipment. Take that road, and drive between the buildings. It will lead us onto the golf course."

Shir carefully fed gasoline to the idling motor, and slowly the van moved toward the buildings. They could hear the tires crunch as the wheels rolled across the gravel. As they neared the buildings, the coating of gravel thinned out, and soon they were driving on hard-packed dirt and grass.

The equipment storage buildings were white-painted wood structures. Once they had maneuvered the van between the buildings, they came to a hard grass road used by the course groundkeepers and the maintenance people for the Thames Water Ring Authority.

Hossein anger faded away. Off in the distance they could make out the aboveground building for the water reservoir. The only source of illumination was a single security light attached to the building.

Shir needed no orders from Hossein; he applied pressure to the gas pedal and drove the van down the road in the center of the golf course. Thick stands of oaks trees lined the outer edge of the course. Lights from the homes built around both sides of the fairway and Honor Oak Street lamps twinkled through the trees devoid of their leaves.

As they slowly drove down the hard-packed road, they passed small raised concrete platforms at regular intervals. Off to the side, their wide headlight beams briefly highlighted more platforms. Each was roughly five foot square; Hossein thought they might be other access places to the reservoir, but he was not sure how the complicated system was laid out underground.

Finally, they reach the center of the open fairways and the large access building. Shir brought the van to a stop once again and waited for more instructions. Hossein turned off his flashlight and started to fold the map he no longer needed. In the dark interior of the van, he had trouble determining the proper way to return it to the original neat, folded condition. After wasting precious seconds, he simply crushed it into a loose ball and tossed the map to the floor of the van.

"Drive around back to the loading dock. We will force open the overhead door at the dock and take the barrels into the building that way."

Shir again fed gasoline to the engine and slowly steered the van around to the back of the building. They found the dock area. A single incandescent light bulb screwed into a porcelain fixture mounted to the overhead roof extending from the building provided a small measure of light. There was no deck area in front of the overhead door. The outer edge of the concrete floor of the building and the overhead door both met together. The floor must have been four feet above ground level. Off to the side of the dock was a set of concrete steps leading up to a steel walk-in door.

Shir turned the van around to align the rear doors with the loading dock. He shifted the transmission into reverse and eased the van back toward the dock. When he was about five feet away, he stopped the van. Hossein quickly hopped out and hurried back to open the rear doors of the panel van. Shir carefully backed the van until the open doors were almost touching the outer wall of the dock and building.

From his vantage point, Hossein could not see the problem, but Shir knew they would have to find a different way to unload the heavy barrels. When Shir did not turn off the motor, Hossein walked back to the passenger door and stuck his head inside the open window.

"What is the problem? We are hours behind schedule."

Shir simply pointed over the barrels toward the open doors in the back of the van. The level of the building floor and the floor of the van did not meet. The building floor rose at least a full two and one-half feet higher than the bed of the van, leaving only about eighteen inches of open space in the van doorway to slide the barrels into the building. There was no way the wide barrels would pass through the narrow opening.

Hossein swore again as his anger returned. "Pull the van out far enough to allow room for us to lift the barrels up to the floor of the building."

A minute later, both men were standing on the ground between the rear of the van and the closed overhead building door. The building floor was more than four feet above the ground. In addition, landscaping engineers included a trench drain system in the ground at the base of the dock to assist with groundwater drainage. It lowered their elevation another six inches. They would have to lift the heavy barrels from the van up to the building floor once they opened the door. With each barrel containing over three hundred pounds of the densely packed powder, this unforeseen problem was going to cause another change in their plan.

"We had the forklift in the building to load the barrels," Shir said. "What do we do now?"

Hossein allows his anger to spill out. "How the hell do I know? Give me time to think." He stepped out from between the van and the building to have a better view of the problem, but nothing was coming to him. He turned to look at the concrete steps. They were planning to force the walk-in door open and then open the overhead door from inside the building.

"Let's force the door open. Maybe we can find some equipment inside the building to help lift the barrels up from the van."

Forcing the old steel door open was relativity easy. Two swipes with their twenty-pound sledgehammer broke the deadbolt lock. The door flew open on its hinges and slammed loudly against the inside wall of the building.

Hossein used his flashlight to locate the light switch next to the doorframe. He flipped the small toggle lever, and overhead fluorescent light fixtures came to life to bathe the open dock area.

The dock was located on one end of the rectangular building. Inside they could see a tubular steel railing running down the center of the building. As they walked toward the railing, a huge pit dividing the center of the building and running the complete length of the building became visible. Down in the pit was the wide water pipe, nearly twenty-four inches in diameter. Each section of pipe was twenty feet in length and connected to the next section of pipe with large round steel flanges bolted together with eighteen heavy-duty machine bolts. Neoprene gaskets pressed tightly between the flanges kept water from leaking from the pipe joints. The flanges, painted blue, contrasted with the galvanized finish of the steel pipe.

In the middle of the exposed piping system was a huge Apex GC vertical inline centrifugal pump, capable of moving three hundred liters of water per second. The cast-iron pump, painted royal blue, was held in place within the piping system by two large flanges on each end, an inlet and discharge flange, and extended above the main pipe. The pump was in line with the water flow; the motor rested atop the pump. They could hear the pump running, but the perfectly balanced single-stage impeller was vibration free. Beneath the pump was a thick concrete reinforcement pad to support the weight of the pump and eliminate strain to the pipe and flanges.

Down in the pit on each end of the building, they could see where the pipe disappeared into the wall system. On their end near the dock, the pipe left the building to continue on to Brixton and connect into the Thames Water Ring Main system. On the far end of the building, they could see the pipe enter the underground storage tank. They could only see a very small part of the huge underground reservoir, but what was important was the large access hatch above the pipe. It was square, with a flange around the outer edge, and bolted down to the steel casing used for that part of the tank. Beyond the access hatch, the tank reverted to its famous brick construction. A heavy steel walkway with side railing crossed over the wide pit above the water pipe to provide a path to the access hatch. The railing had a built-in door near the access hatch that technicians could swing open on heavy-duty hinges to reach the access hatch cover.

Hossein looked throughout the entire lighted interior of the building. They would need to find a way to bring the barrels into the building and then dump the powder from the barrels into the storage tank through the access hatch. He looked at his watch. They were way behind schedule. Maybe Mohammad and his men would arrive soon to help with the work. Originally, his plan called for an entire weekend to do all of their work. Now they had only this night.

Chapter 50

London
Thursday, December 3, 2015
6:55 p.m.

Randy Fisher was moving around the War Room, trying to watch the operators' activity and stay out of their way. Marion Bellwood was almost constantly on his cell phone updating his people back at Langley and receiving any new information gathered from their own sources. Occasionally the two men would meet in the center of the room and watch the images on the large center screen. The scene at Trafalgar Square was still organized chaos. Only recently, the number of dead had increased by one.

The screen reflected the rescue efforts; ambulances and other emergency vehicles still clogged the roads around Trafalgar Square. The number of police cars and vans had increased by large numbers in the short time since the explosion and gunfight. Bobbies now blocked off the entire area from pedestrians. The investigation would continue for many more hours tonight and over the next several days.

Constance Langhorne approached Randy and Marion holding several photographs. "Senator Fisher, we have snaps of the two terrorists in the van. No identification yet, but we're almost certain they are not your two men."

She handed the pictures to Randy as Marion look over his shoulder. Randy took one quick look and knew these were not either of the men from the Jubilee Bridges. The picture of the man inside the van simply showed him with closed eyes. The photo of the other man outside the van was worse. His head appeared terribly distorted by the large-caliber bullet that impacted through the top of his skull. "The man killed inside the van is way too big, and the one outside has a mustache and longer hair. They look nothing like the men I tangled with last Saturday."

He handed the photos of the dead men back to Constance. He looked into her eyes. "You need to tell your people to keep looking. We still have two more terrorists to locate."

Constance simply nodded her head and turned toward the communication desk to contact DC Shepard, still at the scene. He needed the new information immediately. They were after two more terrorists.

"Damn," Marion muttered. "I was hoping we were over this part of the mess."

Randy shook his head. "All this effort to find these bastards and we're still no closer to finding them or discovering whatever else they are planning."

He stood, his hands clenched into fists resting on his hips, while he continued to stare at the center screen. *What to do next?*

A new thought suddenly entered his mind. "Marion, whatever happened to the list you sent to Langley? Were they able to interpret the words?"

Marion reached inside his inner suit coat pocket and removed a folded piece of paper. "I was coming here to give this to you, but I walked into the War Room just as the crap hit the fan in the square. My people translated the words. The list only contains other cities in England. They could not come up with any significance as to the meaning or their relationship."

Randy took the offered sheet of paper and scanned the two columns. The paper detailed the English translation on the left side.

The translators had listed the foreign words in another column across from the English translation.

Kempton	كمبتون	
Kew	كيو	
Mogden	Mogden	
Holland Park	هولند ، بارك	
Walton	ولتان	
Hampton	ه امبتون	
Barrow Hill	ه لي باروو	
Surbiton	سوربيتون	
Hogsmill	Hogsmill	
Raynes Park	بارك	Raynes
Merton	مرتون	
Brixton	بريكستون	
Honor Oak	يونور طلاك	
Streatham	سترهام	
Battersea	بلتيرسي	

He held the sheet of paper so Marion could see the words. "Why are some of the Arabic words the same in English?"

Marion flipped his right hand up to indicate he had no clear answer. "I asked that same question of my people. Some English words have no translation into Arabic."

That made sense to Randy. He once hired a man named Carlos Ramirez, born in Miami, for a sales position. The man's parents were Cuban immigrants. Randy's employee spoke both English and Spanish fluently. Many times when he worked with Carlos, the man would be talking with a customer in Spanish. Several times, he would suddenly switch back to English for only one work. Randy asked him later about the reason, and Carlos simply told him the English word did not exist in Spanish.

Randy saw Constance talking on a telephone. "Let's find out if our English friends know if there is any relationship among these cities. The terrorists couldn't possible try to hit all of these cities."

The two men walked across the room to Constance as she hung up the phone. She informed them that DC Shepard had received the new information and ordered a renewed effort to find the two terrorists still loose in London.

Randy showed her the note. "This is the translation we got from the notebook. Do they mean anything to you?"

Constance took the sheet of paper in her right hand and quickly scanned the words and their English translations. She spread the fingers on her left hand to run them through her dark curly hair.

She confirmed what Randy and Marion already knew. "They're towns and cities in the outer boroughs of London. I haven't a clue as to their significance to this whole nasty affair."

Randy pointed toward the front wall screen. "Can we bring them up on one of the monitors and see how they lie in relation to Trafalgar Square?"

"Yes … of course."

Like newborn puppies following the mother dog, the two men walked behind Constance over to a monitor station in the back corner of the War Room. She showed the list to the young man sitting in the chair.

"James, can you plug these cities into your computer's geographical program and show us their locations?"

He gave the list a very quick look. "Sure. No problem. It will just take a few minutes."

The few minutes seem much longer to Randy; he worried where the next attack would take place. He had no doubt there would be another attack.

James's fingers flew over the keyboard as he entered the information into the system. Finally he pressed the enter button several times. The screen changed to a map of Central London and the surrounding boroughs. The computer reduced the resolution to allow the entire map to appear on one screen.

The screen showed all the names of the towns listed on the sheet of paper. Nobody seemed to learn any new information from the map. Randy pointed at the various cities. "Can you connect the dots between the cities to see what the pattern would look like?"

James bobbed his head. "Sure, easy enough." He entered more instructions into the computer using his keyboard. This time it took less than a minute to bring up the new map.

Now a red line connected all the cities on the map. It stretched north to Burrow Hill and down to Brixton and then generally southwest to four or five other cities, ending at Kempton. It reversed the course toward the northeast back to Burrow Hill. The line did not create any pattern that made sense to the people looking at the monitor. It certainly was not a circle, square, rectangle, or pyramid. Just a line bent to connect the cities.

Everybody was silent when Booker and Reader walked over to look at the screen. They had been sitting in the back of the room watching the large monitors and talking quietly. Randy was about to ask them if anything on the screen made sense to them from their point of view. He was a politician. They were the security experts.

As Randy opened his mouth to speak, Charlie Reader took a sip of water from the plastic bottle in his hand. Randy noticed it was the same brand found in the backpack.

"Where did you get the water, Charlie?"

Everyone turned to the young black agent. Charlie looked embarrassed, not quite knowing what he had done wrong.

"I … um … got it from the café on the lower floor. Sorry, Senator. I did not check to see if anybody else wanted something to drink. I'll be glad to go back down to get whatever anybody wants."

Constance was wondering why anyone, least of all the senator, would be worrying about Charlie getting water. "We have a small canteen right here on this floor. There is no reason to go all the way down to the third floor to the general canteen."

Randy turned away from the group. He needed a few moments to put together the new idea that suddenly flooded his mind. *Water? Why was water so important to him just now?*

He turned quickly around to face the others. "How does London get its water? Do you have one single treatment plant or are there many facilities?"

The others in the room stared toward him with blank looks on their faces.

He stepped closer to the twenty-seven-inch monitor. "People. Think about it. Those three terrorist were dressed in the uniform of some water company. What was it?"

"Thames Water Utility," Marion said. He knew where Randy's thinking was taking them. He stepped toward James at the desk. "Can you bring up the water delivery system for Central London on your screen?"

James looked at Constance. She simply nodded for him to comply with the request.

The operator turned back to the keyboard and started to enter commands. It took longer than the first two minutes of his original search of the cities, but finally he sat back and watched the screen refresh to a new image.

It was almost the same image as before.

"No," Charlie said. "We want to see how the water system flows. Not the cities on the sheet of paper."

James took his index finger and thumped the screen, causing the twenty-seven-inch monitor to bounce slightly on its pedestal stand. "This is the layout of the Water Ring Main around London."

Randy spoke next. "What do you mean 'Water Ring Main'?"

Constance jumped into the conversation. "London gets its fresh water from a variety of rivers and lakes but mostly from the River Thames. The London Water Authority has spent billions of pounds to clean up our water and build the Thames Water Ring Main to deliver the water to all of London and the many inner and outer boroughs."

"That's it," Randy said. "That's their target. The potable water system."

Phillip Booker could not stop from blurting out the first thought in his mind. "You've got to be kidding me. With all the bullets and bombs in the world, you think this whole thing is about water. Senator, please do not take this as a sign of disrespect, but look at the screens on the wall. That is what terrorist do. They shoot people, blow up buildings, and use car bombs to kill more people. How do they kill people with water?"

Randy moved away a few steps and then turned back to explain his thinking. "All right. What I am proposing is a little farfetched. I want you to consider two historical events. The Japanese attacked Pearl Harbor in 1941. Their sneak attack destroyed or heavily damaged our Pacific battleships fleet. Their primary targets were the three aircraft carriers the US Navy had in the Pacific, but the ships were not in Pearl

Harbor at the time of the attach. Our country lost 1,177 sailors plus a lot of army personnel at Hickam and other places on the island.

"But we recovered. By the end of the war, the United States Navy possessed almost one hundred aircraft carriers.

"Let's look at more recent numbers. Look at the destruction caused by two jet airliners in New York City on 9-11. The United States suffered 2,997 dead from the attack. It was terrible. We will never forget Pearl Harbor or 9-11. All that damage—but we recovered. The president of the United States was in New York City in less than ten days after 9-11, telling people to come visit New York."

Randy pointed toward the large group of center monitors still showing the devastation to Trafalgar Square. "That is a terrible mess that will be talked about for months and years to come, but how much of London will be able to operate normally tomorrow morning?

"The long-term effect of what these terrorist did to your city is not permanent. Maybe their real target is the Thames Water Ring System. How would that attack affect the entire population of London, and how long would it take to repair the damage?"

Marion Bellwood pointed at the monitor. "Constance, you need to get security people to those installations—and right now."

She shook her head. "Everything is focused right now on Trafalgar Square. It would take time to organize multiple operations to get heavily armed forces to each of these facilities. I'm worried that we don't have very much time."

Marion spoke again. "You're correct. If Randy's has identified the correct target, then Trafalgar Square was a diversion from their actual target. We may already be too late."

Randy pulled Marion off to the side. When they were able to talk quietly, he laid out the next idea he had. "Marion, you've got those extra embassy culture attachés just sitting around on their butts. Let us use those men to check out these locations. They've got cars and GPS equipment, and I assume they are capable of handling this type of situation."

Marion was quiet for a few moments. "American security forces running around England chasing terrorists? How will that play out in the news back home, or even here?

Randy responded quickly. "If they find these guys and stop them, then who cares? We saved our cousins from across the pond. If there is nothing to find at these locations, then your men were out sightseeing, just like any other tourist."

Marion made a quick decision. "All right, let's get them moving."

Together they walked back to where Constance and BookReader were waiting. Marion quietly cleared his throat to get their attention. "I've got some men at the American Embassy we can utilize in this situation. Constance, we would need your assistance to coordinate their activity. Will you help us?"

The young Englishwoman did not hesitate. "Absolutely. What do you need?"

Randy interrupted. "Constance, of these fifteen locations, which one would be the most important?"

Marion looked at his friend but kept his mouth shut for the moment while Constance looked back down at the monitor on James's desk. "They're all important in the scheme to deliver water and handle waste from London. If any one was taken out, it would cause a disruption in services."

Randy pressed her for a better answer. "I realize they're all part of the system, but certainly one of them has to rank higher as a target for the terrorist. We need your best guess."

Constance looked at Randy and then at the young man at the desk. "James … What do you think?"

The younger man simply looked at the screen. "Sorry, Constance, but I don't really know much about the water ring. We turn on the tap and water magically appears."

Constance felt the pressure growing. She believed the senator had a real strong theory, but they needed directions for focusing their limited resources. Finally, she pointed to the large reservoir on the screen. "Honor Oak. That would be my first target if I were a terrorist."

Randy smiled—he knew Constance had put herself into the role of a terrorist. "Why?"

"Two reasons. It is one of the world's largest underground storage facilities for drinking water. It can supply water for up to eight hundred thousand people each day. If it was taken out, the effect would be long-term and costly to repair."

Booker spoke before the others. "What is the second reason?"

Constance gave a sheepish smile. "I was raised not too far from that area. It's the one place on the list I know the most about."

Randy pointed to the spot in the southern portion of Outer London. "All right. That is where I'm going."

Marion broke his silence. "What the hell do you mean 'you're going'? You're not a security agent."

Randy pointed up toward the main screen. "I'm done standing around here watching all of this mess. If Honor Oak is where my suspect is, then that is where I am going. You and BookReader are not going to stop me."

Marion saw the look of determination on Randy's face. He decided they needed to get their operation in motion rather than stand and argue with each other. He turned to Phillip Booker. "Phil, I want you to stay here and contact our people at the embassy. You, Constance, and James can coordinate their approach to each of the other locations."

He pointed at Constance. "I need you to supply the address for each location to these men and contact any local police to meet them at the locations. Warn the local LEOs they might be facing armed terrorist."

James looked from his screen to the CIA deputy director of operations. "Local LEOs?"

Phillip provided the answer. "Local enforcement officers." He looked toward his boss. "What are you going to do, sir?"

Marion pointed at Randy. "Charlie and I are going with Randy to Honor Oak to keep him out of trouble."

Constance grabbed a memo pad from James's desk and quickly wrote down some information. "Here is the address for the Aquarias Golf Course. Honor Oak is buried beneath the golf course."

Randy grabbed his heavy coat and slipping it over his right shoulder. When his right hand popped out the end of the sleeve, he grabbed the note from her hand. "Let's move guys."

Constance looked at the three men preparing to leave and then her eyes fell on Charlie. He gave her a quick smile, but she needed more. Constance took the three steps that separated them, grabbed his coat collar, and pulled his head down to her own. "You take care of yourself, Charlie Reader." She planted a quick kiss on his lips and ran her right hand over the top of his head against the thick stubble of his short hair.

Charlie flashed her a quick smile and looked over toward his boss. Marion just gave him a shake of his head and turned to follow Randy Fisher out the door. In less than ten minutes, the three men were inside their rented car and driving out of the VIP parking spot at the rear of the Scotland Yard building.

Chapter 51

Chesapeake, VA
Thursday, December 3, 2015
2:10 p.m.

News of the terrorist attack in London flashed around the world. The British press had known something was causing the local security authorities to increase their vigilance. The violence at Trafalgar Square caught them by surprise as well as the British population.

At the Washington CNN office, coverage shifted from the filibuster in the Senate and the president's road trip from Richmond to Chesapeake, Virginia, to the massacre in London. Their London associates carried the broadcast workload, reporting from just outside of the Trafalgar Square area.

US-based reporters were trying to get comments from members of Congress and the president just before the Secret Service decided the open bus tour was now too dangerous for their protectee.

The president said as he was stepping off the bus, surrounded by a mass of agents, "This is a sad day for our friends in England and specifically London. We offer our sympathies to the survivors of the victims who lost their lives in this cowardly act of terrorism. Since 9-11, we know all too well the effects of an act of terrorism like this. I pledge to provide all possible support to the British government to find the people behind this terrible deed."

Harold Miller allowed the agents to escort him to his personal armored limousine, which had been shadowing the bus, when a reporter called out a question he could not ignore.

"Mr. President, in light of today's terrorist attack in London, do you think the three Davids should stop the filibuster?"

Miller knew he needed to take great care not to try to make any political gain from the tragedy in London. However, the opportunity to apply more pressure on the three senators holding up his legislation was too great to pass.

"Any person who wastes the time of the United States Senate or the House of Representatives should be ashamed of themselves. Is it any less shameful when our attention at this minute should be with our friends in London? I will leave that answer to the American public."

In his limousine, out of sight of any reporter, Miller could not keep a smile from forming on his face. He looked across the seat to Alison Warden, packed inside the vehicle by the Secret Service. "Make sure our three friends in Washington are bombarded by that last comment I made in front of the reporters."

Chapter 52

Washington, DC
Thursday, December 3, 2015
3:00 p.m.

Avery Doaks hurried to his Senate bench desk, glancing over at Senator Chip Saunders, the current floor-holder in the filibuster. He was about to throw the hardest verbal punch to date against the three renegade senators.

Saunders had returned to the original six reasons why the Senate should not allow the Fair Share Bill to move forward. He had been going with this list since his shift began at noon.

Doaks waited until Saunders had finished the list for the countless time and used his voice for the first time in several days on the floor of the Senate.

"Will the senator yield for a question?"

Saunders knew he could only yield the floor to either Handley or Laird. The one exception was to yield temporarily to another senator for a question. Any other activity he allowed could cost him control of the floor.

"I yield to Senator Doaks for a question only."

Doaks looked at Chip Saunders but directed his question to the other Senate members in the chambers and to the press gallery again filled to capacity.

"Is the senator aware of the tragic events that have occurred in London?"

Saunders took a moment to prepare his answer. So much time passed that Senator Doaks was about to ask if Saunders was yielding the floor.

"I am aware of the tragedy in London, Senator Doaks. I would like to ask the Senate to observe a full minute of silence to pay our respects to the dead and wounded, but Senate rules will not allow me to go a full minute without speaking. Therefore, I will use the next minute to say a prayer for the dead and wounded victims and their family members aloud."

Asking every person in the Senate Chamber to bow their head, Chip Saunders offered an eloquent soliloquy to express his heartfelt sorrow for the victims in London.

He took almost a minute after finishing the prayer to return to the original list of reasons.

Again, Doaks spoke to the Senate. "Will the senator yield to another question?"

Saunders turned a small and tired smile to the Senate minority leader. "Yes. I yield for a question only."

"Do you, Senator Saunders, believe it is proper to continue to hold this floor in light of the tragedy in London?"

Saunders gave the minority leader a hard stare. "No. I do not think this or any filibuster is the proper way to conduct business on the floor of the United States Senate, but until I have your word, Senator Doaks, that you will kill this outrageous tax bill, you give me no choice. Therefore, I ask you right this moment to give me your word on the floor of the Senate. Will you kill this bill right here and now? You have forty-five seconds to answer, Senator."

Doaks was furious. His play to damage Saunders's image had not worked as he planned. "I didn't start this filibuster, Senator Saunders. I will allow the voters of our state and the American people to determine if you should be returned to office or perhaps be recalled by our state to explain your conduct."

Saunders turned to the president pro tem of the Senate. "Mr. President. I believe Senator Doaks is out of order. He is not asking a question but attempting to take the floor away from me. I ask the president to order Senator Doaks to sit down."

In addition to the two senators raising their voices, the people in the gallery had begun to talk. Senator Cynthia Woodside from Maine, the current president pro tem of the Senate, gave the gavel a hard thump against its heavy wooden base to restore order in the chamber.

"The Senate will come back to order." She raised and dropped the gavel once again. "This chamber will come to order." After a count of ten, she admonished the gallery. "Let me remind the people sitting in the gallery that you are here as guests of the Senate. There is no question as to how you will conduct yourselves. If there is another disturbance, I will clear the gallery."

She looked down at Saunders and then over to Doaks. "Senator Doaks, the rules allow you to ask a question or respond to a question asked by Senator Saunders. Nothing else. Please be seated."

She looked back at Senator Saunders. "Reluctantly, Senator Saunders, I must give the floor back to you."

Chapter 53
Honor Oak
Thursday, December 3, 2015
8:15 p.m.

Lifting the barrels up the concrete steps one step at a time was backbreaking, time-consuming work that sucked energy from both men.

Each barrel was four feet tall and almost thirty inches around. The heavy molded plastic barrels were solid, one-piece construction with an open end where a heavy plastic lid threaded into grooves until the lid was flush with the sides of the barrels. There were two recessed handle grips in the lid for unthreading the lid out of the recessed ledge. A person could wrapped their fingers around the grips but they did not have the strength for moving or picking up the barrel.

They had backed the van up to the wide concrete steps and carefully turned the barrels on their sides inside the van before lifting each in turn onto the first concrete step. They had found no forklift or wheeled dolly to move the barrels. They each took one end of the barrel and lifted it, one step at a time, up the four steps to the stairway and then onto the concrete floor. They were able to get the first four barrels into the building and roll them far enough away from the door to allow room for the next five barrels. However, on the sixth barrel, Shir lost his grip on the lip edge; the barrel broke free, rolled back down the steps, and bounced off the end of the van. It hit the right back door, forcing it back on its hinges to the stops. The barrel lodged between the doorframe and the bottom step. Pulling for all they were worth did not break it loose. They had no choice but to move the truck forward far enough to allow them to free the barrel and start the process over again. This time they had to lift the barrel the full five steps.

When the sixth barrel was finally inside the building, Shir released his grip. Hossein rolled the barrel next to the other five barrels. He turned to see his partner leaning against the doorframe wiping sweat from his face with the back of his uniform sleeve. Hossein wanted to yell at him to move back to the van, but he was just as tired. He simply told him they had to keep working to get all the barrels inside the building.

They continued the arduous process until they finally had the twelfth barrel inside the building. They were exhausted but satisfied. It seemed the hardest part of their scheme was behind them. Now they simply had to roll the barrels down the concrete floor and start to work on opening the hatch.

Rolling the barrels was fairly easy for the two men. They stood side by side and manually moved and directed the barrels about forty-five feet to the steel walkway across the wide pit. It required another twenty minutes to set six barrels upright and remove the lids from the two closest to the catwalk. Shir found a two-gallon plastic bucket with a wire handle to use to dip the powder from the barrels and haul it to the hatchway after they had removed the access cover.

Consumed in their work, they did not realize anyone had arrived at the building until a voice spoke from behind them.

"Hello there chaps. Everything all right here?"

Hossein and Shir spun around to see two constables standing inside the walk-in door. The men were dressed in standard uniforms under winter coats and billed caps with black-and-white checkerboard hatbands. Both officers seemed to accept their uniforms and the van's markings, assuming they were employees of Thames Water Utility.

Shir gave Hossein a quick look and saw his head bob. Quickly turning toward the two officers, he slowly moved in their direction, blocking their view of Hossein with his own body.

His accent was near perfect as he warmly greeted them with a friendly smile. "Good evening, constables. We are getting ready for a work crew to come here tomorrow. Just a little preventive maintenance on the pump. Nothing serious, as long as we take care and are prepared. You know how it is."

One of the constables stepped away from his partner to try to look around Shir at the barrels. "If you're going to be working on the pumps, what's in all them barrels?"

Shir was almost to them when he raised his left hand to distract their attention from his right hand as he slipped it into his uniform pants pocket. "My friend can answer that better than I."

He turned around to look at Hossein, who gave him another little head nod. "Yes. I've got that answer."

As soon as Hossein finished speaking, Shir took two fast steps forward, using his left hand to shove the officer closest to the door against the frame. He removed the titanium Browning quick-opening knife and depressed the release lever in the same motion, allowing the blade to snap out and lock into position. With no hesitation, he shoved the four-inch blade into the officer's stomach. Before Shir pulled the knife from the body, he felt warm blood pouring from the deep wound.

As Shir made his move toward his target, Hossein brought his own right hand around. He had removed the Korth automatic handgun from his back pocket and fired two rounds into the chest area of the second constable. The explosions rang loudly inside the building.

The second constable, who had been looking at his partner, had no time to react. He staggered backward several steps from the impact of the two powerful bullets, and then his legs collapsed. He lay on the concrete floor as his lifeblood flowed from his body and pooled around his chest, soaking into his uniform. Hossein walked over to the officer in time to see life leave his eyes.

He ignored the lifeless eyes staring up at him and looked over to Shir and the second constable. The officer took almost a minute to die. Shir quickened his death by shoving the knife into the officer a second time while holding the man's body against the doorframe. When he could not feel a heartbeat, he removed the knife for the second time and allowed the body to slide down the doorframe to the building floor.

Shir Mohammad allowed his right hand, still holding the knife, to drop to his side as he stepped back from his victim. He sucked in deep breaths of air and tried to calm down. This was his first kill.

Hossein stepped up to his partner and laid his hand on Shir's shoulder. "Good work. You distracted them long enough for me to get to my weapon."

Shir's breathing was slowing down. He used his left hand to run his fingers through his hair to help release the tension inside his body. In doing so, he knocked off his Thames Water Utility uniform hat.

"I was concentrating on our work. I never heard their vehicle approach. I certainly was scared, brother."

Hossein reassured his partner. "We both performed well. The Elder would have been proud of us."

He stepped away from Shir and turned to look for where they could dispose of the bodies. "Let's move the bodies against the wall past the overhead door. They will be out of our way."

Shir nodded in agreement. He wiped the blood off his knife and slowly closed the blade back into the handle. He slipped the knife back into his right front pants pocket.

Each man grabbed one of the constables under the arms and pulled them roughly away from the doorway and over to the wall. Without any regard for the bodies, they simply released their grips and allowed the bodies to fall to the floor.

Hossein looked back toward the doorway. There were still six barrels to roll over to the catwalk where the other six now stood. "Let's get the access cover off and start to transfer the powder into the reservoir. Once we've emptied the first six barrels, we can roll the second group over and finish this job."

Shir nodded, hurried over to the catwalk, and crossed to the middle where the access cover was located. He opened the door built into the sidewall of the catwalk and swung it around, out of his way.

The square, heavy steel access plate, roughly twenty-four inches in diameter, was held in place by a series of large machine bolts located every six inches. Along the edge of the access cover, they could see the black gasket that sealed the panel where the two pieces of steel came together.

The tighten bolts were galvanized to prevent rusting. It would take a large wrench to loosen the bolts and remove the access cover. He walked off the catwalk to his tool bag next to the edge of the pit. He opened the bag and saw the Uzi machine gun and the explosive device placed inside by Iraj Malek-Mohammadi. The tool he was looking for was not inside. He remembered there was another tool bag with the equipment to remove the bolts.

While Hossein was removing the lids from the first six barrels, Shir hurried outside to the van. He returned a minute later with the second tool bag. After setting it down next to the bag containing the weapon and bomb, he opened the second bag and located his set of combination wrenches. The hand tool received its name because it had an open end and a closed end. The open end allowed the wrench to slip around the bolt head, while the closed end slipped over the bolt head and provided a stronger grip onto the bolt head.

Shir grabbed the largest wrench in the set that ranged from 6.35 mm, or a quarter inch, to 28.575 mm, or one and a quarter inches. He took the wrench and tried to place the closed end over the bolt head. It would not fit. He reversed the wrench to try to slip the open end around the bolt head. Again no luck. He walked off the catwalk.

Hossein looked up from his work. "What is the problem?"

Shir held out the combination wrench. "It's too small. I will need to use the pipe wrench. I only hope it's large enough."

He let the combination wrench slipped from his hand to the floor beside the tool bag. He regretted the loud clanging noise as he reached inside for the other wrench. Being the largest item, it had settled on the bottom of the tool bag. Working his fingers among the other tools, he grabbed the heavier straight pipe wrench and pulled it out into the light.

Every plumber in the world had a similar tool. Plumbers argued over whether the cast-iron or aluminum bodies were best. Most sided with the cast-iron as the strongest, although the lighter-weight aluminum would remain rust-free. The wrench came in lengths as short as six inches, or eighteen centimeters, and as long as sixty inches, or 152 centimeters.

Shir's model was the cast-iron style with an I-beam handle and a full floating forged steel hook jaw with a line of teeth for gripping power. The jaw width would adjust for different sizes by way of a round steel ring enclosed into the back of the I-beam handle, which would thread onto the hook jaw, causing the jaw to open and close.

Shir looked at the fourteen-inch wrench. It had a maximum jaw opening of two inches, large enough to wrap around the bolt heads. He walked back onto the catwalk to the chest-high access cover. He placed the new wrench on the first bolt head and adjusted the ring to close the jaw tightly around the bolt head. Once satisfied with the wrench, he gave the handle a counterclockwise pull to twist the bolt loose.

Nothing moved. Shir readjusted his body for better leverage and applied more pressure to the handle. The bolt still would not move.

He removed the wrench and moved it to a different angle that would allow him to apply his arms and shoulder muscles combined with his body weight to force the bolt to move. For the third time, he applied all of his strength and body weight against the handle. Once again, he was unable to move the bolt.

Hossein could hear Shir grunting in his efforts to remove the first bolt. Seeing his failure, he walked onto the catwalk and stood next to Shir. "Here, let me try it."

The two men changed positions, and Shir handed the wrench to Hossein. The leader placed the wrench on the same bolt, and with all the strength and determination he possessed, he tried to twist the first bolt. Grunting from the strain, his success was the same as Shir's. The bolt would not move.

Cursing in his native language, Hossein wanted to throw the wrench across the open floor space but instead calmed himself and tried to determine what they needed to do.

Shir spoke first. "Alone the wrench is too small. We need to find a length of pipe that will fit over the handle to increase our leverage."

Hossein nodded in agreement. "Surely there must be a length of pipe around here that we can use. Let's look and see what we can find."

Chapter 54

Honor Oak
Thursday, December 3, 2015
8:30 p.m.

Traffic was thinning slightly after the combination of rush-hour congestion and the effects of the attack on Trafalgar Square. Randy Fisher, Marion Bellwood, and Charlie Booker finally broke free of the congested area around Scotland Yard and pointed their rented Ford Focus in the direction suggested by the window-mounted GPS system.

As they made their way toward the fourteen locations of the Thames Water Ring Main, Phillip Booker kept Marion updated on all the other American security teams.

Marion's men were bored waiting at the embassy. Most had been there since arriving on Sunday and forced to stay close to the embassy and their cell phones in case the situation changed. Having to watch helplessly as the attack went down on Trafalgar Square added to their frustration. Phillip Booker argued for the need to send two-man teams to each location. Moreover, the sudden need for more transportation than was available for the extra security agents only made things worse.

Marion, realizing the need, reached out to the US ambassador and permanent deputy chief of mission, briefly discussed the plan, and request the embassy loan his men additional vehicles and security personnel. With the combination of Marion's extra men plus security personnel already assigned to the embassy, they were able to mount two-man teams for each location.

Constance Langhorne and Phillip Booker were ready to assign targets and locations by the time the American security teams from the embassy were finally ready to move out. Agents quickly programmed the locations into the GPS equipment inside each car.

The GPS in the car conveying Randy and his friends finally brought them to the outskirts of Honor Oak. Traffic was almost nonexistent. Most of the British population huddled on the sofas in their living rooms watching the reports coming in from Trafalgar Square.

They arrived at the golf course via the same streets used by the terrorists and entered the parking lot, with the clubhouse on their right and the equipment sheds to their left. Charlie allowed the car to coast to a stop, and they all rolled down their windows to listen for any noises in the damp night air.

Randy was in the back seat and slid across to the passenger side to look among the buildings toward the reservoir. He thought there was a light coming across the open fairway.

"Kill your headlights, Charlie."

The agent complied. They sat in the dark. Only a few security lights mounted on wood poles some distance away provided any illumination. The light Randy had seen now showed brightly in the distance. It was still too dark to make out the golf course fairways.

Off to both sides through the stands of trees, they could see more lights from the homes along the edge of the golf course, but only a single light shone from the huge black area in the center of the fairways.

"That must be the pump house building over the reservoir," Charlie whispered. "How far away do you estimate it to be? I'm guessing about seven hundred feet."

Marion still had his cell phone out. He quietly informed Phillip Booker they were going silent. He would call him back once they determined if the terrorists were at the location. Ending the call, his used his left hand to point toward the outer sheds. "Move the car over to the equipment buildings, where we won't be seen by anyone inside the pump house."

Charlie guided the car by the weak lights from the housing developments in the distance. The overnight sky was completely black; rain was again threatening to fall. The heat from inside the car quickly dissipated as cold air poured through the open windows. Randy felt a shiver run up his back. He was not sure if it was the cold night air or fear of what they might discover.

The three men climbed out of the car and walked through the wet grass to the end of the first building to get a clear view of the pump house. The light from the building's windows illuminated the nearby grounds but did not project away from the building more than a few meters.

"No van or any other cars," Randy said.

Marion said, "I think the overhead photo I saw showed a loading dock on the other side of the building."

Randy said, "We need to move closer."

He started to take a step forward but Marion grabbed his arm. "Where the hell do you think you're going?"

Randy roughly pulled his coat free of Marion's grip. "I'm going to walk over there to see what is going on inside the pump house."

Randy could barely see Marion shaking his head. "Oh, no you're not. You are a United States senator and have no business getting involved with what might be a dangerous situation. You are staying right here. Reader and I will check out the pump house. Besides, you're not even armed. We already know these bastards are not afraid to kill anybody."

Randy looked from his friend to Charlie, but Marion was not having any of it. "Don't look to Charlie for help. He works for me."

Charlie's bright white teeth shone between his thick lips in the dark. "Sorry, Senator, but you've got to sit this one out."

Randy knew they were right, but he hated to stand on the sidelines while others walked into harm's way. "All right … all right. Let's move over to the farthest building to get a better angle on the other side of the pump house. I can watch you from there and call for any help."

Marion spoke quietly. "Agreed, but you stay put and out of sight. I don't want your silhouette showing up and the wrong person seeing you."

The three men retraced their steps back toward the front of the buildings and moved west to the last of the equipment sheds. The largest building held the tractors and larger mowers used for grass cutting. They worked their way to the far side and then moved along the building until they reach the end facing the golf course fairways.

From this angle, it looked like there were two vehicles parked near the loading dock. No sight of any people.

Randy's eyesight was near perfect, but he could not see any lettering or logos on the cars through the dark night. Just as he spoke, heavy raindrops hit the top of his bare head. Marion was also hatless. Charlie pulled his wood cap down to cover the tops of his ears.

Nobody could see Randy shaking his head. "I can't make anything out on those cars."

Marion's voice came back in a whisper. "We need to get closer. Charlie, you circle farther to the west and make your approach to come in directly at the cars. I will work my way in from here to the building, away from the door, and circle around to the cars from the other side. We'll meet up and hit the door into the pump house together." Marion turned to Randy. "If the shit hits the fan, you call for help."

Randy bobbed his head reluctantly and muttered his acceptance of Marion's instruction.

Charlie quietly stepped away from the building, and Marion started to make his way toward the pump house. From seven hundred feet away, it would take Marion less time than Charlie. The black agent needed to take a longer curved path to come in from a different direction.

Marion intended to walk his path to the building in two sections. He would quietly make about half the distance and then wait until Charlie had moved west and was in a position to make a straight line to the pump house. Once they were able to coordinate their arrival together, he would begin the second part of his approach.

Charlie moved away from the building, leaving Randy to watch alone as the two men began their approach. Charlie had covered about twenty-five or thirty feet when he approached a medium-size tractor. In the dark in heavier rain that was falling again, he could make out the silhouette. The front tires faced the clubhouse. The top of the rear tires appeared to be about chest height. He paused at the first front tire, accessed his progress, and took a good look at the pump house. He could not detect any motion from inside the building, but he was still a long way off.

He started to move toward the rear tire on his side of the tractor and only took his eyes away from the pump house to walk around the rear of the tractor. Watching the pump house, his eyes adjusted to the light from the interior. When he looked away, his eyes were unaccustomed to the darkness and he failed to see the brush hog attached to the hydraulic lift arms of the tractor. He stepped on the mover's surface, which enclosed the two rotating blades. He misjudged the distance and tripped forward. As he tried to shift his right foot, the leg slipped inside the right hydraulic lift arm of the tractor. He fell forward, forcing his body weight against the ankle. The snapping of his right anklebone reached Randy's ears by the storage shed.

Charlie lost his grip on his Glock G-19 9 mm automatic weapon and fell to the side of the mower, landing hard on the ground. When he came to a hard stop, he could not prevent a grown of pain from escaping between his clenched teeth.

Marion Bellwood heard the sounds of Charlie's weapon glancing off the mower's side shield and the thump of his body hitting the ground. The rainfall helped to muffle the metallic sound. He could only hope no one inside the building had heard.

He watched as Randy's dark silhouette moved out from the shelter of the building and knelt down next to Charlie Reader. From his position, the men's shapes blended into one. At least twenty or thirty seconds passed before a dark figure rose from the ground and moved on to make the turn toward the pump house. From his distance, Marion could not tell if the moving figure was Charlie Reader or Randy Fisher.

He cursed under his breath but waited until the man was in position. As he saw the figure begin the next part of his journey, Marion rose from his kneeling position and started the second part of his approach to the pump house.

Chapter 55

Honor Oak
Thursday, December 3, 2015
8:45 p.m.

They heard a strange noise. Hossein Rahim Bonab and Shir Mohammad Moez Ardalan both stopped their work to look toward the open door toward the sound coming from the darkness outside.

They had found a length of pipe large enough in diameter to slip over the I-beam handle of the pipe wrench. Working together, they could finally apply enough pressure to move the bolt heads. The work progressed slowly; they were still behind Hossein's schedule. They had removed six of the machine bolts but still had many more bolts to loosen and remove. They slowly removed the extra length of pipe from the pipe wrench handle and stepped away from their work.

Both men stepped off the catwalk. Hossein laid the length of pipe down on the floor and picked up his Uzi machine gun. Shir laid the pipe wrench on top of one of the plastic barrels and looked for his tool bag. It was several steps away. He moved quietly around the barrels, opened the bag, and removed the Korth handgun.

Hossein turned to Shir and gestured for Shir was to take cover behind the barrels. Hossein planned to cross the open space and take a position on the other side of the doorway. If anyone came in, the intruder would be in a deadly crossfire.

Shir moved two steps back behind the six barrels. The thick powder packed inside would act as a perfect shield for his body. Hossein moved close to the wall and slowly worked his way toward the doorway. He stopped and kneeled down to listen for any sound of approaching footsteps but could only hear the rain hitting the roof tops of their van and the dead constables' vehicle. Maybe Mohammad and the others had finally made it to the pump house.

He waited for an internal count of thirty and then leaped from his position. He moved quickly past the doorway and spun around to take a new position by the constables' bodies. He waited to see who might be coming through the door.

Randy Fisher saw a man scamper across the open doorway in a crouched position. The light inside the building gave him good visibility. He was certain the man held a weapon against his body. The terrorists at Trafalgar Square had Uzi machine guns. He had to assume the man had the same type of weapon. He looked for Marion, but his friend was still around the corner, out of sight. Marion could not have observed the armed man from his position.

From the equipment shed, Randy had both seen and heard Charlie fall to the ground behind the tractor. He had crossed the open ground and knelt down next to the stricken agent. Charlie held his bent knee up next to his chest, trying not to cry out from the pain. Randy had bent down next to Charlie's ear and only whispered one word. "Broken?"

Charlie had simply nodded. As he tried to get up from the ground, his facial muscles pulled into a grimace of pain. Randy gave the downed agent a gentle grip on the shoulder and looked for the lost handgun. Locating the weapon in the wet grass, he picked it up. From his training in the army and working as an auxiliary deputy, Randy was familiar with the Glock G-19 9 mm handgun. The rubber grip was wet but fit his hand, and he laid his right index finger alongside the trigger guard.

He checked the position of the safety. It was on, but he could move it with his thumb in less than a heartbeat. He carefully pulled the slide partway back to ensure there was a round in the chamber. In the available ambient light, he could see the shiny brass casing of the bullet. He felt the end of the clip, flush with the gun handle. He assumed the clip held the standard fifteen rounds.

He moved back toward Charlie and knelt down again next to the agent. "You're on the sideline now, my friend."

Without another word, he moved off in the direction outlined by Marion. He was about twenty feet from the van backed up to the steps when he saw a man move across the open doorway.

He stopped and checked again for Marion. His friend had arrived at the corner and was peeking around to see the car and van, checking for who was making the approach from the other direction. When Marion saw Randy Fisher approaching the building, he pulled back from the corner and leaned against the building. *Damn. Fisher is not supposed to be here.*

Marion held his 9 mm Smith & Wesson handgun in a two-handed grip close to his chest. He had carried the same weapon on field operations since he had first joined the CIA. He leaned out and watched Randy move around to the back of the police cruiser. Marion decided to make a move to the doorway and up the concrete steps. He needed to reach the building before Randy Fisher. He planned to stop just outside the pump house door.

Randy saw his friend heading toward the doorway, knowing a terrorist waited inside the building. He tried to wave Marion off. Marion's eyes stayed focused on the doorway and steps. He was looking away from Randy as he made the short run to the doorway. Randy knew the man who had crossed the open doorway could not be a police officer. Only armed British forces would carry a rifle or any other type of heavy weapon. Marion was walking into a trap.

Calling out a warning would alert the terrorist and maybe confuse Marion. Randy took the biggest risk of his life. He rose from his crouched position. Using his left hand to steady the weapon in his right hand, Randy aimed the handgun toward the closed overhead door. He fired off four rounds through and across the door, spacing the spread pattern of each round about a foot apart and just above the building floor.

Hossein was crouched down low to the floor on one knee, watching the agent approach the doorway. He was aiming his Uzi and applying pressure to the trigger when the bullets from another weapon came through the lightweight aluminum overhead door. The first two bullets hit the concrete floor, ricocheted across the pit, and embedded into the soft bricks of the far wall. Dust and small concrete chips caused him to pull the gun up and away from his target when his finger pulled the Uzi's trigger. As the machine gun fired bullets into the brick wall next to Marion's head, the last two bullets from Randy's weapon found a human target.

Marion instinctively pulled back from the doorway as the bullets chipped away pieces of the brick wall. He caught sight of the man who only a second before had trained the machine gun on his body. He took another quick look inside and moved to check the status of the terrorist. He could see the man was down on the floor, lying on his right side. He sightless eyes were looking back at Marion. A lifeless right hand with the index finger still inside the trigger guard gripped the Uzi.

Marion heard a handgun discharge to his left and felt a stinging pain high on his left arm. He quickly pulled back to safety, but he lost his balance and tumbled down the concrete steps.

Randy sprang forward, trying to reach his friend, but not before Marion's head struck the edge of the bottom concrete step. In the light shining through the open doorway, he could see his friend's closed eyes. He reached Marion and felt for a pulse. It was regular and strong. Marion was only stunned but out of action for a while.

He stepped over Marion's body and leaned against the doorframe. Inside to his right was the body of the man who had hit him from behind on the Jubilee Bridge. Beyond the body of the terrorist were the bodies of two constables. No doubt, they belonged to the police cruiser. To his immediate left and just inside the door a few feet away were six yellow plastic barrels. Five were standing on end; one still lay on its side. He reached to move them, but their heaviness made that impossible with only one hand. They would make good protection, he thought.

He felt cold rainwater run down the inside of his coat collar. With the back of his left hand, he wiped water off his forehead and out of his eyes. He stole a quick look inside the building to his left and caught sight of another man hiding behind more yellow plastic barrels.

He saw movement from the terrorist and pulled back just in time. A bullet clipped the wall only a few inches from his head. He took a moment to calm down and then shouted into the doorway. "It's over. Your friend is dead. I have more help on the way. It will only be a few more minutes until British SAS troops will be here. They will not give you a chance to surrender. They will simply storm the building with more weapons than you could possibly handle and they will kill you. If you surrender now, you might live past this day."

Randy was hoping Charlie had been able to use his cell phone to call for backup support. He did not want to have to take this man alone, and he wanted him alive. They needed whatever information he possessed about this attack and the attack three years ago in South Carolina.

A voice inside the building interrupted his thoughts. "You are the American? You are the senator who killed my brother?"

Randy did not like the tone of voice. It did not sound like someone debating whether to surrender. He decided not to answer the question. "You only have a few minutes before my backup arrives. Surrender now and you will get a fair trial."

A laugh came from behind the plastic barrels. "If you are here, American, then my friends at the square must have failed, but I bet they took many lives with them. There will be no fair trial for me. I will be judged by Allah. He will approve of my actions by how many of his enemies I can take with me."

Randy called back, "Surely you don't want to die needlessly like this."

When the voice spoke again, the words sent a chilling tremor up Randy's spine. "I only wish that I had lived to see the next attack on your precious American soil. I can promise you they will not fail like my brother. They will destroy much more than your precious little state in America. They will kill millions of Americans."

Randy thought he could hear other noises inside the building. A new though took over his mind. Was the terrorist stalling? Attempting to keep Randy from attempting to enter the building?

He took a quick look through the doorway back toward the terrorist. The yellow barrels inside the doorway gave him an idea. He kept his body low and took two long steps through the doorway. As he moved, he kept his eyes fastened on his target near the end of the building. Just as he ducked down behind the barrels for protection, he caught a glimpse of the terrorist pulling a brown canvas tool bag back behind the barrels.

Randy crouched behind his own upright barrels, thinking fast. The terrorist in the center of Trafalgar Square was carrying the same type of tool bag to hold the explosive device. *Does this bag also hold a bomb?*

Randy looked back toward Marion. His friend was moaning; he would not be any help in the next five or ten minutes. Randy did not feel he could wait that long.

He spotted several broken bricks lying on the floor next to the doorway. They must have been part of the outer wall of the pump house at one time. He selected the largest. It was about two-thirds the size of a full brick. He tried to shift his position. He wanted to use the brick as a diversion, but he was right-handed and needed to use it to hold the Glock. He would have to use his left hand to throw the brick back toward his left to divert the terrorist's attention. However, the angle was all wrong.

Randy laid the brick down and checked again around his area. One of the yellow barrels was on its side. He reached to try to shift the standing barrel next to him. It would not budge. It was too heavy.

He looked again at the barrel on its side. Of the six barrels, it was the only one on its side. If he could move two of the upright barrels just enough, he could move between them to the barrel on its side. Its path was directly toward where the other six barrels were protecting the terrorist. Randy could see tracks in the thin dust coating on the floor from when the other barrels had rolled across the floor.

He shifted to lean his back against the doorframe and placed both feet against the bottom of the upright barrel on the right end. Using his leg muscles, he applied force against the barrel, trying to push it farther to the side. At first, the barrel would not budge. He shifted his body slightly to bring it more in line with the barrel and reset his feet. Once again, he exerted force against the barrel. This time it shifted. He reset his feet again and shoved. The barrel moved at least a full foot and provided part of the space he needed to get to the barrel on its side.

He moved to place his feet against the second upright barrel. After several attempts, he was able to slide it to the right about eighteen inches. When he pulled back to the doorway, there were two barrels to the right of the barrel on its side and three more standing upright to the left, providing a wall of protection.

He positioned his back against the other side of the doorframe, this time facing where the terrorist was hiding. He placed both feet against the top of the barrel on its side and slid down low so he could bend his knees to propel the barrel across the floor. When he was ready, he checked his weapon one last time. He had to assume there were only eleven bullets left in the gun.

He pulled several breaths deep into his lungs, visualizing what he wanted to achieve with the barrel. Summing up every ounce of strength, he reached deeply within himself and gave out the loudest yell possible. With every fiber in his body, he shot his legs out and sent the barrel rolling across the floor.

The barrel rolled faster than he could have hoped. It crossed the open space, staying on target for the terrorist stooped down behind his own barricade. Randy quickly rolled to his left and rose to kneel behind the three upright barrels.

Shir Mohammad heard the yell and thought the British SAS was charging the building. He had been trying to reach the detonator with his left hand, but the bomb was in the bottom of the canvas tool bag under his Uzi. From the corner of his eyes, he saw something moving in his direction. He rose from behind his wall of barrels and fired at the moving target. Six or seven times his fingers pulled the trigger of his weapon as he tried to kill his enemy. The building filled with noise and smoke from the multiple gun blasts swirled heavily around his body, making it difficult to see his target.

He stood, aiming the gun toward the barrel. It came to a stop about four feet in front of him. He could not believe it was one of their own barrels and not a British soldier. He looked up to see the American holding his own weapon, both hands resting on top of one of the upright barrels. He saw the determination in the eyes staring toward him across the open space. There was no lack of conviction in the voice.

"Make the slightest move and I will kill you. Drop the weapon now."

Shir took a moment to gauge the look in the eyes. This man was responsible for his brother's death. In all the public records he had read of the account, the man had claimed his brother had fallen on his own knife and killed himself. This American had never actually killed before.

Shir looked at Hossein lying on the floor and then at the two constables. He remembered how it felt to jam the knife into the soft body of the one he had killed. He looked back at the American. A smile formed on his lips as he started to bring the gun up. He would kill this American just as easily. The hand with the gun had moved only an inch when two explosions from one gun filled the pump house once again.

Chapter 56

Washington, DC
Friday, December 4, 2015
6:00 a.m.

Randy Fisher felt the wheels of the British Gulfstream jet touch down on the runway at Dulles International Airport. He had dropped into a deep slumber almost immediately upon takeoff from Heathrow and used the transatlantic flight to catch up on a lot of lost sleep. As the only passenger on the Gulfstream provided as a courtesy by the British government for services rendered, he had been no trouble for the two flight attendants.

In Honor Oak, Charlie Booker had called for backup as soon as he could get his cell phone out of his back pocket. His call to Constance Langhorne had resulted in a slew of emergency vehicles arriving on the scene. Upon inspection of the open barrels, another call when out for an emergency HAZMAT team that closed off the building and started their own special investigation.

Marion and Charlie received transport by ambulance to Kingston Hospital in southeastern London. A lightweight plastic boot now enclosed Charlie's broken ankle. The bullet fired from Shir Mohammad's gun had grazed the back of Marion's left shoulder, deeply grooving his skin. The bleeding had been heavy but the wound was not serious. He also had a large lump on the back of his head where it had struck the concrete steps after his backward tumble. He was kept overnight for observation.

A hospital staff member provided Randy with a clean shirt. His had been soaked with rain and sweat. While he waited for the doctors to examine and treat Marion and Charlie, he reflected on his gun battle with the two terrorists.

He had never killed a man before, much less two in as few minutes. His hands shook as he waited in the cold rain for backup support and a medical team to attend his friends. During the ride to the hospital in the back of the ambulance, Marion assured his friend the tremor was only nerves and adrenaline. It would all go away in a short time.

Randy had sat in Marion's hospital room listening to the cell phone conversation between Marion and Marci Bellwood. His friend tried to explain to his wife why he would be away for a few more days. When the call was finished, Randy had to bring up the subject of Marion's wounds. "It seems I might have evened the score today. You've been reminding me for years how you saved my life twenty-some years ago in Germany."

"All right, MP. We are even. Maybe I still own you one. You took out two bad guys today." He saw Randy's face darken as the younger man remembered the deaths only a few hours earlier. "You all right with what happened tonight? It's not every day you face a terrorist with guns and a bomb."

Randy looked at his hands. The shaking had finally stopped. "I'm fine, but I'm also worried by that man's last words. He said there would be another attempt to destroy a large part of the United States. I wanted to capture him alive—any of them, for that matter. Now we have five dead terrorists and no leads."

"Whoa, big guy," Marion said. "We've got lots of leads to follow. We will have forensic evidence from the five terrorists, fingerprints, and DNA. The VIN numbers from the vans led the British to the rug company. The two buildings will be filled with evidence." He looked over at Charlie. "What have I missed, Charlie?"

Charlie Reader sat in a chair near the foot of the bed, his damaged ankle stretched out in front of him. "The SAS boys who came to the pump house told me those handguns were very expensive. They can trace each serial number back to the original owners. Someone with a lot of money purchased those guns, and we always follow the money."

"Right," Marion said as he shifted his body into a more comfortable position. "Listen, MP. We have plenty of evidence to follow. It might not happen tomorrow, but we are a lot closer to finding out who was behind today's attack in London and our own incident three years ago. Believe me. We will find out who did this."

There was a light tap on the door, and Constance Langhorne walked in, followed by Deputy Commissioner Shepard. Constance smiled at all three men before she wrapped her arms around Charlie Reader's wide shoulders and planted a fat kiss on his forehead.

DC Shepard smiled but kept his enthusiasm at a more controlled level. "Well now. You all look almost first rate. I thought you would like a recap of what we have learned to date. Our first examination of the rug company has convinced us there were only five terrorists in the group. So with your two at Honor Oak, we got the lot. There are tons of material and papers to go through at the rug company, so it will be some time before we can learn everything possible. However, I can assure you we will put a lot of people into the effort."

Marion broke into DC Shepard's recap. "I assume whatever you find will be fully shared with my agency?"

Shepard nodded. "Absolutely. You have my word on that."

Randy asked the biggest question on his mind. "What was the powder in the barrels?"

Shepard's expression darkened somewhat. "The powder is still being analyzed by our medico people, but it appears to contain some sort of protozoa that at normal strength can cause serious gastrointestinal illness. Our people are running tests, but they seem to think the protozoa could have caused many people to get very sick. Maybe even die. We will have more information in a few days. Thanks to the efforts of you three men, we are very glad the drinking water for 800,000 Londoners was not contaminated. If the terrorists had been successful in poisoning the drinking water, we might have not determined the cause until hundreds or possibly thousands of people got sick or died. Then we would have faced the problem of preventing people from using the contaminated water and cleaning the poison from the reservoir."

Constance looked at Charlie and then Marion and Randy. "You blokes are big heroes. Wait until my mum hears that my Charlie drove the car to the reservoir."

Charlie laughed. "Yeah, and fell flat on his face."

Randy spoke up next. "I think it would be better for all if our involvement in this affair was kept quiet. I think my CIA friend here would agree."

Marion was already nodding. "Yes. I think keeping this under wraps for now is best. I'll have to inform my superiors in Washington, but the less said the better."

Shepard agreed. "We will try to keep information of your involvement out of the hands of the press both here and abroad. However, Mr. Fisher, I know of one special person already notified of your efforts in today's activities. She has requested your presence before you leave the country."

Randy's reminiscences of what had happened a few hours later were interrupted by the flight attendant's normal "Welcome to Washington" speech. He thought it was amusing, since he was the only passenger on the flight.

The meeting with the Queen had taken place shortly before his Met driver whisked him away to the airport. She had smiled and offered her hand, which he had softly taken within his own. They spoke for almost a quarter hour, in which time she asked if Randy would be happy to return to America and his wife Annie. Randy had been surprised someone had taken the time to learn about Annie, and he thanked the Queen for her inquiry. "I'm surprised with all the chaos over the last few hours that your staff was able to take the time to learn about my family."

The Queen had smiled, and Randy saw a little twinkle in her eye. "We like to keep track of foreigners who will soon rise to high positions."

The plane came to a stop in a VIP area away from the main concourse buildings. One of the flight attendants released the exit door lock and prepared to lower the door that converted to a set of stairs for leaving the plane. Waiting for the passenger door to open, Randy thought about the number of e-mails he had received in the last twelve hours. Most had been from Sally LaSalle, informing her boss the filibuster was taking an ugly turn. Senators were tired of the whole mess, and name-calling was becoming common. She sent her last e-mail shortly before Randy got on his plane. Only the subject line was filled in. ***"When are you coming back to the Senate?"***

Randy had sent a short reply that he was boarding a jet for Washington. He asked Sally to call Annie to update him with his new schedule. He had talked with her only briefly from the hospital, promising to provide more details when he got home.

The cabin door finally opened, and Randy walked down the stairway. He noticed a black limousine pulling up near the bottom of the steps. The back door opened, and Annie Fisher stepped out and ran up to the stairway to greet her husband. After a long hug and kiss, she broke away from his strong grip. Her face beamed with delight. "Well, it's about time the hero returns home."

Randy smiled back and gave her another hug. He broke away as a tall man stepped out of the car. He wanted to ask Annie what she meant by the hero returning, but it would have to wait until they were alone.

He recognized the British ambassador to the United States. "Ambassador Hordern. It is a pleasure to have you meet me here at the airport. Thanks for bringing Annie along."

Michael Hordern was in his third year as the British government's highest-ranking representative in Washington. His relationship with the Miller government was excellent. The tall sixty-two-year-old man was slender and had a full head of white hair.

"It's my great pleasure, Senator Fisher. After all, we cannot have you arriving this early at the airport without several friendly faces to greet you. I received a call from the prime minister himself, asking that I arrange this meeting with England's newest hero."

Randy was confused. How could they know so much about his small part in the terrorist plot?

Seeing his confused look Ambassador Hordern opened a large folded piece of paper. "This is a copy off the embassy printer. It's the front page of an early morning edition of the *Times*."

The headline told Randy all he needed to know.

AMERICAN SENATOR HELPS SCOTLAND YARD FOIL TERRORISTS ULTIMATE TARGET

Randy quickly scanned the first few lines. It seemed Jasmine Ainsworth, the CNN reporter, had been closely watching Scotland Yard and had seen Randy and his friends leave the headquarters' building. They had not been able to follow their car, but the reporter had been able to put together pieces of information, along with several quotes from unnamed sources.

Annie smiled up at her husband as she slowly shook her head. "Just couldn't keep your head down over there, right?"

Chapter 57
Washington, DC
Friday, December 4, 2015
8:15 a.m.

United States Senator John Laird had replaced Roberta Hanley and was just starting his speech to hold the Senate floor for the next four hours. He felt deeply in his tired body that today the Senate would vote to break the filibuster and then vote again to allow the Fair Share Bill to go to the Finance Committee. They had held off the vote for more than four days, but the three senators were tired, and the others senators wanted the filibuster to end.

He stopped to collect his thoughts and was about to begin again when he felt someone softly take hold of his left arm above the elbow. He turned to find his friend Randy Fisher standing in the aisle with a warm smile on his face.

Randy leaned in to whisper in John's ear. "Tired, John?"

John gave a little snort and a quiet laugh. "Just a little. I read in the papers you've been very busy yourself the last few days."

Randy just smiled back again and stepped over to his bench seat across the aisle from the Republican. He picked up the copy of the Corporate America Fair Share Tax Bill that had been lying on his desk since Monday morning. He gave the cover a quick glance and sat down in his seat.

As Senator Laird resumed his speech to hold the Senate floor, Randy thought about the last forty-five minutes. He felt better now that he had taken a shower, shaved, and was in a clean suit. He had received an update from Sally LaSalle, Brad Guilliams, and Renee Stockli in his office and then met with Tom Evans and a few other senators in the majority leader's office next to the Senate chambers. Shelba Mace from North Carolina was a good friend. Margaret Anderson of Iowa chaired the Senate Foreign Relations Committee, Amy Carlson was the junior senator from Tom's state of California, and Senator Timothy Richards was chairman of the Senate Finance Committee.

After fending off their questions about the events in London, Randy was finally able to ask a few questions of his own.

"I assume nobody in this room wants to see this Fair Share Bill go to Tim's committee? Am I correct in my assumption?"

Richards sat in a smooth leather chair in the left corner of the office behind Tom's desk. The majority leader sat at his desk, and the three women were sharing a couch against the wall to Tom's right. Randy had refused the chair in front of Tom's desk and was pacing the room. It felt good to be walking around the familiar office of the majority leader after being cramped inside the Scotland Yard building for almost three days, followed by a six-hour flight from London. He was anxious to end the filibuster and have the bill killed. After that, he would enjoy a long three-day weekend with his aunt Frances, who had stayed with Annie until Randy returned from London.

Senator Richards spoke for the group. "Hell … None of us in this room wants to see this bill come to my committee. I do not even think most of the House Republicans who voted to pass it were really in favor of the dang thing. They were just afraid to go up against the president. His White House drum beaters did a real number to build up support for the bill from the very beginning."

Shelba Mace voiced her opinion. "The latest polls show the public is tired of the filibuster, but they are starting to listen to the three Davids. Support for the bill is slipping."

Anderson leaned forward on the end of the couch closest to Tom's desk to look at Senator Mace. "When the president didn't finish his bus tour in Virginia, the steam seemed to go out of their engine. I think we can get this thing killed today."

Randy looked at the majority leader. "Tom, you've been quiet in the Senate and in the news about the bill. If we can get the three Republican senators to allow a vote, do we have the support in the Senate to stop the bill?"

The six-foot five-inch Democratic presidential candidate leaned back in his chair to stretch. The former pro basketball star normally tipped the scales at 285 pounds but to improve his public image had recently gone on a diet and exercise program. Over the last four months, he had dropped forty-five pounds. He was almost back to his playing weight. He was sixty-three years of age and still sported blond hair with very little gray mixed in. He shifted forward to lean against the edge of his desk. "I've tried to keep presidential politics out of this, but it's time to end the filibuster. Besides, I need to get back out on the campaign trail."

There was a light round of laughter from the friends in the room. Tom looked at Randy but spoke to the group. "We can end this today, but we have to get the three Davids to trust us. I have been waiting for Randy to get back from England because he has a close relationship with all three senators. Can you get the floor away from them, Randy?"

Randy was looking over Tom's wide shoulders out the window. "Who has the floor now?"

Mace answered for the group. "If they are still maintaining the same schedule, then John Laird will take over at eight o'clock."

Randy nodded. "I can work with John. He's a good man." He paused for a few moments and looked around the group. "A lot of the American public still supports this bill. We need to present a case that builds trust with the three Republican senators so they'll allow me to have the floor and at the same time change the public opinion about the bill." He paused again to organize his thoughts. "Here is what we are going to do."

Randy's thoughts about the earlier meeting in Tom's office were broken when Senator Doaks suddenly stood at his bench seat. In a voice still full of authority, he asked if Senator Laird would yield to a question.

Senator Laird stopped his speech and looked over at his fellow Republican. He was wary of another ploy by the minority leader to take the floor away.

Randy stood at his Senate seat across the aisle from John Laird. "Will Senator Laird yield to a question from a Democrat?"

A small smile appeared on John's tired face. "The senator yields for a question from his friend from South Carolina."

Randy turned slightly and observed the frown on Senator Doaks face as the minority leader sat down.

Randy turned back to Senator Laird. "Let me first apologize for my absence from the important work undertaken in the Senate Chamber. It was unavoidable."

He waited a moment and then asked the man across the aisle his question. "Senator Laird. I find myself siding with your position against the president's Fair Share bill. I must ask the good senator if you have an end-game strategy to stop this bill."

Randy remained standing while John Laird prepared his response. "Our strategy is to prevent this bill from progressing any further in the Senate. We are determine that this bill die right here on the Senate floor."

Randy nodded in understanding. "If I pledge my support to your cause, will you yield the floor to me?"

Laird was quiet for several moments. The Senate Chamber was very quiet, even the packed visitor gallery. "Will Senator Fisher pledge to continue the filibuster with Senators Saunders, Hanley, and myself until we have enough support?"

Randy smiled back at Senator Laird. "You have my pledge, sir. Therefore, I ask you, will you yield the floor to me?"

John Laird looked carefully at the Democratic senator. He wanted to bring Randy Fisher into their camp along with any other Senate members Fisher could bring with him. Randy had a strong reputation for bringing opposing sides together to a satisfactory agreement on many issues. He wished Saunders and Hanley were in the chamber. They would indicate their willingness to risk losing the Senate floor.

He waited almost a full sixty seconds. He looked around the Senate Chamber and up into the visitor gallery. The news reporters filled their seats. As he looked around the gallery, he noticed that very few seats were empty in the sections reserved for foreign dignitaries and the public.

He was about to look back to Senator Fisher when a familiar face in the foreign dignitary section caught his attention. He had to look twice to make sure the smiling face of Annie Fisher was looking down at him. Annie was sitting next to Ambassador Hordern; she gave a very small wave of her hand. That helped to make up his mind.

"The senator yields the floor to Senator Randy Fisher."

Gasp, groans, moans, and applause broke out around the chamber and up in the gallery. The president pro tem slammed the gavel down several times to restore order as John Laird gratefully sat down in his bench seat. Thinking quickly, he summoned a page girl standing at the back of the Senate to come to his desk. He whispered a few words into her ear, and she turned quickly for the closest exit door from the chamber.

Randy Fisher waited until the noise level in the chamber returned to normal. He took the time to look around the chamber and up into the gallery. He was happily surprised to see Annie and his aunt Frances sitting next to the British ambassador. He sent them a wink and looked back at the senators around the chamber.

A quorum was required to conduct business, and the Senate leaders had worked out a schedule to maintain the required number of senators inside the Senate Chamber during the filibuster. However, as planned by the group in Tom Evans's office, more members were slowly making their way into the chamber. Randy was about to speak when he noticed Senator Hanley make her entrance back into the chamber. She had only left a few minutes ago. She stopped briefly to speak to Senator Laird and then moved over to her own seat.

"Thank you, Senator Laird. I can appreciate the hard work you, Senators Hanley, and Saunders have done over the past several days. To take on a bill submitted by the White House and approved by the House of Representatives by a large majority is no easy task. To take on a bill that has received a high favorability rating from the American public is not done without a lot of forethought.

"I have to ask the members of the Senate why this bill is necessary. Why is it important to the president to force American companies to pay more taxes via this particular method?"

Randy waited for a few moments; he noticed more senators walking into the chamber.

In the White House, presidential press secretary Alison Warden hurried into the Oval Office. The president and his chief of staff were receiving an update from the director of national intelligence about the terrorist attack in London.

"Mr. President. Senator Laird had yielded the floor of the Senate."

Miller sighed with relief. "Well, it's about time. Now Doaks can move the bill to the Senate Finance Committee."

Alison shook her head. "I'm sorry, sir. Senator Laird turned the floor over to Senator Fisher."

"What?" He turned to the DNI. "You just told me Fisher was at the water reservoir south of London. How the hell can he be on the floor of the Senate?"

The president did not wait for a reply. "Turn the television on to C-SPAN. Let's see what that little bastard is up to now."

Alison picked up the television remote and pressed the power button. The television's tuner was already set to C-SPAN and the Senate Chamber. The screen quickly showed them the floor of the Senate. They could hear Senator Fisher talking.

Randy Fisher was listing reasons why the president was behind this bill. "We know the president is required to reveal his campaign finance fund balances. He had a sizeable war chest already in the bank for his reelection campaign. What he doesn't have in the bank is votes."

Randy paused briefly. "How do you move your image more toward the center of the political spectrum and draw more votes from the majority of the American voters?

"How about passing a bill to force big business to pay more taxes? Every American who pays their fair share of taxes wants to hear that someone has finally put their thumb down on big business. Yes, that will bring in the votes for the president next November. That will get him another four years in office."

In the Oval Office Harold Miller was red-faced with anger. "I'll bury that son of a bitch if it's the last thing I ever do."

Fisher was holding up his copy of the Corporate America Fair Share Tax Bill. "A lot of Americans want the big corporations to pay more taxes, but is this the right way to make it happen?"

Randy continued to hold up the ninety-seven-page bill. "This bill is like a patient with a compound leg fracture. The doctor, bandaging the wound, keeps applying more disinfectant. However, the leg needs real attention. It needs surgery to repair the damage, not more Band-Aids, and medical tape."

Randy paused again as he prepared to move into the next part of his speech. "American corporations didn't pass the current tax laws. No doubt, they had their paid lobbyists working behind the scenes trying to insert tax loopholes into the system, but they were not on the floor of the Senate or the House of Representatives. We were or the men and women who came before us."

Randy reached into the inside pocket of his suit and pulled out several sheets of papers prepared quickly by Renee Stockli and Brad Guilliams. "This is a summary of a bill entered into the House of Representatives nine years ago. It is a bill dealing with farm subsidies when the south and southwest of our country were struggling with the effects of the terrible drought that lasted almost two years. It was so bad the water level in Lake Lanier north of Atlanta was thirty-five feet below normal levels. The city was so pressed for water the mayor and council members were discussing having rolling water shutoffs around the city. In Texas, the water levels were so low they passed laws to replace plumbing fixtures with low-water-usage fixtures. The water utilities were paying people to replace high-usage toilets and faucets with models that used far less.

"Our farmers were no less hurt by the water shortage, so the House of Representatives took up this bill to provide financial relief so they could plant new crops the next year. It was a very favorable bill at the time since it assisted American farmers when they really needed it.

"But how many people know about the amendment added on to the bill here in the Senate and passed by the House? It had nothing to do with farm subsidies but with tax deductions for big business. It was very simple. Corporations could set up a subsidiary in a country with a low tax rate and claim a large percent of their expenses for manufacturing in that country. Their income would be higher in a country with a low tax rate structure. They'd save hundreds of thousands of dollars in taxes back here in the United States."

Randy paused to take a few breaths and then continued his remarks. "Kind of sneaky, I think. Something that politicians used to do years ago in back rooms filled with thick cigar smoke."

He flipped through the pages of the summary still in his hand. "I was wondering who would sponsor this bill. In the House of Representatives, several members supported the amendment, all of whom are still there except for Leonard Graham. He was the speaker of the House at the time. He retired several years ago. Larry Frey received the support of the House members to be the new speaker. I have worked with Speaker Frey. He is a good man and worthy of his position.

"On the Senate side were a few members. I will not list their names except for one key person involved in the amendment. It was the senior senator from New York—senator then ... president now."

Randy paused to allow his words to be absorbed both by the other senators in the chamber and by the viewing audience in the Senate gallery and over C-SPAN.

"If the president wanted to do something about making large corporations pay their fair share, why did he support this amendment nine years ago?"

Randy tossed the pages down on his desktop. "I think we need a new federal income tax structure for corporations and for the American public. One that is fair to all."

He looked around the Senate Chamber as he continued. "The current tax code is many hundreds of pages long. Far too large for the average person to read. I think we need to create a personal federal income tax code that is fewer than one hundred pages long so every American can take a weekend to sit down on their front porch swing and read it. I think we need a corporate federal tax code for US corporations and foreign businesses operating in our country that is fewer than one hundred pages long so they do not need an army of professionals to tell them how to avoid paying taxes. It's really that simple, folks, but it will take time to do it correctly."

Randy picked up the copy of the Corporate America Fair Share Bill. "We don't need another Band-Aid like this." He lifted the top lid of his Senate desk and dropped the bill inside. He allowed the lid to drop down against the desk. The sound was loud in the quiet Senate Chamber.

Randy looked around the room. During the time he had been speaking, many of the absent senators had returned and taken their seats. He saw Senator Saunders sitting beyond Hanley and Laird. The senator was only a year or two older than Randy was, and he gave the South Carolina senator a little head bob and small smile.

"I'm not in favor of the Fair Share Bill. I think this body should vote not to send it to the Finance Committee. Do you agree with me? If you do, stand at your desk."

Almost immediately, the three Davids rose together. Senators Evans, Mace, Anderson, and Richards, along with a few more scattered around the room came to their feet.

Randy put a polite smile on his face. "We're not going home today unless we stop this now. I will ask again. Do we have the votes?"

This time more senators rose from their chairs to stand behind their desk. Randy would have guessed enough were now standing to allow the vote to take place, but he wanted more of a showing.

"Now is not the time to be timid. Now is the time to show America that we will not stand for this type of politics ever again. I will ask one more time. Do we have the votes?"

The chamber floor filled with standing bodies as a large majority came to their feet. Randy looked down the chamber toward Tom Evans, who gave him a smile and a little nod.

Randy turned to the president pro tem. "Ms. Pro Tem. I yield the floor to allow the United States Senate to vote for or against sending the question before us to the Finance Committee."

Chapter 58

Washington, DC
Friday, December 4, 2015
12:15 p.m.

Harold Miller was having a quiet lunch alone. It was rare not to have lunch guests to discuss important matters of state or receive a briefing from a senior staff member. In fact, he had canceled his scheduled lunch plans to have this brief time alone.

His plan had failed. Perhaps it would make reelection more difficult; the press would review the old farm subsidies bill and pass judgment on his involvement to their viewers.

Earlier, the director of national intelligence had quickly completed his briefing on the London terrorist attack and left the Oval Office. Miller's only instruction was for the DNI to provide every piece of information about Fisher's role in the affair. Maybe there would be something to use against the senator later.

Alison Warden and Warren Fletcher, alone with the president, had expressed their disappointment in the bill's failure. It had been Alison's idea to send the Fair Share Bill to the Congress, but Harold had fully embraced the plan. She had offered her apology and even hinted that he might want her resignation, but Harold had only offered a small smile and told her they would just regroup and come back fighting tomorrow.

Warren Fletcher listed a few things they could do to soften the political blow the Miller Administration had just taken. He spoke to both the president and Alison, but Miller just sat quietly as his press secretary made notes in her portfolio.

Fisher. The man had been a constant thorn in his side ever since he came to Washington. After his first burst of outrage, Harold had sat in the Oval Office almost in a trace as the man had calmly spoken on the floor of the Senate where Harold had spent many years. In the very short time he spoke from his Senate desk, Randy Fisher had unraveled months of carefully planned work to move Miller's image toward the center of the American political spectrum.

He remembered Tom Evans's face after the Senate president announced the vote. He revealed a small smile, knowing the president had just lost a major vote and would experience a setback in the election process. Already Evans had told the reporters outside the Senate chambers he was heading back to the campaign trail.

Miller was having half a BLT sandwich with a bowl of tomato basil soup, along with a cup of coffee, at the Resolute Desk in the Oval office. He scanned the calendar desk pad, even though he had the primary election schedule memorized. The Iowa caucuses were only a few weeks away. He was running unopposed and would win the Republican vote. Evans, facing at least eight or nine other Democratic candidates, was expecting to pull out a solid victory.

He removed the pen from his suit coat pocket and wrote a few notes. He would need to get Lewis Drake, his campaign manager, into a meeting very quickly. They would need to work out a new strategy.

Chapter 59

Harrisburg, PA
Friday, December 4, 2015
12:50 p.m.

The two-story brick Tudor home on the outskirts of Harrisburg, Pennsylvania, was set back on a deep lot. The closest homes on both sides were almost a half-mile away. The well-tended front lawn next to the city street was lined with Douglas firs that prevented passing motorists and people walking along the street from seeing very much of the expensive home.

Former Speaker of the House Leonard Graham was just finishing his lunch. There was only one guest at the table, plus his wife of many years. After dinner, the servants removed the dishes, and his wife went to her study to make some telephone calls.

Leonard walked beside his guest as they returned to his study, located on the other end of the house. Mrs. Graham would not disturb them in their work.

Barbara Harrison took a seat at the Queen Anne desk set at a ninety-degree angle to Leonard's own expensive wooden desk. Both desks had a computer, but Barbara's was a laptop version that would leave with her. They also had a telephone with separate lines to allow both to make calls, as well, of course, as their smart phones. It was an age of technology, and they were just as adept as everyone else was.

Barbara flipped her long, thick, luxurious blond hair back over her shoulder as she opened her portfolio to write down Leonard's instruction. The thirty-three-year-old beauty was five feet three inches tall and with Leonard Graham had watched the C-SPAN coverage on the television in Leonard's study. They had quietly listened to the comments of Senator Randy Fisher as he destroyed the president's Fair Share Bill.

Leonard quietly cleared his throat to announce he was ready to begin. Barbara had her pen ready. "We will start with the largest donors in the manufacturing sectors. Automotive, electronics, and energy. Of course we must not forget any other big business either here in the United States or outside our borders." The sixty-five year old man, slender in build, with wavy brown hair streaked with gray, spoke calmly. His skin tone still held his summer tan from months of playing golf. He projected a look of competence and calm authority.

"The president's plan failed completely, and now he has isolated big business from supporting his reelection plans. It will never be a better time to enter the race for the Republican nomination."

He looked at the beautiful woman. There was no physical relationship between the two. They had worked together for some years when he was speaker of the House. They had made a great team during their time together in the lower chamber in Congress and would do so again after Leonard's election to the White House.

"You will be my official campaign manager, but always check with Harry before you make any major decisions." Harry was Leonard's younger brother and current governor of Michigan.

"Once we are in the White House, you will be my chief of staff once again."

Barbara Harrison displayed her very white teeth at the prospect of working again in the White House. Until a few months ago, she had been assistant White House chief of staff. A mistake on her part during the confirmation process for the chief justice of the Supreme Court had caused the president serious embarrassment. It had been very embarrassing personally when she cleaned out her desk under the watchful eyes of Secret Service agents. Leonard Graham would be her ticket back into power.

"Your papers are ready for the Iowa caucuses?"

Leonard smiled back to his beautiful assistant. "Absolutely. They will be filed tomorrow."

Leonard Graham had lost the bid for the Republican Party nomination in 2012 to Harold Miller. He would not lose this time.

Chapter 60

Former Vice President of the United States Jerrod Wyman tossed the television remote control onto the round glass-top table on the patio overlooking the Gulf of Mexico. A tiled roof extended from his house and provided enough shade to see the CNN logo fade away on the screen. He had watched enough of the news network's coverage of the Senate and the terrorist attack in London.

The former vice president and former governor of Texas looked over at his lunch companion. Pamela Collins had been his chief of staff in the Texas state government and followed him to Washington, DC, when he was the vice president under Harold Miller. He had resigned his position immediately after the midterm elections over disputes with the president over the illegal immigration bill and border security bill introduced into Congress in 2014.

Wyman was in his midfifties, with thick, prematurely gray hair. His waistline was flat, his shoulders wide, and his teeth were perfect. Many people claimed he looked like the perfect Texas cowboy.

Pamela was in her midthirties, with long black hair and a slender body that came to the shoulders of six-foot-one Wyman. He thought her slightly upturned nose was cute. They had become lovers during his second term as governor and had kept their relationship secret

338

throughout their time together in Washington. No doubt, the Secret Service agents knew about the affair, but they kept what they saw and heard to themselves. Pamela was still married to a Texas state senator, but they had no children. Wyman was divorced long ago and childless. Together they made a great political team.

"Miller blew it," Wyman said as he looked over toward Pamela. She was dressed for a swim in the Gulf, but he knew she would only walk along the water's edge, allowing only her feet and ankles to get wet. She hated the water when the temperature dropped below seventy degrees.

Pamela picked up the brown folder lying on the table, flipped the cover open to reveal the several sheets of papers inside, and neatly typed lines of information. It was her checklist of things done and things to do. Most of the items were marked completed.

"We're all ready for your press announcement on Monday. I have given the campaign press manager his news release. You should have full coverage when you step before the cameras. After that, we are off to Iowa, New Hampshire, South Carolina, and Florida. They all vote in January." She flipped to the second sheet of paper in the thin file. "We've got a number of Republican governors waiting on the sidelines to endorse you and a full e-mail and social media campaign ready to go. The president will never know what hit him."

Wyman looked out toward the waves rolling in onto the private beach along the width of his property. He possessed a net worth estimated at $4 billion dollars, and he was prepared to spend whatever was necessary to defeat Harold Miller for the Republican nomination.

"Miller thinks he's only got Tom Evans to worry about."

Chapter 61

Tehran, Iran
Monday, December 7, 2015
4:00 p.m. Coordinated Universal Time

The Elder poured the green herbal tea into his ceramic cup and dropped in a few small squares of sugar to mix with the blend. He looked outside his office. The sky was cloudy and a cold wind was blowing. He doubted the temperature would reach the projected high forties but was almost certain it would drop below freezing after the weak sun slipped below the horizon.

He picked up the report his people had compiled on their London operation. They had operatives in England, watching from afar and reporting what they had observed. All the information gathered from the news services was included in the report.

He was mildly disappointed in the operation. Their main target, to destroy the precious water supply to London and kill thousands of people, had failed to materialize. The damage to the confidence of the English people in their government to keep them safe would be cause for discussion for many months to come. The minor damage to Trafalgar Square was quickly repairable, but memories of those people gunned down after the explosion would linger for many years.

All five members of the team were dead, a loss, but it was better than if they had been captured and forced to talk. Besides, more followers, loyal to their cause, were waiting for the next opportunity to kill the British and the Americans.

He read the information learned from private sources about the American senator. Twice now, the man had foiled his operations. Was it just luck, or was Allah's hand behind any of it? It would require prayer and contemplation on his part before they launched their next mission.

He had plenty of time to determine the fate of the American senator. His people were still getting the next mission organized, scheduled to take place shortly after the next American presidential election, when they hoped a new American government might be in place. The attack would have a better chance to succeed when the new government was in transition.

He pushed himself out of the old steel swivel chair and walked into the closet built against an inside wall of the building. A large floor safe filled most of the space. He worked the combination lock until he heard a faint click. He spun the handle with five steel spokes until it stopped and slowly pulled the heavy door open. Inside were many folders with lists of men and equipment. Others contained hand-drawn plans to bring the end to the Americans' influence throughout the world. The Elder did not know if he would see the end of the Americans in his part of the world, but he took great solace in knowing that would happen with one of the many plans contained in the safe.

He removed the thickest folder, standing on its edge between two thin metal dividers on the right side of the second shelf. He turned back to his desk and sat down in his chair. He placed his old fingers against the outside of his teacup. The brew was still hot, and he took a full sip. Satisfied, he set the cup off to the right side of the desk and opened the folder's cover. Across the top of the first page was the name he had selected for the operation. He thought it was very fitting for the complex web he planned to unleash on American soil.

In Arabic, it was دازرهش, Operation Scheherazade. One thousand and one tales to confuse the American intelligence system—but only one would be true.

Chapter 62

Washington, DC
Monday, December 7, 2015
7:45 a.m.

Senator Randy Fisher was dressed and ready to attend an early morning ceremony to commemorate Pearl Harbor Day. It was sad to think the Pearl Harbor Survivors Association had disbanded on December 31, 2012. The official ceremony, held for many years at the Pacific naval base, ended simply due to the ages and deteriorating heath of the men and women assigned to the beautiful island on that fateful morning in 1941.

Randy believed, along with millions of fellow Americans, the day should never be forgotten. Not that he or other Americans still held a hatred for the Japanese but because they should always learn from history. He had used the example of the Pearl Harbor attack to convince the people in the War Room that the attack on Trafalgar Square was a diversion and they needed to keep looking for the terrorists.

He stood near the back of the crowd, away from the large temporary stage at the World War II Memorial on the National Mall. At center stage, the secretary of defense and the chairman of the Joint Chiefs of Staff conducted the quiet ceremony. Many senior officers from the various military branches were standing off to the side.

Randy looked around at the hundreds, perhaps thousands, of uniformed military personnel mixed among the many civilians who had come to pay their respects. Those who had served in the war made up a very small number; the number of actual survivors from Pearl Harbor, if any, was smaller still.

At 7:48 a.m., the official time when the Pearl Harbor air attack began, a bugler began to play "Taps." The tune was sometimes called "Butterfield's Lullaby" or the first line of the lyric, "Day is Done." *Stay vigilant! Never forget!* The words roamed through Randy's mind as he listened to the musical piece. Yes, he would stay vigilant, and so too would millions of other Americans. He silently vowed to never let another Pearl Harbor or 9-11 happen again while he drew breath.

At eight thirty, the ceremony concluded. He decided to walk the long distance back to the Capitol building. He could easily see it off in the distance past the Washington Monument.

The sun was shining brightly even though the air was cold, and a light breeze blew. He pulled the collar of his winter coat up higher to protect his neck from the cold. The long walk would do him good; he had only been out running once since he had returned home from London.

Would the US intelligence organizations, along with British counterparts and those of other friendly nations, discover more information that led them to the people behind the attacks in London and his own state of South Carolina? Randy was hopeful. He had great faith in his friend Marion Bellwood. Until then he would stay vigilant.

Author's Notes

In 1993, in Milwaukee, Wisconsin, 880,000 citizens of the city's 1.61 million residents were threatened by cryptosporidium oocsts from March 23 through April 8. It was the largest documented waterborne disease outbreak in United States history. The Howard Avenue Water Purification Plant was contaminated, and treated water showed turbidity levels well above normal.

Authorities have never officially identified the official root cause of the epidemic. Some experts suspected cattle genotype due to runoff from pastures were behind the outbreak. Another possibility was that melting ice and snow-carrying cryptosporidium may have entered the water-treatment plant through Lake Michigan. The Atlanta-based Center for Disease Control (CDC) determined the outbreak was caused by cryptosporidium oocsts that passed through the filtration system of one of the city's two water-treatment plants. The material came from the discharge outlet of a sewage treatment plant two miles upstream in Lake Michigan.

Over the two-week span, an estimated 403,000 people became ill with stomach cramps, fever, diarrhea, and dehydration caused by the pathogen. At least 104 deaths resulted from the outbreak, mostly among the elderly and immuno-compromised people, such as AIDS patients.

The authorities closed the water-treatment plant after April 8, 1993.

LEVELS

✰✰✰ OF ✰✰✰

POWER

The

Vice President

By Mike Gilmore　　　　**A Randy Fisher Novel**

Levels of Power
The
Vice President

Millions of Americans are closely following the presidential election process as President Harold Miller faces two late-entry challengers from his own party for the nomination at the upcoming Republican Convention.

Jerrod Wyman, former vice president, and Leonard Graham, former speaker of the House of Representatives, have drawn enough delegates away from Miller during the primary elections to force a contested convention. Miller finds himself in a fight for a second term. Will the pledged delegates stay with the embattled president during the convention, or must he make a deal with one of his opponents?

Democratic Senator Tom Evans has already locked up the votes needed for his nomination during the upcoming Democratic Convention in Baltimore. There is little doubt in his mind that South Carolina Senator Randy Fisher is the right man to be his running mate. Together, he is certain they can displace the sitting president.

All their plans appear to be working as they leave the Democratic Convention and make the run for the White House. The polls are showing a growing tide of support for the Democratic team. They appear to be unstoppable until an event never considered possible derails a perfectly planned campaign.

Levels of Power: The Vice President tells the behind-the-scenes story of politics at the highest level. The story will keep you turning pages to the very end.